TASSOS

Titles available in this series

Yannis
Anna
Giovanni
Joseph
Christabelle
Saffron
Manolis
Cathy
Nicola
Vasi
Alecos
John
Tassos

Greek Translations

Anna

published by Livanis 2011

TASSOS

Beryl Darby

ISBN 978-0-9574532-3-4

Printed and bound in the UK by
CPI Antony Rowe, Chippenham

First published in the UK in 2013 by

JACH Publishing
92 Upper North Street, Brighton, East Sussex, England BN1 3FJ

website: www.beryldarby.co.uk

In memory of Katie.

My cover girl for ANNA, my role model for Annita.

A much loved friend who will be missed by all who knew her.

Family Tree

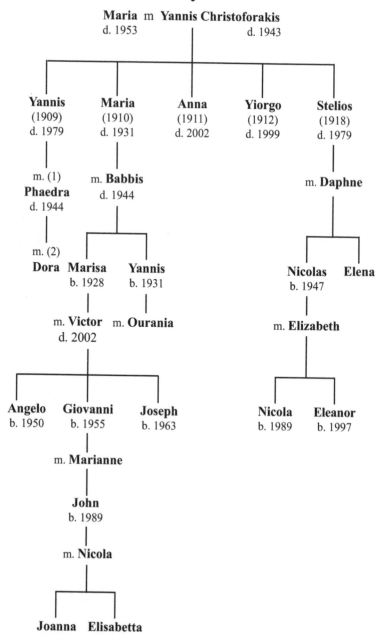

Family Tree

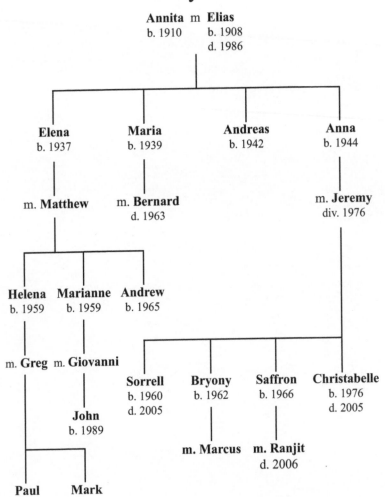

Acknowledgements

My thanks to

Yvonne Payne for her information regarding Kritsa Gorge

Sheila and Roger Sharman for taking me to Mili Gorge (2010) and sending me her photographs to refresh my memory

Ronald Smith (once supplier to many prestigious establishments in England and America and many private clients) for the information he gave me about the techniques for painting on enamel, the subsequent firing and mounting of his work.

Mr Sfyrakis (Dimitris Steak House, Omirou 2, Elounda) for allowing me to use his taverna for the cover photo.

Author's Note

When the leprosy sufferers were sent to Spinalonga a quantity of wooden bath tubs were supplied for their use.

Some men found a secondary use for them – they used them as makeshift boats to float across to the mainland. A number escaped in this fashion. Once a bath tub was found abandoned on the shore a full scale search took place, and once found, the leper was returned to Spinalonga.

There was one man who was never found. Did he manage to hide away and escape detection or was he swept out to sea and drowned? There is no way of knowing, but I would like to think that he survived the trip and went on to live a happy and useful life.

I hope I have given Tassos a plausible way of evading recapture and a believable life story. There is no reason at all to associate him with Mili, but I found the ruined village in the gorge so beautiful and evocative that I had to incorporate it into this book.

All the characters in this book are entirely fictitious. Any resemblance to actual persons, living or dead, is entirely coincidental.

September 2009

John had finished reading most of the notebooks that his great uncle Yannis had written after he had left Spinalonga. He was not surprised that Yannis's widow had asked for certain details not to be included in the publication of his memoirs. To have such intimate thoughts and feelings disclosed to casual readers was a violation of his privacy and John felt guilty for reading them.

In the published version of his life Yannis had glossed over his childhood and the time he had spent in Aghios Nikolaos living with his cousin, Annita, and her family whilst attending the High School. In his notebooks he had described how he had disliked the work on his father's farm, preferring to search for pottery in the fields or sit and read.

Whilst living with Annita's family he was expected to go to sea at the weekends to help his uncle who was a fisherman. He confessed to being frightened of a rough sea and the night time trips his uncle made to Spinalonga to collect the smuggled goods that had been stored there, petrified that he would come face to face with one of the incarcerated inhabitants or be inadvertently stranded on the island.

His indescribable joy when he was told he had gained a scholarship to the Gymnasium in Heraklion and the relief of knowing that his teacher, Yiorgo Pavlakis would join him there and they would lodge in the same taverna. He described his journey up to Heraklion, the excitement he had felt at making the journey and also how nervous he had been when he had first arrived alone in the bustling town, as Yiorgo had missed the bus.

There were details of the friends he had made at the Gymnasium, his visit to Knossos and the discovery that the girl his teacher was enamoured of was one of the town's prostitutes; his horror and disbelief when he had been diagnosed as suffering from leprosy when he returned from a prolonged visit to his family, destroying his hopes and dreams for the future. He had contemplated returning to his family or hiding in the hills along with other outcasts who had been diagnosed, but he also knew that eventually he would be discovered. The doctor at the hospital had held out hope of a cure, so he had surreptitiously crept away from his lodgings, telling no one of his destination.

His initial meeting with Father Minos had not been documented in the published book and John found it fascinating to read about the compassion and understanding the priest had shown to his parishioners. Yannis had expressed his utter disbelief when Father Minos had joined them voluntarily on Spinalonga. How the priest had later told Yannis that he had suffered from a guilty conscience due to lack of knowledge of the fate of the leprosy patients and finally decided he had been called to Spinalonga to live amongst them.

John found Yannis's description of the conditions endured in the hospital in Athens unbelievable and was not surprised the patients had demanded better conditions. That their requests should have been met by being forcibly placed in strait jackets and sent to Spinalonga to fend for themselves was inhuman.

Yannis had described in detail the conditions he had found on the island when he first arrived. All the houses that were habitable were already occupied, with people using the churches and the tunnels for shelter from the burning summer sun and the freezing rain and cold winds in the winter. His determination to make life bearable for himself and the others shone through as he related how he had cajoled and threatened until, with his friend Spiro's help, he had organised the rebuilding and repair of the buildings.

Although John knew this had taken place he had never fully appreciated the amount of work that had been necessary and how they had begged the boatmen who delivered their supplies of food and water for materials.

Doctor Stavros had made a difference to their well being when he began to make regular visits offering rudimentary treatment and basic medication. With the pension Yiorgo Pavlakis had arranged with the government came a modicum of independence and pride and Yannis had described the various trades and occupations the islanders became involved with.

Their suffering during the war was unimaginable, and on every page of the notebook, covering the second year of deprivation until Crete was liberated, were the names of those who had succumbed to starvation. John had tears in his eyes as he read of the death of Yannis's wife. It was no wonder that after his daughter also died he took to drinking.

There was a gap in Yannis's writing then, no doubt he had little memory of events that took place during his dependence on alcohol. There was so much he had wished to forget. When the notebooks continued he described the improvements the government implemented, but his greatest joy was finally being able to receive visits from his family.

The wedding of John's grandmother, Marisa, was described in detail and John wondered if she would like him to read it to her. She and Ourania were the only people left now that he knew had visited the island on a regular basis. How he wished he had asked Aunt Anna for more details of life over there before she had become senile.

Yannis's protracted fight with the Government for the new medication for the treatment of leprosy to be made available to them had been a part of his life story, but along with the notebooks were the original letters and articles sent to him by Annita and Elias. John found them fascinating, despite having little knowledge of medicine, and his respect for his great grandmother grew. He was sure Saffron would be interested in looking at them.

After four weeks of reading the neat hand writing John now returned most of the books to his uncle. The ones he kept were labelled with the name of an islander and the event they had been directly involved in. Yannis described how he had used a bath tub to sail across the short stretch of water and visit the mainland. He had not been alone in this venture and John was curious to find out the fate of the others who had attempted such a hazardous trip.

He read first the book labelled 'FLORA', having met the shy, reclusive woman occasionally in Aghios Nikolaos and was touched by Manolis's devotion to her. That she had survived the amputation of her arm without anaesthetic was nothing short of a miracle. He would have to ask his father and uncle for more information and wished the old fisherman was still alive.

The next book he tackled was entitled 'ADONIS'. It described the argument that had taken place between Adonis and Christos over a piece of cheese. Christos finally hit Adonis with the length of wood he used as a crutch and Adonis had retaliated by knocking the man to the ground. Before either could do any more damage to each other they had been separated. Adonis had become sulky and morose. Christos taunted him daily with references to cheese until Adonis decided he could no longer bear to be on the island with the man. One night he had taken his bath tub down to the jetty, climbed inside and hoped the current would take him across to the mainland.

Yannis described how the bath tub could be seen wedged amongst the rocks just along the coast from Plaka and was immediately spotted by the men as they brought the barrels of water out to the island. Having deposited the water barrels they made a detour, sailing as close to the rocks as they dared, looking for any sign of the man.

The information that an inhabitant of the island had escaped to the mainland was passed to the other boatmen who delivered supplies, the fishermen and finally the authorities in Aghios

Nikolaos. From his vantage point on Spinalonga Yannis could see the searchers combing the area, but it was not until a week later that Adonis was found and returned to the island. He had hidden in one of the caves, but without easy access to water or food he had finally been forced to emerge and make his presence known.

John frowned. He would have liked to know how the enmity between Christos and Adonis was settled or if it developed further. He searched through the books, but there was not another that bore either man's name. He had to conclude that there had been no further animosity between the two men and therefore nothing that Yannis had felt was worth recording.

The next book recalled how Theo had tried to leave Spinalonga. His freedom was short lived as he did not reach the shore until daylight and was seen by the boatmen and returned. Apparently he had been philosophical and declared he would not bother to make the effort again.

The description of Yannis's own journeys across the stretch of water had been published in his book. He had not planned to escape, merely wishing to visit his family, particularly his mother who had suffered a stroke.

John opened the final book, marked TASSOS. This was far more interesting. Yannis had described in detail Tassos's plan for returning to the mainland, evading recapture and the occupation he intended to pursue. Yannis ended by saying that he wished the man well and hoped one day to hear he had been successful.

John closed the book in frustration. What had happened to Tassos? The mystery niggled at him. He borrowed all the notebooks from his uncle again, but there was no mention of Tassos returning to Spinalonga.

'What are you doing, John?' Nicola leant over her husband's shoulder. He had a pad of paper and old Uncle Yannis's notebooks before him.

'I'm still trying to track down Tassos.'

'Oh, I thought you might be making a list of the guests we have to invite for our party.'

'There's plenty of time. It isn't until April.'

'They need enough notice to get time off work and flights arranged. We need to know who's coming so we can arrange suitable accommodation We could ask Vasi if we could use the Katerina for the older people, and I'm sure his father, Cathy and Marjorie will be able to stay at the house with him and Saffie. The others could go to the self catering units if your Dad's agreeable, but we ought to have sent out invitations by Christmas at the latest.'

John shrugged. 'I thought you were going to get it organised.'

'It was your idea.'

'No,' John shook his head. 'You promised your Mum we'd have a party, so it was your idea.'

'What you really mean is that all you want to do is sign your name at the bottom of an invitation.'

John grinned at her. 'I could probably manage that.'

'You're hopeless. How do you expect to track down this missing man? If there's nothing in old Uncle Yannis's papers you're not likely to find any information about him anywhere else.'

'I'm looking through to see if there is any mention of a man called Tassos Nevrakis. According to old Uncle Yannis he escaped from Spinalonga. He never mentions him again. I'd like to know if he was caught and sent back and died on the island or was amongst those who went over to Athens.'

'Why don't you ask Doctor Papanakis if there's a list amongst the documents Doctor Stavros left? He's probably never looked at them, but there could be mention of the man in there.'

'That's brilliant, Nick. I'll go into Aghios Nikolaos tomorrow and ask him. Why didn't I think of that?'

'Because you're a man. Now, can we start on a list of guests for the party? Bryony is keeping the girls amused and there's half an hour before their tea time. Put down my Mum and Dad first with Eleanor. There's Dad's sister, Aunt Elena, my Uncle Bob and my grandparents, then I'm done.' Nicola grinned at him mischievously. 'It's you who has a long list of relatives.'

'They're yours too.'

'Distant relatives,' Nicola corrected him.

'Shouldn't we get Mum and Dad involved? They may know of some we've never heard of, but who would be offended not to be invited.'

'John,' remonstrated Nicola. 'You are only putting the job off. '

John sighed. 'All right. There's my grandmother, her sister Maria and brother Andreas. I'm not sure if anyone knows where Aunt Maria is.' John continued. 'There's Aunt Helena and Uncle Greg. I suppose I'll have to ask Paul and Mark. Oh, and Uncle Andrew. I nearly forgot him. He's another one that I doubt will come.'

'Have they got partners or children?'

'No idea. Mum might know. That's about it.'

'What about your Uncle Angelo and Francesca?'

'I haven't seen them for years.'

'That's no excuse for not inviting them. There's Saffie and Marjorie, and we'll have to invite Vasi and his father and Cathy. How many does that make?

'And Dimitris and Antonia. After all, they're godparents.'

Nicola added them to the list and added it up quickly 'So far that's twenty four. Then there's your Mum and Dad, Grandma, your grandmother, Uncle Yannis and Aunt Ourania, Bryony and Marcus. If everyone comes that will be thirty six if you include us and the girls.'

'I invited Doctor Gharcia and his family and they said they might come over at Easter.'

Nicola sighed. 'I suppose we'll have to send everyone an invitation card.'

'Why? We can pick up the 'phone or just ask those who live here.'

'People like to receive a proper invitation to events like this.

They keep it as a souvenir.'

John raised his eyebrows. 'Is that it?'

Nicola shook her head. 'No, you're on bath duty tonight. Bryony helped me yesterday. Your turn tonight. You can write this list out decently and check it with your Mum whilst I give them their tea. We can order some cards to be printed next week and we should be able to get them written and sent off before people start to send their Christmas post.'

John nodded absently; he could not be enthusiastic about the arrangements for an event that was six months away. He wanted to turn his attention back to the notebooks. He must read through the chapters in old Uncle Yannis's book that covered the time when the survivors were sent to the hospital in Athens. Tassos might be mentioned there.

'Did you check the list with your Mum?' asked Nicola as she lifted Joanna from the bath and wrapped her in a towel.

'No, I thought it would be more sensible to do it later when Dad was around. We can ask him about the self catering at the same time. Lisa, if you wriggle like that I shall drop you back in the bath.'

Elisabetta looked up at her father and smiled as if understanding his threat. She loved her bath and would kick and splash, often crying when she was finally taken out.

'I'm sure she's going to be a good swimmer,' announced John. 'I'll be able to take them in the sea next summer. Lisa will love it.' John rose to his feet, his daughter wrapped in her towel in his arms. 'I'll have to lay her down on the bed to put her diaper and nightclothes on. I can't manage on my lap like you do.'

'I'll do her diaper, you just put her vest and sleep suit on. Don't start tickling her and getting her excited. It's bed time, remember. They need to be quiet and calm or they won't sleep.'

'You tell me that every night.'

'I know, and still you insist on playing with them when you

should be just rocking them gently or cuddling them. Then you leave me with the job of quietening them down.' Nicola placed Joanna in her cot and patted her back. 'Mamma will be back in a minute and Pappa will go and get your bottle. Then we'll have a *quiet* cuddle whilst you drink your milk.' Nicola looked at John sternly. 'No clucking or quacking and definitely no jiggling up and down. The last time you did that Elisabetta was sick.'

John grinned. Every night he was in trouble with Nicola when he helped her to put the girls to bed. He could not resist playing with them, pulling faces at the one he was feeding, making her smile and writhe around trying to touch his nose and usually resulting in a bout of hiccups.

'We were looking at our guest list earlier on and I wanted to check with you that we hadn't forgotten anyone.' Nicola handed the list to Marianne.

Marianne looked down the list of names. 'Aunt Maria. I haven't seen her for years. We can't ask Grandma if she knows her address or she might suspect something. I'll try 'phoning Uncle Andreas and see if he knows where she is. I'm not sure if he will come, but I know Grandma would love to see him again. Having a party for the girls is a perfect excuse to invite everyone over without her suspecting that we plan to celebrate her birthday.'

'He ought to come. It will probably be his last chance to see his mother.'

'John!' Marianne exclaimed in horror.

'Well, you know what I mean. Grandma is going to be a hundred. He could regret not coming over for the party if we had to send him bad news a short time afterwards.'

'I'll see how my mother feels about him coming when I 'phone her. She'll be able to travel with Helena and Greg; maybe they could all meet up somewhere and travel together.'

'I bet Paul won't want to come. He'll probably think I'll put a crab in his bed again.' John grinned. 'He howled like a baby and he was ten!'

'That was a wicked thing to do to him. Whatever made you think of it?'

Nicola and John exchanged glances and Nicola giggled. 'You've always got me into trouble.'

'Nick put one in my bed the day she left.'

'Nicola!'

'He put one down my swimming costume the day before,' Nicola excused herself. 'I was just getting my own back.'

Yannis cleared his throat. 'If you are planning to invite all these people over here where they going to stay? We haven't enough rooms in the house.'

'We thought we would ask Vasi if Marianne's mother, Uncle Andreas and Aunt Maria, if they both come, of course, could stay at the Katerina along with Elizabeth's parents. Everyone else can stay in the self catering units.'

'I'm not sure if Helena and Greg would be happy in the self catering,' frowned Marianne.

'They'll go to the hotel,' Giovanni replied firmly. He had never liked his sister-in-law and did not get on well with Marianne's mother. She had never forgiven him for marrying her daughter so she stayed in Crete.

'I suppose that would be better,' Marianne frowned. 'I wonder if Andrew will come and if Paul and Mark come that will make five rooms needed at the hotel and eight units.'

'Eight? Paul and Mark can share so that makes seven,' corrected Giovanni.

'Eleanor will be thirteen. She's a bit old for sharing with her parents. She ought to have her own room.'

Giovanni shrugged. 'All right, eight units.'

'What about Doctor Gharcia? I kind of gave him an open invitation to visit whenever it suited him. Maybe we should send him an official invitation and include him in the numbers.'

'Better to send him an invitation. Then it will be up to him if he wants to come for a family party or later just for a holiday. Either way he and his family can stay at the self catering. I'll include him in the numbers until we hear definitely from him.'

'We need to decide on the date. We can't have a celebration until after Easter Monday. I thought the following weekend would be about right. Do you agree?' John looked at his father.

Giovanni nodded. 'It will be right at the beginning of the season. I suppose we'll have to offer everyone at least a week. You can't expect relatives from America to spend a couple of days here and return home again. If we offer them a week we'll have to do the same for Angelo and Francesca and your Aunt Elena. I hope it won't mean we have to turn any guests away.'

'If we do it could make them book up even earlier next year.'

'Or they decide not to bother to come to us and go elsewhere,' replied Giovanni gloomily.

'Don't be such a pessimist, Dad. Thanks to Mum forcing that creep's father to pay compensation we're back on our feet. This time next year you'll probably be wondering how to avoid paying an enormous tax bill because of the profit you've made.'

Saffron had discussed her idea for a gift shop with Vasi in detail and she approached Giovanni tentatively. If he turned down her proposal out of hand she could hardly approach the owner of other premises in the area and would be forced to abandon the project.

'Giovanni, can I talk business with you?'

Giovanni raised his eyebrows. 'What kind of business? Is Vasi thinking of opening a self catering hotel?'

Saffron smiled. 'I shouldn't think so. He has enough to do at the moment.'

'Vasilis is no better?'

'Vasilis is progressing well. There's no reason why he should not resume the management of the Central. In fact Vasi and I are planning to visit England in December and see Marjorie. Providing Cathy does not have another fall we are determined to ignore any protest Vasilis may make. I'm sure once he is back organising the conferences he will realise how much he missed being completely in charge.'

Giovanni nodded. 'So what business do you wish to discuss with me? I'm sure you will not want to work as a chambermaid next season.'

'Certainly not.' Saffron shook her head. 'It must be awful having to do cleaning every day when it is so hot. No, I want to ask you about your new shop units. The one opposite Uncle Yannis is still empty, isn't it?'

'At the moment. I'm hoping someone will want to rent it next season.'

'I would like to.'

'You?' Giovanni stared at Saffron in amazement. 'Why should you want a shop?'

'Whilst I was in England with John I kept thinking what I could do to pass my time over here and not be bored. During the season Vasi's only at the house over night and at the weekends so I don't have cleaning and cooking to do every day. I've driven to just about everywhere and I don't want to spend most of my days sitting in the car.'

'You are always welcome to visit us.'

Saffron smiled. 'I know, and I'm grateful, but I can't spend every day down here. I'd like to open a gift shop. I'd only want to rent it for next season. I couldn't take on a long term agreement until I knew if it was going to be a success.'

Giovanni shook his head. 'Uncle Yannis has the gift shop.'

Saffron leant forward intently. 'I wouldn't sell any of the goods that he stocks. He has quality glass and china ware, silk scarves, handmade leather goods and the family sketches. I'm thinking more of small, good quality souvenirs for the visitors to take home.'

Giovanni frowned and Saffron continued. 'Jewellery, not cheap rubbish, but not the kind you would visit a jeweller to buy.

A middle range. If I stocked any china it would be small, hand decorated pots and dishes, nothing over ten Euros, suitable for a child to take home as a gift for their grandparents. I also talked to John about photographs. I know people take their own, but John has the advantage of knowing the best composition and when the light is right to get the best effect. I could have a selection, the island, the local churches, a market scene, animals; there's no end to the possibilities. I wouldn't try to sell anything you stock at the taverna and general store. If people wanted postcards or guide books I'd send them to you.'

Giovanni nodded slowly. Provided Saffron was not taking trade away from his aunt and uncle or himself her shop could be an added attraction to the area.

'It takes a considerable amount of money to stock a shop,' he cautioned her.

'I know, but I have my savings and the allowance that Vasi gives me. I've talked to him about it and he sees no reason why I shouldn't make the investment for a season and see if it's a success. If I lose money then I have to give up the idea, that's why I don't want a long term agreement with you.'

'You'd still have electricity and water to pay for.'

'I know, but I shouldn't need to use very much water and the electricity will only be for air conditioning. If I'm only there during the summer I shouldn't need any heating or light. I could contact suppliers and place orders using the computer at home.'

'Did John think it was a good idea?'

Saffron nodded. 'He did at the time, but since he's been home he's been occupied with trying to find out about the man who went missing from the island. I needed to talk to Vasi and get his opinion. If John does agree to supply me with photos I'd pay him a commission on the sales, of course.'

'One season might not be sufficient to know if the project was going to be a success.'

Saffron shrugged. 'If I manage to cover my costs the first year

I'd be happy to continue. I have to be realistic. I don't expect to make a fortune, but I can't afford to run a shop at a loss forever just to keep me occupied.'

'So how much rent are you prepared to pay me?'

For the first time Saffron looked uncertain. 'I don't know. I understand the rent depends upon the square metres of the building and also the location. That shop is not as large as the other two that are rented out, but the location is better.'

Giovanni smiled at her. 'I can't make any decision until I have spoken to Uncle Yannis. If he objects to you opening a gift shop opposite him then I cannot rent the premises to you. Ask me again the next time you visit and I will let you know what he says.'

'Thank you. I understand. There's just one thing I would like to ask you – do you think it would be successful provided Uncle Yannis agrees?'

Giovanni shrugged. 'Who knows? Tourists are fickle creatures, but there is no reason why they should not patronise you, at least until the novelty has worn off.'

Doctor Papanakis considered John's request to look at the medical records he had inherited from Doctor Stavros.

'I'm not at all sure where they are, or even if they are in my possession. I took over the practice in nineteen seventy four and I imagine my predecessor had disposed of any earlier records. They were not relevant to me when I took over the practice. The island had been closed for years and the inhabitants dispersed.' Doctor Papanakis frowned. 'Doctor Stavros may have sent them to the hospital in Athens or simply destroyed them.'

John's face fell. 'Would it be possible for you to have a look? I realise you are probably busy and I'd be willing to do a search if you would allow me. I'm only interested in tracing one man, so I wouldn't be reading confidential notes about anyone else who lived over there.'

Doctor Papanakis raised his eyebrows. 'Surely you have all

the information about your great uncle?'

John shrugged. 'Probably, but it isn't him I'm looking for. I want to find out what happened to Tassos Nevrakis.'

'Was he also a relative?'

John shook his head. 'I was reading old Uncle Yannis's notebooks and he says that Tassos Nevrakis used his bath tub to float over to the mainland. He planned to walk openly around the villages as a pedlar thinking the authorities would be looking for someone hiding away in the hills. Uncle Yannis doesn't mention if he was ever found by the authorities and returned to Spinalonga. I'm sure he would have written the information down. I'd like to know if the man survived the trip and if he did what happened to him.'

'So how would Doctor Stavros's medical notes help you? He's hardly likely to write anything about a man who isn't on the island.'

John spread his hands in despair. 'I just don't know where else to look for information. I thought if he had drowned Doctor Stavros might have recorded that.'

'Surely the Doctor would have told the islanders of the man's fate? Your uncle would have noted the fact and I would have expected the islanders to have held a service for him.' Doctor Papanakis rose. 'I'll have a look around in my cellar when I have time and see if I can find anything that might be of use to you, but somehow I doubt it.'

December 2009

Marjorie was delighted when Saffron 'phoned and asked if she and Vasi could stay with her for a couple of weeks.

'I've finally managed to persuade Vasi that his father is quite well enough to take over the running of the Central whilst we are away. I'm sure Vasilis could have done so since the end of the season, but he's become used to spending his day at home with Cathy. I'm hoping that when we return he'll be happy to continue being the manager. It will take some of the pressure off Vasi.

'I've so much to tell you. John and Nicola are busy arranging their party, and at the same time they are planning to throw a birthday party for Grandma. It's being kept a big secret from her as they want it to be a surprise. You're invited to both parties, of course. I'll tell you all the details when we come over. You'll stay with us, of course, along with Vasilis and Cathy whilst they are in Elounda. I'll make a booking for you whilst I'm in England so you won't have to worry about that and one of us will meet you at the airport.

'I also want to tell you about my idea for a gift shop, but that can wait until I come over. Nothing is definite yet. I might have to forget about it. I don't know anything about being a shop keeper.'

'Nor do I,' replied Marjorie, 'but if I can help you I will, you know that.'

Marjorie listened with interest to Saffron's idea of a gift shop.

'Provided you're not too ambitious I don't see why it shouldn't be a success. I'll try to think of some souvenirs that I would expect to find on offer. Have a look in the museum gift shop whilst you're there.'

Whilst Saffron and Vasi visited the British Museum Marjorie began to compile a list. By the time they returned she was feeling extremely pleased with her ideas. She would present Saffron with her thoughts whilst they ate the roast beef she had cooked. Saffron had requested that Vasi sampled traditional English food whilst they were there, but she was pleased they were not staying for Christmas and she would not have to tackle a turkey and all the conventional trimmings. It was so much easier to take advantage of the Goldsmith's offer to join them on the day when all she needed to prepare was a trifle to take with her.

Saffron frowned. 'I've thought of some of those things and we looked in the museum shop. They have little dolls dressed as beefeaters or guardsmen. I'd thought of dolls dressed in Greek traditional costume, but not of evzones. I hadn't thought about statues at all. If I could get some miniature ones that are replicas of those in the museum in Athens or Heraklion they could be a success.'

'What about those attractive vases made from onyx? They seemed to be in all the shops when I was over there and some of those are museum copies rather than original designs. You could stock both kinds,' suggested Marjorie.

'I'm not sure how Uncle Yannis would feel about that. I've promised not to stock anything that he or their self catering store sells. It wouldn't be fair, but it does cut out things like postcards and maps that would draw people in.'

'Tourists will always look; you'll just have to make sure your window display makes them want to come inside to see what else you have.'

'I'm going to drag Vasi around the shops tomorrow,' Saffron admitted. 'I'm hoping I can get some good ideas from the shops in the West End.'

Vasi raised his hands in mock horror and Saffron laughed. 'I promise, only one day at the shops, besides whilst you're here you ought to at least have a look at the famous ones. John couldn't believe them when I took him.'

'What did he buy?'

'Nothing. Everything was too expensive. He was looking for presents for the girls. He bought all their duck and chicken clothes when I took him to the shops that specialise in baby wear. Their prices were far more realistic.'

'We need to look at items that are a souvenir from England. I want ideas. I'm thinking of those white dishes. There are similar ones here with a transfer of Buckingham Palace or the Queen. Where would I be able to get a transfer of Spinalonga put on them?'

Vasi smiled patiently. 'I haven't any idea.'

Saffron frowned. 'Am I being very foolish, Vasi? Suppose the shop is a failure and I end up losing a good deal of money?'

'It is your money.' Vasi spoke seriously. 'I would prefer you to invest in a business than waste your money on expensive clothes that you will wear once and throw away. If your shop is a failure you will still have the stock and would be able to sell that on to a shop in Aghios Nikolaos. You would not get all your money back, but nor would you lose everything. We will not be dependent upon you making a profit for us to have food on the table.'

Vasi very much wanted Saffron's shop to be a success. If she was occupied and happy to fill her days dealing with the tourists she would have no reason not to settle in Crete. She insisted that was the only reason she was refusing to make any marriage plans with him. She did not want to find she was bored and unhappy after a while and want to return to England.

'I'm going to ask the shop if they will give me the name of their supplier,' said Saffron firmly. 'I can explain that I am setting up a gift shop in Crete and want local scenes. I won't be in competition with them.'

Vasi waited patiently whilst Saffron explained her requirements to the assistant who then asked her to speak to the manager. He listened politely to her and finally said he was unable to help. The shop was part of a chain of stores throughout England and she would have to contact their head office and ask for the information she required from their buyer.

Saffron placed the card he gave her in her purse and shook her head at Vasi as they left the shop. 'That was such a waste of time. That manager could have given me that information immediately, rather than making me spend half an hour explaining my ideas to him.'

'Where do you want to go now?'

'We'll have some lunch. You must be so bored, Vasi. I promise we'll only spend today going around the shops. Tomorrow we'll go to the Tower. They keep the Crown Jewels there.'

'And you are thinking of having replicas made to sell?' Vasi raised his eyebrows quizzically at her.

Saffron laughed and shook her head. 'I'm sure no one would be allowed to make full size replicas and who would buy them? You could hardly go out shopping wearing a crown.'

'In the jewellers they have tiaras.'

'Those are for very wealthy people and special occasions. They can't be compared with those the Queen has. Hers are a unique design that no jeweller would be allowed to copy. Where would you like to eat?'

Vasi shrugged. 'Wherever you suggest.'

Saffron looked at him mischievously. 'Shall we be truly extravagant and go to Fortnum and Mason? My treat to make up for you having such an uninteresting day. We could look at the souvenirs they are offering and then go to Harrods and Selfridges to see if they have anything different.'

Saffron made sure Vasi did not see the bill she paid for their lunch. He would have been horrified at the cost and she regretted her rash decision. She steered him quickly past the menu on display at the entrance where he would have been able to see the prices and headed towards the jewellery department.

'I know there will be nothing here that I could possibly afford to stock, but I might get some ideas and be able to find a way of purchasing some that are similar at a reasonable price.'

Vasi looked over her shoulder. He hoped she would be enamoured of a particular piece and he would be able to give it to her as a present. He swallowed hard. The prices on most of the items were hidden, but those he could see were more than their combined flights to London had cost.

Saffron moved from one display case to another. The necklaces and bracelets were all made from gold and set with precious stones and she moved past them rapidly until she came to those set in silver and sighed. They were far too expensive for her to consider and even if she was able to find a supplier who used coloured glass they would probably still be beyond her price range.

'I think I'm wasting my time here,' she smiled. 'I'll have just a quick look over there, then we'll go.'

Vasi followed her to the counter display where a young man, smartly dressed in a suit and tie, stood smiling a welcome, hoping he would be able to make a sale.

'Can I help you, madam?'

Saffron shook her head. 'I'm really just looking for ideas.'

'For a gift? We have a selection of pendants with hand painted designs.'

He pointed to enamel pendants of various shapes and sizes, each one painted with flowers or animals. 'If there is a particular design you would like I am sure we could get it made up for you. You can choose whether to have the chain in gold or silver and we will fit it for you.'

'How do they make them?' asked Saffron. 'Is it a transfer?'

The salesman shook his head. 'No, they are all painted individually by hand. You will never find two that are exactly the same. It is a very skilled and exacting process.'

'It's amazing.'

'There are very few artists who are capable of carrying out the work to such a high standard. We accept only their perfect examples.'

'What happens to the ones that you reject?'

'I have no idea. I expect they have another outlet somewhere that is not as particular as us.'

'I suppose it wouldn't be possible to be given the name of the workshop?'

The salesman shook his head. 'You would have to speak to our head buyer. I am only a sales assistant.'

'Can I do that?'

'I will ask a floor walker to speak to him and ask if he can spare you a few minutes.' The man raised his hand to attract the attention of a young woman who appeared to be browsing jewellery also and Saffron realised that she was actually an employee watching for shoplifters.

'What are you thinking, Saffie?'

'I've two questions. The artists might be willing to sell the ones Fortnum and Mason reject at a reduced price. I'd also like to know if it would be possible to shrink down a photograph of Spinalonga and fix it to a pendant in some way. I'm sure the only person who would be able to answer my question would be the artist.' Saffron continued to look and admire the pendants, moving to the end of the display counter where there were small boxes with a painted design on the lid and delicate silver edging.

'Those are pretty.'

'They come from the same workshop,' the assistant informed her.

'That could be a more practical idea,' said Vasi, becoming interested.

'I'd need to find an artist with the ability to paint Spinalonga as a miniature.'

Vasi shook his head. 'I was thinking of shrinking down a photograph.'

Saffron looked at him excitedly. 'Do you think John would be able to do that?'

'I've no idea. You'd still have to find someone who was able to attach it to the lid. You couldn't just stick it on. It would peel off in no time.'

The buyer arrived at the counter and looked at the couple standing there expectantly. 'I understand you wished to speak to me. Is it for a special commission?' he asked hopefully.

Saffron shook her head. 'Not really. I have a gift shop in Crete so I'm always looking for new ideas. If I could contact the artist who supplies you I would like to know where he purchases his enamels and how much he would charge to paint some for me and send them out.'

The buyer pursed his lips. Fortnum and Mason did not have a monopoly on the goods and there was no reason why he should not pass on the address of the artist to Saffron. 'Some of the designs are exclusive to us.'

'I'm sure he would tell me which designs were not available. I wouldn't dream of using any that were contracted elsewhere. In fact it's highly unlikely. I wouldn't want anything except flowers or butterflies that are found only in Crete. I'm also interested in the boxes, but I need to speak to the man who makes them to see if my idea is practical.'

Reluctantly the buyer pulled a card from his pocket. 'Their workshop is fairly close to London. I am sure you would be able to speak to him over the telephone.'

Saffron placed the card safely inside her purse. 'Thank you for your help. Goodness, is that the time? We really must hurry or we'll miss our train.' She took hold of Vasi's arm and propelled him towards the door.

'What train are we catching?' asked Vasi.

Saffron smiled at him. 'We're not. I just wanted to get out of there once I had the artist's card. I didn't want to tell that buyer any of my ideas in case he decided to pass them on and then claim they were exclusive.'

'He would do that?'

'It's possible. Let's see where this artist is based. He has an e-mail address so I could mail him with my questions. That would be easier than trying to explain my ideas over the 'phone.' Saffron slipped her hand into Vasi's. 'We'll visit Harrods and Selfridges and then go home unless there's a shop you want to visit.'

Saffron found it difficult to explain her ideas succinctly in an e-mail and sighed in exasperation at her lack of knowledge. 'I can picture exactly what I want, but I don't know how to put it into words. I don't want to give him the wrong impression. He'll either think I want to buy hundreds from him or poach his ideas.'

'Why don't you say that you'd like to meet with him so you can explain yourself fully?' suggested Marjorie. 'He's based in Sussex. It would probably take you no more than an hour to drive down and you did say you planned to hire a car for a few days.'

'Do you think he would meet me?'

'I don't see why he shouldn't. You're a prospective customer.'

Saffron smiled wryly. 'I doubt it, somehow.'

Saffron drove confidently through the outskirts of London. She had studied the map and knew she would have to look for a turning that took her off the motorway and into the countryside and she did not want to miss the sign and drive miles out of her way. Jack Morrison had agreed to see her between eleven and twelve that morning and she did not want to arrive later than eleven thirty.

She was surprised when she finally drew up outside the address she had been given to find it was a private house; she had been expecting a small industrial premises. She parked a short distance down the road, ensuring she did not block any of the entrances to the other houses and took a deep breath.

'I'm so glad you're with me, Vasi. It's a bit risky a woman visiting a man on her own at his house.'

'So without me you would not have made the journey?'

'I would have asked Marjorie to come with me. There's safety in numbers.'

'I'm sure you have nothing to worry about, but I'll not leave you alone in the house. Whenever you want to leave you only have to look at your watch and say we have to drive to another appointment.'

Saffron smiled at him gratefully as she locked the car and they walked up to the door. Vasi shivered as they waited for their knock to be answered. 'I hope he has his heating on.'

'Bound to have at this time of year. He wouldn't be able to work if his hands were frozen with the cold.'

A woman answered the door to them with a smile and Saffron felt her earlier apprehension recede.

'Do come in. Jack is looking forward to meeting you. Would you like some tea or coffee?'

'Coffee would be very welcome.' Saffron and Vasi followed the woman into the lounge where a man sat at the table, small cardboard boxes stacked up before him and some pamphlets at his side. He rose and shook their hands before asking them to sit at the table with him.

'I understand you are interested in purchasing some of my work,' he indicated the boxes. 'I have some samples here to show you.'

Saffron shook her head. 'I don't want to mislead you. I would like to ask you some questions about your work. I didn't know how to express myself in an e-mail.'

'You are an artist?'

'Goodness, no. I live in Crete and I'm planning to open a gift shop. Whilst we were looking around the shops for ideas I saw your pendants on sale in Fortnum and Mason. The ones they have on sale there are way out of my price range, both for purchasing and selling. They belong in a jewellers; not a gift shop.'

Jack smiled and waited for her to continue.

'The buyer explained that some designs are exclusive to them and they only accept perfect examples from you. I wondered how much it would cost to purchase the ones they do not want or those with other designs.'

'They are still expensive. Even those that are not considered perfect are of a very high quality. It is also an expensive process. The simplest of designs can take a week from the initial painting to the firing of the finished article.' Jack opened a box and withdrew a cellophane packet.

Saffron placed her coffee cup on the table and examined it carefully.

'This is beautiful,' she exclaimed as she looked at the small bunch of violets, their stems held together with a matching ribbon.

'It is imperfect.' Jack handed her a magnifying glass and she looked again.

'I still can't see anything wrong with it.'

'One petal is slightly larger than the others,' he smiled.

Saffron looked at him in amazement. 'Flower petals are often irregular.'

'In nature, yes, but not when you are reproducing them as jewellery.'

'Do you use a magnifying glass when you paint them?'

Jack shook his head. 'I don't need to, although some of my artists find it helpful.'

'You use other artists?'

'We all have our own particular talent. One woman is excellent at painting animals, another birds, and a colleague specialises in insects.' He took some more packets from the box and handed them to Saffron. 'You can imagine how long it would take to paint a fox. The base colour has to be completely dry before you add the brush strokes to give the fur effect, of course. There is also a limit to the amount of time you can concentrate so intensely.' He sighed. 'You can imagine how devastated the artist feels when the piece they have lavished such care on misfires or slips from its mount in the kiln and is damaged. Two week's work is lost.'

'So what do you do with the ones you consider imperfect?' asked Saffron, hoping he would say he threw them away and she would be able to make him an offer.

'I take them to Craft Fairs. They still fetch a good price.'

'If I found an artist in Crete who was capable of doing such delicate work where would I be able to purchase the materials?'

A smile twitched at the corner of Jack's mouth. 'I can put you in touch with the supplier but you will need to find an artist who can paint using a brush with one hair, knows the composition of the specialised paint and has a kiln that has been designed to hold and fire small items like these. Without the knowledge the materials are worthless.'

Saffron hesitated. 'I did have another idea.'

Jack raised his eyebrows.

'If it was possible to shrink a photograph down small enough would you be able to fix it to an enamel to make a pendant?'

Jack shook his head. 'I don't see how you would attach it. No, you would have to find an artist to paint a copy of the photo directly on to the enamel.'

Saffron pulled a face. 'I think my idea for pendants is out of the question. What about the boxes? I saw those in Fortnum and Mason. Again, I'm thinking of a photograph on the lid rather than a painting.'

'That would be possible. I make my own boxes with the design painted onto enamel and then fitted into a leather or silver surround. I'll show you.' Jack rose and went to a cupboard at the side of the room, removing a tray from a shelf and placed it on the table in front of Saffron.

Saffron looked at them thoughtfully. 'They could be more practical. What do you think Vasi? Would they sell?'

Vasi lifted one carefully. 'May I open it?' he asked.

'Go ahead.'

Vasi pushed up the small silver clasp. Inside the lid was a

replica of the painting on the outside and the box itself was lined with velvet. 'This is for jewellery?'

Jack shrugged. 'That is the intention, but who knows what people use them for.' He handed another to Saffron. 'This is a less expensive item. There is no lining and the picture is only on the outside of the lid.'

Saffron turned the box over in her hands. 'I couldn't afford silver boxes. A photo could be stuck on the lid of a wooden box and a silver trim placed around the outside to hold it permanently in place. It wouldn't need a clasp.'

'You would need a layer of Perspex to protect the photo,' Jack advised her. 'If you have the items where people can handle them a photo will soon become marked. If you are interested in boxes I can give you the name of a supplier, also the one where you can purchase the silver trim and the tools for applying it. You need someone who has a good eye for detail and hands capable of doing the delicate work. It is not the same as nailing two pieces of wood together.'

'I think I could probably manage it with a bit of practice.'

Jack raised his eyebrows. 'It is quite an intricate process. You need a good eye and a steady hand.'

Saffron smiled. 'I use to be an orthopaedic surgeon. I have both.'

Saffron and Vasi placed the two boxes carefully back on the table and Jack replaced them on the tray.

'I would be grateful for the supplier details,' said Saffron. 'I couldn't possibly consider the silver boxes or ask you to paint designs for me, but if John can reduce the photo I have in mind the wooden boxes are a distinct possibility. Then it would come down to the cost.' She looked at Vasi and sighed. 'How much would a tourist be prepared to pay for such a souvenir?'

Vasi picked up the cheaper of the two boxes and looked at it again. 'I have an idea, Saffie. If John can reduce a photograph to the size you require it does not have to be only of Spinalonga.

John is planning to take photographs of donkeys, cats, churches, village streets.' He shrugged. 'Almost anything you can think of. All of those would be suitable for on the lid and appeal to different tastes. How much you could charge I do not know. Uncle Yannis would be able to tell you how much profit he expects to make on the goods he sells and you could price yours accordingly.'

Jack was listening to their conversation with interest. 'I wish I was able to be involved. It sounds an exciting venture. How many shops will you be in competition with?'

Saffron smiled. 'Where I'm planning to open there is only my uncle selling very expensive items. The local people go to him when they want to buy a wedding or anniversary present. We won't be in competition with each other.'

January 2010

Giovanni had spoken to his uncle Yannis about Saffron's idea of opening a gift shop opposite his in Plaka.

'Is she trying to put me out of business?' asked Yannis.

Giovanni shook his head. 'I don't think so. She is planning to sell small cheap items, nothing like you sell. She only wants to rent the shop initially for one season. If you find she is encroaching on your business you only have to tell me and I'll not rent to her again.'

'What exactly does she plan to sell?'

'She mentioned jewellery, small items of china, photographs taken by John. I could ask her to come in with a full list of her proposed stock and we could discuss it with her. If there's anything you don't want her to sell we can tell her. It will be part of the rental agreement that she only sells items we know about and approve. She told me she wouldn't stock guides or postcards or anything we sell at the general store.'

'I don't want her selling glass or ceramics. I'm planning to stock some cheaper items myself this year to attract customers in.'

'Then we ask her to bring us a sample or photograph of anything she wants to sell and if you're not happy she has to forget that idea. It's up to you, Uncle. I'm sure she has no intention of being in competition with you.' Giovanni was anxious to have the retail unit let and it would be considerably easier to impose restrictions on Saffron than on an experienced trader.

After her visit to London, Saffron had spent many hours on the internet investigating the variety of items that were being offered as tourist souvenirs. She had found a workshop in Heraklion that specialised in hand painted miniature pottery. These were replicas of the larger items on display in the museum and Yannis sold either full size copies or smaller ones with a certificate to guarantee they were authentic copies. With Vasi's help she requested a sample to be sent to her.

She downloaded photographs of ash trays, condiment sets and small dishes. She was particularly interested in some plain white dishes that the manufacturer claimed could have a transfer or design of the purchaser's choice applied and was guaranteed to withstand continual washing and asked for further details and the price she would be expected to pay.

The books were no problem. She simply looked at a web site and made a note of any novels that said they featured the island of Spinalonga in their story. She planned to order half a dozen of each title in English. If they sold well and she was asked for them in other languages she could expand her stock later.

The jewellery was more difficult and she finally decided that she would only sell silver. Anything with a gold setting was above the budget she had set herself. Silver chains with a pendant set with semi-precious stones or bracelets, sometimes with earrings to match were more practical to stock than rings; rings could easily be lost and a variety of sizes were needed. She listed the pieces she found most attractive and planned to ask the opinion of both Nicola and Bryony, they would no doubt have different tastes.

John was quite happy to present Saffron with a selection of photographs; a couple he had enlarged to show how a finished work would look, but the others he had only reproduced to an A4 format as examples of the variety of subjects that were available to her.

Armed with her samples and information she drove down to Yannis's house and hoped she would not meet with stubborn opposition from the elderly man.

Saffron spread John's photographs on the table and arranged each item next to the brochure describing the goods available. Yannis gave the photographs a cursory glance and dismissed them.

'She can stock as many of those as she wants,' he said to Giovanni, 'along with the key rings, ash trays, bottle openers and dolls dressed as Greeks.' He placed the items to one side. 'I'm not interested in jewellery.'

Yannis picked up the miniature hand painted pot and examined it carefully. He looked at the various designs offered in the brochure and the cost. It could be worth his while investing in a hundred. They were cheap enough and he should be able to make nearly a seventy five percent profit.

'I'm planning to stock those,' he declared and Saffron's face fell as he placed the sample and brochure next to his elbow. He debated whether to demand that he also had the monopoly on the condiment sets and hors d'oeuvre dishes and decided to compromise.

'Saffron can sell the small dishes. I will have larger ones and matching plates. I don't know what she thinks she'll do with those plain white ones. No one will buy those.'

Giovanni wrote the information down so he could relay it to Saffron accurately. Despite Yannis being a relative she felt resentful that he had taken advantage of the research she had done. Had she been a stranger renting the shop she could have stocked whatever goods she pleased without consulting him. She watched with growing annoyance as he picked up the miniature pot and the brochure and left her to pack up the remaining items.

'I do wish he hadn't decided to stock that little pot,' she complained to Giovanni. 'That was one of my best items.'

Giovanni shrugged and smiled. 'Uncle Yannis is a business man. Do not try to compete with him.'

'I wasn't,' protested Saffron. 'I'm sure he hadn't thought about those pots until he saw mine.'

'He could have also claimed the condiment sets and hors

d'oeuvre dishes. Look through your brochures again. You could well find something to take their place that he isn't interested in.'

Saffron nodded. She had not mentioned her visit to the English artist and the boxes with photographs she wanted to stock. John was still experimenting with reducing a photograph of Spinalonga. The previous evening whilst looking on the internet she had spotted some little trinket boxes made from silver with a semi precious stone set in the lid. She would get some of those and if Yannis protested she would claim the items were jewellery.

John had heard nothing more from Doctor Papanakis and decided he would visit the doctor again with his request. It was quite possible the doctor had forgotten his enquiry and not looked for any archived medical papers.

John stood hesitantly in the consulting room. 'I'm sorry to bother you again, but I just wondered if you had had the opportunity to look for any papers belonging to Doctor Stavros.'

Doctor Papanakis nodded. 'There are a load of his old papers downstairs. The patients are dead. Their details have to be kept for a number of years in case the family ask for an enquiry at a later date or there's any question of foul play. They could probably all be thrown away. I've never found the time to sort through them.'

'So there could be papers relating to the occupants of Spinalonga?'

'It's possible.'

'Would you allow me to look at them? I'm trying to trace one man. I'm not interested in any of the others.'

Doctor Papanakis considered. It could save him the onerous task of checking the dates of the medical records. 'I suppose so. I'd have to rely on your discretion and trust you not to read details about other patients.'

'I'm sure they'd be of no interest to me. All I want to know is if a man named Tassos Nevrakis who escaped from Spinalonga was ever found and brought back. If he was, did he survive the war and was he sent to Athens with the other survivors when the island was closed. All I want to do is check the names.'

'If he went to Athens I would imagine his medical records went with him. Be prepared to find nothing at all relating to the man except the date of his death.'

John smiled. 'If I manage to find that I shall at least know what happened to him.'

John spent three days in the cramped and gloomy cellar beneath the doctor's premises. To his surprise the records appeared well ordered, divided into years and tied together in bundles. He was not sure where he should start and pulled a large collection from the top shelf. The piece of paper wrapped around them said 1960 – 1961 and when John opened them he understood the old doctor's method of filing. When a person died he just placed their record on the top of the pile and at the end of each year he bundled them together. They were certainly not in alphabetical order. Pleased that it appeared a simple task of looking for records before nineteen fifty seven John replaced them on the shelf.

He worked his way backwards, checking the years as he looked along the shelves. Three quarters of the way along he found a small bundle marked 'SPINALONGA TRANSFERS'. Delighted he took them over to the small table and began to examine them.

These were in alphabetical order and John read the medical details relating to his old uncle Yannis with interest, but little understanding. According to the doctor he was '*f & h, ment al, alc add o'come. Reg dent t'ment. Tfr 1954.*' John looked at the cryptic entries and wished he knew their meaning. He copied them down in his notebook with the intention of asking Saffron later. She might well know what the doctor had been recording.

John looked through the remainder of the records, but could not find anything relating to Tassos Nevrakis amongst them. He checked a second time. There was a man named Tassos Iliopolakis and he checked the lettering carefully before having a quick look at the man's medical record.

According to the doctor the man had lived on the island since nineteen thirty five, having arrived at the age of twenty seven. At intervals over the years Doctor Stavros had added small amounts of information. *'dg r.h. - s.'* About a year later there was an entry *'amp 2 dg r.h. to ass dext.'*. John again copied the entries to ask Saffron at a later date if she knew their meaning. Tassos Iliopolakis's records finished with his transfer to Athens in 1954. It was unlikely he was the man John was searching for.

John worked his way steadily back through the records for the previous years, finally finding the name Tassos Nevrakis. He opened up the notes eagerly. The date Tassos had arrived on the island in 1939 was recorded and again there were some medical notes that he copied into his notebook.

'irreg skn pig; l ind amp.'

There were no more entries regarding Tassos's medical condition, nor was there a date that the man had died, just a red line drawn across the page.

John looked through all the remaining records, gratified that those relating to Spinalonga were bundled up separately from the other patients on the mainland. That had certainly simplified his task. He would be able to tell Doctor Papanakis that at least one shelf in the cellar could be cleared with impunity.

He imparted the information to Doctor Papanakis as he thanked him.

'Did you find what you were looking for?'

'Well,' John hesitated. 'Yes and no. I found out when the man had been admitted to the island, but there's no record of his death or transfer to Athens.'

'Have you asked at the Town Hall?'

'Why should they have medical records?'

Doctor Papanakis smiled. 'They wouldn't have medical records, but they may have a record of the pensions paid to the islanders.'

John's face lit up. 'I hadn't thought of that. Manolis was their book keeper. When they left the island that duty would have passed on to someone else in Athens, but there must be the old records. If the Town Hall can't help me they should be able to tell me the name of the bank where the money was held and they should certainly still have records of the transactions.'

Doctor Papanakis nodded. 'It's quite possible, but be prepared to be told that the information you are searching for is in Athens.'

John sighed. 'If only Manolis were still alive. I'm sure he would know what happened to him.'

John approached the reception desk in the Town Hall and smiled at the woman who was talking on the telephone. She frowned at him and he took a couple of steps backwards and tried not to listen to the conversation. Within a few minutes he realised that it was a private call she was making to a friend, discussing where they would meet that evening and certainly not a part of her duties. He waited patiently for almost ten minutes and when she showed no sign of curtailing the call he approached her desk again.

She scowled at him and turned away, still talking animatedly. John looked around. There was no one else in sight, but there was a bell on the counter that said "Ring for Attention". He placed his hand on it and pushed the plunger up and down three times. The woman continued talking on the telephone and ignored him. John rang again and this time a man emerged from a side room.

Before John could greet him and make his request known the man declared the Town Hall would be closed in five more minutes and no further business could be transacted that day. John shook his head.

'My business will not take more than two minutes and I have already been waiting here for fifteen.'

The man shook his head. 'I'm sorry. I have to start to lock up now, so I have to ask you to leave.'

Furious, John turned on his heel and left the building. He knew there would be no point in arguing. He would just have to return earlier in the day and hope the receptionist would not be busy talking to her friend on the telephone.

'Hello, is that Marianne Pirenzi?'

'No, she's engaged elsewhere at the moment. Can I help you?'

'I really need to speak to her. Would it be convenient if I called back in an hour?'

'That should be fine. What name shall I tell her?'

'It's Mark, her nephew.'

'Mark! It's Bryony here. How are you?'

'I'm sorry. I didn't expect you to answer the 'phone.'

'I do when Marianne is busy. Am I able to help you?'

Mark hesitated. 'No, I think I ought to speak to Marianne.'

'Is it about coming over for John and Nicola's party?'

'Yes, but I still need to speak to her before we make a final decision.'

'I do hope you will come, and Paul, of course. Goodness knows when the whole family was last together.'

'I can't remember, so I was probably a baby. I'll call back in an hour and hope to speak to Marianne then.'

The telephone went dead and Bryony looked at the receiver in annoyance. Why was it necessary for Mark to speak to Marianne? He could have told her if he and Paul were planning to come and she would have passed the message on.

Mark called again later in the morning and once again Bryony answered. 'Hold for a minute. I'll get Marianne for you.'

Bryony handed the receiver to Marianne, who sighed and saved the details she had been entering on the computer. Surely her nephew could have left a message earlier; he was probably going to say he was not coming to Crete.

'Hi, Marianne? Good to speak to you after so long. First I want to say thanks for the invite. I'm speaking for Paul as well. We'd both of us like to come over, but there are a couple of things I'd like to ask you about.'

'I'm pleased you'll both be able to come. I know how much John is looking forward to seeing you both again.'

Bryony suppressed a giggle, having heard how enthusiastic John was about his cousins visiting.

'Yeah, be good to see him, too. The thing is, it's obviously rather a long way for us to come just for a week. I wondered if we would be able to stay in your self-catering units for a bit longer. Not for free, of course, but we thought we could hire a car and make a holiday out of it. We all like walking, so we would be out all day and can look after ourselves for food and everything. All we really need are beds and a shower.'

Marianne frowned. 'Are you thinking of two weeks as well as the one we offered to everyone?'

'That would be fabulous. We'd like to spend some time in the area, then go and stay somewhere else for a while and see what other parts of Crete are like. We haven't been over since we were children. I remember the wonderful swimming and being dragged around Knossos, but not much more. We didn't think we should just assume we can take advantage of your accommodation and go off to do our own thing without discussing it with you first. You could be fully booked up.'

Marianne smiled. At least her nephew had some manners. 'Your mother hasn't mentioned staying longer to me. Has she changed her mind?'

'It's nothing to do with Mum. She wouldn't want to walk anywhere. That's the other thing I wanted to ask; could our partners come with us? They don't have to come to the parties or anything, although I'm sure they'd like to meet everyone.'

Marianne shrugged. There was no reason why her nephews and their partners should not stay on, particularly if they were prepared to pay.

'That's no problem, Mark. I had put you and Paul down to share a room, but I'll allocate you two adjoining units and your partners will be welcome to come both parties.'

'That's great. Thanks Marianne. I'll tell Teri and Ron they have to bring something decent to wear. Will it be warm enough to swim in April?'

'I can't guarantee that. Bring your trunks; they won't take up much space and we can always let you have beach towels.'

'Fabulous. Thank a lot. I'll let the others know. See you in April. Bye.'

Marianne replaced the telephone and turned to Bryony. 'Mark says he and Paul would love to come over for the parties and asked if it would be alright for Terry and Ron to come with them. They plan to hire a car and want to stay on for a couple of weeks.'

'Terry and Ron?'

'Their partners. I'd better let Giovanni know.'

Giovanni raised his eyebrows and frowned at the same time. 'I'm not sure I'm happy about having that sort of relationship under my roof.'

Marianne shrugged. 'It's acceptable these days. I could hardly refuse on those grounds. We've had same sex couples sharing the chalets in the past. We don't enquire into their relationships before we agree to them staying, besides Uncle Andreas lived with Laurie for years and they were a delightful couple of gentlemen, devoted to each other. '

'Is your uncle coming over?'

'He says he will.'

'In that case he'll know how to deal with them.'

Marianne looked at her husband in amusement. 'You don't 'deal' with them. They're no different from you or me.'

Giovanni looked at her sceptically. 'Does Grandma know?'

'I have no idea. Helena has never mentioned their partners to me so I doubt that she has told Grandma. Don't worry, Giovanni. They'll only be here for the parties and then they plan to go off walking each day.'

John was not amused when he was told that his cousins were

coming over and bringing their partners. 'They're just taking advantage of our hospitality. I didn't like them when they visited us before.'

'You were all children then. Mark sounded a very decent, responsible young man. He's offered to pay for their accommodation.'

'I bet they still cheat and hate losing. What about Uncle Andrew? Is he coming?'

'I haven't heard from him, but there's still time.' Marianne consulted her list. 'We'll have to ask Vasi to reserve four rooms. There's your grandparents, Aunt Eleni and Uncle Andreas, and Nicola's grandparents. Vasi's father and Cathy will stay at the house along with Marjorie. Everyone else can stay in the self catering apartments. I'll make sure there are a couple of spare room ready in case Andrew or anyone else turns up unexpectedly.'

'Like who?' asked John.

'Your Aunt Maria could decide to come over.'

John snorted in derision. 'That's not likely. Even Grandma hasn't heard from her for years.'

'Well we're still waiting for a reply from both Bob and Andrew. It doesn't mean they won't arrive. Their replies could have been lost in the post.'

'So could their invitations. Provided Nick has her mum and dad here for our party I'm sure she won't mind if aunts and uncles are missing.'

'Dad has said he will go up and collect your grandmother, Helena and Greg from the airport. He's asked Angelo to arrange his flight to arrive near enough the same time so he can collect him and Francesca and not have to make more trips up and down than necessary. We're still not sure when Nicola's parents and grandparents are arriving. At least Mark and Paul plan to hire a car and drive down.'

John pulled a face. 'It would be far simpler if everyone was told to check into a hotel in Heraklion for the night and we collected them the following day. Why don't you ask Vasi if they can stay at the Central for the night?'

'Someone would still have to meet them at the airport. You can't expect visitors to come all that way and be left to fend for themselves.'

'Mum, they're not children,' protested John. 'Vasi could meet them at the airport and take them back to the Central or taxis could be arranged and Vasilis could meet them at the hotel. For what it will cost in gas going up and down that arrangement could work out cheaper.'

'I suppose so.' Marianne looked at John doubtfully. 'I am rather dreading them all arriving at different times on the same day. If they all came at the same time I could have refreshments ready and not have to spend time rushing around and replenishing plates and making drinks.'

'That's the answer then.' John beamed. 'I'll speak to Vasi and see if he wants me to 'phone his father or if he'll make the arrangements if I give him a list.'

'You'll still have to speak to Vasilis,' protested Marianne. 'After all, it's a courtesy. You're asking him to do you a favour.'

'A favour we will be paying for,' John reminded his mother. 'Of course I'll phone Vasilis, but I want to ask Vasi first if rooms will be available and if his father is willing to have them occupied for only one night. He could refuse. No hotelier likes one-nighters. You know how you complain if people want self catering for three nights rather than a week. Leave it with me. I'll let you know if Vasi and his father agree and then I can e-mail everyone and tell them the arrangements.'

Marianne frowned. 'I'm not at sure there'll be enough room in the people carrier for all of them and their luggage. They're bound to have a fair amount with them.'

'Mum,' John looked at her in exasperation, 'Will you stop seeing difficulties where there aren't any. If they don't all fit then we hire a taxi or two. It's still better than Dad having to make endless trips up and down to the airport and if there are any flight delays he could be waiting around for hours. Leave it up to Vasi and me to organise and stop worrying.'

'I just want everything to be perfect for Grandma, and you and Nicola, of course. It's such a big family occasion.'

February 2010

John returned to the Town Hall in Aghios Nikolaos two weeks later. He had composed a letter implying he was undertaking research for the television series that was being made about Spinalonga. He hoped it would not be necessary to produce it, should a Town Hall official wish to check his claim was authentic the Italian film company would certainly say the application had not been made by them. He had made a list of questions and was hoping that a certain amount of bluffing on his part would gain him the information he wanted.

The same woman was in attendance at the reception desk and John approached her with a broad smile.

'Good afternoon. I do hope you may be able to help me. You know there is a television series being made about Spinalonga, yes, of course you do, everyone knows. It's the talk of the area. Everyone is really excited. I've been asked to check a few facts.'

The woman frowned. 'How can I help?'

John pulled his typewritten sheet of questions from his pocket. 'I was hoping to be able to speak to someone who could confirm the original number of inhabitants who were living there in nineteen forty one. How many of them survived the war? How many were sent to the hospital in Athens? The company want to make sure their basic information is accurate.'

The woman shook her head. 'I've no idea.'

'Is there anyone employed here who might be able to help?'

'Maybe Spiro might know,' she replied tentatively.

'Would it be possible to speak to him? If he has the information I need it should only take a few minutes of his time.'

'I'll see if he's free.' The receptionist lifted the receiver of her telephone and dialled an extension number. When it was answered she turned her back on John and held a quiet conversation, finally announcing that Spiro would be able to spare him no more than ten minutes and he would have to wait until the man was free.

John thanked her profusely and took a seat a short distance away from the desk, wondering how long he would be kept waiting. He took out a notepad, hoping it made him look professional, and consulted his list of questions again. To many of them he already knew the answer, but had thought it could be diplomatic to profess ignorance. During the next half an hour two people entered the building and deposited some paperwork, but there was still no sign of anyone coming to attend to him.

He cleared his throat and looked pointedly at the reception desk and then down at his watch. The woman ignored him and John decided he would curb his impatience for a further quarter of an hour before approaching her again and reminding her of his request.

A door to one side opened and the most corpulent man John had ever seen strolled out. He raised his eyebrows at the receptionist and she pointed to John with her pen. John rose, held out his hand and grasped a sweaty palm.

'I appreciate you being able to see me, sir.' John resisted the urge to wipe his hand down his trousers. 'I'm sure I won't need to keep you very long.'

The man waddled back to the door and John followed him through into a small office. The chair creaked as the man lowered his weight on to it and mopped his brow. A fan was blowing cold air into the room and John shivered inadvertently. The man must have a serious problem during the summer months if he was finding a February day hot.

'What do you want?' he wheezed.

'Just a few facts about Spinalonga. How many people were living there in nineteen forty one?'

Spiro wrinkled his brow. 'I wasn't working for the government then. I wouldn't know.'

John nodded understandingly. He knew the answer to that question from Uncle Yannis's papers. 'Would you know how many sufferers were still alive after the war?'

'Forty or so.'

'You can't be more accurate?'

'Why should I be expected to remember?'

'So you're not able to tell me how many finally went over to the hospital in Athens?'

The man shook his head and mopped his brow again. 'If you need accurate figures you'd have to consult the archives.'

'Yes?' John looked at Spiro eagerly. 'Am I able to see those?'

'They're not here; they'd be in Heraklion or Athens.'

'What about their pension records?'

'Same place, I expect.'

'So you have nothing here at all?'

Spiro shrugged. 'Not that I know of. The bank may have some pension records, but they'd be confidential.'

'Of course,' agreed John. 'I'd only want to know how many people were in receipt of a pension before and after the war. That would give me the information regarding the number who survived. I don't need any financial details.'

'Why don't you ask the Doctor? He should have a record of the deaths.'

'I have asked him. He has the records left by Doctor Stavros. He allowed me to look through them. There's a record for one man, but no date of death. He suggested I asked here at the Town Hall.'

'Well we can't help you.'

John rose and steeled himself to take hold of the sweaty palm again. 'Thank you for your time. I'll contact Heraklion as you suggest and see if they can help.'

John returned home feeling decidedly dispirited. It had been too late in the day when he had left the Town Hall to approach the bank, so that would mean another journey into Aghios Nikolaos.

'I'm sure I'll have to go to Heraklion eventually. I'm not going to find out anything down here,' he complained to Nicola. 'Someone must know what happened to the man.'

'Don't despair until you've tried the bank. If you can't get any information from them you can go up to Heraklion next month and check the accommodation arrangements with Vasilis at the same time.' Nicola squeezed John's hand. 'I think it's quite possible he drowned and that's why Uncle Yannis never mentioned him again.'

John shook his head. 'I'm sure Uncle Yannis would have recorded that. The information would have reached the island eventually.'

'Maybe his death wasn't recorded by the doctor and he didn't tell them because he thought it would upset them,' suggested Nicola.

John looked at his wife scathingly. 'I doubt that would have entered his mind. Besides, Manolis would have had to be told as he was the book keeper, whoever found the body would have talked about their discovery and sooner or later the islanders would have heard; someone would have been sure to tell them.'

Nicola giggled. 'You are obviously so like your old Uncle Yannis. He was obsessed with rebuilding and then getting everyone the new medicine. You've become obsessed with this man Tassos.'

John grinned sheepishly at her. 'It's just not knowing. Did he reach the mainland; did he become a pedlar; did he evade the authorities?' John frowned. 'He may have been found, of course, and sent to the leprosarium at Chios, but he could have walked straight out of there. Chios is a large island and the leprosarium was on the mainland'

'You could approach the authorities on Chios and see if they have any record of him.'

John shook his head. 'I'm sure that would be a waste of time. Chios is miles away, almost in Turkey. No, I'll go to the bank next time I can get to Aghios Nikolaos and if they tell me their archives are in Heraklion I'll have to make a trip up there.'

'And if they say their archives are in Athens what are you going to do then? Go over there?'

'I'd write or telephone them first. They could have destroyed everything, of course, and then it would be a wasted journey.'

'And a waste of money. I know you put a substantial sum aside for the girls and we've agreed never to touch that unless it's a dire emergency, but the amount it's going to cost us for this party is certainly going to eat into your balance,' Nicola warned him.

'It won't be that much. Remember, Dad is paying half as it's Grandma's birthday. We only have to pay Vasilis for the rooms at the Central and Vasi for the days people spend at the Katerina. The self catering is free and five hundred Euros should cover the food and drink easily. If everyone comes we're only feeding thirty people.'

'Don't forget you have to pay Pappa Lucas to conduct a blessing and he'll expect a taxi to take him to the church in Plaka, and to come back here to join the party.'

'Nick, stop worrying. We've plenty of money.'

John walked into the bank at Aghios Nikolaos and asked to speak to the manager. The chief clerk frowned. He was sure this young man was not one of their customers.

'If it's to open an account I am able to deal with the formalities. There is no need to trouble the manager.'

John smiled. 'No, I have a bank account elsewhere. I want to find out about some past accounts that were your responsibility.'

'Has a relative died?'

John shook his head. 'It's far more complicated than that, although the answer is very simple. I want to know if you have the records here of the pension that was paid to the inhabitants of Spinalonga?'

The clerk's eyebrows shot up. 'The island was closed in the nineteen fifties.'

'I know,' John nodded. 'That's why it's a little complicated. I imagine if you do have the records here I would need the manager's permission before I could look at them or be given any details. I'm happy to tell you exactly what I'm looking for, but I'll probably only have to repeat myself to him. If you don't hold the records please tell me and I won't waste any more of your time.'

The clerk looked at the serious young man. 'Are you an inspector?'

'Inspector? No. Whatever gave you that idea?'

'It is not usual for people to come in and ask us about our customers' records.'

'I am only interested in one man, but you won't be able to help me if the records are no longer here.' John sighed. Why did officials find it so difficult to answer a simple question?

'I'll see what I can do.' He pressed a button on his intercom and a disembodied voice asked how they could help. 'Please could you come to the counter for a moment. I believe you may be able to answer a question for the gentleman who is with me.'

The clerk turned back to John. 'I have asked Panayiotis to come in. He's been with us for over forty years and may remember something.'

John sat and waited, his heart was racing in anticipation when Panayiotis eventually appeared and shuffled through the door.

'How can I help, sir?'

'The gentleman is enquiring about the pension records for the inhabitants of Spinalonga. Do you know what happened to them after the island was finally closed?'

Panayiotis nodded slowly. 'They were stored downstairs until three years ago. We were under no legal obligation to keep them any longer and planned to dispose of them. The head office in

Heraklion thought they should be kept a bit longer, due to the interest there is now in the island.'

'So do you still have them?' asked John eagerly.

'No, as I said, we had them until three years ago. As far as I know they're in Heraklion now.'

'I suppose you don't remember if there was an account for a man named Tassos Nevrakis?'

'I never looked at them. No reason for me to do so.'

John shrugged resignedly. 'Oh, well, thank you for your help. At least I know where they are now.'

'What's your interest?'

'I'm just involved in some research.'

'Oh, yes, something to do with that film company, isn't it? My daughter-in-law told me you'd been to the Town Hall.'

'That's right. Well, I won't take up any more of your time. You've been very helpful and I'm grateful.' John was now in a hurry to leave before he was asked any further questions about the film company.

Panayiotis nodded slowly. Something was not quite right here. According to his daughter-in-law the young man had wanted to verify the number of inhabitants on the island before and after the war. Now he only appeared to be interested in one man. He shrugged as he left the office. Whatever the young man wanted was none of his business.

John had shown the cryptic entries he had copied from Doctor Stavros's notes to Saffron and she had smiled when he transcribed the letters from Greek to English.

'It's pretty simple, just a form of medical shorthand. Shall I read it to you? You'll kick yourself for being dense when I do.'

'Go on, then. You're the clever one in the family.'

'There's nothing clever about it. I imagine doctors do it all over the world. It saves a considerable amount of time and keeps the records somewhat confidential from the patient. They don't always understand that long words for simple complaints are nothing to worry over. If I said you were suffering from rhinitis what would you think I meant?'

John looked at her in alarm. 'Some disease I'd picked up from a rhinoceros?'

'Idiot! I've not seen a single rhinoceros in Crete. It would mean you had a common cold.'

'Really!' John looked at her in surprise.

Saffron indicated the letters with her finger. 'This is old Uncle Yannis's record?' and John nodded.

'Well, he was fit and healthy, mentally alert. Had overcome his alcohol addiction and received regular dental treatment.'

John looked at Saffron in amazement. 'It says all that?'

'It also indicates that he went to Athens in nineteen fifty four.'

John nodded. 'That's what he says in his books. He was one of the first to go over as he had been such a nuisance to the authorities. What about this next one? I'm pretty sure this isn't the man I'm looking for. The name isn't right, but I was intrigued by the doctor's notes.'

'I'm guessing a bit here,' admitted Saffron, 'but I think it says that the digits, they're your fingers, on the man's right hand had lost some of their sensitivity. This entry a year later implies that two digits were amputated to help him regain the use of his hand.'

'How would that help?'

'Bend two fingers into your palm, John, and then try to pick something up.'

John followed Saffron's instructions, experimenting with different fingers. 'That is so difficult,' he admitted. 'They get in your way.'

'Exactly. They're no longer any use to you. Take them away and it increases the amount you are able to do with your hand. You'd be able to lift a spoon to your mouth without spilling everything.'

'This is the entry I found for Tassos Nevrakis.'

Saffron looked at it and frowned. 'Irregular skin pigmentation – in other words he had some discoloured patches. That could have been due to anything. Left index amputated. I wonder when that was done?'

'It's the only entry under his name so it could have been done before he arrived. There's nothing else, no record of him having died on the island or being found drowned anywhere.'

Saffron shook her head. 'I can't help you any more, John. At least if you come across medical shorthand again you'll have an idea how to interpret it.'

John wrote to the medical authorities in Heraklion and asked if it would be possible for him to have a list of the men and women who had lived on Spinalonga and survived the war. The authorities replied that they had no such list; if it was still in existence it would be at the hospital in Athens. John wrote to Athens and waited impatiently for their reply. Politely they explained they could not send him a list due to patient confidentiality, forty three patients from Spinalonga had been admitted to the hospital during nineteen fifty four and fifty seven.

The government were no more helpful when John wrote and asked about the pension that had been paid to the inhabitants of Spinalonga. Again he was told that no information of that kind could be disclosed to him. John tried again. How many lepers from Spinalonga were paid their back pension after the war ended? He received a curt reply saying that everyone had been paid whatever was owed to them and it would be far too late for him to try to claim on behalf of a relative now.

John composed a letter to the bank in Heraklion hoping he would be able to persuade them to open their records to him and he might find when the pension paid to Tassos Nevrakis was discontinued. He explained that he was doing some research into the government grant that gave the islanders a pension for the remainder of their lives. All he wanted to know was the number of people who received their back pension, personal details were not necessary.

When John finally received a reply from the bank he read it through three times, then looked in his file for the letter from the Athenian hospital. It was as he thought when he had first read the reply from the bank. There was a discrepancy. According to the hospital a total of forty three patients had been admitted, but the bank claimed that forty four people had been paid their pension arrears.

A delighted smile on his face he waved the letter at Nicola. 'There's something wrong with their records,' he announced. 'The hospital says forty three and the bank says forty four.'

'Forty three what?' asked Nicola. 'Can you put the girls' toys back into their playpen? They've decided it's a great game to throw them out and then howl. I want to get the ironing finished.'

John bent and picked up the stuffed rabbit and gave it to Elisabetta. She promptly threw it back again.

'I see. If you throw them out, I'll throw them in.' He tossed the rabbit back into the playpen so that Elisabetta had to reach as far as possible and finally toppled over with a surprised look on her face. She wriggled helplessly and John placed her back in a sitting position where she held up her arms for him to lift her out.

'Oh, no. If I take you out Jo will want to come out as well.' He pushed a toy dog up to her. 'Woof, woof, woof. Skele has come to say hello.'

Elisabetta stretched out her hands for it and Joanna promptly tried to take if from her. 'No, you have the cat, Jo. Miaow, miaow. Listen, Nick. I've had a letter from the bank to say they paid forty four people a pension, but the hospital claim that only forty three people were admitted from the island.'

'Someone fiddled the books,' replied Nicola nonchalantly.

John shook his head. 'It's possible, of course, but suppose Tassos wasn't admitted to the hospital with the others? He may have already been there and claimed his pension when he found the others were receiving theirs.'

'Sounds logical.'

John ducked as a Joanna threw a soft ball out of the playpen. 'How did they discover this game?' asked John as he returned it to her.

'I think we have to blame Marcus. He was encouraging them to throw a ball to him.'

'Then I suggest he comes and sits with them and throws the toys back. If I write to the bank again do you think they'll tell me if Tassos received a pension?'

'I don't know. You can try, but be prepared for them to insist the records are confidential.'

'Maybe if I went up to Heraklion and called on them I could get an answer.'

'John,' Nicola looked at her husband in concern. 'It's only two weeks until the big parties. Can't you forget this man for a while?'

'Two weeks is plenty of time. I'll go up next week, check with Vasilis that there's no problem with the accommodation at the Central and call at the bank at the same time.'

Nicola unplugged the iron and placed it safely on the side to cool. 'John, will you promise me something? If you don't get any information from the bank you'll stop trying to find out what happened to him.'

'If I can't get any useful information from them I don't know where else to turn so I'll have to give it up,' replied John morosely. 'Can these two be set free now?'

John entered the bank and approached the desk confidently. 'Excuse me, I was told I could gain access to your archived records for the inhabitants of Spinalonga. I have a letter here from the manager.' He waved the letter at the clerk, hoping the man would not read it and realise he had not actually been granted permission to look at the archived accounts.

The man glanced at it briefly and handed John a form. 'Fill that in. You won't be able to take any personal information about any one of them away with you unless you can prove you're a relative.'

John filled in the form with his name and address and his request to examine the ledgers relating to the pension paid to the islanders. The man took the completed form from John and scrutinized it.

'You'll need to be more specific. There are twenty ledgers stored downstairs. You'd need a week to go through them all.'

John frowned. He should have realised there would be more than one ledger covering the transactions. 'Are they in alphabetical order?'

'No. New islanders' names were added when they arrived.'

'I'm really only looking for one man. I just want to see if his name is amongst those who had his pension arrears paid to him after the war. I spoke to the doctor in Aghios Nikolaos but he said the medical records of the survivors had been sent to Athens and suggested I asked the bank for the information I'm seeking.'

'Why didn't you say so?' grumbled the bank clerk and handed John a new form. 'Fill that in with your details as before and where it says "reason for request" write in "pension arrears payment records".

John did as he was requested and added Tassos's name.

'Is that the person you're looking for?'

John nodded. 'Tassos Nevrakis.'

'Never heard of him. What's your interest?'

'My great uncle was living on the island. He kept diaries and said that Tassos had floated over to the mainland in his bath tub. There's no record of him having been recaptured and returned to the island. According to my uncle he was going to become a pedlar. I'm just trying to find out if he survived. I haven't managed to find out anything specific, but the Athenian hospital said they had admitted forty three patients and the bank told me they had made forty four pension arrears payments. If one of those payments was to Tassos Nevrakis the man must have survived.'

'And if a payment was not made to him?'

John spread his hands. 'Then I'm at a total dead end.'

'You say he's not a relative?'

John shook his head. 'I don't need any private financial details. You can look in the ledger for me, just look for the name and tell me if the bank records paying him.'

'I'll have to ask the manager. I'm not sure I have the authority to give you any information. How do I know what you plan to do with it?'

John sighed in despair. 'I don't plan to do anything with it. I just want to know whether the man survived the trip across to the mainland.'

'Wait here.'

John waited in an agony of impatience until the man returned accompanied by the manager. Once again he had to explain his interest in Tassos Nevrakis and finally the manager agreed to consult the ledger.

'You can come with me, but I can't allow you unlimited access, you understand.'

'If you'll just look for the name, please.'

John followed the manager through a locked door and along a corridor. Rooms led off, each with a paper label attached to the door. Stencilled boldly on the label was the year the records related to, becoming older as they went further down the corridor. Finally the manager stopped outside a door that had 'archives' painted on it and took out a key.

'You can look over my shoulder as I turn the pages, but you cannot make any notes without my permission.'

John nodded. He was certain he could memorise anything relevant that caught his eye.

The manager looked along the shelves and finally pulled out a thick ledger which he placed on the large wooden table. He opened it and began to flick the pages over quickly and John was convinced he would miss the name altogether.

'Could you go a little more slowly, please?'

The manager ignored his request and continued until he was almost at the end pages. He then slowed and looked at the name on each page. John saw the name Yannis Christoforakis and was tempted to ask how much his uncle had received. Automatically John counted the pages as they were turned and he felt unreasonably disappointed when he had counted forty three without coming across the name Tassos Nevrakis when the end of the ledger was reached.

'He's not there.'

'I'm afraid not. We obviously cannot help you.'

'Oh, well.' John shrugged. 'That's it then. There's nowhere else we could look, I suppose?'

The manager shook his head and closed the ledger. As he did so a loose page fluttered down to the floor and John retrieved it. He gave it a cursory glance as he was about to hand it to the manager and then looked at it more closely. Clearly written at the top of the sheet was the name TASSOS NEVRAKIS and beneath it the words COMPENSATION CLAIM 1945.

'This is it!' John was elated. 'This is the man. What was the compensation he claimed? Are you able to look in the nineteen forty five file for me?'

The manager took the sheet of paper from John, slipped in back into the front of the ledger and shook his head. 'If there was a compensation claim filed the records would be with our legal department in Athens.'

John groaned. 'I don't believe it. Just when I thought I'd finally tracked him down. Is there any way you could get the details sent over to Heraklion for me?'

'Not without a legal request from your solicitor. Even then you could have a problem getting permission as you say you're not a relative.'

'Isn't there anyone here who would know why Tassos was paid compensation rather than just his arrears?'

The manager furrowed his brow. 'You could ask Kyriakos. He might remember. He would have been working here about that time.'

'Yes?' John's face lit up. 'Where can I find him?'

The manager shook his head. 'He retired years ago. I can't give you his address or telephone number without his permission.'

John sighed in exasperation. 'Would you be able to telephone him and ask if he's willing to meet me? I only want to ask him if he remembers anything about Tassos.' He slipped his hand into his pocket and drew out his wallet.

The action did not go unnoticed by the manager.

'I suppose I could telephone him,' he agreed as John placed some notes in his hand.

John sat in the taverna, a glass of beer before him and waited. He hoped desperately that the man would arrive soon and be able to help him. He had promised Nicola he would check at the Central that Vasilis had received the confirmation they had mailed to him regarding the final number of rooms they wanted reserved for their relatives the following month.

The simple task would take at least an hour as he would be bound to accept hospitality from Vasilis. He then had to drive back to Elounda and would prefer to negotiate the highway whilst it was still light. It was always busy with the coaches transferring visitors to their hotels, but the later the hour the more anxious the drivers were to dispose of their passengers and would often drive recklessly.

A silver haired man, leaning heavily on his stick, shuffled into the taverna and looked around. John rose to his feet. 'Good afternoon. Are you Kyriakos?'

The man nodded. 'Are you the young man who's asked to meet me?'

'I am. Can I buy you a drink, sir?'

'A whisky, make it a double.'

John raised his hand to the bar tender and placed the order. Kyriakos sniffed the glass and took a sip, smacking his lips and smiling in satisfaction.

'So what's this old claim you want to ask me about? Can't guarantee I'll remember it. I was only a junior cashier back then.'

'It's the claim Tassos Nevrakis made. I understand the bank paid him compensation in nineteen forty five.'

'What's your interest in him? Are you a relative?'

'No, I'm Yannis Christoforakis's nephew. He lived on Spinalonga until the island was finally closed and he kept notebooks detailing events over there. He recorded that Tassos Nevrakis floated over to the mainland and escaped. After that there's no mention of him. I've been trying to find out if he survived the journey and if the authorities ever found him.'

Kyriakos looked into his empty glass and John hurriedly ordered another drink for him. 'Tassos Nevrakis.' Kyriakos shook his head. 'I do remember him. He opened a bank account to have his disability pension paid in each week. A bit later a very large sum was credited to him by the government.'

'What was that for?'

Kyriakos shrugged. 'It said compensation. It wasn't my place to ask what for.' He tapped his head to indicate that Tassos was deranged. 'He insisted on withdrawing the full amount in cash. I referred him to the manager, of course, but we couldn't refuse to pay him the money. His war disability pension continued to be paid in and then a few months later he withdrew that and closed the account.'

'Why was he receiving a war pension?'

'I don't know. Some injury he'd sustained whilst fighting, no doubt.'

'What happened to him?'

'I've no idea.' Kyriakos insisted and looked ruefully into his empty glass. 'I simply recorded the amounts in the ledger. That was the end of the matter as far as I was concerned.'

'Did he return to his family?'

'I've told you, I don't know what happened to him.'

John frowned. 'The compensation money; are you sure you can't remember any details about it? If it came from the government there must be a record of it. Where could I go to find out?'

'What for?'

'It might just give me a clue to where he went or how he spent the money.'

'Probably went off to America. A lot of families went over there after the war.'

John nodded. 'Very likely; but would I be able to read any relevant papers?'

Kyriakos sighed and looked at his empty glass again. 'I suppose I could ask at the Town Hall. It was over sixty years ago. He's unlikely to be around to object, even if he stayed in Crete.'

John returned to Elounda elated. 'I've got him,' he announced to Nicola. 'I've found Tassos.'

Nicola looked up in surprise. 'Really? Where is he?'

John shook his head. 'I doubt if he's still alive, but at least I know what happened to him at last. After the war he was given a large sum of compensation money by the government.'

'That could have been awarded to him for a war injury.'

'I don't think so. He was receiving a war disability pension and that was being credited to his bank account. No sooner had the compensation money been credited to him than he withdrew it all in cash.'

'Wow! He must have thought himself a millionaire.'

John's brow creased in a frown. 'I should have asked Kyriakos if he knew what disability warranted receiving a war pension. I must remember to do so when I meet him again.'

'Didn't you say that in the doctor's notes it was recorded that the man had a finger missing?'

'That's hardly a disability that would entitle you to claim a pension, besides, according to Doctor Stavros's records his finger was missing when he lived on the island.'

'What did he do with all his money?'

'I've no idea. Kyriakos thought he may have gone to America.'

'John! You haven't really found him then.'

'Kyriakos is going to ask at the Town Hall if they have any papers relating to the compensation payment. They might give me a clue. He said he would 'phone me at the end of the week. Whilst I'm waiting to hear from him I can look on the internet at the old shipping lists for Greeks who went abroad after the war.'

John closed his computer with a sigh. 'There doesn't seem to be any trace of him. His Spinalonga pension account was closed by the government and I can't think where else to look for him now. It's frustrating, but at least I know he survived his bath tub voyage.'

Nicola smiled. 'So that's the end of the search for Tassos. Now maybe you'll concentrate properly on the arrangements for our party.'

John shook his head. 'Not until I've been up to Heraklion and seen Kyriakos again.'

John sat at the taverna waiting anxiously for Kyriakos to arrive. The man appeared to be in no hurry, stopping to greet acquaintances as he walked past the tables. John rose to greet him.

'Whisky?' he asked and Kyriakos nodded.

John returned to the table, a double whisky for Kyriakos and a beer for himself. 'Did you manage to get permission for me to look at the papers?' he asked.

Kyriakos shook his head. 'The request was refused.'

John's face fell. 'Why didn't you tell me that over the 'phone? When you said you would meet me again today I expected you to have gained permission for me.'

'I spoke to Zak. He can't come here, but if you're willing to visit him he said he'll tell you what he remembers. We'll need to take a taxi.'

John was about to say that he had his bike parked only a short distance away when he realised the old man would not be capable of riding pillion, particularly through the Heraklion traffic. 'I'll find one,' he said.

They drew up outside a shabby apartment building on the road leading towards the airport and Kyriakos led the way round to the rear of the building. Zak opened the door at their knock and led them into the living room. An elderly woman sat in a chair, her eyes closed, and John guessed she was the reason why Zak had been unable to meet with them at the taverna.

'Take no notice of Maria,' he said. 'She doesn't know what day it is. Kyriakos said you'd been asking about the compensation payment paid to Tassos Nevrakis. What did you want to know?'

'Anything. Anything at all that you can tell me about it. I've tried to find out what happened to him after he escaped from Spinalonga.'

Zak shrugged. 'I don't know how he evaded the authorities. After the war he obviously thought it worth the risk to be tested for leprosy and get an identity card to comply with the new laws.'

'He was taking a hell of a risk.'

'All I can tell you is that there was a good deal of wrangling between the bank, the government and the medical authorities. That's why I remember. Apparently a large sum had been credited to him that was his arrears of the disability pension he'd been entitled to as a leprosy sufferer. The problem was, having papers to prove he was free from the disease, the government said he was not entitled to it. He could not receive a pension as a leper if he did not have the disease and should only be in receipt of his war pension.'

John nodded. That was logical. 'So did he have to pay it back?'

'He refused. He said it was compensation for misdiagnosis and if they insisted the money was repaid he would sue the medical authorities. The doctor who'd been in charge of the island at the time backed his claim.'

'So what happened?'

'The government backed down. They realised he could be awarded a far larger sum than the amount of his pension arrears if he took his case to court. He continued to receive his war disability pension, of course, so he was no worse off.'

'Why was he receiving a war pension? What was his disability? Did it say?'

'He'd only one hand. He lost his right hand during the war.'

'Poor chap. He was already a finger short on his left.'

Zak shrugged. 'He was probably finding life difficult. That could have been why he decided to have the tests. Had he proved positive he could have claimed accommodation in the hospital, lived there for free and had money in his pocket.'

John shook his head. 'Somehow I don't believe that was the reason. He'd left Spinalonga, planned to travel around as a pedlar to avoid the authorities and now he's suddenly prepared to be readmitted to a hospital.'

April 1939

Tassos was convinced that he was not leprous. He had had dry, scaly patches of skin behind his knees and the bend of his elbows since he was a child. His mother had rubbed olive oil into the areas and it had seemed to help with the irritation he suffered and also to soften the skin. Sometimes a dry, itchy patch developed elsewhere on his body and due to his scratching he would have ugly red scabs where he broke the skin. Despite the discomfort they always disappeared after a few weeks.

Working with his father in the cobbler's shop he had sliced off the end of the index finger on his left hand whilst he was cutting leather and when septicaemia subsequently set in he visited the doctor. The doctor amputated the infected finger and a week later had insisted on giving Tassos a thorough examination to ensure the infection had not spread elsewhere. On seeing the white, scaly areas, cracked skin and a small amount of pus erupting from the sores he had immediately suspected leprosy.

Tassos had been stoical and not flinched when the doctor had pricked the afflicted areas with a pin. He now realised the mistake he had made. Insensitivity in an area was a sign of leprosy and the doctor had no hesitation in diagnosing the illness. Despite all Tassos's protests that he had suffered from the skin complaint since he was a child and it was nothing to be concerned about, the doctor was adamant that he must be sent to a leprosarium for treatment.

Tassos cursed his stupidity in believing the doctor when he

said he would be sent to a hospital and receive treatment. A cart had arrived at his house and he had been ordered to collect his possessions and bid his family farewell. Still trusting the doctor he had not resisted and assured his parents he would only be away for a short time. What a simpleton he was!

He had been taken to Heraklion, placed in an ambulance and driven for over an hour. He had no idea where they were taking him and was surprised when they finally arrived at a fishing village and he was ordered into a boat. Now he was on Spinalonga amongst all the other leprous men and women who were incarcerated over there and probably would be for the remainder of his life. When he looked at his companions who were afflicted he was convinced he was not a leper, he had none of the disfiguring nodules, his remaining fingers were straight and nimble and he had no trouble walking due to nerve damage in his toes.

When he was a boy Tassos had watched as the travelling scissor grinder and knife sharpener worked. Sparks shooting off the wheel in a cascade of bright colours as the man turned the handle of the grindstone. He would then test the sharpened edge with his thumb and finish the blade on his whetstone. It had been exciting, each time Tassos had held his breath, waiting to see if the man would cut himself.

It was not as exciting as when the man had come through the village with his dancing bear. He had always kept a safe distance away, despite the bear being muzzled, as it stood on its hind legs and pirouetted, its large paws outstretched. He had not been afraid of the chimpanzee who was dressed as an old lady. The very first time he had seen her he had screamed and buried his face in his mother's skirt, but once he realised she was an animal dressed up to look like a woman he would place a drachma in her hand, feeling the dry, leathery skin.

He had dreamed of travelling around the villages from one end of Crete to the other with a bear or chimpanzee when he was old enough. It would be an adventure. He had no idea where you found bears or chimpanzees on Crete. He knew when he did find one he would have to catch it and then train it. He would like to have asked advice from either of the men who owned animals to see if they could help him, but once they had collected the coins people threw at them they were always in a hurry to move on.

His childhood dreams were over. He no longer wanted to travel the country with a bear or chimpanzee. He wanted to be back in his village, working with his father as a cobbler, even if it did mean living with Damara. He had been away for over a year. Neither he nor Damara, the carpenter's daughter, had wished to marry each other. The arrangement had been made between the families when they were children.

Tassos's mother had done her utmost on her son's behalf to cancel the betrothal. In the white of Damara's left eye there was a distinct brown mark. It had to be a sign that the devil had touched her. Due to his wife's persistent nagging, Tassos's father had spoken to the carpenter, suggesting that the marriage might not be as suitable as they had first thought and maybe the childhood betrothal should be forgotten. Damara's father was furious, he explained that the mark in his daughter's eye was the same as having a brown mole on your skin; she had inherited it from her grandmother. If Tassos's family wished to break the agreement that had been made fifteen years ago they would have to pay substantial compensation for the insult that it would be to his daughter.

Tassos's father was in no financial position to pay any compensation demanded of him and finally agreed the arrangement should stand. Damara's father had finally conceded that the marriage should not take place for a further two years to enable the couple to get to know each other better, but a betrothal party had been held and he and Damara had become reconciled to spending the remainder of their lives together.

When Tassos had been diagnosed with leprosy his mother was convinced that Damara had cursed him for delaying their wedding.

She berated her husband for not standing out more firmly against the marriage agreement or paying the compensation demanded of him so the ceremony would never take place.

At first Tassos had asked the doctor who visited the island weekly, to take a blood sample or skin scrapings from him, but the doctor had refused. He explained that he had no facilities to conduct the detailed examination the samples would need. Tassos had been examined and diagnosed. Sadly he must now accept his fate and spend the remainder of his life living amongst the exiles.

Unconvinced by Doctor Stavros's excuses Tassos had appealed to Father Minos. The priest had regarded him sadly. 'I am unable to do anything more than pray for you, my son. We all have burdens to bear in this life and unfortunately yours is a particularly heavy one.'

'Couldn't you speak to the doctor?' pleaded Tassos.

Father Minos shook his head. 'I am not a medical man. I cannot challenge the diagnosis and demand that you are re-examined. The only advice I can give to you is to accept your fate. Once you have come to terms with your illness it will not be so hard to bear.'

His island companions seemed to be accepting of their lot; they even appeared happy now most of them had somewhere weatherproof to live and the doctor visited regularly. When they began to receive a pension from the government their spirits had lifted even further. Small shops had been set up along the main road, hens provided eggs, others supplied home grown vegetables and fruit; Panayiotis kept some goats and supplied milk to the hospital patients; there were two barbers, a dressmaker and four tavernas. Tassos had declared that he would work as a cobbler. He wished he had brought his tools with him, rather than leaving them with his father. It would have saved him having to purchase new equipment.

Manolis was being kept busy. Having agreed with Father Andreas that he was willing to become the book keeper for the lepers on Spinalonga he had spent weeks purchasing the items and equipment the islanders wanted to enable each of them to start their own business. He had to find out where he could purchase the goods on their behalf most cheaply and all of them fretted at any delay.

Having found out the cost Manolis then had to check that the islander was willing to pay the amount he quoted. When the sale had been agreed Manolis would make the purchase and enter it into the ledger under the person's name and deduct the cost from the amount of pension available. Once a week he would visit the church and present them with a list of suppliers to be reimbursed and the accounts to be debited. It had been time consuming to compile the ledger, but now the system was underway it was working smoothly and efficiently.

Tassos pursed his lips as he looked at the list Manolis handed back to him. 'A stitching awl costs that much?'

Manolis nodded. 'No doubt prices have risen since you bought your first one.'

'Are you making a profit for yourself?' he asked suspiciously.

'Not a drachma. I get a small allowance from the government for acting as the book keeper. I don't need to steal from you,' replied Manolis, hurt that his honesty should be questioned.

Tassos shrugged. He was not convinced. 'I'll think about the items and let you know.'

Manolis nodded. 'Whenever you're ready.' He knew the only way the man would be able to purchase any goods from the mainland was through him and he was being kept busy collecting the items others had asked for. He had more than enough to do each day without buying anything for Tassos.

Tassos sat at the side of the road and looked at the list of items with Manolis's prices beside them. If he was to set up as a cobbler and repair the boots of the islanders he needed a sharp knife, stitching awl, needle and thread, along with a small hammer, a leather hide and boot polish. There was no way he could afford a wooden last or marking wheel.

He added up the amount it would cost him to buy the items. He knew he had seven drachmas a week paid in to his account the same as everyone else. His brow furrowed in concentration as he tried to calculate the balance that would remain on his account after purchasing the necessary tools and the price he would be able to charge for his services.

He was a cobbler, not a boot maker. Would he run out of customers before he was able to recoup his expenditure? There was a limit to the number of times an old pair of boots could be patched before they fell to pieces. He would never become a rich man, but what would he do with riches anyway if he was on Spinalonga for the remainder of his life?

'All right, Tassos?'

Tassos nodded. 'Just trying to work out if I've enough money to buy a last.'

Michaelis sat down beside him. 'A last what?'

'A cobbler's last. You put the boot over it and it makes repairs easier.'

'You could ask the bank to give you a loan,' grinned Michaelis.

'I'm sure they'd oblige!' Tassos rose to his feet. 'I must get up to the hospital. Spiro said he would pay me if I'd give him some help with the cleaning a couple of afternoons a week.'

'What do you need more money for?'

'I told you. I'd like to be able to have a last. I'd be able to make new boots if I had a last and marking wheel.'

Michaelis shrugged. The man was a fool. Many of the islanders had cut away the sides of their boots so they could manage to get their misshapen feet inside. They would not thank Tassos for sewing them up again and would certainly not want new boots made.

Manolis frowned as he arrived at the jetty, accompanied by Flora and saw Tassos waiting for him.

'Have you decided which items you want me to buy for you?'

Tassos nodded. 'I can't afford a last yet, so I've crossed that off. I've made a new list for you. I need a stitching awl, cobblers' thread, glue, a small hammer and a sharp knife. According to you I've enough money on my account to buy those.'

Manolis nodded. 'I should have them by this time next week.'

'I'll have another week's pension in my account then, won't I?' asked Tassos anxiously.

'I've told you, seven drachmas a week. You get the same as everyone else.'

'Would you be willing to get me a piece of leather on credit?'

Manolis shook his head. 'Once I give one person credit everyone else would want credit as well. If you have enough money in your account I'll buy whatever you want.'

Tassos shrugged and turned away. It would not have hurt the fisherman to buy a piece of leather for him and be paid later. He could hardly run away. He looked across at the mainland and wished he was able to swim.

Tassos waited impatiently for Manolis to deliver the goods he had ordered and expressed his satisfaction with the purchases. 'Have you found out the cost of a piece of leather for me?'

'My uncle works at the tannery and he says he could pick up a piece for you for about twenty drachmas.'

'Pick up as purloin or will he pay for it?'

Manolis glared at the man. 'He'll pay for it. I'll bring you a receipt.'

'How much will that leave on my account?'

'Your balance at the end of this week will be eighteen drachmas. You'll have to wait another week before you can afford the leather. If you pay twenty drachmas for the leather you'll be left with five drachmas.'

'So I'd have enough for another stitching awl?'

'What's wrong with the one I bought for you?'

'Nothing. A second is always useful. I could break the first one and after a while the needle gets blunt. Another knife would be handy as well. One to use and one to lose.'

Manolis nodded. 'I'll see what I can do. I'll buy the leather for you as soon as your pension has been credited to your account, but you'll have to wait until there's a bit more on there before I can buy you another knife and the awl.'

Tassos considered. 'Get me some more thread. The knife and awl can wait another week or two, unless you'll take cash.'

Manolis shook his head. 'You know I'm not allowed to take actual money off the island. The shopkeepers would refuse to touch it.'

Tassos continued to help Spiro up at the hospital, the money he earned he placed in a pot in his house. He was not going to be misled like some of the islanders and immediately visit the taverna and drink his savings away. Whilst he repaired the boots that were brought to him he was able to immerse himself in the work and pretend that he was still in his home village with his father, but if he had nothing to keep him occupied he sat and brooded.

His chin on his hands Tassos thought deeply. He was not as accepting of his fate as the other inhabitants and not prepared to spend the rest of his life on Spinalonga. He examined his body regularly. Despite the removal of his left index finger the others showed no sign of clawing and they had lost none of their sensitivity. He still had the cracked, dry skin behind his knees and at his elbows which would itch and the small spots would discharge a small amount of pus. Occasionally patches still appeared on other parts of his body, but after a few days they would dry up and disappear. He had none of the disfiguring signs of leprosy that were evident on the other men and women on the island.

He knew it would be impossible to return to his village of Gazi and resume his work with his father. The villagers had been made aware of his fate and would not accept him back amongst them, but there was no reason why he should not visit his family and creep away into the hills. It would just be a question of evading the authorities, but he needed to be patient and plan carefully.

July 1940

Tassos sat down beside Yannis, hoping he could glean some useful information from him.

'You know this area, don't you?'

Yannis nodded. 'I used to live over in Plaka when I was a boy.' He pointed to the small village that was just across the water.

'How far away are the other villages?' Tassos waved his hand in the direction of the mainland to where clusters of houses could be seen up on the hills.

Yannis shrugged. 'About an hour from Plaka and then they're only a short walk from each other. Why?'

'Just curious. What's over there?' Tassos indicated the arm of land that ran parallel to the mainland shore and almost touched the island.

'Only the mills. You can't see them from here.'

'So is there a village?'

Yannis shook his head. 'No one lives over there as far as I know. Manolis might know if there's a village on the other side. He used to sail that way round until Doctor Stavros bought a motor for his boat. Now he's able to cut through the canal without having to lower his mast each time. Takes a good hour off his journey.'

Tassos sat and contemplated the information Yannis had given him. 'So what else is down there apart from the mills?'

'The salt pans and Manolis says they've built a carob factory with machinery. Ships are down there continually loading up. I'm sure my father's pleased that he can take our carob crop there. He used to take it in to Aghios Nikolaos each year. My brother would have to do it now. Since my father broke his leg it's doubtful if he could walk there, although he'd be able to ride back on the donkey.'

'How much further is it to Aghios Nikolaos?'

'From Plaka it would take about three to four hours. It's not far away, but walking up and down the hills takes time.' Yannis smiled. 'I thought Aghios Nikolaos was wonderful when I lived there with my cousins. There were shops selling everything you could possibly imagine, not like in Plaka where there was just the general store. There was even a library where you could borrow books to read.'

'That's where Manolis buys the things we ask for, isn't it?'

Yannis nodded. 'You can buy just about anything you want in Aghios Nikolaos. They have a proper school with trained teachers, not like in the village where the priest passes on whatever knowledge he has. There are doctors, dentists, even a hospital there.'

'If they have a hospital there why can't Doctor Stavros take some tests from me to prove I'm not suffering from leprosy?'

Yannis shrugged. 'You'd have to ask Doctor Stavros.'

'I have and he says he hasn't got the facilities. Why can't I go to the hospital? They must be able to do the tests there?'

'Tassos, you have to accept that once you have been sent to Spinalonga you are here forever. There's no way the doctor would be able to take you to the hospital at Aghios Nikolaos.'

Tassos sighed heavily and shook his head. 'There has to be a way and I'm determined to find it.' He rose and looked longingly over at the mainland.

At the end of the week Manolis found Tassos sitting down on the quay waiting for him.

'What have you forgotten to ask me to add to the shopping list?'

Tassos shook his head. 'Nothing. I just wanted to ask you a

couple of questions.'

Manolis released Flora's hand. 'Let me put this in the boat.'

He jumped down into his fishing boat with the heavy ledger that had the records of the money paid to the islanders and the bills he paid on their behalf. He stowed it safely inside the small cabin and climbed back onto the quay.

'So, what did you want to ask me?'

Tassos considered. 'Well, I've been watching the way the water ripples. Is that due to the currents or the breeze?'

'Bit of both. You can't always see it when you're down level with the water, but if you go up on the fortress walls you can usually see quite clearly which way the current's running.'

'Does it always run the same way?'

'More or less. Why?'

'Just wondered. I thought I might go for a dip in the sea and I wouldn't want to be swept away by the current.'

'Keep close to the shore and you won't have a problem. If you start trying to swim across to Plaka you could be caught in the cross current and that will take you down to the canal,' warned Manolis.

'What's down there?' asked Tassos innocently, waving his hand towards the canal that could not be seen from the island.

'The salt pans, olive mills and carob factory.'

'So are people working down there every day?'

Manolis nodded. 'Usually.'

'What about the other side of the headland?' Tassos pointed to the spit of land that jutted out.

'It's rocky everywhere around there. No one lives or farms over there. What's your interest anyway?'

Tassos shrugged. 'Just curious.'

Manolis regarded him suspiciously. 'Well if your curiosity has been satisfied can I go home now?'

'Thanks for your time.' Tassos walked back through the arch towards the ramparts of the Venetian fortress. He would have to look again at the ripples on the water. Obviously to try to sail down to the canal and expect to go ashore unseen was definitely out of the question. He needed to talk to Yannis again.

'Yannis,' he began tentatively, 'When you floated over to Plaka, where did you land?'

'You mean where was I washed up on to the rocks! About there.' Yannis pointed across the short stretch of water to the mainland.

'Was that where the current took you?'

Yannis nodded. 'I had a piece of wood with me, but I found I couldn't keep my balance if I tried to use it to steer or paddle.'

'Did you tip over?'

'No, just rocked alarmingly.' Yannis smiled at the memory. 'After that I just sat still and hoped I would drift in to the shore and not out to sea.'

'How long did it take for you to get over there?'

'I've no idea. It seemed like hours. I left here when it was dark and it was still dark when I arrived. My brother and father hadn't gone to bed, so it can't have been that late. I had a good meal and a brandy.' Yannis smiled at the memory. 'My brother gave me some dry clothes and I spent the night sleeping in the stable with the donkey.'

'Why didn't you stay there with them?'

'To hide away in a cave and be dependent upon them for my food?' Yannis shook his head. 'I only wanted to visit my mother. I had no plans to stay on the mainland.'

'What happened when the authorities found you there?'

'I wasn't at the farm. My sister told me the bath tub had been found and the boatmen were searching for me. My father ordered me on to the cart and covered me with grass. My brother took me to the outskirts of Elounda and then I started walking. No one challenged me until I was almost through the village, then the villagers began to throw sticks and stones at me. I just carried on walking towards Aghios Nikolaos and they followed me, calling out to anyone we met on the way that I as a leper.'

Tassos frowned thoughtfully. 'No one took any notice of you when you walked through the village?'

'Not for a while. People were busy about their own business. It wasn't until word reached them that there was a leper from Spinalonga in the area that they realised I was him.'

'So if you had been carrying some farm implements you could easily have been ignored?'

'Possibly. Why? What's your interest?'

Tassos ignored the question. 'Is Manolis trustworthy?'

'Of course,' replied Yannis scornfully. 'We all trust him to purchase items for us and charge us the correct amount.'

'I mean could he be trusted not to go to the authorities if he knew one of us was planning to leave the island?'

'I'm sure he could. When he brought me back from Aghios Nikolaos he said I should have told him my plan and he would have collected me from Plaka and saved me the walk.'

Tassos looked out at the sea. 'It looks calm enough, but I need to know if there are any dangerous currents that you can't see.'

'Ask Manolis, he would know. You haven't answered my question. Are you planning to make the trip?'

Tassos nodded. 'I'm thinking about it.'

'Adonis tried and he found it impossible to survive without help.' Yannis had a disturbing thought. 'I couldn't ask my family to help you. If the authorities found out they'd suffer repercussions.'

'I wouldn't ask it of them. I'll be willing to take my chance. Adonis hadn't planned properly.'

'And you will?'

Tassos nodded and smiled. 'I'm gradually getting it worked out in my head. I still think the canal could be the safest landing place to make for.'

'That's quite a distance to sail in a bath tub. There will be people working down by the canal in the mills and salt pans.

There's also the carob factory so there's bound to be someone around all the time. You'd be wiser to make for Plaka, besides if you capsize it isn't so far to swim to land.'

Tassos shrugged. 'Makes no difference. I can't swim.'

'You can't swim?' Yannis looked at the man in horror. ''You're thinking about sailing across that stretch of water and you can't swim? What happens if you capsize?'

'I'd just have to hang on to the bath tub. It's wooden so it will stay afloat.'

'Is it really worth the risk, Tassos? Even if you reach the shore once your bath tub is seen by the fishermen there will be a search for you.'

'Then I'll have to make sure they don't see it.'

'How do you propose to do that?'

'I've various ideas.' Tassos rose. 'Thanks for the information. I'll let you know what I decide.'

Yannis looked after him and shook his head. The chances of the man escaping detection if he did reach the mainland were slim.

Tassos licked the stump of his pencil. According to the ledger Manolis kept by now he should have over two hundred drachmas at his disposal along with his savings that he kept in a pot. He began to compile a list. He could not have anything too heavy or bulky. Needles, sewing cotton and buttons were essential, along with screws, nails and string. He decided to add some pot menders and wicks for oil lamps. Once he had seen the cost of those items and also the amount of space they took up he would decide whether he could afford to add some crochet hooks, embroidery silks and ribbons. The other item that was a necessity was a leather bottle in which to carry a supply of water.

He smiled to himself. Manolis was going to be puzzled when he presented him with his shopping list this week and the quantity he required of each of the items. He already had two sharp knives for cutting and shaping leather, but he would ask Manolis to buy him some more strong needles, three extra balls of thread and another awl. A whetstone would be essential for sharpening his knives and those belonging to others and he must invest in some more leather. He scratched his head. He would need a notebook in which to keep account of his money and purchases. He also needed to have some money in his pocket and he would be able to use the savings that had accumulated in his pot. He would ask Manolis to bring him whatever remained on his account to add to the amount. He knew the quantity of goods he would be able to transport across the water were minimal. Once he had made a few drachmas he would buy some pots and pans, spoons and any other small, easily portable goods that villagers could need.

Manolis frowned when he saw the list of items. 'Why do you want two notebooks?'

'One to use and one to lose,' grinned Tassos.

'Are you sure you wouldn't like two water bottles? Why do you need one anyway?'

'Save me having to queue up first thing each morning at the drinking fountain.'

'They're expensive, four drachmas.'

Tassos shrugged. 'There's enough money on my account, isn't there?'

Manolis nodded. 'Are you sure you want a hundred sewing needles?'

Tassos nodded. 'Exactly as the list says.'

'Are you opening up a general store?'

'Something like that.'

'I still don't see why you'll need a hundred needles.'

'One to use and one to lose. People put them away somewhere safe and then can't find one when they need it so they buy another. I need a small tin to keep them in along with the buttons.'

Manolis shrugged. 'It's your money, but I would have thought you could have cut down on the quantities and bought some other bits and pieces. You want nails and screws but you haven't added a hammer or screw driver to the list.'

'I can get those later. I plan to start in a small way.'

'When do you want to open up?'

'How quickly can you get everything?'

'A couple of weeks.'

Tassos nodded. 'I'll need whatever money is left on my account after I've paid you. I'd like at least twenty drachmas in small value notes.'

'You may not have two drachmas left after I've bought this lot for you,' grinned Manolis.

Tassos shrugged. 'In that case you can bring it to me the following week when my pension has been paid to the bank.' He tried to appear unconcerned, but now he had finally made his decision he was anxious to put his plan into effect and take advantage of the summer weather.

Tassos examined everything that Manolis brought over to the island for him and spent a considerable amount of time listing the items and their cost in the notebook. He was pleased he had asked Manolis to bring him two. In one he would keep account of his income and expenditure and in the other he would list the villages he visited. Now he needed to plan how he would manage to transport his goods in the confined space of a bath tub. The sack he had washed in the sea would hold the roll of leather, safely wrapped in his woollen cloak, along with a spare pair of trousers, two shirts and a jacket.

Tassos placed the goods on the floor of his house and looked at them critically. They were a small and measly collection. He wrapped the screws and nails around with some scraps of leather, not wishing for them to make holes in his trouser pockets, then unwrapped them. It would be more practical to remove the buttons from the tin and replace them with the nails and screws. With the leather scraps he would make a pouch with a drawstring, large enough to keep his money and identity papers safe and he could hang it around his neck during the journey and tie it to the belt of his trousers later.

Having made one money pouch he decided to make a second. It would be sensible to have two. If he should inadvertently lose one he would still have money at his disposal.

He placed the reels of cotton, buttons and pot menders into a pocket of his spare trousers and the ribbons, crochet hooks and skeins of embroidery silk in the other before wrapping the trousers around his cobbler's tools. His precious whetstone he wrapped first in his spare shirt and then again in his jacket, before folding his blanket and placing it on top. By the time he had finished the sack was quite bulky and he knelt on it to ensure nothing stuck into his knees. He was sure the short journey across the water was going to be unpleasant and he certainly did not want to make it painful also.

Finally he sought out Yannis. 'Are you willing to help me?' he asked.

'What needs to be done?' Yannis's thoughts immediately turned to a roof repair or something similar in Tassos's house.

'I'm leaving. I thought I'd go tomorrow night. It should be calm, there's a half moon to give me a bit of light and I've packed my sack.'

'What are you taking with you?'

'Everything.'

Yannis frowned. 'You mean your cobbler's tools? Is that wise? If you're caught they'll send you back here with nothing and you'll have to buy them again.'

Tassos shook his head. 'I don't plan to get caught. Once I've reached the shore and removed my sack I'm going to fill the tub with stones and push it far enough out so that it sinks.'

Yannis eyes him doubtfully. 'There are some large stones on the beach at Plaka, but if you land up on the rocks you won't find any.'

'Then I'll pull it inland and hide it beneath some bushes. If that isn't possible I'll tip it over and push it out to sea. It will be less noticeable upside down.'

'So once you've disposed of your bath tub what will you do then? Take to the hills?'

Tassos shook his head. 'You told me no one challenged you until they heard there was a leper around. Provided they don't find the bath tub too quickly no one will be looking for me. I'm going to walk into Elounda and stand in the square and announce my arrival. I'm going to be a pedlar and a travelling cobbler.'

Yannis shook his head in disbelief at the man's audacity. 'When the authorities find you've escaped they'll ask if there has been a stranger around.'

Tassos smiled confidently. 'And everyone will say they've not seen a stranger, only the pedlar. Besides, by the time they're asked I shall have moved on to another village. If I'm challenged I have goods with me to sell so why shouldn't people believe I'm anything but a genuine travelling pedlar? I'll have a bit of money with me so I can buy some food and not have to beg and draw attention to myself that way.'

'Suppose no one buys anything from you?'

'Someone will need to have their boots repaired or their scissors sharpened. My mother often waited weeks looking out for the knife grinder to visit the village.'

'Where will you go after Elounda?'

'I'll ask someone for directions to the next village and keep on moving. That's another thing that will confuse the authorities if they do start to look for me. They will expect me to hide in the hills and make my way towards Gazi. I'm going in the opposite direction to begin with; then I'll gradually work my way back up the coast.'

Yannis looked at the man in admiration. 'You really have planned carefully. If you're ready to go why are you waiting until tomorrow?'

'Manolis should be bringing me my money from the bank

tomorrow when he comes over. That's the last thing I'm waiting for; then I shall be off.'

Yannis nodded. 'I'll help you with your bath tub and I'm sure Spiro will also. All I can do is wish you a safe journey and a prosperous new life as a pedlar.'

August 1940

Tassos was waiting anxiously for Manolis to arrive on the island. He had looked round his small, sparsely furnished house and decided there was nothing more he needed to take with him. He placed his pencil and bent spoon on top of his sack. He would add those to his pocket at the last minute.

'I've left one drachma on your account,' announced Manolis as Tassos signed his name to acknowledge the transaction.

'Why?'

Manolis shrugged. 'You might be grateful one day, besides I can't remove your name from the ledger without a letter from the doctor declaring that you've died.'

'So my pension will continue to be paid to me?'

'Why shouldn't it be? You're entitled like everyone else here.'

'Suppose I don't draw any more money from it?'

'Then it will just sit there until such time as you want it.'

Tassos nodded slowly. 'That's good to know.' He had no idea how he would be able to access his money without returning to Spinalonga, but he was sure he would be able to find a solution to the problem if necessary. 'Thanks, Manolis.'

'When are you going?' asked Manolis.

Tassos frowned. 'What do you mean, when am I going?'

'I'm not stupid. All the information you asked for about the currents and the coast line started me thinking. Then the quantity of small items you've asked me to purchase along with a water bottle and now wanting all your remaining money tells me that you

have something in mind other than starting a general store here.'
Manolis smiled. 'Good luck. If I see your bath tub I'll sink it.'

'Not whilst I'm in it, I hope. I can't swim.'

Manolis looked at him in horror. 'You're going to float over to the mainland in a bath tub and you can't swim? You must be mad.'

Tassos shrugged. 'What have I got to lose? I'm not prepared to spend the rest of my life over here as an outcast. I'd rather take the chance that I capsize and drown.'

Manolis shook his head sorrowfully. 'I wish I could help you, but you know what would happen if the authorities found I had given you a ride. When do you plan to leave?'

Tassos considered his answer. Could he trust Manolis not to go to the authorities and tell them his plans? 'I haven't decided yet. I'll see what the weather's like.'

'Said to be set fine with a light wind for the next few days. I'll be moored up each night before it's dark and spend the evenings in a taverna.' Manolis winked at Tassos. 'I know nothing.'

Tassos smiled in relief. 'Thanks,' he said and walked away, clasping his money in his hand with the intention of placing it in his money pouch once he was back in the privacy of his house.

As soon as it was dark Yannis and Spiro helped Tassos carry the bath tub down to the jetty where he placed his sack inside. Carefully they lowered it into the water where Manolis usually moored his boat and Tassos climbed in, kneeling on the sack, the tub rocking precariously as he did so.

'You're awfully high up,' remarked Yannis. 'You'll have to be careful you don't tip over the side.'

'Once you've pushed me away from the jetty I'll keep still and wait for the current. After that I just have to take my chance.' Tassos settled himself as comfortably as was possible, holding tightly to the sides. 'I'm ready,' he announced. 'Give me a push to start me off.'

Yannis and Spiro watched as the bath tub bobbed up and down

gently on the water, appearing unwilling to leave the island. Tassos held the sides and rocked himself forwards and then gently backwards and the makeshift boat moved a few inches. His progress was slow, but eventually he felt the current catch him and the tub began to move without any further movement from him.

'Do you think he'll make it?' asked Spiro.

Yannis nodded. 'Provided he doesn't panic he shouldn't have a problem.'

'How long do you reckon before he's found and brought back?'

Yannis shrugged. 'If his plan works he won't be coming back. Provided he's successful in getting rid of the bath tub no one will even know he's left the island.'

'We should have arranged for him to send a message to us.'

'How would we have done that?'

'I don't know; something cryptic to Father Andreas with instructions to send the message on to Manolis who would deliver it to Father Minos.'

'Well, it's too late now. We should have thought of that earlier. Now I guess we'll never know what becomes of him.'

Tassos gripped the sides of the bath tub. Despite his bravado he was petrified that he would fall out and be unable to cling to the wooden bath tub. He had never joined the other boys when they went to the beach in the summer months. He had been self conscious about his skin condition and the sun and the salt water had made the irritation worse; consequently he had never learnt to swim.

Although there was a certain amount of light from the moon Tassos could only make out the dark shape of the mainland. He did not dare to turn round to see how far he was from Spinalonga. He just had to hope that he would drift in somewhere and be able to go safely ashore with his precious sack.

The tub bobbed and dipped with the current, sometimes moving quite quickly and at other times seeming motionless.

He wished he had a way of calculating how long he had been on the sea. He knew the boats from Plaka took only half an hour to reach the island, but he was sure he had been at sea for far longer than that.

He peered across the dark expanse of sea, hoping he would be able to spot any jagged rocks that would probably tip him out of his precarious craft. The moon reflected off the water in places and in others it seemed to be a solid black mass. There was a grating noise below him and he held his breath. If he was grounded this far from the shore he would have no choice but sit there until the first fishing boats came into the area when it was daylight. That would ruin all his plans.

To his relief after the initial sound the bath tub progressed reasonably smoothly on its way and Tassos realised he was very close to a rocky outcrop, but if he could manage to avoid it there seemed to be an area of clear water that led to the shore. Risking capsizing he straightened up as far as he could whilst in his kneeling position and as he reached the first of the rocks he pushed himself away with his hands.

The bath tub rocked violently and sweat came out on Tassos's brow as he clutched again at the sides. The tub stabilised and when he drifted near to the rocks again he risked giving it another push. This time he was prepared for the unsteady motion and also realised that he had made some progress towards the shore. Alternately pushing and waiting, he eventually felt the tub grind to a halt beneath him and he could see there was only a short stretch of water between him and the land.

Tentatively he rose to his feet and placed one leg over the side. The water came half way up his leather boot. Hoping he would not suddenly find that he had misjudged the depth he swung his other leg over and grasped his sack. He would take that to safety and then return to deal with the tub.

Feeling cautiously for a footing in the shallow water he waded ashore and placed his sack on a high, dry rock. Smiling happily he turned and made his way back down to the water's edge. To his horror he saw the bath tub had disappeared and he could just make out the shape of it as it bobbed back out to sea now it was relieved of his weight. For a moment he wondered if he could wade in and retrieve it, then decided that would be foolish. By the time he reached it the water could be above his head. He would just have to hope that it was holed by a rock and sank.

Tassos returned to where he had deposited his sack and rubbed his boots against it. He did not want them to be stained by the salt water. Once it was light he would use some of his precious polish to ensure that any white marks were erased. He decided it would be wise to try to make his way off the beach and find somewhere to hide. If he sat there until day break he would be spotted by the first boat that sailed past the area.

He shouldered his sack and tried to find the easiest route to leave the small cove. As he struggled over the rocks he hoped he was not damaging his boots too badly. He ended up at the base of a cliff, and although not high, it was impossible for him to scale. He followed the base of the cliff until he finally found a rough path, probably made by goats, which he would be able to scramble up, pushing his sack before him. Panting and sweating from his exertions he threw himself down to rest when he reached the level ground.

As soon as he saw the sun begin to rise over the hills he knew it was not safe for him to stay there any longer. He needed to be in Elounda and have taken up a stance in the square by the time the villagers began to emerge from their houses.

Manolis arrived early on Spinalonga and sent Flora to find Yannis. He greeted him with a broad grin on his face. 'Is Tassos around?' he asked. 'I think I have something that belongs to him.'

'Maybe. Do you want me to find him?'

'You'll have your work cut out unless you plan to follow in his footsteps.'

'What do you mean?' frowned Yannis.

'There's quite a gathering in the square over in Elounda. I imagine a pedlar must have arrived in the village, or maybe a cobbler.' He winked at Yannis. 'I found a bath tub floating down towards the canal. Fancy helping me to bring my catch ashore before any of the other boatmen arrive?'

'That must mean he landed safely at any rate.' Yannis was relieved. Once he and Spiro had lost sight of Tassos into the darkness they had no way of knowing if he had reached the shore.

Manolis had passed a rope through the handle of the bath tub and it now hung lopsidedly against his boat.

'If you take that side and pull, between us we should be able to get it on board.'

'Why don't you just put it on the jetty?'

Manolis looked at Yannis and shook his head. 'It will be easier to do that from the boat once we've got it out of the water.'

Yannis nodded. He could only just reach the tub from where he stood on the jetty, whereas Manolis was standing on his boat. 'Can't you get any closer?' he asked.

'Not with the tub in the way.'

Yannis looked around. The water boats were leaving Plaka and they would have less than ten minutes to get the bath tub onto the jetty before the boatmen would be able to see their endeavours.

'Can I come aboard? I can't do anything from here.'

Manolis glanced over at the boats that were approaching from Plaka. 'Better be quick about it.'

Yannis stepped cautiously down into the boat. It was a long time now since he had jumped into a fishing boat. Yannis pulled at the unwieldy wooden tub whilst Manolis hauled on the rope he had used to secure it, finally able to grasp the handle and pull it over his guard rail where it sat on the deck.

'Get back on the jetty. You pull from that side and I'll push. Once we've got it ashore you can take it back up to your house.'

'I can't manage it alone. Where's Flora?' asked Yannis.

'She can't help you carry it. She isn't strong enough.'

'I wasn't suggesting that. I was going to ask her to go and fetch Spiro.'

'There's no time for that. The boats are too close.'

Manolis picked up his fishing net and dumped it on top of the bath tub, pulling bits of the net down over the sides until the tub was completely hidden. He looked at Yannis and grinned conspiratorially.

'I wonder if that pedlar will be in Aghios Nikolaos when I return. I could do with some buttons for my shirt.' He winked at Yannis. 'I'll let you know if I bought any when I come tomorrow.'

Tassos replaced his unsold items back into his sack as the small gathering of villagers who had come to view and purchase his goods dwindled. He was not sure how much money he had taken, but he would certainly have enough to buy a meal without opening his money pouch. A man asked where he had come from and he had waved his arm vaguely in the direction of Plaka.

'Walked in over the hill earlier this morning. Is there anywhere here where I can get a meal before I walk on to the next village?'

'Are you going along the coast?'

Tassos nodded. 'Can't get lost whilst I can see the sea. Thought I'd taken a short cut over the hills earlier, but I think I walked in circles.'

'Easy done if you don't know the area. Keep going that way and you'll reach Aghios Nikolaos eventually.'

'How long will it take me to walk there?'

The man shrugged. 'Three hours, maybe; depends how fast you walk. Go down towards the salt pans and you'll find a taverna there that caters for the workers.'

Tassos followed the man's directions and walked along the shoreline. He was conscious the whole time that Spinalonga was only a short distance away, but he did not want to draw undue attention to himself by appearing anxious to leave the area.

He entered a hot and airless wooden shack that called itself a taverna and ordered a dish of fish stew and bread. It appeared to be the only dish available. He carried it over to a vacant table and immediately two men joined him. They looked at him curiously.

'Where have you come from?'

'Heraklion.'

The man looked at him in disbelief. 'You weren't here yesterday and you couldn't have walked that far this morning.'

'Oh,' Tassos smiled easily. 'I left Heraklion almost a week ago.'

'Are you looking for work?'

Tassos shook his head. 'I'm a pedlar, going round the villages. I was selling up in the square a bit earlier. Thought I'd have something to eat before I moved on.' He dipped his bread into the fish stock.

The man eyed Tassos's sack. 'What are you selling?'

'Needles, thread, screws, nails, ribbons for the ladies.' Tassos answered with his mouth full, then added. 'I can mend your boots and sharpen knives for you. What are you interested in? If I haven't got it with me now I can bring it for you in a couple of weeks when I come back this way.'

'You must have more than that in there.' He pushed at the sack with the toe of his boot.

'A blanket and a clean shirt along with my cobbler's tools.' Tassos took another bite from the bread. He had not realised how hungry he was.

'We've got a cobbler in the village.'

Tassos grinned. 'Wondered why no one wanted their boots patched. Maybe I'll have better luck elsewhere. So what's your occupation?' he asked, wishing to turn attention away from himself.

'Depends. I'm working at the carob factory this year. Last year I was at the salt pans .

Tassos nodded. 'This stew is pretty tasty. Better than the meal I had last night.' He bent over his plate, hoping he would be left to eat in peace and not be asked any more questions.

'What happened to your hand?'

'I told you. I'm a cobbler. Sliced my finger off when I was cutting leather. The doctor had to cut it off completely.' Tassos flexed his hand and straightened his fingers. 'I'm used to not having that one now. Glad I had four, one to lose without making any difference to me. Good job I'm right handed otherwise I may have had to learn to cut with my left; probably ended up losing all my fingers then.' He grinned to make light of the situation.

'Accidents happen. Makkis nearly lost his hand when he got it trapped in the oil press.'

'Nasty.' Whilst talking and listening to his companions Tassos had been eating steadily. He mopped his empty dish around with the bread and belched in satisfaction. He pushed back his chair. 'Well, I must be on my way. I understand it will take me about three hours to reach Aghios Nikolaos.'

'Sounds about right. If you're coming back this way I could do with some tobacco.'

Tassos nodded. 'I'll remember.' Give me a week or two.' He lifted his sack and placed it over his shoulder. Tassos had no intention of returning to Elounda. He did not want word to reach the village that a leper had escaped from Spinalonga; he would be easily identifiable with a finger missing from his left hand.

Once away from the straggle of houses he sat down on the bank and counted his money. He smiled with satisfaction; despite having paid two drachmas for his meal he had increased the money in his pouch by four drachmas. He entered the six drachmas into his notebook and deducted two. He would have to replenish some of his goods and he also wanted to increase his stock. To the best of his knowledge Manolis had purchased his list of items from Aghios Nikolaos so he should be able to do the same. He also hoped he might also be asked to mend a pair of boots. He needed to make at least four drachmas a day so he would have enough money to buy a meal and continue to replenish his stock without encroaching on the pension money in his pouch. He was prepared to sleep in the open until the end of the summer, and by then he planned to be back near Gazi and hoped to be able to find a permanent lodging.

Tassos looked at the goods on display in the hardware shop and considered the most practical items to purchase. He had sold four screws earlier, so would buy another ten, along with two sets of hinges, a hook and eye door fastening, ten wicks for oil lamps, two paintbrushes and ten boxes of matches. As he was about to leave his eye alighted on a wheelbarrow.

He studied it and lifted it up onto the wheel. It appeared to run easily. He placed the legs back down on the ground and considered. If he had a barrow in which to place his goods he would not have to carry them in his sack. He would also be able to carry more stock and some larger items. He returned to the man who had been watching him carefully from behind the counter.

'How much is the wheelbarrow?'

The shopkeeper hesitated. The man looked like a beggar, despite having paid for the goods he had selected without demur. How badly did the man want a wheelbarrow? Should he put an inflated price on it and maybe miss the sale or charge him his original asking price?

He licked his lips. 'Ten drachmas.'

Tassos looked at the wheelbarrow again and shook his head. 'I can't afford that much.'

'How much are you willing to pay?'

'No more than eight.'

The shopkeeper pursed his lips and pretended to consider. 'Nine?' he suggested.

Again Tassos shook his head. It was a considerable outlay on his behalf and if he planned to fill the barrow with saleable items he needed to budget carefully. It would also make him far more noticeable should anyone be searching for him. He hefted his sack onto his shoulder and turned to walk out of the shop.

'All right. Eight drachmas,' the man called after him, knowing he would still be making a profit of three drachmas.

Once outside he tested the weight of his sack. He could certainly add some items and not find it an insurmountable inconvenience to carry. He returned inside and the shop keeper looked up eagerly, the man had obviously decided to purchase the wheelbarrow.

'I'll have another set of hinges, a larger size with the screws to fit, ten cup hooks and two chimneys for oil lamps.'

'I thought you wanted the wheelbarrow.'

'Can't afford it,' replied Tassos cheerfully. 'Can you wrap the chimneys in a bit of newspaper or cloth? I don't want them to get broken.'

'I could charge you for packaging,' grumbled the shopkeeper.

'In that case don't worry. I'll wrap them in my shirt.'

Grudgingly the man pulled a crumpled sheet of newspaper from beneath the counter and wrapped each chimney separately. 'You wouldn't like the screws wrapped as well?' he asked sarcastically.

'I'm sure they won't break. Thank you for your trouble.' He waited whilst the man added up the total and handed over the exact amount. The chimneys had cost two drachmas each, but he should be able to add a drachma to the price when he sold them.

From the hardware shop he walked to the chemist and bought twenty bars of cheap soap and ten combs and on to the haberdasher to replenish the reels of cotton and embroidery silks he had sold earlier. He hesitated and then bought a small pair of scissors suitable for snipping the ends off embroidery threads. Satisfied that he had purchased enough items he walked back to the town square and looked for a suitable place to set out his goods at his feet.

As people passed he called out to them, listing the goods he had for sale and saying he was also a cobbler and would grind their knives and scissors to razor sharpness. Some hurried past after a cursory glance in his direction; others looked at his meagre display and shook their heads, until he was beginning to despair of making a sale. There was no call for a pedlar in a town. Yannis had been correct when he said there were plenty of shops there for people to purchase whatever they required. In future he would only try to sell his wares in the villages. He knelt and began to re-pack his sack in readiness to move on.

'Have you got any buttons?' A woman had arrived whilst his back was turned.

'Only shirt buttons, I'm afraid. Nothing fancy.'

'That's what I want.'

Tassos rummaged in his sack and brought out his container of buttons and needles. 'Six for two drachma.'

'But I only want four buttons.'

Tassos shook his head. 'I could sell you three for one drachma. That means you'd be a button short. If you take six you have four to use and two to lose.'

The woman hesitated. It was not her money. She would charge her nephew for the purchase later. 'Very well.'

'Do you need a needle or cotton?'

She shook her head. 'I've got that, thanks.'

Tassos placed the buttons in her hand and her drachma in his pocket. 'Well, I'll be off. See you the next time I'm in town.' He placed his goods back in his sack and walked down the hill. He considered going to the harbour to try to sell some items to the boatmen and thought better of it. If his bath tub had been found the fishermen would be looking for him and word of his escape would have been passed amongst them. Manolis would also be returning from Spinalonga soon and he did not want to meet him or the doctor and be recognised.

As he walked along the track away from the town he knocked on the door of any cottage he came across.

One man asked him for four screws and Tassos handed him five. 'Four to use and one to lose,' he had explained to the purchaser who had grinned and admitted that once he had dropped one he could rarely find it again. In exchange for the extra screw the man gave Tassos a bunch of grapes.

Tassos continued on, he was not sure how far it was to the next village or even if there was another hamlet that he could reach before it was too late to expect people to answer their doors. He decided that the next house he came to he would ask for directions.

He knocked and young girl came to the door, before he could speak she returned to the kitchen. Tassos stood and waited, hoping the girl's mother or father would come to ask what he wanted. The woman arrived, wiping her hands on her apron.

'What do you want?' she asked.

'Just some information, please, ma-am. I've come from Aghios Nikolaos and I wanted to know the name of the next village and if I'm walking in the right direction. I'm a pedlar and new to these parts.'

'What are you selling?'

Tassos place his sack on the ground and began to lift out his small collection of goods. 'I'm also a cobbler and knife sharpener.'

The woman hesitated. 'I'll have a new lamp wick.'

'One drachma, please.'

She handed over the money and pointed along the rough road. 'Keep going in that direction and you'll reach Istro.'

'How far is that? Will I get there before dark?'

She frowned. 'It's a good hour or so.'

'Thank you, ma'am. I'll see how far I can get before nightfall.' Tassos replaced his goods into the sack, raised his hand in farewell and walked back to the pathway.

He had gone only a short distance when the girl who had opened the door to him called. 'Mamma says wait a bit.'

Tassos stopped and turned to see the girl approaching him holding a pair of boots. He smiled at her and stretched out his hand for them.

The girl kept her hold on them. 'Mamma said to ask how much.'

'I need to have a look before I can give you a price.'

Reluctantly the girl passed her father's boots to him and waited whilst he examined them. Tassos shook his head. 'They're pretty thin down each side.'

'That's where Pappa rides his donkey.'

Tassos nodded. That explained the wear. 'I can do a quick job for five drachmas or charge ten drachmas for a really good job that will last.'

'I'll tell Mamma.' She snatched the boots back from Tassos and ran back to the house. Tassos sighed. He would wait five minutes, then if she had not returned he would continue on his way.

To his surprise the girl returned quickly. 'Mamma says a good job. When you've done one boot I have to take it to her and if she isn't satisfied she'll expect you to do the other one for nothing.'

'Drives a hard bargain, your Mamma,' smiled Tassos. 'She'll be satisfied. Are you going to wait whilst I do them?'

The girl nodded and sat down on the grass nearby. 'Mamma said I was to stay and if you walked off with them I was to run and tell her.'

'I'm not a thief,' replied Tassos indignantly. He unrolled the leather and placed the boot on it. 'If I was going to make a quick patch I'd just cover the thin area, but as I'm doing the good job I'm going to place a new piece of leather all over the foot.'

Deftly he cut the piece of leather to size and then placed it over the boot, nodding in satisfaction. He cut a second piece and replaced the roll of leather into his sack. The girl watched as he stitched the new piece of leather first down one side and then the other until it joined at the heel. He waved it at her.

'What do you think of that?'

She nodded. 'What about that bit? It's all loose.'

Tassos winked at her. 'So what do you think I should do about it?'

'Sew it like you did the other piece.'

'Clever girl. I'm going to stick it in place first, then I'll stitch it. When I've finished you can take it to your Mamma and see if she's satisfied. Whilst you're gone I'll make a start on the other one.'

Tassos sat and stitched whilst the girl returned to her home with the repaired boot. He had turned the rough edge of the leather under and using his awl with a running stitch had covered the foot of the boot with a new layer of leather. The loose piece he had stuck to the ankle of the boot so there would be no stitching to rub the man's foot and he had finished the boot with a quick polish. He hoped the woman would be satisfied with his craftsmanship. It was worth five drachmas and he doubted if she would have found anyone else to do a better job.

The girl returned and handed him a stick of bread with caraway seeds. 'Mamma said to give you this.'

Tassos smiled. 'Thank her for me.'

'It's fresh from the oven.'

'In that case I'll eat it now. It would be a shame to let it get cold.' Tassos placed the boot on the ground and took a bite from the bread. 'That's really good. Tell your Mamma I've not had anything that tasted that good for a long time.'

The girl smiled shyly. 'Mamma said you had done a good job.'

'I've been a cobbler for a long time.' Tassos picked the boot up again and continued to stitch assiduously. He frowned when he was about to stick the leather around the ankle. 'Could you bring the other boot back to me?' he asked.

'What for?'

'I want to make sure I stick this one in the same place. Your Pappa doesn't want them to look odd where one is stuck higher than the other.'

The girl scrambled to her feet, returning moments later with the other boot and another bread stick. 'I told Mamma what you said about her bread and she said to give you another.'

'Nice lady, your Mamma.' Tassos place the boots side by side and nicked a small piece of leather off the one he was repairing so he could turn the edge under smoothly. Finally he placed them together on the ground in front of him and eyed them critically. It would have been easier if he could have placed them on a last whilst he worked, but he had made them look like new.

'There we are. Your Pappa should get some years of wear out of those before they need to be repaired again.'

The girl nodded and placed ten drachmas on the ground before picking up the boots and walking back to her house. Tassos considered following her and thanking the woman for the bread, then decided she might think he was after some more. He knelt and wrapped his cobbler's tools safely before placing them back in his sack and continuing down the cart track towards Istro. It would be too late by the time he arrived in the village to try to sell any of his wares. He would be sensible, find a sheltered spot off the track, spread his blanket and sleep until daylight.

When Manolis returned to Aghios Nikolaos he looked for Tassos, but there was no sign of the man.

'You owe me two drachmas,' announced his Aunt Eirini as soon as he walked through the door.

'What for?'

'I bought some buttons for your shirt.'

'How many did you buy? There are only four missing.'

'I know, but I bought six for two drachmas.'

'Six! For two drachmas! You can buy ten for one drachma from the haberdasher.'

'How would you know how much buttons cost? I need four and the pedlar said he could sell me three for a drachma, but if I bought six I would have two to lose; besides I felt sorry for the man. No one seemed to be buying anything from him and he had a finger missing. He probably has no other way to make a living?'

Manolis looked at her in disbelief and then threw back his head and laughed.

'What's so funny?'

'I know him. One to use and one to lose!' Still chuckling to himself Manolis handed over the money. 'I'll bring my shirt down on my way out.'

'Where are you going?'

'When I've had my meal I've a bit of shopping to do; then I'll probably call at the taverna. I might see One To Lose in there.'

Eirini frowned. What was her nephew talking about? Had the sun affected him?

Tassos was woken in the early hours by a rustling in the grass. He sat up cautiously, hoping it was not a snake, then smiled at his foolishness. Snakes did not go hunting at night; being cold blooded they were dependent upon the sun to raise their temperature. It was probably a mouse or hedgehog looking for a meal. He rolled himself up in his blanket again and closed his eyes. There was no point in rising until the sun was coming up.

When he woke again it was long past dawn and he squinted at the sun to judge the hour. He cursed himself for not rising earlier when he had first woken, now he would have missed any villagers going off to work in the fields. The walking he had done the previous day must have tired him more than he had realised at the time. He wished he knew the area and where it would be practical to go from Istro. He did not want to walk back to Aghios Nikolaos if he could avoid it. It would be his bad luck to bump into Manolis or Doctor Stavros, but nor did he want to end up lost in the mountains.

He smiled ruefully. For all his careful planning he had omitted some very important items. Short of following the coast road until he reached the outskirts of Heraklion he did not have the faintest idea how to reach the town. Nor had he thought about food and water. He was accustomed to rising and walking down to the storeroom to supplement his food stocks, eating when he pleased. Now he was feeling hungry and he did not know when he would have his next meal. Even more important was his thirst. He had drained his water bottle when he woke and he hoped Istro was not too far away and that there would be a pump or water fountain in the village square where he could get a drink.

Tassos folded his blanket and placed it in his sack; brushed down his rumpled clothing and shook out his boots before placing them on his feet. He ran his fingers through his hair and rubbed his hand over the stubble on his chin. He must look like a dirty, unkempt beggar. If they had a barber's shop in Istro he would treat himself to a haircut and a shave. He had deliberately allowed his hair to grow and only trimmed his beard occasionally whilst he was on Spinalonga, being worried that if he nicked his skin whilst shaving he could easily pick up an infection. Being clean shaven would make him feel better and also alter his appearance.

He hoped he would sell enough items to cover the cost of a barber and a meal without having to use any more of his savings. He wanted to save money for when the weather turned cold and he would have to pay for shelter over night. He sighed. He would have to get used to having only one meal a day accompanied by water.

Istro was a disappointment to him. There was a straggling line of houses and few women opened their door to him, shaking their head when he listed the goods he had on offer, although one willingly gave him a jug of water to slake his thirst and filled his water bottle for him. Only one woman had asked for her scissors to be sharpened and bought a reel of cotton from him. He stood hesitantly before her.

'Could you give me some directions, please? I don't know this area. I'm looking for a village where I could visit a barber and get a meal. If I carry on walking down this track which village will I reach?'

She frowned. 'I'm not sure if there are any villages down that way. You'd do better to take the road to Pirgos and then cut across to Mardati. Go back up the track until it branches off to the left and it will lead you to the village. You may find a taverna and a barber there.'

Tassos thanked her, shouldered his sack and continued on his way. His stomach was rumbling as it demanded food. He consoled himself with the thought that he should at least be able to buy a loaf of bread and some cheese in the village, even if he had to move on elsewhere to find a barber.

Manolis sat in Flora's small house with the ledger open in front of him. 'One To Lose really does have a nerve,' he grumbled. 'I sold him ten buttons for one drachma and he charged my aunt two drachma for six. I've a good mind to deduct it from his account.'

'I don't understand how you can deduct it from his account. Surely your aunt should ask for her money back if she thinks she was overcharged.'

Manolis shook his head. 'It's not as simple as that. He was just a pedlar who was passing through and she felt sorry for him.'

'That was kind of her.'

'No it wasn't,' Manolis contradicted her. 'She knew she could ask me for the money as they were buttons for my shirt. They didn't cost her anything.'

'So if he was a pedlar you can't deduct it from his account anyway. You only deal with our money.'

Manolis was about to explain that Tassos had left the island and set up as a pedlar when he thought better of it. Flora would be bound to tell one of the other women and before you knew it the whole island would know that Tassos had escaped. Word would reach Doctor Stavros and he would have to inform the authorities who would instigate a search. Better for him to keep the information to himself and when the Doctor eventually discovered one of his patients was missing it would be too late to find him in the area.

'Yes, you're right,' he smiled. 'Why don't we close your door and put the latch across? I don't appear to have many customers this morning and they can always come back later.' He raised his eyebrows suggestively to her.

Flora giggled. 'Shall we?'

'Why not? You're my wife, so you have to do as I say. I'm telling you to latch the door and take your clothes off.'

'Suppose I don't do as you say?' Flora closed the door and lifted the latch into place.

'Then I would have to spank you before I tore your clothes off. Come here, Flora, let me help you with the fastenings.'

'I can manage.'

Manolis seized her and swung her to face him. 'I know you can manage, but I want to undo your blouse and remove your skirt. You can unbuckle my belt.' Manolis bent and kissed her. 'You'd better be quick about it. I'll have your skirt off in a second.'

The cluster of houses at Pirgos did nothing to raise Tassos's hopes of a meal or a barber. At the side of the road was a water pump and Tassos took a long drink before splashing water over his face and rubbing his hands to get them as clean as possible. He dried himself on the sack and looked around. There would be no point in standing in the road and shouting his wares, the place was deserted. Once again he would have to resort to knocking on doors and hoping to find a customer.

After an hour he had sold only three lamp wicks, a box of matches and a reel of cotton. He was asked for a saucepan, another woman wanted a pair of knitting needles, having snapped one of hers a few days earlier and a third asked him for a scrubbing brush. He must make a note and invest in more stock, even if it did mean returning to Aghios Nikolaos.

Tassos walked up the hill towards Kritsa feeling disheartened. He had hailed a man who was working in his fields and asked if he was on the correct road for Mardati. The farmer had asked why he wanted that village and advised him to make for Kroustas which was nearer. Tassos had heeded the farmer's directions to go to Kroustas, on to Kritsa and then back down the hill to Mardati. Tassos also asked if he would find a taverna in Kroustas where he could buy a meal, but the farmer did not know.

He reached some isolated houses and commenced knocking on the doors and offering his wares, selling mainly cotton, needles and buttons to the ladies who answered him. He asked a woman how much further it was until he reached Kroustas and she looked at him in surprise.

'This is Kroustas. Do you mean Kritsa?'

Tassos nodded. 'Yes, my mistake. I'm not familiar with this area and get confused by the village names.'

'Kritsa is up the hill. Not very far.'

'Will I find a taverna there?'

The woman nodded. 'There are two tavernas in Kritsa, but they might not be open until the evening,' she warned him.

As Tassos walked up the main street of the small town he saw a taverna; there was also a baker, greengrocer, general store, cobbler and blacksmith. Tassos grimaced. He was unlikely to sell any of his goods here. He took five drachmas from his money pouch and placed the notes in his pocket. There was no need to advertise that he kept most of his money in a pouch hanging around his neck. As he entered the taverna the owner looked at him suspiciously and Tassos smiled.

'I know I look like a beggar. I've been travelling down from Heraklion. If there's a barber in the village I'll be only too pleased to make use of his services for a haircut and shave.'

'He's along at the end. Clean yourself up and you're welcome to buy a meal.'

Tassos nodded. 'I'll be back in a while.' He would have preferred to have had a meal first, having realised that since his fish stew of the previous day he had only eaten two small bread sticks and a bunch of grapes and it was now late afternoon. He would have to buy a loaf, some cheese and a few olives before he left the village. If he then found himself somewhere deserted over night he would at least have some food for the following day.

'How much for a haircut, wash and shave?' he asked the barber.

The barber looked at Tassos's unkempt locks and matted beard. 'Three drachma for a haircut and two drachma for a shave.' He expected Tassos to say he did not have that kind of money to spend and leave the shop. To his surprise Tassos walked over to the chair and sat down.

'I'd like my beard shaved off completely and my hair short.'

'Your moustache? Do you want that off?'

Tassos hesitated. 'Yes. If I don't like being without it will soon grow again.'

The barber stood there. 'I'd like to see your money before I start.'

'No problem.' Tassos extracted the notes from his pocket. 'I charge one drachma to sharpen a pair of scissors so if you want me to do a pair for you the cost can be deducted from my bill.'

'My scissors are sharp enough,' the barber assured him.

Tassos smiled. They might be sharp now, but by the time they had dealt with his matted locks they would have little edge left to them.

'I might be able to interest you in some of the goods I have for sale,' offered Tassos as a towel was placed around his neck. 'I'm a pedlar.'

'Where are you from?'

'I've been walking down from Heraklion, calling at the villages on the way. I haven't been around Kritsa yet. I thought I'd like to be cleaned up a bit first. I don't want to be mistaken for a beggar.' Tassos smiled easily and the barber grunted. The man might have enough drachmas for a haircut and shave, but that did not mean the money was honestly come by.

The barber began to cut jagged lumps of hair from Tassos's head. 'No point in washing it all if it's going to be cut off,' he stated and Tassos suffered the indignity until his head was finally pushed forward into the basin and water poured over his remaining hair. Whilst bending over the basin Tassos kept tight hold of his money pouch. It would be too easy for the barber to cut the leather thong and steal it. The strong fingers of the barber rubbed at his scalp until he began to feel quite sore and he was relieved when his head was raised and the towel wrapped around his head.

Again before tackling Tassos's beard the barber took his scissors to it and clipped it as short as he could, before washing it vigorously and stropping his razor. Tassos looked at the cut throat razor nervously and held up his hand.

'Could I do that?'

'I'll do a better job than you can and I won't nick your skin.'

Tassos swallowed nervously. He had never been shaved by a barber before, always trimming his beard growth himself. He crossed himself and leaned back in the chair, closing his eyes. He did not want to see the lethal looking razor approaching his face.

'All done.' The barber whisked the towel away from Tassos's neck and held up a mirror for him to see the finished effect. Beardless and with his hair short his appearance had changed dramatically.

Tassos nodded. 'Thanks. That looks better. I thought it could wait until I returned to Heraklion, but my hair grows more quickly than I realised and I've not had an opportunity to give it a proper wash. I began to worry that I would end up with lice. Would you like to have a look at the goods in my sack before I go back to the taverna for a meal?'

The barber shook his head. 'You'd not have anything in there that I wanted.'

'Now, you don't know that until you've looked,' smiled Tassos and began to open the neck of the sack.

'I've told you I'm not interested. Go and peddle your goods elsewhere.' The barber waved his arm towards the door and Tassos shrugged and walked away. He couldn't force the man to buy anything from him; maybe he would have better luck with the taverna owner.

As he waited for his meal to arrive Tassos made some entries in his notebook. He entered the cost of his visit to the barber and the amount he had been quoted for his meal. He listed the items he had sold and the amount of money he had taken from customers and shook his head. He had certainly not covered the cost of his expenses for that day. In his other notebook he entered the names of the villages he had visited, how long it had taken him to reach one from the other and if he had made sufficient sales for the journey to be considered profitable on another occasion. When he finally found somewhere to spend the night he would count the money he had in his pouch. As he ate he day dreamed. Once he had returned to Heraklion he would investigate the possibility of purchasing a small four wheeled cart. Ideally he would eventually like to make enough money to have a donkey and full size cart so he would be able to carry a proper grinding wheel for sharpening knives and scissors and also a far greater variety of goods to tempt the villagers.

'Three drachmas.' The taverna owner broke Tassos's reverie and he felt around in his pocket for the money.

'Can I interest you in any of the goods I have with me?' he asked. 'I sharpen knives and mend boots also.'

The taverna owner shook his head. 'Not unless you charge less than Thranassis for sharpening.'

'How much does he charge?'

'Two knives for a drachma.'

'I charge the same. How often do you ask him to sharpen them?'

'About once a month.'

Tassos nodded sagely. 'If I did them you'd not need them done again for at least two months.'

The taverna owner considered the offer and shook his head. 'You could do a poor job and I'd never see you again. If I'm dissatisfied with Thranassis I take them back and he does them again for nothing.'

Tassos shrugged. 'Your choice. I've never had any complaints. Can you give me directions to the next village? I don't think I'll make any sales in Kritsa.'

'Are you going up into the hills?'

'No, I'm working my way back to Heraklion.'

'Then you'd be best to go down to Mardati and on to Aghios Nikolaos from there. There's nowhere between here and Flamouriana and that's some distance away. You'll certainly not get there before dark.'

Tassos sighed. 'I'd best be off, then. Thanks for the meal.'

Once back in the town of Aghios Nikolaos Tassos visited the hardware store again. The owner looked surprised to see him back so soon. If the man thought he could get the wheelbarrow for less than eight drachmas he was mistaken. He scowled at Tassos from across the counter.

'What can I do for you?'

Tassos consulted the list he had made earlier. 'I'd like some more screws, different sizes and a couple of screw drivers. Two hammers, good strong ones and a box of nails. Four saucepans, medium sort of size and three of the little ones to brew coffee; three scrubbing brushes; five knives, five forks and ten spoons.'

Tassos was amused at the surprised look on the owner's face. 'I've made a note of the items the villagers asked for so I thought it would be a good idea to come back and buy them,' he explained.

'Where've you been?'

'Along the coast as far as Istro. I was told it was pretty deserted after that so I turned up to Pirgos, walked over to Kritsa, back down to Mardati.'

'Where are you making for now?'

Tassos hesitated. Why was the man interested in his journeys? 'Back to Kritsa.'

'Thought you said you'd been there?'

'Promised a lady I'd get a saucepan for her. I can drop down to Flamouriana from there.'

The hardware owner shrugged. 'I'd have thought you would have done better to go along to Elounda and go up over the headland. Lots of little farmsteads and small villages up there.'

'That was the route I used to walk here I think. I know I dropped down to the coast and found myself in Elounda. Actually I could do with a map. I have to keep asking directions to the next village. Any idea where I could buy one?'

'Try up in the Square. There's a kiosk there that sells newspapers. They may have one.'

Tassos nodded. 'Thanks for your help. How much does that lot come to?'

'Twenty two drachmas.'

Tassos swallowed. He had not realised he had spent that much. 'How much are the saucepans?'

'Three drachmas the larger ones.'

'My mistake, I thought they were two drachmas, same as the small ones.'

'Do you still want them?'

'Oh, yes. I promised the lady I would get one for her and no doubt one of her neighbours has also decided she wants a new one. These ladies like to keep up with each other.' Tassos handed over the notes. He had not intended to walk back towards Elounda and go over the headland, but if the hardware owner was correct that there were a number of potential customers in the area it could be worth his while.

He called at the haberdasher and bought three sets of knitting needles and debated asking at the kiosk to see if he could purchase a map, finally deciding he could not afford to spend any more money that day and could continue to manage without. It would be prudent to avoid Elounda and Plaka and he was sure he would be able to find a route that circumvented both the villages. He filled his water bottle, purchased some cheese and stale bread and made his way out of the town. All he needed now was somewhere sheltered to spend the night.

Tassos took to a goat track that led up into the hills behind Aghios Nikolaos. Within a short time he found he had to turn back. The gradient was too steep and the ground too rough for him to negotiate with his sack on his back. His sack was considerably heavier now than when he had first arrived on the mainland and he shifted it regularly from one shoulder to the other.

He would take the road to Elounda, but not stop in the village. He had seen the three small villages from Spinalonga and also a number of isolated dwellings only a short distance up the hill. There was bound to be a reasonable cart track he could use. If his luck held there would be a track from one village to the next and he would eventually end up on the headland.

The hill leading up to Kato Elounda was steep and he sold little to the inhabitants, hoping he might do better in Pano Elounda he continued up the hill. He asked directions for the next village and was told that down the hill lay Mavrikiano or if he continued on he would come to Kato Pines. He decided he would risk visiting Mavrikiano despite its proximity to Elounda and Plaka, and return to Pines and make his way across the hills towards the headland.

The sales in Mavrikiano were good, but he found it disconcerting to be able to look down on the island of Spinalonga where he had been living such a short time earlier. He needed to leave the area as soon as he physically could. He had sat with an old man and discussed the most practical route for a pedlar to take, not too steep or rough, but he did not want to spend time travelling a road that ended in a town. He had realised he could not compete with the prices the shops in the towns were able to charge and a pedlar would not be patronised.

The old man scratched his head. 'If I were you I'd go from Pines to Fourni. There are a number of small villages up there.'

'What's the track like? I tried one elsewhere and had to turn back.'

'It's well used. You shouldn't have a problem.'

'Anywhere nearby that I can buy a meal?'

'There's no taverna up here, but I can sell you a few olives and a bit of cheese.'

Tassos nodded gratefully. He had inspected the fields as he passed, but most of them seemed to have only olive or carob trees growing. He was convinced that when he was closer to Heraklion he would find some fruit and vegetables that he could purloin to supplement his meagre diet.

He had looked down on the island of Spinalonga one last time with a feeling of elation. He was no longer a prisoner over there, but a free man. No one had challenged him and whenever he had seen anyone with a newspaper he had asked for the latest news. Nowhere was there any mention of a leper escaping from Spinalonga, all the media attention seemed to be centred on Europe where a war had been raging since the previous year. Tassos ignored that. It did not affect Crete.

September 1940

Doctor Stavros checked that his records were up to date. Each Sunday, when he returned from church he would go through the record cards of the patients he had visited on Spinalonga, making a note of any change he had seen in their condition. Many just had a date and a tick indicating that he had not noticed anything worth recording. Every so often he wrote the date of death on a record card and placed it in a separate pile in his cupboard, never to be looked at again.

He would tell Manolis of the fatality when he saw him so the person's name could be struck through on the ledger and he would fill in two forms, one would go to the church and the other to the bank. His duties were then completed.

Now he tied the cards together and placed the pile at the end of the stack in the cupboard. He worked in strict rotation, moving the piles of cards up each week and only adding one to the pile for the following week if he thought the patient's condition would have deteriorated in that time. This ensured that he fulfilled the obligation entrusted to him to examine every sufferer once a year. If he saw the man or woman working and they appeared fit he would place a tick on their card and that constituted an examination.

He knew he was not truly fulfilling his duty as the doctor in charge of the island, but he had little choice. To give everyone over there a full examination regularly was impossible when he was only able to visit for one day each week, sometimes missing two or three weeks' visits due to the weather during the winter months. It was better that he concentrated on alleviating the suffering of the chronically sick and left the others until he was needed.

Doctor Stavros looked at the record cards. There were five men and a woman included that he had not seen around during his last visit. If he did not spot them when he went over on Thursday he would ask Father Minos if he had seen any of them in church the previous Sunday. If they were fit enough to attend the church service they could receive a tick on their card.

Father Minos listened to the names the doctor read out to him and agreed they had all attended church except Tassos Nevrakis. 'I expect he was up at the hospital helping Spiro.'

'Did you see him there when you visited the patients?'

Father Minos shook his head. 'I did not go up until the afternoon. If he was working during the morning he would have returned home by then.'

Exasperated the doctor placed the card with the details of Tassos Nevrakis to the bottom of the pile. He would have to track the man down the following week.

Father Minos looked at the doctor's retreating back. Now he thought about it, he could not remember when he had last seen Tassos. The island was not that large and in the course of a week he had usually exchanged a greeting with everyone at some time. If the man, who appeared to be the fittest on the island, had been taken ill and admitted to the hospital Spiro would have alerted him to the fact. What had happened to Tassos?

It took Tassos three more weeks to reach Amnisos and to be told he was not far from Heraklion. Whilst travelling around the small villages and isolated homes on the headland he had realised it would be impossible to follow the coastline to Heraklion. He had made a detour inland and found himself in Neapoli where he had been able to replenish his stock of goods and eat a substantial meal before walking to the outskirts and spending the night in an outhouse.

He sharpened two pairs of scissors and a knife before moving on from Amnisos towards the suburbs of Heraklion. Once there he again sought out a hardware shop and bought screws, nails, hooks, hinges and a scrubbing brush to replace the ones he had sold in the villages during his journey. At the haberdashers he spent ten drachmas on ribbons, embroidery silks, buttons and cotton, before entering the chemist and buying a quantity of cheap soap.

He would make a gift of some of the embroidery silks to his mother when he finally reached Gazi. He contemplated her reaction when he finally knocked on the door and she saw who was standing on her scrubbed step and smiled. She would not be able to believe her eyes.

Tassos decided it would be fruitless to try to peddle his goods in the town of Heraklion. There seemed to be even more shops now than when he had made his occasional visits with his father in the past. The town dwellers would need nothing that he was carrying with him. Everywhere was busy, people hurrying about their business and he felt quite bewildered.

Down towards the waterfront he found a shabby taverna and pushed open the door. Inside a young woman with a girl sitting beside her looked up and eyed him speculatively.

Tassos smiled at her. 'Would I be able to buy a meal, please?'

She seemed disappointed by his request and waved him to an empty table. 'What do you want?' she asked.

Tassos was surprised by her question. He was used to being told which two dishes were available. 'Stuffed tomatoes?'

She shook her head. 'Not the season for the tomatoes. I can make some stuffed peppers.'

'That would be fine. I've not had the dish in a while.'

'A glass of wine whilst you wait?'

Tassos hesitated. He had not had a glass of wine since leaving Spinalonga. This could be a celebratory meal; he had been a free man now for over a month and all being well he would see his mother again tomorrow.

He nodded. 'That would be very acceptable. I suppose you don't have a newspaper that I could look at? I couldn't see anywhere to buy one on my way here.'

She shook her head. 'Anna can go and get one for you. Anna, the customer wants a newspaper. Be quick about it.'

Anna slid off her chair and ran out of the door without answering her mother. She knew if she did not do as she was asked immediately she would not be allowed out to play with her friends when they called for her. She ran along the road and around the corner to the kiosk, realising as she arrived there that she had not brought the money with her.

Biting her lip, knowing she would be in trouble with her mother, she hurried back. Louisa was standing very close to their customer, smiling and talking quietly to him. She looked up in annoyance as Anna entered.

'Where's the newspaper?' she asked and took a step away from the table.

'I need some money,' mumbled Anna.

'Stupid child! Take a drachma from the till.'

'No. Wait.' Tassos took two drachmas from his pocket and handed them to her. 'Here you are. A drachma for the newspaper and one for yourself for your trouble.'

Anna smiled warily at him. She was not used to being given money of her own to spend. She clutched the money tightly in her hand, desperate not to lose it. When she returned to her bedroom she would wrap the drachma note in a piece of paper and hide it in her chest amongst her clothes. It would be safe there whilst she decided what she could spend the meagre amount on.

When she returned she handed Tassos the newspaper. 'Thank you, sir,' she said quietly as she pushed her dishevelled hair back with her hand.

As Tassos looked up at her he saw the disfiguring red mark on her neck and frowned. Was the girl leprous? For a moment he felt inclined to leave the taverna before his meal arrived, then realised his stupidity. He had lived for almost a year amongst leprosy sufferers and had no ill effects. It would not make any difference if he was in the company of another for a short while.

Tassos poured a glass of wine from the carafe that had been placed on the table and looked at the headlines of the newspaper. It was all about the war in Europe that appeared to be spreading outwards at an alarming rate. The Italians had tried to invade Greece and been pushed back into Albania; but the situation was tense and further outbreaks of fighting were inevitable.

He turned the page and saw that the Cretan people were complaining about the rising cost of their food. Transporting goods from the ports to the inland villages had become more costly due to an increase in fuel prices and Tassos shook his head. The old ways were best. He had seen some of the lorries, loaded with produce, rumbling along the ill-made roads and belching out black smoke. The donkey and cart that had brought sacks of flour to his village each week had made little noise and certainly did not give off obnoxious fumes. Even the donkey droppings, despite their objectionable smell, were hastily cleared away and used as fertilizer.

As his meal was brought to the table Tassos pushed the newspaper to one side and poured himself another glass of wine. It had been a waste of a drachma to purchase a newspaper. There was nothing in there that interested him. He would use it as wrapping paper for the glass chimneys that fitted the oil lamps. He continued to glance down the columns, but they held little interest and to his relief there was still no mention of a search being made for a man who had escaped from Spinalonga.

He ate his meal in a leisurely fashion. Despite the exterior appearance of the taverna the food was good. He wiped his mouth with the back of his hand, pushed the newspaper into his sack and walked up to the counter.

'How much do I owe you?'

'Four drachmas.'

Tassos frowned. It was more than he had expected to pay.

'You had a carafe of wine,' Louisa reminded him. She turned to her daughter. 'Go out to play for an hour.'

Tassos nodded and placed the coins on the counter.

'There are other services available here. We let rooms.'

Tassos shook his head. 'I'm only passing through.'

'They can be let for a very short time. Only five drachmas an hour. Lonely travellers often like to take advantage of some company before they move on.'

Tassos suddenly realised what she was offering him and why she had sent her daughter outside. He let out a bark of a laugh. 'I'd expect more than an hour for five drachmas.'

Louisa glared at him. 'Everyone has always agreed they received value for their money.'

Tassos raised his eyebrows. The offer was tempting. He had made a few fumbling attempts with Damara and she had made it quite clear that she was not interested. He had experienced better luck with Aspasia from Kavrohori and had tumbled her regularly, reckoning it was worth the hour's walk each way and the drachma he gave her. He enjoyed his time in her company. Since being sent to Spinalonga he had been celibate, frightened that one of the women over there would infect him with leprosy. His body was telling him that he needed a woman urgently.

'Very well,' he agreed and Louisa went across and shot the bolt on the door to the taverna.

Tassos followed Louisa up the wooden stairs and into a room with a large bed in the corner. He sat and lifted his feet to allow Louisa to remove his boots. He lifted her skirt and looked at her nakedness, feeling himself stirring immediately. Now the moment had arrived there was no time for finesse. He pushed her onto the bed and entered her roughly, only to erupt, with a roar of delight a few moments later.

He laid panting and sweating beside her, watching as she

removed her blouse and unlaced her skirt, unbuckled his belt and pulled down his trousers, then waited patiently to find out if he intended to take her again. Tassos raised himself up on one elbow and looked at her. Her breasts were round and firm, the nipples standing up, hard and provocative. He pulled at one gently and lowered himself to take it in his mouth, running his tongue over it and then sucking hard. Louisa drew in her breath. This was how she expected her customers to behave, not a frenzied attack like she had suffered a short while earlier.

She allowed him to explore her body leisurely, waiting for him to be aroused again. This time he entered her gently, able to enjoy himself as he thrust into her deeply time and again until he could control himself no longer. He rolled off her and Louisa sat up with her back to him. His finger traced the three little moles on her back before his hand slid round to cup her breast.

'Your hour is up,' she announced.

'It can't be,' protested Tassos.

'There's some water over there in the basin if you wish to wash,' she announced, ignoring his comment. She picked up her skirt and stepped into it, lacing the waist to hold it firmly before slipping her blouse over her head. Whilst Tassos gave himself a cursory wash she brushed her hair and tied it back with a grubby ribbon, impatient now for him to leave.

Tassos replaced his clothing and forced his feet back into his boots. Louisa held out her hand.

'Five drachmas.'

Without demur Tassos placed the notes in her hand. 'How much do you charge to rent a room for the night?'

'There are no rooms available at present.' She knotted the money into a corner of a shawl, placed it in a chest and opened the window. 'I need to unlock the taverna,' she announced and opened the bedroom door, a clear indication that Tassos was expected to leave.

As Tassos walked along the road towards the harbour he heard a cry.

'There he is. That's him.'

Tassos resisted the urge to run. His heart sank. He was so close to Gazi and making a brief visit to his parents. Surely he was not going to be stopped now. Coming towards him was the little girl from the taverna holding the hand of a man and pointing to him with the other.

Yiorgo Pavlakis smiled. 'Thank you. That was kind of you to give my daughter a drachma.'

Tassos swallowed hard. 'It was nothing. She ran an errand for me.'

'I went to the kiosk and bought a newspaper,' announced Anna.

'It meant I was able to catch up on the news whilst I waited for my meal.'

'I trust you enjoyed it. My wife is a good cook.'

Tassos hoped his flush of embarrassment was not noticed, thankful that he had a covering of fresh beard growth. 'It was excellent.'

Yiorgo Pavlakis gave a delighted smile. 'I am the luckiest of men. My wife is not only beautiful, but also a wonderful cook. I hope you will call on us again.'

Tassos nodded. 'I certainly will the next time I'm passing through,' he replied. 'I didn't see a name outside. If I have a problem finding it where should I ask for?'

Yiorgo waved his hand airily. 'Just ask for Louisa's place. Everyone seems to know it. Where are you making for now?'

Tassos shrugged. 'The next village along the coast.'

Yiorgo frowned. 'That would mean walking to Linoperamata. You'll not get there before dark.'

'No problem. I'm used to sleeping under the stars.'

'I'm sure we could rent you a room for the night. Return to the taverna with me and I'll ask Louisa.'

Tassos shook his head. He certainly could not return to the

taverna and accept a bed there for the night. He would be haunted by the thought of the man in front of him in bed with the beautiful girl for whose services he had paid highly such a short while ago.

'I'm a pedlar. I don't have money for taverna lodgings, but thanks for the offer.' He lifted his sack higher on to his shoulder, walked around the man and girl and continued on his way. No wonder the girl had said his hour was over if she knew her husband was due home.

Tassos had no intention of going to Linoperamata before he had visited Gazi. Another hour saw him on the outskirts of Heraklion just as the sun slid down the sky into the sea. He placed his blanket on a level stretch of ground beneath some olive trees, wrapped his cloak around him and sat hugging his knees. He had enjoyed the girl at the taverna and the urge to repeat the experience was on him again.

He hoped Aspasia was still around and as willing as she had been in the past. He was sure he was not the only man she obliged, but she was always willing to spend hours in the fields with him, encouraging him to further exertions until his appetite was completely sated. He enjoyed being with her and wished with all his heart that she had been the girl who had been betrothed to him when he was a child. He could forgive her previous loose behaviour if she would promise to keep herself solely for him. He longed to feel her delicate touch encouraging him to further exertion.

Finally Tassos lay down to get some rest. He still did not know how he was going to approach his parents the following day without alerting the whole village and broadcasting his presence to the authorities.

Tassos woke early and had just finished his rudimentary ablutions when a flock of goats and sheep arrived out of nowhere. He heard the shrill whistle of the shepherd and hastily gathered his belongings together. Goats were notorious for eating anything, edible or not, and he did not want one of them to nibble his sack or deface his boots.

He stood on the rise of the ground to gain his bearings. He could see the sprawl of Heraklion to the right and in front of him was the sea. He was sure if he walked along the main road that led from Heraklion to Rethymnon he would eventually see a track that led to Gazi. If he missed the turn he would end up in Linoperamata and have to turn back. He wished now he had stopped at a barber in Heraklion, he would also have been able to use the public baths and clean himself up properly. He hesitated, then decided he would return to the town, but certainly not venture anywhere near the taverna that was known as Louisa's place.

Tassos entered his father's cobbler's shop nervously. He had bathed and visited the barber before donning a clean shirt and trousers and rubbed his boots with the end of his sack to remove the dust, now he stood waiting for his father to look up from the repair he was completing and recognise him.

Lambros spat the nails he was holding in his mouth into his hand. 'What can I do .... Tassos! Tassos, my son, welcome home.' He opened his arms and Tassos returned the hug before pulling out of the embrace.

'Don't say my name again. I shouldn't be here. I've escaped. If word gets around that I'm in the village the authorities will come looking for me and send me back.' Tassos spoke quietly to his father.

'Escaped? You mean you've left the hospital without permission?'

'Something like that. I'll explain to you later. Close the shutters tonight before you light the lamps and lock the door. I'll come in at the back and lock the door behind me. Tell Mamma to expect me when it is dark, but that she is to tell no one.'

Lambros frowned and shook his head. 'I don't understand.

Why can't I close the shop and we go home now? Your Mamma will be faint with happiness.'

'No one must know who I am. I'm just a pedlar, travelling through the village. If anyone asks I called in here to see if you needed your knives sharpened. You sent me away and have no idea where I went. I'm going now and I'll talk to you tonight and tell you what has happened to me, but remember, tell no one who I am.'

Tassos turned and left the cobbler's shop with tears in his eyes. It had been good to see his father again and feel his strong arms around him. Now he needed to leave the village and sit where no one would notice him until the evening darkness closed in.

Tassos walked back into the village of Gazi and past his father's shop to the small house where he had lived all his life until he had been sent to Spinalonga. He noticed that the shutters were closed and continued down the road. Once he was certain there was no one around he would sneak round to the rear of the house and let himself in.

The door creaked familiarly as he pushed it open and he latched it firmly behind him. He placed his sack just inside the door and took a deep breath, both his father and mother had risen when they heard the door opening and he held out his arms to them, hoping he would be able to keep his emotions under control.

Lambros released him first. 'Let the boy have a seat. Maria, serve the supper. He looks in need of a substantial meal.' Lambros poured a glass of wine for each of them and held his up in silent salutation to his son.

Dabbing her eyes with her apron, Maria withdrew the moussaka from the oven and placed it on the table. 'It used to be a favourite of yours,' she whispered.

'It still is, Mamma, but I've not tasted one as good as yours in a long time.' Tassos piled a liberal helping onto his plate and broke a piece of crust off the homemade loaf. Maria looked at her son's left hand where his finger was missing.

'If only you hadn't cut your finger,' she sighed.

Tassos shrugged. 'One to use and one to lose; it's no problem being one short. Luckily the doctor amputated before the poison spread or it could have been my hand or even my arm that I lost.'

Maria frowned. 'If he cut your finger off to stop the – infection – spreading why did you have to go to the hospital?'

'He thought my skin condition was a sign of leprosy, nothing to do with my finger.'

'And now they've found out they were wrong?' asked his father hopefully.

Tassos shook his head. 'No one cares whether they're right or wrong. I was sent out to the island to live amongst all the other incurables although I know I am not leprous.' Tassos flexed his fingers and held them out straight to prove his diagnosis.

'Why didn't you ask the doctor to examine you?'

'He told me he didn't have the facilities to make a full examination. He comes once a week, leaves a supply of Chaulmoogra Oil tablets and does whatever he can to help the chronically sick.'

'So who nurses them?' asked Maria.

'No one. They look after each other.'

'That can't be right.' Maria shook her head.

'That's the way it is. I spoke to the priest and asked him to speak to the doctor. He was sympathetic but told me I must learn to accept my affliction as everyone else has. I refuse to accept an illness that I am convinced I do not have.'

'Are you going to the hospital in Heraklion?' asked Lambros.

'Certainly not. They would send me straight back to Spinalonga. Now I've escaped I'm determined to stay a free man. That's why you must tell no one that I've visited you.' Tassos leaned forwards across the table and spoke earnestly. 'I used my pension to buy some cobblers' tools and bits and pieces that I could sell. When I decided the time was right I floated over to the mainland in my bath tub and I've been travelling around as a pedlar. No one takes any notice of me and that is the way it has to stay. I can't come back here to live. Someone in the village would be bound to tell the authorities I had returned and they'd come looking for me. I have to keep moving on.'

'Do you make enough money to live on as a pedlar?' asked Lambros.

'Enough for a meal each day and an occasional visit to the barber.'

'No wonder you're looking thin.' Maria ladled another helping of moussaka onto Tassos's plate.

'What about Damara?' asked Lambros.

'What about her? We never did care for each other. I hope her father has found someone suitable to marry her, but she means nothing to me. If I was able to return I would refuse to marry her. I'm a man now and can make my own decisions.'

Maria and Lambros exchanged glances. 'Her father is refusing to release her from the betrothal agreement unless I pay him compensation.'

Tassos shrugged. 'I'm sorry, Pappa, but that is not my problem. If I had enough money I would pay whatever he wanted just to be rid of her, but I'm a poor pedlar. He should be grateful we had not already married and he can find another husband for her.'

Maria shook her head. 'I don't think he can find anyone willing to marry her, that's why he keeps asking for compensation. The village knew you were not happy to become betrothed to her and the wedding had been delayed. After you went away there was a rumour around that she had given you the evil eye and caused your sickness. The young men avoid her.'

'Where did that rumour start, Mamma?' asked Tassos sternly and his mother had the grace to drop her eyes.

Lambros poured another glass of the rough village wine for each of them. 'What will you do if the war comes to Crete?' he asked.

'Why should it come to us? The problem is in Europe.'

Lambros shook his head. 'The Germans are in Africa and the Italians want to march through Greece. We've refused them, of course, but if they decide to make a fight of it, will we be able to hold them off? They could decide to come up from Africa or down from Italy. They shot the 'Elli' out of the water the other week. We can't just sit here and do nothing if they start blowing our ships out of our harbours.'

'I'm not a military man, just a poor pedlar. I'll just keep moving around.'

'I've heard they are persecuting the gypsies and driving them out of their countries.'

Tassos shrugged. 'I'll be careful. If necessary I'll fight for my freedom. I'm determined never to be a prisoner again.'

'You haven't been a prisoner,' protested Maria.

'Mamma, we were all prisoners on Spinalonga. Why do you think they sent us to an island? They thought we couldn't escape.' Tassos frowned. 'If the war should come to Crete will you and Mamma be safe?'

Lambros shrugged. 'No reason why we shouldn't be. I'm just a cobbler. I could be useful to them. They'll no doubt need their boots repaired.'

'Do you want a bed for the night?' asked Maria.

Tassos shook his head. 'It's a very tempting offer, Mamma, and I'm grateful, but I'll finish my wine and leave. I'm used to sleeping out in the open.'

His mother looked at him in horror. 'But in the winter – won't you be cold?'

'I'll find somewhere for a bit of shelter. There are plenty of stables and outhouses that will be warm and dry for the night. You don't need to worry about me, Mamma.'

'Do you need some money?' asked Lambros, fumbling in his pocket. 'I've a bit put by you can have.'

Tassos shook his head. 'Thank you, but no, Pappa. You save whatever you have towards that compensation Damara's father wants. I have enough for my needs. I'll only take from you if I'm starving.'

Tassos rose from the table. 'I'm planning to move around; up to the Rethymnon area and then I'll come back down to Gazi in a few weeks and visit you again. Just remember, you tell no one that you've seen me.'

Lambros clasped his son to him and Tassos could feel his mother's tears on his cheek as she kissed him goodbye. He was reluctant to leave his family, but conscious that if anyone should visit, even at this late hour, they would be curious about the three plates and glasses that were in evidence.

Tassos collected his sack from inside the back door and closed the door quietly behind him. He walked back to the main street and out of the village looking for a sheltered spot where he could spend the night. The next day he would make his way to Kavrohori and from there he would be able to walk to Tilisos. If he managed to spend an hour or so with Aspasia it would be an added bonus.

He entered Kavrohori and was delighted to find that it was market day. There would be plenty of people milling around and someone was bound to want to purchase some of his goods. He took up a stance at the corner of the road and began to call his wares. As he had anticipated, business was brisk and he very quickly sold out of screws and lamp wicks. He held up a scrubbing brush in one hand and a saucepan in the other, ensuring the sun reflected off the saucepan and drew attention to him.

At the end of an hour his sack of stock was almost depleted and he realised he would have to return to Heraklion and purchase more goods before he could move on to Tilisos. There had been no sign of Aspasia in the market and the depressing thought came to him that she could be married and have moved on. He knew which house she lived in with her father and grandmother and decided to risk knocking at the door. If she was not there he could offer to show her father the goods he still had available for sale in his sack.

'Hello, Aspasia. I haven't seen you for a while.' He spoke quietly when she opened the door to him, not wishing to alert her blind grandmother who was sitting in her chair staring into the black void that constituted her world.

Aspasia smiled and raised her eyebrows, beckoned Tassos inside and indicated he should follow her out through the back door. She leaned against the wall where the outhouse abutted and gave a certain amount of privacy.

'Where've you been?'

'Travelling around. I decided I was bored with Gazi so I became a pedlar. Have you missed me?'

'Only by about five drachmas a month.'

'You're cheeky as well as wicked.' He leaned closer to her and slipped his hand beneath her skirt.

'And you love the cheek and enjoy the wickedness.' She ran her hand across his crotch. 'Is this what you came for?'

Tassos nodded and lifted her skirt whilst she parted the folds of his trousers. Her hands caressed him and he smiled with pleasure.

'Long time without?' she asked.

Tassos nodded, conveniently forgetting he had spent an hour with Louisa a couple of days earlier, as he pushed her legs apart. 'Not easy when you're travelling from village to village.'

'Makes it all the better when the time comes. Oh, Tassos. Oh!'

'Shh.' Tassos hushed her rapidly. 'Do you want to tell the whole village what we're doing? Oh, that feels so good.' Tassos closed his eyes, his body relishing in the rhythmic movements Aspasia was making. He could no longer resist moving within her, pressing her back harder against the wall and moving faster and faster until his relief came.

He stood there, feeling himself going limp and shrinking out of her.

'It was good whilst it lasted,' commented Aspasia. 'You used to manage to stay for longer.'

'Next time,' he promised. 'I'll come this evening and we'll go into the fields as we used to.' He squeezed her buttocks hard. 'We could be disturbed at any minute here.'

Aspasia gave a laugh. 'I would tell them the pedlar was showing me his goods.'

'Showing is one thing, sampling is another. Let go of me so I can straighten my trousers.'

'I was only admiring what you have to offer,' she removed her hands reluctantly.

Tassos made himself decent and then pulled Aspasia to him. 'As soon as the sun begins to go down I'll be there waiting for you. We can do a lot of admiring of each other then.'

Aspasia kissed his lips briefly. 'Don't be late.' She longed to be lying on the soft grass in the field, feeling Tassos's weight on her and enjoying his attention, but she did wonder how he would receive the news she had for him.

Aspasia lay on the grass beside Tassos. She had removed her blouse and was relishing in the soft touch of his hand on her naked breast.

'What happened to your finger?' she asked.

'I cut it off.' He lifted his left hand and showed her, 'One to lose, one to use.' He lifted his right index finger and wagged it at her.

Aspasia giggled. 'Show me how you use it.'

'You know how.'

'Show me again.'

'Aren't you ever satisfied?'

'No. Are you?' Aspasia lifted his hand and placed it beneath her skirt. 'Oh, yes, Tassos, just there.' She closed he eyes. 'I could lay here forever with you doing that to me.'

'You'd soon be dissatisfied and demanding more.'

'Mmm. I'm ready for more whenever you are.' She stretched out an exploratory hand and was not disappointed.

Finally Aspasia sat up and retrieved her blouse. 'I'll have to get back and settle Dimitris down for the night.'

'Dimitris? Who's Dimitris?'

'Your son.'

'Mine!'

Aspasia nodded. 'I know he's yours, he's the very image of you. I thought you knew and that was why you went away.'

Tassos shook his head. 'I had no idea. You should have been more careful.'

'Me! *You* should have been more careful.'

'Why didn't you marry one of the village lads?'

Aspasia snorted in derision. 'No mother would let their son marry me. They don't mind their boys using me for their pleasure, but they would never accept me as their daughter-in-law. Had it not been for my grandmother my own father would have thrown me out when I started to show. The villagers turn their backs on me when I walk down the street.'

'I am sorry, Aspasia.'

Aspasia shrugged. 'It's too late now, what's done is done.'

'You didn't think about going into Heraklion and finding someone who could help you?'

Aspasia shook her head. 'I thought about it. I didn't have the money, besides, who would have looked after Grandma whilst I was gone for a couple of days?'

'Couldn't your father have helped?'

'He said it was my own fault. He knew I liked the attention of the boys. He'd caught me a couple of times with a hand up my skirt and threatened to thrash me within an inch of my life if I brought dishonour on his name.'

'Did he thrash you?'

'No. He cried and that was worse than a beating.'

'But it hasn't stopped you?'

Aspasia sighed and rose to her feet. 'I can't help enjoying

myself, it's only natural. I refused the boys' attentions whilst I was carrying Dimitris. If I was going to have a child I didn't want him harmed in any way. Now I'm a mother the boys don't want to know me. They think it could happen again and I might claim one of them is the father.'

'How old is Dimitris now?'

'Nearly two.'

'And you've been a good girl all that time? No wonder you were pleased to see me.'

'I'd always be pleased to see you, Tassos. You're special. You're willing to give me pleasure, not just take what you want and leave as fast as you can.'

'I have to move on tomorrow,' Tassos warned her.

'Why? Surely as a pedlar you can please yourself how long you stay anywhere.'

'I need to go back to Heraklion and buy some more stock. I'm planning on visiting Tilisos and there's no point in me going there empty handed.'

'How long will you be away?'

Tassos shrugged. 'Who knows? I want to go up to the Rethymnon area. There are plenty of villages up there. I'll call in on you again on my return.'

In the darkness Aspasia nodded. She could not expect Tassos to marry her any more than one of the village youths. She was just a woman who would be used as a convenience by men until she was too old to be attractive to them, but she was hurt that he had not asked to see his son.

'Well, you know where I am,' she said resignedly, as they reached the outskirts of the village.

Tassos tilted her face towards his and kissed her whilst he pressed five drachmas into her hand. He had spent that much on the prostitute in Heraklion and she had not given him any pleasure. He realised he actually cared deeply for Aspasia.

Tassos walked back to the field where he had spent the evening with Aspasia. He felt guilty that he had unwittingly fathered a child and left Aspasia to deal with the unfortunate situation alone. Had he not been sent to Spinalonga he would have insisted he married her to give his child a name and respectability. Now he was in no position to do that.

Unable to sleep he decided to start walking back to Heraklion. He could always stop somewhere on the way if tiredness overcame him. He could make his purchases and walk back to Kavrohiri and see Aspasia again. It was only right that she should know his true situation. If she never wished to see him again and wanted to keep his identity a secret from their son he would have to accept her decision. Cursing the doctor for his arbitrary diagnosis he strode out purposefully, walking off his anger and trying to think of a solution to the problem.

Tassos went from shop to shop and made his purchases. He had made money on the goods he had sold in Kavrohiri, but he had spent an unnecessary five drachmas on the girl at Louisa's place. He did not begrudge the money he had given to Aspasia; he could excuse that as a gift for his son. He added up the amount of profit he had made and his expenditure that morning. He deducted the amount he had paid for his bath and his gift to Aspasia. According to his notebook he had made a profit of seventeen drachmas since becoming a pedlar. He could certainly not afford to indulge himself more than once a month.

He found his feet dragging as he walked back towards Kavrohori and finally decided he must rest. He lay and looked up at the sky where a few white puffs of cloud were visible. It was a sign that the summer was coming towards an end and soon he would have to think about finding somewhere to shelter at night during the winter months. There would be no point in travelling around the villages and ending up with pneumonia. He would look for a shepherd's hut, not too far from a village, where he could stay dry and reasonably warm. It was possible that Aspasia would know of somewhere close to Kavrohori; that could be very convenient.

Tassos woke a couple of hours later, pleased he had thought to purchase some bread and cheese before leaving Heraklion. The bread was already hardening, but he poured a small amount of water on it and it was certainly soft enough then to be palatable. Finally he rose, squinted up at the sun to judge the time and brushed the crumbs from his clothes. Now he had made his decision he hoped Aspasia would be able to meet him again that evening.

He knocked at Aspasia's door late in the afternoon and when she answered there was a small boy clinging to her skirt. He looked up at Tassos with round, wondering eyes. Tassos felt a lump come into his throat as he looked down at a small replica of himself.

'If anyone asks the pedlar was going around knocking on doors touting for sales. I'll call at some other homes in the village then I'll go up to the field. Can you meet me there?'

'Can't keep away now, can you? I'll need to feed my father when he returns home. I can't meet you for at least a couple of hours or so.'

Aspasia closed the door and Tassos moved on to the next house. To his surprise he sold a pair of knitting needles, two reels of cotton and sharpened a pair of scissors before walking out of the village and up to the field where he hoped Aspasia would soon be joining him. He had almost given her up when he heard her stumbling towards him in the semi darkness.

'Pappa was late home, Dimitris wouldn't go to sleep and Grandma was difficult,' she announced as she sat down beside him and prepared to remove her blouse.

Tassos stopped her. 'No, Aspasia. We have to talk. Once you start enticing me I can't think straight.'

'Who's asking for your thinking to be straight?' She stretched out her hand. 'We can talk later.'

Tassos shook his head and clasped his knees.

'I can't marry you, Aspasia.'

'I hadn't asked you to.' She tossed her head defiantly.

'No, listen. I'd like to marry you, but I can't.'

'You married that girl back in your village – the one you said your mother called a witch?'

'I'm not allowed to get married.'

'Not allowed? Who's stopping you? You're a big boy now.' Her hand strayed again and Tassos took hold of it.

'The government. It's against the law.'

'Since when? There's no law against getting married when you're of age.'

'Aspasia, please, listen to me. I'm trusting you to know the truth and never say a word to anyone. The only other people I've told are my parents. No one else must know.'

In the gathering darkness Aspasia looked at Tassos in concern. 'Are you a criminal?'

'Not the way you mean, I'm not a thief or a murderer. When I cut my finger it had dirt in it and the poison spread. The doctor had to cut it off or I would have lost my hand, maybe my arm. When I went back for him to make sure I was healing properly he examined me. He saw those white, itchy patches that I have and decided I had leprosy.'

Tassos felt Aspasia pull away from him.

'I swear I'm not leprous, Aspasia. I have a skin complaint, but it certainly isn't leprosy. Have you ever seen anyone who has the disease?'

Aspasia shook her head.

'It's horrible. Open, running sores, nodules just waiting to erupt and finally the disfigurement and crippling of your hands and feet.'

'Is that why you became a pedlar?'

Tassos ignored her question. 'I knew no better at the time. The doctor said I had to go to the hospital for treatment and I believed him. I was sent to Spinalonga. Everyone there has leprosy so I know exactly what it looks like. I asked the doctor who comes out to the island to examine me and take tests but he said he didn't have the facilities. The priest was no help, he said he would pray for me and I must accept that I was a leper. I kept looking at myself and my body is clear. I have no nodules, no open sores, nothing. I swear to you I am not leprous, Aspasia.'

'Where's this Spinalonga place?'

'Down the coast; quite close to Aghios Nikolaos. It's an island where everyone who suffers from leprosy is sent. The authorities think they can keep you a prisoner over there, but I decided to escape. I planned carefully, managed to get back to the mainland and I've been travelling around as a pedlar ever since. No one takes any notice of me. I'm here one day and gone the next. If the authorities find out where I am they'll send me back. That's why you must tell no one, Aspasia.'

'Are you sure you're not infected?'

'I'm positive. I would never have tried to escape from Spinalonga if I was ill. Sooner or later the signs would have become obvious. I wouldn't be able to hide away forever and I certainly would not have risked coming here and infecting you.'

'So what are you going to do?'

'I told you, I'm moving on to Tilisos, make my way up towards Rethymnon, then I'll come back down here before I visit the villages the other side of Heraklion. I'll keep coming back to see you, Aspasia, and give you some money for Dimitris, for his clothes and things. Is there any chance you'll be faithful to me?'

In the darkness Tassos could just see her grinning impishly at him. 'That could depend upon how long you stay away. If you're moving on tomorrow, you'd better give me something so I'll remember you.' She lifted her blouse and pushed her breasts towards him. 'One finger to lose and one to use,' she breathed in his ear and Tassos was only too happy to comply.

November 1940

Tassos had walked from Kavrohori to Tilisos and then over the hills to Gonies. From there he had meandered from village to village, selling his goods as he went and replenishing his stocks whenever he was able to find a supplier. The cost of purchasing the items seemed to be rising each week but he had passed the increase on to his customers and they had accepted his prices with no more than a shake of their head. Trade had been good and by the time he had reached the outskirts of Rethymnon he had thirty two drachmas in his money pouch along with the money he had brought from Spinalonga.

He felt like a rich man and was tempted to buy himself a new shirt and then he thought of Dimitris. The boy would probably need some warm clothes for the winter. He calculated carefully. He should always have ten drachmas in his pouch for emergencies. On his way across the countryside he had picked apples and pomegranates from the trees, treated himself to two substantial meals each week and lived the remainder of the time on bread, cheese and olives. Now the winter was approaching and once it became really cold he might have to pay for an occasional night's lodging if he was unable to find anywhere suitable to shelter from the elements and he would need a hot meal more often.

On reaching Rethymnon he had purchased more stock, deciding he could not be parsimonious about that. It would be better to overspend a little rather than be short of the goods the villagers wanted and lose sales. He had decided he could afford to spend twelve drachmas on items to add to his sack and when he returned to Kavrohori he should be able to give Aspasia at least ten drachmas.

Having visited Aspasia he would make the journey to Gazi to see his parents and then return to the numerous profitable small villages between Heraklion and Rethymnon. There were many he had not yet set foot in. If he could find a cave or shepherd's hut to live in during the winter he would decide on a route where he could return to the dwelling each evening, rather than have to sleep in the open. He would not travel down towards Aghios Nikolaos, there were fewer settlements in that area, and he had no wish to ever set eyes on Spinalonga again.

On reaching Kavrohori he began to knock on the doors of the villagers' houses and offer his goods, making sales mostly of lamp wicks, matches, needles and cotton. He reached Aspasia's house and knocked gently. Once again Aspasia opened the door with the small boy clinging to her skirt.

'Can I interest you in any of my goods?' asked Tassos raising his eyebrows to her.

'Are they good quality?'

'Excellent quality,' Tassos assured her. 'You'll be satisfied with anything you have from me.'

'Really!' replied Aspasia. 'I'll meet you this evening,' she added quietly.

Tassos picked up his sack. 'Maybe you'll want something the next time I pass this way.'

'I'm sure I shall.'

Tassos grinned at her. 'I'll see you later. You may find something amongst my possessions that you need.'

'I'll know just where to look,' she said and indicated parting Tassos's trousers with her hands.

'Any chance I could come through to the back?' he asked.

Aspasia shook her head and pointed to Dimitris. 'Not whilst he's around. Save it for later.'

Tassos turned away as Aspasia closed the door. He continued knocking on the doors in the village, making a few more small sales, before going up to the field.

Tassos had wrapped his cloak around himself to ward off the evening chill and sat waiting in the field for Aspasia to join him. He determined to ask her if she knew of a cave or hut nearby where he would be able to spend the night. He counted his money and considered carefully the amount he could afford to give to Aspasia, finally deciding that provided he had fifteen drachmas in his pouch he had sufficient to live on for a few days. He placed the notes in his pocket. He would give them to her when he walked her back to the village.

Aspasia arrived, walking quietly and carefully across the rough field, lit only by the light from the moon. She let her cloak fall to the ground and sat down beside him. Tassos immediately enveloped her in his arms.

'The pedlar's goods are waiting for you,' he whispered in her ear.

'I thought they might be on show,' she giggled.

'Very nearly.' He pushed her down and lifted her skirt, whilst her hands parted his baggy trousers.

Finally satisfied they lay in each other's arms, Tassos caressing Aspasia's breasts whilst she revelled in the pleasure he was giving her. 'It will be too cold up here in a few more weeks. Is there a shelter anywhere we could use?'

'I don't know. I'll look around.'

'Where did you go with the others in the winter?'

'Just out the back. They were always in a hurry. I only ever came up to the fields with you.'

'You won't do that this winter whilst I'm away, will you?'

Aspasia snorted. 'It's not likely anyone will come calling on me. You've done it again, Tassos.'

'Done what?'

'I'm pregnant again.'

Tassos groaned. 'I don't believe it. Are you sure?'

In the darkness Aspasia nodded. 'I'm sure. In May Dimitris will have a brother or sister to keep him company.'

'What does your father say?'

'I haven't told him yet.'

'Suppose he wants to know who the father is?'

Aspasia shrugged. 'I'll say I don't know. I was walking in the fields and someone grabbed me from behind. They pushed me down and threw my skirt over my face so I couldn't see who it was.'

'Will he believe you?'

'No, but he won't be able to prove any different.'

'I wish I could stay here with you,' sighed Tassos.

'You know you can't. I'll just have to make do with seeing you whenever you pass through.'

Tassos wrinkled his brow. 'I'll have to try to find some regular work. I'll start asking in the villages.'

'You don't have to worry about us. I can sell my weaving. I'll manage.'

'I don't want you to manage. I want you to be able to live decently as you would if I was still working as a cobbler.' Tassos pressed the paper money into her hand. 'Put that somewhere safe. It's not much, but it's for some warm clothes for Dimitris. Next time I'm back this way I'll be able to give you some more.'

Aspasia held the notes in her hand. 'What about you? Have you got enough for a meal tomorrow?'

'I've plenty for my needs,' Tassos assured her. 'If I can find a bit of casual labour and make a bit extra all to the good.' Tassos ran his hand over Aspasia's still flat stomach. 'You're quite sure you've got one in there?' he asked. 'I can't feel it.'

'You won't for another couple of months.'

'We won't have done any damage, will we? You said when you were expecting Dimitris you wouldn't accept anyone else in case they damaged him.'

'They were always so rough. I was frightened they would hurt him and he would be born with something wrong with him. You're not rough with me, besides, you put this one there so you won't hurt it.'

'If you're sure...'

Aspasia giggled. 'I'm sure. Make the most of me whilst you can still get near me. In six months time I'll be waddling around like a duck.'

Tassos left Aspasia with mixed feelings. He was not sure if he wanted to be a father again and not be there to see his children grow up. He tried to conjure up a scheme whereby he would be able to stay in the village with her, but he could not think of anything that was practical and would be believed. If they claimed to have married in another village he would be asked to produce the papers declaring their union official. There was no way her father would allow him under his roof without those.

He was in no position to ask her to leave her village and live with him. He had no home to offer her and she could certainly not be expected to travel around Crete on foot as he did, particularly with one small child and another on the way. Even if he did have a house and regular work it would be impossible for Aspasia to leave Kavrohori; she had her blind grandmother and father to look after.

Aspasia was known as the loose woman of the village, proving her reputation by having a child, and she still held her head high and ignored the jibes and comments that were made about her. She might not wish to marry a pedlar. He could see no immediate solution to the problem unless he found a sack of money lying beneath a bush or could think of a way to access his pension that was accruing in the bank.

Tassos walked on in the direction of Rethymnon, visiting as many small villages and isolated dwellings as possible each day. Wherever he stopped now he asked if there were any odd jobs the occupant would like him to do or if there was any work available on their farm. He repaired a stretcher on a weaving frame in exchange for a hot meal and another time he spent the day chopping firewood and stacking it in the outhouse. The woman gave him five drachmas in payment and Tassos looked at it in disgust; for the ten hours he had worked unremittingly he deserved double the amount.

He had increased the prices of the goods he offered for sale and the purchasers grumbled as they handed over their money for lamp wicks, matches and soap. These were necessities and buying from the pedlar saved the long walk into the nearest small town where they might find the items were not available and they had had a wasted journey.

Tassos replenished his supplies when he reached Rethymnon. In the town all anyone was talking about was the war that was raging in Europe. After the refusal of the Greek government to allow the Italians to march through the country they had tried to enter Greece by force. Having been repelled they were now calling on their German allies to help them. Opinions were divided. Greece was a poor country, it had no oil or minerals so the Italians would find their request refused; others felt that Germany would invade any country just to add the name to its growing list of conquests and territory.

Tassos listened to the arguments put forth by the old men who sat in the cafes. Even if Greece was invaded there was no reason for the Germans or Italians to come to Crete. They were safe enough.

It was too soon for Tassos to return to the villages he had visited during the past two weeks and he decided to target the inland villages towards Chania and see if he could find employment picking olives. Whole families would spend the day in the olive groves, but extra help was always appreciated. This time he would state his price for a day's work and not be short changed as he had when he had chopped wood. He would ask for six drachmas, a meal and somewhere dry to sleep at the end of the day. If it became necessary for him to negotiate the price downwards he would still be making more money in a week than he did from his sales as a pedlar.

Tassos asked for work each time he saw activity in an olive grove and was turned away. It was a family affair and they had no need to employ additional help. Finally a farmer offered him four drachmas a day with a meal and a bed of straw in an outhouse each night and Tassos accepted with alacrity.

He was prepared to work hard, despite being ignorant of the procedure. He suggested he shook a number of trees and then they all set about collecting the fallen produce, but the farmer shook his head.

'That's fine for those that are caught in the nets, but once they fall to the ground they are bruised and need to be collected up as quickly as possible and kept separately. The women can't manage the weight of the net, nor can they climb up the tree and prune the branches. Work my way and you'll realise I know best.'

At the end of the day Tassos had to acknowledge that the farmer's system worked well. As the men shook the tree the women began to collect the olives that landed on the ground. By the time the net was full the ground had been cleared and the men could approach, untie the net and gather the edges together, haul it over to the cart and tip the contents in.

As soon as they moved on to the next tree the farmer popped a ladder against the one that had been stripped of its fruit and proceeded to lop off some of the branches, leaving them in an untidy heap on the ground. Once the cart was full of olives his son would drive it to the village, where the crop would be weighed and registered in his name before the pressing of the fruit took place. Tassos was expecting to be able to take a short break until he returned, but he was told to gather the cut branches together ready for collection later. Whilst he stacked the wood the women folded the nets and wound them around the trunks of the olive trees where they would stay in readiness for the harvesting of the following year's crop.

In the evening he ate a bowl of stewed vegetables, supplemented by a small amount of meat with relish, wiping the bowl around with bread and filling his stomach with more bread dipped in olive oil. He suppressed a belch and thanked the farmer's wife before asking if he could be shown his sleeping place. He was not best pleased when he found he was sharing the outhouse with the donkey, but it would certainly be warmer than sleeping outside. His cloak and blanket were not sufficient protection against the cold night air. He piled the straw up into a corner, turned his face towards the wall and within minutes was asleep.

By the end of the week Tassos's body had become used to the manual labour and no longer protested when he rose in the morning. He accompanied the farmer's son to the olive groves, pulling the cart between them, whilst the farmer rode into the village on the donkey. They would load the cut branches on to the cart and wait for the farmer to join them after he had received payment for his olive crop. The donkey would then be tethered to the cart, the wood taken back to the yard to be chopped and stored ready for the winter fires.

Tassos accepted the twenty four drachmas the farmer gave him and asked if there was any chance he could be employed permanently.

The farmer shook his head. 'I only need a bit of help when I pick the olives. Come back next year and I'll employ you again. You're a good worker.'

'You wouldn't know of anywhere I could get regular employment?'

'Not round these parts.'

'I'll make my way to the village then. I'm a cobbler by trade and a good knife grinder so I may be able to earn enough for a meal as I pass through.'

As Tassos walked from village to village it became colder. He often wrapped his cloak around himself as he walked to ward of the bitter wind, and would lay shivering in an outhouse until he fell into a fitful sleep. He still had the money in his pouch that he had earned picking olives and he realised he had to make a decision. He either purchased some warmer clothes to wear or he would have to pay for a lodging each night. To spend all day and all night shivering was asking for pneumonia.

He walked slowly through the village of Koufi. He had sold only a box of matches and a lamp wick all day. He was tired, cold and hungry. The village did not have a taverna in evidence, but there was a church. So far he had resisted accepting charity, but short of continuing to walk to the next village and with no certainty of finding a taverna open there, he had little choice.

Tassos pushed open the door, glad to be inside and away from the wind. He sat on a chair at the back and tried to think of a suitable prayer. He had not been inside a church since leaving Spinalonga. He placed his sack at his feet and leaned on the chair in front of him, his head resting on his hands. The next thing he knew a hand was shaking him gently and the kindly face of the priest was regarding him with concern.

'Can I help you, my son?'

Tassos blinked and shook his head. 'I'm sorry. I think I must have fallen asleep for a few minutes.'

'You were asleep when I arrived to close the church for the night and I have waited for you to wake up for the last half an hour.'

'I'm very sorry.' Tassos stumbled to his feet and groped for his sack.

'Where are you headed?'

'The next village.'

'Both Arhotiki and Karoti are some distance away.'

Tassos sighed. 'I was looking for somewhere I could buy a meal and have a bed for the night.'

'By the time you reach either village the taverna will be closed. You would do better to stay in Koufi.'

'I couldn't find a taverna open here.'

'That is no problem. Come with me and I will ask them to accommodate you for the night.'

Gratefully Tassos followed the priest back along the village street until he stopped and opened a door. Heads tuned to see who had come to join them and when they saw the priest and a stranger the conversation between the men stopped.

'At this time of year the shutters are closed once it is dark. The local residents are used to the routine, but anyone passing through would not know the establishment was open.'

'I didn't' admitted Tassos.

'Find a seat by the fire and I'll ask Panayiotis to serve you some food. It will only be simple country fare, but sustaining.'

'Would he have a room to rent me for the night?' asked Tassos anxiously. 'An outhouse with a bit of straw would do.'

The priest nodded. 'I'm sure something can be arranged.'

'Where've you come from?' asked the man who had moved up on the bench seat to allow Tassos a space close to the fire.

'I left Gonia this morning. I'm a pedlar. I also mend boots and sharpen blades. I'm happy to do any odd jobs.'

'Wouldn't fancy being out on the road myself at this time of year,' observed the man.

Tassos shrugged. 'If I could find some permanent work and a place to stay I certainly wouldn't be a pedlar.'

The priest returned and handed Tassos a bowl of lentils flavoured with pork fat. It was not a dish he would have chosen, but warm and filling and he accepted gratefully.

Sipping from a small glass of raki the priest smiled down at Tassos. 'How long have you been a travelling man?'

Tassos was tempted to say he had been on the road all his life, but he could not lie to a priest. 'About six months now.'

'It's a hard life,' the priest sighed. 'Remember whenever you

152

reach a village and cannot find a taverna to go to the church. You will always receive a meal and shelter.'

'I'd be willing to pay. I'm not a beggar,' Tassos assured him.

'A contribution in the poor box is always welcome. The taverna keeper here can provide you with a small room and mattress where you can spend the night. He would like payment from you before you retire. He does not want to rise tomorrow and find you have already left, you understand.'

'I wouldn't do that, but I'll pay him what he asks as soon as I've finished my meal.' The unaccustomed heat from the fire was beginning to make Tassos feel drowsy and he would be quite happy to be shown the room as soon as possible.

Tassos found the priest was correct when he said he would always be able to obtain a meal and a place to sleep if he called at the village church. He still tried to manage with a hot meal every other day and sheltered in outhouses and stables whenever the opportunity arose, rather than have to spend his hard earned drachmas. Despite asking if there was any permanent employment to be had at every house he visited he was turned away. The apples and pomegranates had been picked earlier and the olive harvest was over. If he returned in the early summer there would be oranges, lemons and limes, followed by grapes and the farmers might have work for an extra hand.

Over the ensuing weeks he chopped and stacked firewood, helped to slaughter a pig, sharpened scissors and mended numerous pairs of boots, but every day saw him walking out of the village and on to the next. He was dispirited, being no nearer to his goal of finding somewhere close to Kavrohori to live so he could visit Aspasia.

He travelled as far as Kambi before making his way back down to Malaxi. The coast appeared to be deserted of settlements of any size and twice during his journey back towards Rethymnon he had been forced to sleep in the open. He struck back inland

and began to offer his dwindling stock and his services to the villagers without a great deal of success.

He still had money in his pouch, but nowhere near the sum he had hoped to accumulate and be able to share with Aspasia. When he reached Rethymnon he spent as much as he dared to replenish his goods; without some items to sell he would be dependent upon cobbling and sharpening blades.

From Rethymnon he turned inland again towards the small villages. On reaching Roussospiti he was told there were few villages further over and he would do better to make his way back down towards the coast. The track over the hills was pointed out to him and he spent the day walking in deserted countryside looking for any sign of habitation. Finally the path led down into a wooded valley.

Undaunted he continued; a path had to lead somewhere, if only to a shepherd's hut. As he descended further amongst the trees he could hear the sound of water rushing and looked behind fearfully. He did not want to be caught by a flash flood. He began to eye the trees, looking for one that he would be able to climb, keeping him safe from the water provided it was not uprooted by the deluge.

The track widened and the trees thinned. Below him Tassos was able to see a river flowing swiftly and he was sure he had caught a glimpse of buildings between the foliage. His spirits rose. If there were buildings there must be people. He should certainly be able to make some sales in this deserted spot.

He increased his pace as the track dropped downwards, finally showing him both houses and mills. It was the noise of the mills using the water power that had made him think he was about to be swept away by a flood. As he stood and looked the wheels of the mills slowed, gradually coming to a halt; and in the sudden quietness he could hear movement on the track ahead of him. As a train of donkeys approached he stood to one side to let them pass, but their leader took them down a side path, their driver following them.

Tassos followed. He could ask the driver where he was and if he was able to get food and a lodging for the night.

The driver looked at him in surprise. 'Where've you come from? I didn't see you on the road.'

'I've walked down from Roussospiti. Can you tell me the name of this village and how far I am from Rethymnon?'

'This is Mili. Carry on down the track and you'll come to Kastellakia. That's no more than an hour's walk to Rethymnon.'

Tassos looked at the rapidly darkening sky. Rain was threatening and it was unlikely he would reach Rethymnon without becoming soaked to the skin.

'Would there be anywhere here I could buy a meal and spend the night?'

The driver of the donkeys considered. 'I expect my wife could give you something to eat, but I've only the stable to offer you.'

Tassos nodded gratefully. 'I'll be happy with that. Any bit of shelter is welcome.'

'You'll have to wait whilst I see to the beasts.'

'Can I help?' offered Tassos.

The driver raised his eyebrows. 'Are you used to dealing with donkeys?' Tassos shook his head. 'Then you'd best wait whilst I stable them for the night.'

Tassos watched whilst the drive tethered each animal to a metal ring before slipping a nosebag over their head and removing the unwieldy panniers from their backs. They were not the usual baskets that donkeys carried on each side to transport goods, but large flat pieces of wood with leather straps to hold them in place over the donkeys' back and under its belly.

'I've not seen panniers like those before,' remarked Tassos.

'More use for carrying sack of flour than a basket. You can stack four sacks on each side. A basket would only carry one.'

Tassos looked at the wooded hillside with the river flowing below. 'Where do you grow the grain?'

'We don't. We're just the millers. We grind it and take it into

Rethymnon each day. Without us no one would have any bread.'

Tassos nodded, pretending to know that. He had never thought about the process of making bread. His mother had bought flour from the grocer and baked a couple of loaves each day in her oven. How the flour had reached the grocer he had never considered.

He watched as the driver removed the strip of blanket from each donkey's back and examined each one for any sign of sores. One was developing a raw place and the drive picked up a bottle and a rag and rubbed copious amounts of olive oil into the place. The donkey lifted her head from the nosebag and curled her lips back as he worked.

'I know, old girl, it hurts. Bear with me. I'll rest you for a couple of days so you heal.' Finally he slapped her rump and she returned her nose to the bag. 'Valuable beasts,' he explained to Tassos. 'Can't afford for that sore to become an open wound and get infected.'

He checked the donkeys' hooves for stones or damage, renewed their water supply, placed an armful of straw into a wooden trough, finally removing their nose bags and releasing them from the rings. 'Keeps them quiet whilst I do whatever's necessary,' he explained.

Tassos turned to go, but the driver began to examine the leather straps that had held the wooden panniers in place. Finally he slung one over his shoulder and hung the others on a hook. 'My job for the evening,' he said gloomily.

'What's wrong with it?'

'Nearly worn though. I need to cut a length out and stitch in a new piece. Follow me.'

Tassos followed the man up the path to the track he had left earlier and almost immediately back down another that led to a house.

'I could do that for you,' offered Tassos.'

'Do what?'

'Mend the strap. I'm a cobbler by trade. I have my tools with me and it would take me no time at all.'

'So if you're a cobbler why aren't you working as one?'

Tassos shrugged. 'My father is the village cobbler.'

'What made you learn the trade then?'

'My father said it would mean I could take over from him when he was no longer able to work. He's fit and well, I'm pleased to say, so there's no job for me there yet.'

The driver nodded as he opened the door to his house. 'Anna, I'm home and we have a guest.'

A diminutive woman appeared from the dark recesses of the room and peered short-sightedly at Tassos before nodding a greeting to him.

'I'll add a couple more potatoes,' she said and delved into a sack.

Tassos stood in the room uncertainly. Was he expected to sit down with them or would he be given a bowl of food to eat out in the stable? To his surprise the donkey driver thrust a glass of wine into his hand and waved him towards a chair.

'I'm Costas. What's your name?'

'Tassos.'

'Well, Tassos, I'll light the lamp and then you can show me how adept you are at repairing a strap. You can work for your supper.'

Tassos removed his stitching awl and thread from his sack. 'Do you have a new strip of leather?' he asked and Costas produced a length.

'Cut off what you need, but don't waste it. Costs money.'

Tassos nodded. He did not need to be told not to waste leather or money. He examined the strap carefully and finally cut out the worn piece. 'Does the wear always occur in the same place?' he asked.

'More or less. It's where the strap goes through the hole in the wood.'

Tassos sat with the damaged strap in his hands. 'I could replace this with a double piece and it should last twice as long. Why don't you bind the holes in the wood with leather? That should stop the strap from chafing.'

'We tried that. The leather still wore out with the continual friction. Put a double piece and I'll see how long that lasts.'

'I'll splice it,' Tassos promised. 'That will make it stronger still.'

'We'll eat first.'

Tassos was not sorry to put the repair to one side and enjoyed the home made meal of goat meat and potatoes, with plenty of bread to mop up the gravy. Afterwards he sat as close to the oil lamp as possible and Costas watched as he first cut out the worn strip and measured a new length. Costas had frowned when he saw the strip Tassos had cut was considerably longer than the piece he had removed.

'I said not to waste it,' he grumbled.

'I need double the length if I'm going to sew in a double piece,' explained Tassos patiently. 'It also needs to be a bit longer so I can splice it. No good me sewing a new piece to the worn bit. It would break away within a few days.'

Costas watched as Tassos thinned the centre of each end of the old leather strap, leaving the outer edge untouched. Deftly he joined the new leather over the old, making sure it was firmly sewn to the edge of the leather he had thinned. He repeated the process at both ends and then sewed the sides together and stitched across the joins on both sides. Finally he handed the completed job to Costas who scrutinised his work and tested it for strength.

'That's a pretty good job, better than I could have done,' admitted Costas.

Tassos shrugged. 'It's my trade. I don't know anything about donkeys, but I know how to work leather. Do you want me to have a look at the other straps tomorrow?'

Costas nodded. 'Good idea. Maybe some of the others would like you to do a repair for them.'

'You supply the leather and I'll do the repair. I charge two drachmas for each one. This one is free as you've given me a meal and offered me a place to sleep.'

'You can bed down in the corner.'

'If there's a taverna here I'm happy to spend the night there rather than inconvenience you.'

'They don't have rooms.' Costas shrugged. 'The choice is yours, the corner or the stable.'

'I'll accept the corner gratefully. I've slept with a donkey before. I didn't appreciate the experience and you have six out there.'

Costas grinned. 'Wise man. Tell me about yourself. Where've you travelled?'

'Around Heraklion and Rethymnon, up as far as Chania.' Tassos decided not to mention he had been anywhere near Aghios Nikolaos.

'Do you sell much?'

'Depends. If the village is near enough to a town for the people to shop they only use me for emergency goods, something broken or lost that they need immediately. If they have a long journey to make for supplies they usually take advantage of the goods I have to offer. Provided I make enough for a meal and a bed I'm not complaining.'

Costas shook his head. 'I don't think you'll sell much in Mili. We go into Rethymnon every day so bring anything back we need. I don't remember the last time a pedlar came though here.'

'I'll doubt you'll see me again then if that's the case. No point in making a wasted journey.'

'Where are you headed from here?'

'Buy some bits and pieces in Rethymnon and head back towards Heraklion. There are plenty of villages on the way until I reach Livada. After that it's pretty deserted for a while. I'll drop back down to Heraklion, buy some more goods and start working the inland villages the other side of the town.'

'You obviously enjoy life on the road.'

Tassos snorted. 'I'd give it up tomorrow if I could find

permanent employment. It's not that bad in the summer months, but I'm finding the winter hard going.'

'Same with all of us,' Costas agreed. 'The trees drip all over you and the track is wet, muddy and slippery during the winter. Going up and down there in all weathers to Rethymnon isn't much fun.'

'At least you know you'll have a regular amount of money coming in each week. If it's raining too hard I have to take a day off. Don't want my goods getting soaked as well as me.'

Anna cleared her throat and looked pointedly at the large double bed that took up most of the space in the room.

Costas rose. 'I've an early start. You'll need to be up with me if you're going to check those straps.'

Tassos took the hint, happy to lie down and go to sleep in the warm room. 'I'll make myself comfortable over there.' He wrapped his cloak and blanket around himself, removed two saucepans from his sack to enable him to make a comfortable pillow and then lay down with his back towards the couple. He was still able to hear the noise of the river, but it was a comforting sound and it quickly lulled him into a deep sleep.

Tassos woke to the sounds of Costas dressing and the smell of coffee. He rolled over cautiously and opened his eyes. He did not want to see that Costas's wife was still getting dressed. To his relief the bed was empty. On the table were steaming cups of coffee and a plate of yesterday's bread.

'Help yourself.' Costas proceeded to dip his bread into the coffee to soften it and Tassos followed suit. 'Whilst I prepare the donkeys you can check the other straps.' Costas spoke with his mouth full. 'When we're ready to load up I'll take you down to the mill with the donkeys and introduce you to the other drivers. If they want any repairs done I'll leave you here and see you again this evening. If you decide to move on just follow the track and you'll arrive at Kastellakia. To your left will be Rethymnon and after that you'll have to find your own route.'

Tassos followed Costas and his string of donkeys down to the mill. The one with the sore had looked at her owner reproachfully as he left her behind and brayed until her companions were out of sight.

'She doesn't like to be left out,' grinned Costas. 'Hard workers, donkeys. That's what you need to carry your load, a donkey.'

Tassos shook his head. 'I couldn't afford to buy one and I wouldn't know how to look after it. No, I'll stick to walking and carrying my load myself for the time being.'

Tassos looked around him as they walked and marvelled at the beauty he had been unable to appreciate in the failing light of the previous evening. He was actually in a steep sided gorge, the river running through and abundant vegetation as far as he could see; fruit trees were growing and small patches of land had been cultivated to grow vegetables. On the side of the gorge where they were standing were small houses interspersed with mills, most of them already working and churning the river into a white froth, whilst opposite the cliff rose steeply.

'This is beautiful,' said Tassos, drawing in his breath. 'It's unlike any village I've ever been in.'

'It's a good place to live. We can grow just about anything in the way of food.'

Tassos waited whilst Costas tethered his string of donkeys and spoke to the other men. They eyed Tassos suspiciously, but gradually they nodded and Costas beckoned him forward.

'I've shown them the strap you repaired for me and they're willing for you to check theirs. They'll want to know your charges before they agree to you doing any work.'

Tassos nodded. 'I told you, two drachmas for each repair if you supply the leather. It's the same for them as it is for you.'

Tassos spent almost a month in Mili, repairing straps, bridles and leading reins. After the first night he had moved in to the cottage where Zen lived alone and had a corner allocated to him where he could spend the night to sit and work on repairs. He was sad when he finally had to replace his tools into his sack and bid the villagers goodbye. It was the longest he had spent anywhere since leaving Spinalonga and he had enjoyed the company of the men during the evening. He now counted both Costas and Zen as friends.

'I will come back,' he vowed. 'This place is paradise.'

He accompanied the strings of heavily laden donkeys down the track and along the road from Kastellakia to Rethymnon. There the drivers parted company, delivering their sacks of flour to the various bakers dispersed round the town and Tassos started on his search for supplies; finally leaving the town and walking back to Kastellakia where he turned inland to Giannoudi.

April 1941

Tassos no longer described his trade as a cobbler. Having spent the time in Mili he now claimed to be a leather worker and found his work in demand amongst the farmers who had made unsatisfactory and temporary repairs to their harnesses and leading reins. He increased his prices, charging three or even five drachmas depending upon the extent of the work he was expected to carry out. Along with his meagre income from peddling he was finally beginning to accrue some savings.

He worked out a route which took him to the villages in the countryside behind Heraklion until he reached Rethymnon. He would purchase more goods from the town and from there he would begin his journey back to Heraklion, passing through the villages until he reached Gazi and call in briefly on his parents before going to visit Aspasia the following day. Having made the visits he would start walking back towards Rethymnon, passing through the villages until he reached the town and able to replenish his stock before returning to Heraklion by a different route.

The round trip took him almost two months to complete and each time he visited Aspasia at Kavrohori he was able to give her some money. She accepted gratefully; no longer able to spend the long hours standing at the loom. It was an effort to thread the shuttle from side to side and reach up to block the weft firmly and evenly into place now she was so large and unwieldy and she often undid a few rows that did not satisfy her skilled eye.

Tassos looked at her increasing size in alarm. 'Are you sure it's only one you have in there?'

'I've seen the village midwife and she reckons it's just one again. I'm no bigger than I was with Dimitris or the other women in the village who are expecting.'

'Have you got enough to pay her when the time comes?' asked Tassos anxiously.

'I've been saving up the money you've left with me. Don't worry, Tassos. At least I know what to expect this time so it won't be so frightening. Who knows, the next time you come to visit I could have a flat stomach again and something to show you.' Aspasia grinned at him cheekily. 'With a bit of luck I could be ready for you to show me something interesting.'

Tassos felt himself stirring at the thought and ran his hands across her swollen breasts and enlarged stomach, feeling the baby move beneath his touch.

'It's too far for you to walk up to the fields, but we could go out to the yard,' he suggested as he slipped his hand beneath her skirt.

Aspasia shook her head. 'It's not that I don't want to,' she assured him, 'but I don't know how it would affect this little one now I'm this far on. Besides, Dimitris is around and I don't want him learning his father's bad habits at such an early age.'

Tassos ruffled the boy's hair. 'You don't need to learn what comes naturally. I'll be back again and hopefully you'll have dropped this one and be ready for me.'

Aspasia pressed her body against his as she kissed him. 'It's as hard for me as it is for you,' she assured him. 'I reckon I'll have it in May, if not before.'

Aspasia's eyes widened as Tassos handed her fifty five drachmas. 'Where did you get all that?'

'I've done well over the winter. If I manage to continue to make money at this rate we'll soon be wealthy enough for me to find a little house somewhere nearby.'

Aspasia's lips twitched in amusement. 'What do you want a house for? You spend most of your time wandering around the countryside.'

'You could live there. Be waiting for me whenever I returned. We wouldn't need to go up to the fields or into the back yard.'

'I can't leave my grandmother. Who'd look after her?'

'She could come with you,' offered Tassos recklessly.

Aspasia threw back her head and laughed. 'That would leave my father alone. It would be more practical for you to move in with us.'

'Even if your father agreed the village priest would want to see the papers declaring us officially married. If I hadn't cut off my finger I wouldn't be in this position,' groaned Tassos.

'If you hadn't cut your finger you'd be married to that woman in your village by now so we'd be no better off. Be thankful that you can come and enjoy me and not have to service her.'

'I don't think she would ever have allowed me near her.'

'You could have insisted.'

'Where's the pleasure in that?' Tassos shook his head. 'No, when I've made my fortune your father will be only too pleased to welcome me into his house, married or not.'

Tassos could not believe the amount of goods he was selling. It seemed that every villager wanted matches, soap and lamp wicks. Twice he had to return to Heraklion before he walked towards Rethymnon with a full sack. The items were purchased with alacrity and he bought no more unwieldy saucepans or scrubbing brushes, instead he concentrated on the light and popular necessities that people wanted. He wished he was able to carry twice the amount and thought seriously about investing in a donkey and panniers.

His dream now was to take Aspasia, Dimitris and the baby away to a village where they were not known and live as a family. He doubted that her father would join them, but she would have to bring her grandmother. The old lady would need to have her bed on the ground floor beside the fire where she would be warm during the winter. He needed either a spacious one storey property or one with an upper level that would accommodate him and his family.

He would be willing to do any repairs that were necessary, and although he had passed houses that were no more than ruins whenever he enquired if they were available to rent he was looked at with scorn. No pedlar would be able to afford to rent a house.

He took a detour up to Mili, partly out of the desire to see the village that he found so attractive and also to speak to Costas and ask how much a donkey would cost to purchase and the expense involved in looking after it. If he could carry more goods he would sell more goods and consequently make more money he reasoned. Eventually he would have enough money to buy a small house and not be looking to rent and be turned away like a vagabond.

Costas laughed at him. 'Depends what you want. An unbroken colt that you train yourself is cheaper than one that's been broken to a bridle and leading rein. With the knowledge you claim to have of donkeys you'd best get one that's ready for a harness.'

'How much would that be?'

Costas shrugged. 'No idea. We breed our own here. No need to buy them.'

'How much would you be willing to sell one for?'

'They're not for sale. We can use every one. If we started to sell them how would we get our sacks of flour to Rethymnon?'

'One less wouldn't make much difference.'

Costas shook his head. 'One can make all the difference. There's nearly always one that's sick or lame each week. Take my advice, get to know how to look after a donkey before you buy one or you'll be selling him for meat or the price of his skin within six months. There's more to it than just giving them food and water. Stick to the work you know and forget about donkeys.'

Tassos sighed. 'I thought if I had a donkey I'd be able to carry more goods and make more money. I need to make enough to buy a house.'

Costas raised his eyebrows. 'What does a travelling man need a house for? You'd never be there.'

Tassos hesitated. 'I've a wife and child, another on the way. I need somewhere for them to live.'

'Where are they living now?'

'In her father's house.'

'So what's the problem with her staying there?'

'It's a question of space. Aspasia has her loom and her grandmother has to sleep in the living room. There's hardly enough room for a table and chair. Her father sleeps upstairs and we have the other room. With our mattress and another for Dimitris I don't know where we'll find a space for the babe.' Tassos described an imaginary situation, never having been upstairs in the house. 'I've been asking in various villages if I can rent an empty property, but no one trusts me to be reliable as I'm a pedlar with nothing but a sack over my shoulder.'

'Is there no one who would vouch for you?'

Tassos shook his head. 'I'm not usually in one place long enough to get to know anyone. The month I spent here last year was the longest I'd lived anywhere since I was a boy.' Tassos conveniently omitted to mention that he had spent over a year on Spinalonga.

Costas scratched his head. 'I don't see how I can help you. You dealt fairly with us but I can't tell anyone that you'd have enough money to pay your rent every week. Can't you find a house to rent in the village where your wife lives? Her father could guarantee you.'

'There's nowhere available there.'

'I can't see a solution to your problem, then. Do you want some work whilst your here? You can have a meal and a bed for the night if you'll check my reins and bridles. I'll pay you for any repairs you do. Same rate as before?'

Tassos nodded. 'I'd be grateful. I'll not tell you something needs to be repaired unless it's necessary.'

Tassos spent three days in Mili, staying again with Zen, whilst he did a number of repairs before leaving to make the journey back to Heraklion again. He would have to call in at Rethymnon and buy more thread, and some matches; lamp wicks and soap would be a good investment judging by his previous sales.

He left Kastellakia behind him and walked along the main road until he reached Rethymnon. Provided he completed his purchases swiftly he should be able to reach Giannoudi that night and spend the following morning selling his goods in the village. He would then take the track across the fields to Maroulas and should be back in Kavrohori before the end of May. Provided he timed his journey correctly he should be able to see his new born child and leave Aspasia some more money before moving on again.

Buoyed up with this thought he entered the general store in search of his purchases.

'Any news?' asked the shopkeeper eagerly.

'News? What kind of news?'

'Where've you come from?'

'Walked down from Mili this morning.'

'So you won't have heard. Australian troops are arriving in Chania.'

'What for?'

'Greece has fallen into enemy hands and the allied troops are being moved out.'

'Why are they coming here?'

The shop keeper shrugged. 'How should I know? I'm a shop keeper not an army general.'

Tassos thought about the information whilst he made his purchases. It could be worth his while to walk towards Chania. If troops were arriving they could well need their boots mended. He would go cross country, visiting the villages as usual and return to Rethymnon by bus and then on to Heraklion the same way. He could still be in Kavrohori by the end of May and with a considerable amount of money in his pocket, despite having purchased a bus ticket for the return journey.

Cheerfully he left the town and turned inland to Atsipopoula. At every village he was asked if he had any news of the troops that had been sent to Crete from mainland Greece and had to admit he knew no more than they did. He promised to find out all he could when he reached Chania, despite knowing that he would not be in the area again for a number of weeks and by then any news he had would be out of date.

From the village of Mournies Tassos turned down to the main road that would lead him in to Chania and was surprised at the amount of traffic he encountered. Open backed lorries, crammed with soldiers, passed him frequently and his spirits sank. If the soldiers were being moved elsewhere he had made a wasted journey. He entered the first taverna he saw and placed his sack by an empty table.

Two elderly men were sitting at the far side, their beads clicking as they ran them through their fingers or flicked them from side to side. Tassos walked over and inclined his head to include them both in his greeting. They nodded back at him and regarded him curiously.

'Any news?' asked one immediately.

Tassos shook his head. 'I was hoping you could tell me. I've just walked down from Mournies. When I was in Rethymnon I was told troops had been sent to Chania. Where are they going now?'

The man shrugged. 'We don't know, but there were too many in Chania. Where do they think we're going to find the food to feed them? If it was just a couple of hundred we'd be able to manage, but there's thousands of them. The ships came in and they poured off like water from a pump.'

'Surely they brought some food with them?'

'They may have had some on the ship but they're going round begging now. People have given what they can, but they've their own families to think about.'

'Why are they here?'

A second man leaned forward. 'I've heard they're going to

bring ships to take them back to their own country.'

The first shook his head. 'They're here to defend us.'

'Why should we need foreign soldiers to defend us?' asked Tassos bewildered.

'There's a rumour that the Germans plan to invade us by sea and these troops from the mainland have been sent here to fight them.'

'When are they coming?'

The man shook his head. 'How should I know?'

'No,' he second man spoke again. 'They've done their share of fighting. They're being driven down to the coast to get a ship to take them home.'

Tassos looked from one man to the other. It was clear that neither had any definite knowledge. 'Any chance I could get something to eat here?' He looked around for the taverna owner and the man who had asked him for news rose from his chair.

'I can manage a bowl of soup and some bread.'

Tassos nodded. 'That will be enough to keep me going. I can get a proper meal later.'

'I doubt that,' remarked the man and walked into his tiny kitchen whilst Tassos returned to the table where he had left his sack.

The soup, when it arrived was thin and greasy, tasting faintly of chicken and Tassos guessed it had been made from boiling the remains of a fowl more than once. The bread was stale and he dipped it into the liquid to soften it, wishing he had stopped in the town rather than on the outskirts.

When the taverna owner asked him for four drachmas in payment he was horrified and thought about protesting at the exorbitant price. Grudgingly he took the notes from his pocket and handed them over. If prices had risen to that extent at this end of the island the sooner he returned to Heraklion the better. He could not afford to spend that amount on such meagre and unpalatable sustenance.

Tassos turned his back on Chania and walked along the main road towards Rethymnon. It was too soon to return to the villages he had visited the previous week and he decided it would be sensible for him to take the bus to Rethymnon and work the villages as he made his way back to Heraklion.

He had no idea if the bus was still making its daily journey to Rethymnon or if it had been commandeered to help with the transport of the soldiers. As he walked he was amazed at the number of uniformed men who were travelling in the same direction. Some were helping their companions to walk along whilst others sat resting in the sparse shade afforded by olive trees. One or two held out imploring hands towards him and he averted his eyes. They were obviously asking for help of some kind, but he did not know what and doubted he that he would have whatever they required.

He plodded doggedly onwards, weaving his way around the groups of men, holding his breath as he passed them to avoid gagging on the vile, unwashed smell that came from many of them. Mostly they were walking in silence, but when he did hear them speaking he had no idea of their conversation. One grabbed his arm, pointed along the road and began to repeat the word 'Rethymnon'.

Finally Tassos understood his meaning, pointed into the distance and nodded. The soldier released his arm and asked him something else indistinguishable. Tassos shrugged and hurried on. If the bus had not arrived by the time he reached the road leading to Tsivaras he would abandon his idea of a bus ride and begin to walk across country to Rethymnon. He felt uncomfortable with so many armed men around him and his inability to communicate with them.

He was relieved when he saw a cloud of dust coming down the road, the bus hooting to warn the travellers to move to the side. Tassos stepped out into the road and once it halted he boarded with alacrity and paid his fare.

Every seat was occupied; often a woman was sitting on her husband's lap and their child on hers, with bundles at their feet.

In the aisle people stood crammed together, clutching their possessions as best they could. A woman pushed her sack further beneath the seat and Tassos squeezed himself into the small space in front of her.

'Is the bus always full like this?' he asked.

The woman shook her head. 'I don't know. It's the first time I've ridden on it. My husband said I had to leave Chania as there were so many soldiers around. He said you couldn't trust them if they'd been without a woman for months on end.'

'Where are you going?'

'Rethymnon, my sister lives there. I can stay with her for a week or two.'

The bus shuddered to a halt again and two more people forced themselves aboard, the portly man leaning back on Tassos so he could hardly breathe. He tried to push his sack a little further out, hoping to encourage the man to move forwards, but he was ignored. As they travelled slowly along the main road he was able to see the look of despair and weariness on the soldiers' faces as their rhythmic marching gave way to stumbling forwards as best they could.

Tassos was tempted to force his way off the over-crowded, smelly bus, then he looked at the soldiers again. They were no longer en mass, but either walked alone or in small groups, whilst some were curled up on the hard ground appearing to be asleep. He reminded himself he should be thankful that he was not walking, although at the pace the bus was travelling he would probably have covered the ground more quickly. How long it was going to take these exhausted men to reach Rethymnon he could not calculate.

Suddenly he had an intense desire to be back in Heraklion so he could visit his parents and warn them about the troops coming in their direction. He needed to see Aspasia and impress upon her the necessity to lock her door and stay hidden in the house if the soldiers took a detour through her village. Despite the oppressive heat on the bus he shivered. Did this mean that the war had come to Crete?

By the time they were over halfway to Rethymnon the numbers of soldiers had thinned and the bus was able to increase its speed, despite its heavy load. Having travelled inland and stopping at a couple of villages to allow people to alight they were now driving back down towards the coast and Tassos could catch an occasional glimpse of the sea.

Finally drawing in to the bus station Tassos drew a deep breath of relief and regretted it as he gagged on the fetid smell in the bus. Fortunately, having been one of the last passengers on and having only his sack, he was able to climb down the steps and appreciate the fresh air within a few minutes of the bus grinding to a halt. Feeling thoroughly nauseous he took a mouthful of water and stood taking in deep breaths until he felt capable of moving on.

It was late afternoon and he debated the wisdom of walking to Mali to inform Costas of the troop movement. It would take him at least two or more hours to reach there and he wanted to ensure he was at the bus station when the Heraklion bus departed the next morning. It would not hurt him to sleep on the waste ground in the shelter of the bus for the night. A more immediate need was to refill his water bottle and also to have a meal. The thin soup and stale bread had done nothing to assuage his hunger earlier in the day.

Tassos groaned as he stretched and rose from the hard packed earth. He had moved some stones and spread his blanket, but had not slept well. He consoled himself with the thought that if he was able to get a seat on the bus by arriving early he would be able to sleep during the journey down to Heraklion. He purchased a ticket to Heraklion and studied the timetable, hoping it was reasonably accurate, and decided he certainly had time for a cup of coffee.

Whilst drinking his coffee Tassos watched the buses anxiously to see if a driver was arriving. A number of people began to congregate on the waste ground and Tassos finished his coffee hurriedly and joined them, only to find himself standing there for a further half an hour before the driver finally arrived.

He scrambled aboard and pushed his way through to a seat by the window, placing his sack between his feet. A large woman sat down on the seat next to him and forced herself over so that a girl could sit beside her. Tassos was squashed between the window and the woman. He tried to wriggle to give himself a little more space, but the woman would not budge and Tassos felt unreasonably annoyed. If they ran more than one bus a day it would not be so crowded and the long, bone shaking journey would be more tolerable.

Finally the bus crawled slowly away from the waste ground and Tassos leaned his head against the window and closed his eyes. The woman next to him kept up a non-stop conversation with the girl who answered in monosyllables. Tassos feigned sleep, wishing it would overtake him and make the tedious journey be over more quickly.

Each time the bus stopped in a village the driver would call out the name and a few people would leave, whilst others would take their place. Tassos would open one eye and look out to see if he recognised the area and could judge how much longer he would have to endure his cramped and unpleasant conditions.

It was three hours before the driver finally shouted 'Gazi' and Tassos pushed his way past the large woman who promptly filled his seat. No one else left the bus and within minutes it had pulled away in a cloud of dust. Tassos stretched his stiff body, took a long drink from his water bottle and began to walk into the village. Upon his arrival he went through his usual procedure of calling at his father's shop and then waiting behind a stone wall that bordered the track to the village until darkness fell.

Over a meal of chopped liver and onions Tassos described to his parents the troop movement he had witnessed as he left Chania.

'Where are they going?' asked his father.

Tassos shrugged. 'I've no idea. I was told they had been sent over to defend Crete against a German invasion and I was also told they were here to be taken off by ship and returned to their own country.'

'Well if they walk to Heraklion to find a ship they'll certainly need their boots mended by then.' Lambros smiled in satisfaction at the thought of the extra business he would acquire.

'I'm not sure you want them down here,' Tassos cautioned him. 'A woman on the bus from Chania said her husband was sending her away to stay with her sister. He didn't think she would be safe in Chania with so many soldiers around who hadn't had a woman in months.'

Lambros frowned at his son. That was not the way to speak in front of his mother. Maria looked at her husband anxiously.

'They'll have no reason to come here,' Lambros assured her. 'Tassos said the one that spoke to him was asking for Rethymnon. I don't see why they don't take them off from Chania, save them having to walk anywhere.'

'I think there are too many for the town to cope with. When I spoke to a taverna owner he said the soldiers were begging for food. You can't expect anywhere to have sufficient supplies to suddenly feed thousands more people.'

'The poor men,' Maria shook her head sadly. 'They've been fighting hard and now they can't even have a decent meal.'

'I'm sure the army will have things organised very soon and supplies sent in.' Lambros assured her. 'Now, tell us where else you've visited. Have you been to any new villages?'

Tassos shook his head. 'I have a regular route worked out now. There's no point in me walking all day to reach a village with half a dozen houses or expecting to sell my goods in a town. I call on anywhere isolated that I pass, set up in the square for a while in a village and often knock on a few doors if sales are slow. I know now the items that are usually wanted. I thought about buying a donkey and carrying more goods in panniers, but I spoke to a man who keeps the beasts and he said unless I knew how to look after it I would be wasting my money.'

Lambros leaned forward eagerly. 'Why don't you invest in one of those three wheeled vehicles with a cart behind them? You'd be able to carry a large quantity of goods in one of those. I could probably let you have a bit towards it.'

'Thank you, Pappa, but I can't. I'd need to show my identity papers when I bought it and I can't risk that. If the authorities decided to check up on me they'd soon find out that I'm a fugitive from Spinalonga.'

'It doesn't seem right that you should have to be a pedlar to earn a living. It's more than four years since you were sent away and there's nothing wrong with you. You're a cobbler and there's work here for you.'

Tassos smiled. 'I'm known as a leather worker as well as a pedlar now. I mend bridles and leading reins. That's how I know a man who keeps donkeys, besides, I enjoy being on the move.'

'So you wouldn't want to come back to the village and live here?'

Tassos shrugged. 'Of course I'd like a permanent home, but it isn't to be. At least I know I can visit you when I'm in this area and rely on a good meal.'

Maria sighed deeply. 'You should be married and I should be a grandmother by now.'

'I'd rather be single than married to Damara. Has a suitor asked for her hand yet?'

Lambros shook his head. 'No man has shown any interest in her. I feel sorry for the woman. If we hadn't agreed the original arrangement her father would have been free to approach others when she was in her prime. She's getting past it now. Her only hope is a widower who wants someone to keep house for him.'

'Have you anyone in mind?' asked Tassos curiously.

'No, Yiorgo will have to look outside our village.'

'Well, if he can't find anyone at least he has the consolation that he and his wife will be looked after in their old age.'

Maria pursed her lips. 'That's another reason why you should be married. What will happen to us when we're too old to fend for ourselves?'

'That won't be for a long time yet, Mamma. Besides, who knows, circumstances may be different by then.' Tassos drained his glass of wine. 'I should go and find myself somewhere to spend the night.'

'You could sleep here. Your mattress is still upstairs,' offered Maria.

Tassos shook his head. 'I'd have to leave before dawn. I don't want to risk meeting anyone in the village who remembers me, so it's better that I spend the night in the hills. It isn't cold now. Wrapped in my blanket I'm more than warm enough.'

Tassos kissed his mother farewell. 'I'll see you again in a few weeks,' he promised.

'I'll see you out. I'll lock the door after you.' Lambros rose and Tassos looked at him in surprise. He did not usually lock the door until he and his wife retired to bed.

Lambros unlocked the door leading to the yard and beckoned Tassos outside. 'There's something I want you to take with you,' he said quietly. 'Your mother doesn't know I still have it.'

From behind the dwindling pile of firewood Lambros pulled out a rifle and pushed it into Tassos's hands. 'I didn't hand it in when we were supposed to do so. It's too late now, but under the circumstances you might have need of it.'

Tassos looked at the rifle in surprise. 'Why should I want a gun?'

'I hope you won't, but travelling around you could find it's useful if those Germans do invade.'

'I don't know how to shoot a gun,' Tassos protested.

'Just point it and pull the trigger. Make sure you've loaded it first. There are a few bullets in here.' Lambros pressed the small box into his son's hand.

Tassos shook his head. 'I don't want it, Pappa. I'm already a fugitive. If I was picked up carrying a gun I'd be in worse trouble. You keep it, just in case the Germans do come. You might need to defend yourself and Mamma.'

'That's not likely. We'll be of no interest to them. I'll probably be expected to repair their boots for nothing,' he added gloomily.

May 1941

Aspasia answered his knock and Tassos was shocked at her white, drawn face and the dark circles under her eyes. 'What's wrong?' he asked looking down at her stomach that no longer bulged and strained her skirt.

Aspasia indicated that he should go through to the back and followed him. She leaned against the wall and smiled.

'You've got another son.'

'When?'

'Two days ago.'

'Are you alright? Is there anything wrong?'

'No, why should there be? He's a big boy, bigger than Dimitris was.'

'Is that why you look so tired?'

'Of course. It's hard work giving birth.'

'You should be in bed.'

Aspasia laughed derisively. 'So who would look after the children, my grandmother and my father if I was lying in bed all day?'

'Can't your father help?'

'He could, but he won't. He says they're my problem and I shouldn't have been so free with my favours. Thanks to you I'm able to pay one of the village women to come in and help with my grandmother. She also brings in a meal each night so my father can't complain.'

'Suppose I spoke to him?'

'What good would that do?'

'I could tell him they were mine and assure him I'd marry you if I could.'

'Don't be foolish, Tassos. What do you think he'd do when you told him why you hadn't married me before? He'd go straight to the authorities; you'd be arrested and sent back to that island. I'll have my strength back by the next time you visit. You don't have to worry about me.'

'I do worry,' Tassos assured her. 'Here, I've some more money for you.' He opened his money pouch and took out a handful of the drachmas that remained from his pension money. He pressed them into her hand without counting them.

Aspasia could feel by the thickness that he had given her a considerable amount and she tried to pass the notes back to him. Tassos shook his head.

'If we were married it would be my duty to make sure you and the children had enough to live decently. I've been carrying most of that around since I left the island. I don't need it. I've plenty to buy more stock and a meal each day.'

Aspasia looked at him with tears in her eyes. 'You're a good man, Tassos. I wish you were my husband.'

'Yes, well, you behave yourself as a married woman should. I don't want to find out that you've been accepting a few drachmas from the village men. If you need extra money for yourself or the children you ask me. I'll always give you whatever I can afford.'

'You can trust me not to waste it, Tassos.'

Tassos tilted her face towards his and kissed her. 'I hope I can trust you in every way,' he said sombrely and Aspasia nodded.

'There's no one but you, Tassos, I swear. Do you want to see your son?'

'I'd like to see both of them. I know Dimitris doesn't realise I'm his father, but that's no reason why I shouldn't see him.'

Tassos stood in the yard and waited whilst Aspasia went back into the house and returned a few minutes later with a small bundle in her arms. Tassos looked at the tiny contented face and touched the sleeping child's hand gently. He felt strangely moved to feel he was responsible for this new life.

'Maybe we could have a little girl next time,' he suggested to cover his emotion.

'Maybe you could have a little more self control next time,' answered Aspasia immediately.

'Where's Dimitris?'

'Playing outside. You'll be able to see him as you leave.'

'Promise me you'll get some rest,' Tassos spoke to her earnestly.

Aspasia smiled. 'I'll try.'

Tassos left Aspasia in a sombre mood. He had been shocked at her haggard appearance and given her far more of his savings than he had originally intended, hoping it would enable her to pay the village women to help her for a few more weeks until she had fully recovered from childbirth. He had stood and watched Dimitris playing on the dirt road with his friends and wished he had something that he could give his son. He determined to sew together his scraps of leather and make them into a ball. On his next visit he would show the boy how to toss it into the air and catch it or kick it along the dirt road.

As he passed through the villages he asked again if there were any houses he could rent, and again met with refusal from the owners. The villagers seemed most anxious to purchase soap and matches from him, the embroidery silks and weaving wool being ignored, although he was kept busy sharpening knives.

Each time he stopped he was asked if he had any news of the German invasion and would shake his head. He, too, wished he had some definite information. He certainly did not wish to walk into a battalion if they did invade his country. He had heard rumours that Hitler had decided that gypsies were unclean travellers who should be exterminated and he was concerned that as a pedlar he would be classed as a gypsy.

He returned to the main road at Kastellakia and planned to take the turning leading to Roussospiti. In the olive groves and orchards at the side of the main road tents had been erected for the troops who had not yet commenced their long walk to the harbours on the opposite coast of the island. They lay in them, hoping a couple of days' recuperation would be enough to restore their stamina for the arduous task in front of them.

Two days' later as Tassos arrived back at Kastellakia he saw that many of the tents were being dismantled and their occupants were preparing to depart. Not wishing to be caught amongst the mass of military men Tassos hurried onwards. He would return to Heraklion by way of Giannoudi and use the cart tracks to reach the other villages. He did not know that the men had been ordered back to Chania to repel the sea invasion that was considered imminent and would be walking in the opposite direction from himself.

Ten days later when he arrived in Gazi his mother greeted him with relief. 'Thank God you're safe. When we heard what was happening I never thought I'd see you again.'

Tassos frowned. He had heard little news, moving daily from one village to another, and spending a complete day walking cross country on the path from Astiraki to Tilisos before finally reaching Gazi.

'What's happened?'

Maria looked at her husband and wrung her hands. 'They've landed,' she whispered.

'Landed?'

Lambros nodded. 'They didn't come by sea they dropped from the air.'

'Who did?'

'The Germans. Hundreds of them came floating down out of the sky.'

Tassos looked at his father in disbelief. 'You can't just float down from the sky.'

Lambros nodded. 'I'm told they did. They had something attached to their back, like a balloon, and they just floated down.'

'So why weren't they shot?'

'They were. I understand many of them were killed before they landed, but it didn't stop them. Our men fought hard but they kept on coming. Just as it looked as if the Germans would be forced to retreat our men ran out of ammunition. Whilst the soldiers were fighting there the ships in Souda Bay were bombed and more Germans arrived by sea. The soldiers are still fighting and the townspeople have joined them. It's hand to hand combat. They're using knives, axes, anything they can lay their hands on.'

'How do you know all this?'

'The bus driver from Rethymnon said he'd heard it from the bus driver from Chania. He said the roads were choked with people trying to escape from the town whilst they could. The driver told his passengers and the news is being passed amongst the villages.'

'So what are you going to do?' asked Tassos.

'What can we do? If the soldiers can't stop them what chance do we have? We were told to surrender our arms. We have nothing to defend ourselves with.'

Tassos raised his eyebrows at his father, knowing full well he had a rifle hidden. Lambros shook his head imperceptibly. He did not want his wife to know he had the weapon. One box of bullets would not go very far and as a last resort he would shoot his wife rather than let her fall into German hands.

'It's unlikely they'll come here. No doubt they'll loot the towns, but we're just a poor village. There's nothing of any value for them here.' Tassos hoped he was correct in his assumption. He could not stay in Gazi and defend his parents if the German troops decided to attack 'I saw hundreds of allied soldiers on the road at Rethymnon. They'll defend our country. The Germans may be here now but they'll not be here that long,' he said confidently.

'I hope you're right. What are you going to do?' asked Lambros.

'Me? I'll stock up with whatever supplies I can get my hands on and start walking back towards Rethymnon. If the Germans do manage to spread out towards the area I'll be able to avoid them. They won't know their way on the tracks and trails over the hills. When I return to Gazi in a few weeks no doubt the Germans will have gone and everything will have returned to normal.'

His parents nodded in agreement, hoping their son was correct in his assumption.

Tassos walked over to Kavrohori wondering if Aspasia and the other villagers there knew the Germans had landed. Despite his brave talk in front of his parents, Tassos was concerned that the invading forces could spread out from the main towns and into the surrounding areas if they managed to gain a foothold in the country. The towns would soon run out of food and the troops would be forced to look further afield for supplies.

He stood in the main road unloaded his sack and began to advertise the goods he had for sale at the top of his voice. Within a very short time a small crowd had gathered around him, more interested in the latest news than spending their money. In reality Tassos had very little to tell them, but he wanted to hold the villagers' attention and encourage them to buy from him.

'Well,' he began, 'When I was on the road from Rethymnon there were soldiers everywhere, camped by the roadside. They had been brought over from the mainland to support our fighting men. They looked tough and were well-armed.' He did not mention that they also looked exhausted and many of them were injured. 'As I understand it they fought hard and were driving the Germans back towards the sea when they ran out of ammunition and had to fall back. The Germans took advantage to press forwards. Whilst the fighting was going on the Germans bombed the allied ships that were in Souda Bay and landed their own men who fought from the rear. The townspeople have taken up arms and are fighting along with the soldiers.'

'How can they?' called a man. 'We were told we had to surrender all our weapons.'

'They're arming themselves with anything they can find.'

A ripple went through the crowd. What did they have at home that would make a useful weapon?

'As I came through the villages,' continued Tassos, 'I was sharpening blades; knives, scythes, scissors, anything that was to hand that they could use to defend themselves if the time came. If you want me to sharpen your implements go home and collect them. I'll sharpen two items for the price I usually charge for one,' he added recklessly. 'I've also matches, lamp wicks and soap. It won't hurt for you to stock up as I don't know when I'll be able to obtain further supplies. Once I've sold out it's unlikely I'll be able to purchase more.'

Tassos waited, some pressed forwards to buy his goods whilst others returned to their homes for their hunting and butchering knives and the women brought their scissors for sharpening. He was kept busy for most of the day and when the last of the villagers finally dispersed to their homes he had a pocket full of drachmas and an almost empty sack.

He knocked on Aspasia's door and was delighted when she opened it with their baby in her arms. She indicated that he should go through to the back yard and he complied with alacrity, hopeful that he would be able to pleasure himself quickly and meet her later for a more leisurely encounter.

Aspasia shook her head. 'It's too soon, Tassos. You'll have to wait another couple of weeks at least.'

Tassos groaned. 'I thought now the babe was here you'd be as anxious as I am. I didn't know how to contain myself standing out there in the square knowing you were just over here.'

'I'll make it up to you as soon as I can,' she promised. 'In the meantime you'll just have to be patient. Tell me what you said to the people. You had such a crowd around you and I couldn't hear from the doorway.'

'They wanted to know about the fighting at Chania. I only knew what my father had been told and had passed on to me. I don't know the latest news.'

'Well you seemed able to convince them that they needed to buy everything you had with you and they all wanted a blade sharpened.'

'I didn't see your father.'

'Pappa has a gun.'

'I'd still like to sharpen your knives and scissors. If he runs out of bullets his gun is useless.'

'Do you really think they'll come here?' Aspasia's eyes widened anxiously.

'I don't know, but I hope not. If they do come this way where can you and the children hide? It would be better for you to hide than take a chance that they wouldn't notice you.'

Aspasia frowned. 'I don't know of anywhere. There are no caves or shepherd's huts near enough for Dimitris to walk to and I can't carry him and Yiorgo.'

'Have you got a cellar?'

Aspasia nodded. 'It isn't very big, but we store the food for the winter down there.'

'Can you show me?'

Aspasia looked dubious. 'Pappa will be home soon.'

'It will only take a minute.'

Aspasia led him into the kitchen and opened the door of the cupboard where she kept her flour and other dry goods on one side and fresh vegetables on the other. At the back was another door and she pushed it open to reveal a dark space holding some barrels and half the carcass of a goat. Tassos nodded.

'It will do.' As he walked through the kitchen to the back yard he picked up a knife and took it with him. 'I'm going to sit and sharpen this for you. If your father comes he'll not suspect anything.' Tassos sat down on the ground and took out his whetstone. 'Listen carefully to me, Aspasia, and when I've left I want you to do exactly as I've told you.'

He poured a minute amount of oil onto the stone and began to move the blade backwards and forwards.

'Put something soft at the back of the cellar for you and the babes to sit or lay on. You'll need some food that won't go rotten and some water. If you hear the Germans are coming in this direction put the children in there and join them. Roll those barrels against the door and anything else you have that's heavy. Make sure you have a knife in there with you so you can defend yourself if they do force their way in. Understand?'

Aspasia nodded, her lips trembling. 'What about my grandmother?'

'They'll not be interested in an old lady like her. It's you I'm concerned about. If it weren't for the children I'd insist you came away with me and we could hide out up in the hills.'

'Is that what you're going to do, Tassos?'

Tassos ran his finger over the blade of the knife, testing the sharp edge. 'No, I'm going back to Heraklion to buy some more stock and then make my way towards Rethymnon. I hope I'll hear the Germans have been defeated and in that case I'll come straight back here to tell you. Put the knife back in the kitchen and bring me your scissors.'

Silently Aspasia obeyed him and returned with two pairs of scissors. Within a few minutes Tassos had sharpened the first pair and handed them back to her. 'I'm going to make you a couple of weapons to store in the cellar,' he declared and Aspasia watched as he broke the other pair of scissors apart.

'They're not much good now,' she remarked.

'They will be. Find me two pieces of stout firewood. Not too big or heavy and as straight as possible.'

Whilst Tassos sharpened each blade separately Aspasia searched amongst the firewood that had been left over from the winter months. She held out two lengths to him.

'Will this do?'

Tassos tested the strength of the wood with his hands and declared himself satisfied. Deftly he cut into one end to make a notch deep enough for the scissor handle to sit in and proceeded to bind it firmly into place with the thread he used to repair boots. He handed the finished article to Aspasia and she weighted it in her hand.

'Not too heavy, is it?' he asked anxiously and she shook her head. 'You can use it to stab someone or throw it at them. The blades are as sharp as a knife so be careful. Put them in the cellar now. If you need to hide there in a hurry you may not have time to get the knife.'

Aspasia swallowed. 'I do wish you were going to be here with me.'

'I wish I could stay, but you know it's impossible. I'll be back soon and with good news, I hope. Remember, whatever happens, I love you Aspasia.' He rose to his feet and kissed her, replacing his whetstone into his sack, before pushing a bundle of drachmas into her hand. 'Let me see you place the scissors into the cellar, then I must be on my way.'

Tassos was horrified. Prices in Heraklion had risen alarmingly in just a few days. Previously he had been able to purchase ten boxes of matches for two drachmas, now they cost a drachma for each box. Lamp wicks that had cost one drachma for a pack of five were now three drachmas and it was impossible to buy any soap. He bought as much as he could pack in his sack and carry, before beginning his walk to Arolithos.

Despite the prices he had paid and the inflated prices he now quoted for his goods they were purchased with alacrity by the women and he decided he would spend the night in the village and move on to Marathos the following day. Finding a sheltered spot just off the track he spread his blanket, placed his sack under his head and lay looking at the stars.

At first he thought he was hallucinating, although he had

drunk nothing intoxicating with his meagre meal. The stars were moving and exploding in a shower of sparks. Then the noise came, a distant, muffled sound like someone playing a drum. He felt the earth shake beneath him, there must be an earthquake in the vicinity.

The drumming did not stop, if anything it increased in volume and intensity and when he looked up at the sky again he could not see any stars. Instead there was a red glow in the distance towards Heraklion and it was then that the truth of the situation came to Tassos. The town was being bombed.

Hurriedly he gathered his blanket and pushed it into his sack. He must return immediately to Gazi and find out if his parents were safe. There was no way of telling whether the village, only a short distance away from the city, had been hit. He stumbled over the rough ground back to the track and returned to the village where he was able to join the main road. At first he was able to walk quickly, but as he neared Gazi he was met by people coming towards him. Children clutched at their mother's skirts, their faces white with fear.

Tassos threaded his way through them. There was no point in stopping anyone to ask what was happening. It was clear that they were all desperate to get far away from the area that was being bombed and reach a place of safety. The red glow in the sky grew brighter as he reached Gazi, but to his relief the village seemed untouched.

Uncaring if he was seen by the villagers he hammered on the door of his parents' house until finally the ground floor shutter was opened a crack and the barrel of a rifle glinted.

'Pappa, it's me. Can I come in?'

The shutter was closed again rapidly and Tassos heard the bolt on the door being drawn back. He slipped through the opening and waited whilst his father bolted the door behind him, allowing his eyes to become accustomed to the darkness. Still cradling his rifle Lambros sat on the edge of the bed.

'What are you doing here? I thought you were on your way to Rethymnon.'

'I'd only reached Arolithos. I saw what was happening and came back.' Tassos realised that now he had ascertained that his parents were safe his legs were shaking and he sat down on the chair by the table. 'I couldn't tell if they had bombed Gazi. All I could see were the bombs dropping and then the sky was red with flames.'

'You were lucky I didn't shoot you. I thought you were a German, hammering away at the door like that,' grumbled Lambros. 'You've probably woken the whole village.'

'I doubt if they were asleep.'

'They'll want to know who came calling on me at this hour.'

'Tell them it was a stranger and you sent them away.'

Lambros looked at his son and pursed his lips. If he had turned away a traveller why hadn't the stranger moved on to the next house and tried to raise the occupants?

'Better to tell them that I allowed you to stay for a while and then sent you on your way.'

'Whatever you think best, Pappa.' Suddenly Tassos felt too weary to care. 'Can I sleep in the corner for a few hours? I'll leave before dawn. I can't risk the neighbours recognising me.'

Lambros nodded. 'I would think the authorities would have more important things on their mind at the moment than bothering to look for someone like you.'

Tassos was back walking along the country track towards Tilisos as the sun tried to break through the pall of smoke that hung over Heraklion. An acrid smell was in the air and he hoped that once he was deeper into the countryside the atmosphere would be clearer. A disconcerting thought occurred to him – if Heraklion had been bombed, had the same fate overtaken Rethymnon? Rather than working his usual route he would make a circuit of the inland hamlets that were closer to Heraklion. It would mean he could return to Kavrohori and Gazi more quickly as there was a rough road that led from Krousonas directly down to both villages.

He stopped just outside Tilisos and sat in a field to eat the bread and meat his mother had packed in a clean cloth for him before he continued his journey. It was quite possible that the people there did not know what had happened to Heraklion the previous night. Being the bearer of news, albeit bad, he would be certain to draw a crowd.

As soon as he took up a stance in the square the women left their duties in the house to call their men folk from the fields to return to the village. They listened in silence whilst Tassos announced that Heraklion had been bombed the previous night, but he was unable to tell them the extent of the damage that had been suffered.

'When I was on the road I saw people fleeing into the countryside, but it may have been just the harbour area that was being attacked. If any of you have relatives who live there be prepared for them to come to you for safety. If any of you have weapons hidden get them from their hiding places and check they are in working order. Make sure your knives are sharp. Be ready to defend your women folk and children,' he exhorted them and removed his whetstone from his sack. 'I'll put a razor sharp edge to any blade and I'm offering to sharpen two for the price I previously charged for one. Bring them out to me and I'll work until dusk.'

Each day Tassos moved on to another village and spent his time sharpening the various different implements the inhabitants brought to him. He thought it unlikely he would be able to replenish his usual supplies and was happy to rely upon sharpening blades and repairing boots for his immediate living. With his sack being lighter he was able to walk over the goat trails and donkey tracks more swiftly and easily, although it still took him almost two weeks before he was nearing the turn off to Kato Kalesia and it would take him no more than a couple of hours to reach Kavrohori.

He was both surprised and alarmed when he saw a group of soldiers sitting miserably at the roadside. Did this mean that the fighting had moved inland? One waved a hand at him and he halted in his stride.

The soldier pointed to the track, 'Preveli?' he asked.

Tassos frowned and shook his head. He had no idea where Preveli was situated. He had never visited a village of that name and wondered why the soldiers should want to go there.

The soldier shrugged and returned disconsolately to his companions. Tassos watched as the group rose reluctantly to their feet and prepared to continue walking.

'Kato Kalesia,' suggested Tassos and indicated they should go in the opposite direction.

'Preveli,' the man repeated and added in English. 'I think he said he didn't know. We'll just have to keep going and hope.'

Tassos stood and watched as the weary men continued their walk along the deserted road that would eventually lead them to Krousonas. He moved to the side of the track as he heard a vehicle approaching, hoping it was a local farmer who was affluent enough to own a motorised cart and not a German patrol. There was nowhere for him to take cover and he had nothing with which to defend himself. The knife he used to cut the leather was stowed inside his sack.

The farmer came around the corner and Tassos breathed a sigh of relief as the man raised his hand to him and continued. It was only a short while later that Tassos heard the sound of the cart returning and once again he stepped to the side of the track.

To his surprise the farmer drew up alongside him and cut his engine. 'Do you know your way around these parts?' he asked.

Tassos nodded. 'I'm a pedlar.'

'Do you know your way to the main road?'

Tassos frowned. 'You'll have to drive on to Krousonas and

take the track down to Kitharida. From there you'll need to go back to Agios Mironas. Just outside the village there's a turn for Stavrakia and another track before you reach the village will take you to the main road.'

'Do you know of a quicker way across the fields?'

'You'd not be able to drive across. There's not even a goat trail.'

'I know that,' the farmer smiled grimly. From his pocket he drew out a map and spread it out before Tassos. 'We're here.' He placed his finger on the village of Kato Kalesia. 'The soldiers need to get across to Preveli. That's over there. They've taken the wrong turn and missed the main road. They don't speak Greek, can't even read the name of a town.'

'How do you know what they want?' asked Tassos suspiciously.

'I speak English,' answered Basil.

'They'd be quicker to return to Heraklion and pick up the main road.'

'It's not possible. The road's being held by the Germans.'

'So why don't you show them the way?'

'I need to get to Aghios Nikolaos urgently. I can't waste the time moving at their pace. If you could lead them to Krousonas and get them some food and water from the villagers they'd be grateful.'

'I've just come from there.'

'So you know your way.'

Tassos shrugged. 'They'd do better to go to Kato Kalesia and take the road to Vourtes. There aren't any villages between here and Krousonas on this road and it's a two day walk.'

Basil studied the map and traced the route with his finger. 'If you took them that way you'd end up in Agios Mironhas. You could go on to Pirgou and take the track to Ano Asites. From there it's easy to reach Agia Varvara and it should be safe enough for them to use the main road down to Gortys.'

Tassos shook his head. 'I don't know my way down there.'

'You'd only need to take them as far as Agia Varvara. It's a pretty direct route and you'll know your way back, besides, you can always ask for directions if you get lost.' Basil held out his hand. 'Can I rely on you to help them?'

'I suppose so.' Grudgingly Tassos shook Basil's hand. He had planned to be in Kavrohori with Aspasia that evening and it should be long enough now since the birth of little Yiorgo for them to enjoy being together.

'Jump on, then and I'll give you a ride down to catch them up.'

With one hand Tassos clutched his sack tightly and with the other he held on to Basil's shirt. The journey took no more than a few minutes, despite the slow pace of the cart, but Tassos felt vulnerable and frightened. He had only ever travelled on a bus where, despite being uncomfortable, he had felt safe in the enclosed space. He listened to the unintelligible words the farmer spoke and the equally unintelligible replies from the soldiers.

Basil had taken out the map again and was tracing the proposed route whilst they crowded around him. 'Once you reach Agia Varvara you should be safe to use the main road and then it will be straight down to Gortys. When you reach Agia Varvara ask for the road to Rethymnon and keep going until you reach Agia Galini. No doubt you'll meet up with the troops who are coming down from Rethymnon and you'll be able to find your way along the coast to Preveli together. There's a chance you'll be able to pick up a fishing boat, but if not you'll just have to walk from village to village.'

'Is he coming all the way with us?' asked the soldier who appeared to be in charge.

'He says he doesn't know that area.'

'At least he'd know how to ask for directions,' muttered a man.

Basil shrugged. 'I've done my best for you.'

'Yeah, thanks mate. What's this chap's name?'

'I didn't ask. Hey, pedlar man, what's your name?' asked Basil.

'Tassos. I'm also known as 'One to Lose'.

'Tassos will be good enough for them. Point to yourself and

repeat your name. They'll get the idea and tell you theirs.'

Obediently Tassos did as Basil instructed him and listened as each soldier pointed to himself and said words that were alien to Tassos's ears. He nodded. If he needed to attract their attention he would just call out 'soll-der', one of them was bound to turn around.

Basil climbed back on his farm cart. 'On the way you could teach them a bit of Greek,' he shouted above the noise of the engine and grinned cheerfully at Tassos as he drove away.

Tassos looked at the men standing before him. The enormity of the responsibility that had been thrust upon his shoulders made him tremble inwardly. It was his duty to get them safely to Agia Varvara. The sooner the journey was over the happier he would be.

The soldiers looked at Tassos suspiciously as he led them back the way they had already walked and turned off on a dirt track.

'Hope he knows where he's going,' a soldier said. 'We could end up in the middle of nowhere.'

'That farmer who spoke English seemed to think we could trust him. Besides, we don't have much choice.'

Mopping their brows the small group followed behind Tassos as he strode along the path, finally stopping when a cluster of houses came into view.

'Water,' he said in Greek and led them to the pump. He placed a stone over the outlet in the basin and held his own water bottle beneath the spout as he pumped the handle until the water ran reluctantly. Once his bottle was full he plunged his hands into the water that had collected in the basin and then dipped his face in as far as possible before the water leaked away. He pointed to one of the soldiers. 'Your turn.'

One by one the soldiers filled their water bottles and plunged their hands and face into the basin of water whilst Tassos worked the pump. He knew they would be watched by the villagers and if they were seen to be wasting the water one of them would be out to scold them soundly.

Their cursory ablutions complete and their thirst slaked Tassos indicated they should sit down at the side of the road beneath a tree. He walked over to the first cottage and knocked on the door. A conversation took place between him and the woman who lived there and finally Tassos sat down on the doorstep, opened his sack and removed his whetstone. He proceeded to sharpen a knife for her whilst the soldiers watched and grumbled.

'If he's going to stop at every house we'll never get anywhere.'

Their commander frowned. 'I hope he didn't make that a condition for showing us the way.'

'At least it gives my feet a rest. I wish I could have put them under that pump. I think they're on fire.'

'You'd never get your boots back on once you'd taken them off. I don't need to lace mine up my feet are so swollen.'

Tassos handed the knife back to the woman and waited until she returned with a cloth bundle. He walked over to the waiting men, placed the cloth on the ground and proceeded to hand out a piece of bread and cheese to each man along with half a dozen olives each. He grinned at their surprised faces and mimed sharpening the knife and feeding himself. He joined them, taking no more than his fair share, and was amused to see there was a competition between the men to see who could spit his olive stone furthest. Tassos joined in and won the contest easily. He had not played that game since he was a boy.

Their meagre meal finished Tassos folded the cloth and returned it to the woman at the cottage. As the men passed by each one saluted her by way of thanks and she put her hand up to her face in embarrassment.

June 1941

They reached Ano Asites without incident, Tassos sharpened blades or mended boots in exchange for some local produce and bread for the soldiers to eat and whilst he worked they rested. On two occasions he had sneaked into a field and cut a water melon, slicing it up and sharing it amongst the men to cool them and slake their thirst. Once in the small town Tassos checked with a baker that he was on the road that led to Agia Varvara and asked if there were any villages on the way.

'Only Prinias. You should be able to reach there by the end of a day although it's quite a steep climb in parts. The trail across the fields is flatter and more direct.'

Tassos hesitated. Had he been alone he would have taken the field track, but he could not afford to lose his way whilst leading the soldiers. It could even be beneficial if he allowed them to rest for the remainder of the afternoon and they started walking as the sun rose when it would be cooler.

'How much further is it from Prinias to Agia Varvara?'

The baker shrugged. 'About another day I expect.'

'Would you be able to let us have some bread to take with us?'

'Prices have risen.'

Tassos frowned in annoyance. He had gone out of his way to help these men but he had not expected to have to buy food for them. He was losing money by working in exchange for provisions, but now it appeared he would have to use his precious stock of drachmas as well.

'How much?'

'Two drachmas a loaf.'

'Two!' Tassos was horrified.

'Price of flour has risen along with everything else. How many do you want?'

'I need six.'

The loaves, when the baker handed them to Tassos, were half the size he had been expecting and he handed over his money grudgingly. He walked back to where he had left the men and placed the loaves on the ground. He broke each one in half and handed out the portions, wrapping the remainder back in a cloth and placing them in his sack. They would have to be a meal for the men the following day. If the price of bread was so extortionate he dreaded to think how much a piece of cheese or meat would cost.

Tassos could not tell by the conversation between the soldiers whether they were grateful for the meagre rations he handed out or complaining. He wished he had a way to explain to them that he was not being parsimonious. He would need food on his journey back to Giza and if prices were rising so rapidly he wanted to ensure he was able to give some money to Aspasia. She and the children must be fed.

Tassos led the way to the outskirts of the village and into a field where they would sleep. He was grateful that he had his blanket to wrap around himself at night, despite the fact that it was the summer. During the day the soldiers removed their uniform jacket and rolled up the sleeves of their shirt, but once the heat of the day had passed they replaced them quickly and would wake cold and stiff in the mornings.

He could not think of a way to tell the men that he would expect them up at dawn and ready to continue walking, but he mimed sleep, rolled himself up in his blanket and turned his back on them.

As the dawn broke Tassos shook each man awake. He would be glad to leave this town where the people had regarded the unshaven, unwashed soldiers warily. He had asked the baker if he had any news of the German landings; had the invaders been repulsed or were they in control of the main towns? The baker had shrugged and said he had no knowledge of their progress. There had been no newspapers delivered to the area for a week.

Tassos led the way down the rutted country road. He was hungry and he guessed the men were also. He scanned the fields as he passed for anything edible that was growing and filched some unripe pears and small apples that he handed out and the men ate uncomplainingly. It was something to put into their empty stomachs.

The road to Prinias became steeper and the men were moving slowly. Tassos was on the point of calling a halt for the night when he espied the village in the distance.

'Soll-ders – Prinias.'

They looked where he pointed and began to quicken their steps. They were hopeful that when they arrived at their destination their guide would be able to arrange some food for them. The lethargy they were all suffering was no doubt due to lack of nourishment.

It was dark by the time they entered the village, the houses shuttered for the night and the streets deserted. Tassos walked over to the church and tried the door. It was locked firmly. He would have no choice but to knock on doors and ask the occupants for help.

The farmer he disturbed regarded him warily. He was not used to vagrants calling on him, particularly in the evenings. He listened as Tassos described their dilemma. They had been walking all day with nothing to eat. They were happy to sleep in the open, but would anyone provide them with some food? They would be moving on to Agia Varvara the following day so would not be troubling the villagers again.

The farmer closed his door, telling Tassos to wait whilst he pulled his boots back on. He led the way down the main street and opened a door. The men inside looked curiously at the straggle of men who walked inside and stopped their conversation. Tassos thanked their guide, who shrugged, called out good night to everyone and closed the door behind him.

Tassos stepped forward. 'Good evening, friends. I have been asked to guide these brave and valiant soldiers as far as Agia Varvara. We have walked to Prinias today without a morsel of food. Out of the goodness of your hearts would you be able to provide something for us to put in our stomachs? We will be leaving at dawn tomorrow, but I am not sure if my companions will have the strength to walk at all unless they have some sustenance tonight.'

The soldiers did look as if they were ready to drop at any moment and after a momentary hesitation the local men began to vacate their seats and invite the strangers to sit in their place. The taverna owner hurried out to his kitchen and re-lit his fire. He had some potatoes and onions and it would take no time at all for him to boil them up together and make a thick soup.

'Why are they going to Agia Varvara?' asked a man.

Tassos shrugged. 'I understand they're going to Preveli. They'd missed their way and I was asked to guide them down to Agia Varvara so they can rejoin the main road that leads to Gortys.'

'They've a long walk ahead of them,' observed the man.

'So have I,' countered Tassos. 'I have to walk back to Heraklion.'

'From what we've heard there's not much of Heraklion left. The Germans have been looting from any building left standing and killing anyone who tried to stop them.'

Tassos's face paled and he crossed himself, saying a silent prayer for the safety of his parents and Aspasia. Why had he agreed to walk halfway across Crete with these strangers? His place was with the people he cared about, defending them.

The soldiers moved more swiftly the next morning, revitalised by the heartening meal they had eaten the previous evening, and they had entered Agia Varvara by late afternoon. Tassos begged some stale bread, bought a piece of cheese and three soft tomatoes. He gave the soldiers the food, wrote the name Gortys in Greek letters on a piece of paper, showed them where the main road led out of the town, shook their hands and wished them good luck before walking away rapidly back towards Prinias.

It had taken him a week in the company of the soldiers to walk from Kato Kalesia to Agia Varvara, but he was certain if he used the trails and tracks across the fields he could be back in Kavrohori within four days. He would not stop to peddle any of his remaining goods or offer a sharpening or repair service unless the payment took the form of a meal and bed for the night.

Tassos entered Kavrohori and made his way immediately to Aspasia's house. He was relieved to see that she and the children were safe.

'I was beginning to think something had happened to you,' she said. 'I was expecting you a week or more ago.'

'I was no more than a couple of hours away when I was waylaid.'

'The Germans?' she asked in horror.

'No,' Tassos smiled. 'A farmer stopped me. There were some soldiers on the road. They were making for Preveli, wherever that may be, and he asked me to show them the way to Agia Varvara. I told him I didn't know my way past Krousonas, but he wouldn't take no for an answer. I finally agreed to take them to Agia Varvara and showed them the road they needed to get to Gortys.'

'That could have been dangerous, Tassos.'

Tassos shrugged. 'There was nothing dangerous about the journey. It was just frustrating being so close to you and having to go back down there. I even had to spend my money to buy them food. So, tell me what has been happening here. The last I heard was that Heraklion was in ruins.'

Aspasia shook he head. 'I've only heard rumours. I know

nothing for certain. I've been told that after the bombing the Germans went into the town and looted whatever valuables they could lay their hands on. If the owners protested they were shot.'

Tassos nodded soberly. 'That's what I heard so there must be some truth in it. I'm going up to check on my parents and then I'll be back. I thought I'd spend a couple of days in this area. Make up for the time we've lost.'

Aspasia smiled seductively. 'We could slip out the back for five minutes,' she suggested and Tassos was only too willing to accompany her.

After leaving Aspasia Tassos walked to the outskirts of Gazi and spent the night in a field. There was still the acrid smell of smoke in the air, but to his relief the sky was not lit up with gun fire or bombs dropping.

He walked along to his father's shop and stopped in horror. The place was a blackened shell along with the others on each side. Trembling with fear he ran along the road to the cottage where his parents lived and pushed open the door. The sight that met his eyes was unbelievable. The furniture was overturned and there was blood on the floor and up the wall.

'Mamma! Pappa!' he gasped. 'Pappa, where are you?' He mounted the wooden stairs two at a time and looked into the room he had occupied as a child. He knew there was nothing of any value in there, but the bed had been stripped of its covers and the mattress was propped up against the wall, split from end to end with the stuffing strewn on the floor, the chest where the blankets were stored was open and the contents thrown around the room.

Thoroughly distraught he returned to the ground floor and out through the back door. Where were his parents? If the blood on the floor belonged to them where were their bodies?

'Mamma! Pappa! Where are you? Answer me,' he called again and looked around wildly, pulling some of the wood from the stack where his father had hidden his gun. Finding nothing he returned to the combined kitchen and living room where his parents' large bed stood in the corner. The cover looked undisturbed and Tassos pulled it off. The mattress beneath had been shredded as had his own and he looked at it puzzled. Why had someone put the ruined mattress back on the bed and covered it?

'Mamma! Pappa!' he called again and felt something touch his leg. He jumped back fearfully, wishing he had thought to take his knife from his sack.

'Tassos.' His mother's voice was weak and scared.

He looked down to see her crawling from the storage space beneath the bed and bent down to help her to her feet.

'Mamma, what's happened? Are you alright? Where's Pappa?'

Maria's eyes filled with tears. 'They shot your Pappa,' she whispered.

'Shot Pappa? Why?'

'He wouldn't let them in. He made me get into the storage space and told me not to come out until he said it was safe. They broke the door down and then I heard a shot. I heard them tramping around, knocking things over, but I didn't dare to come out until they left and it was all quiet again. Then I could hear your Pappa groaning. He had a large hole in his chest where they had shot him. I tried to cover it and stop the bleeding, but it was no good. He was too damaged inside.'

'Oh, Mamma.' Tassos enfolded her in his arms and could feel her body shaking as she shed hot tears on his dirty shirt. He waited until she had calmed a little. 'Tell me, what did you do then?'

'I moved the mattress back up on the bed. They had left it lying in front of the storage space and I'd had to push it over before I could get out. I went back and hid in there until the evening, then I went to Pappa Theodore and asked for help. They took your Pappa to the cemetery and he was buried with just the priest saying a prayer over him. I've been hiding since then, all day and all night. Why did they do it, Tassos?'

Tassos shook his head. 'I don't know, Mamma. His shop has

been burnt. They may come back. They could set the house on fire and you wouldn't be able to get out. You can't stay here hiding.'

'Where can I go? There's nowhere safe in the village.'

'I know a safe place,' Tassos assured her. 'You'll have to walk for a while, but I'll carry your bundle for you. Collect together some clothes and anything else you want and we'll go now.'

Maria looked around her ruined home and her tears began to fall again. 'This is my home.'

'I know, Mamma, and when it's safe you'll be able to return, I promise. Just do as I say and let me take you away for a few weeks until the Germans have been driven out. I know someone who will look after you.'

Maria gazed at her son fearfully. 'I don't think anywhere is safe.'

Aspasia looked at Tassos in surprise when she opened her door. The baby was suckling at her breast and Dimitris hid behind her shyly.

'I wasn't expecting you back quite this quickly,' she smiled.

'Can we come in, Aspasia? I need your help.'

Aspasia raised her eyebrows. 'What's new?' she asked as she opened the door wider to admit them.

Tassos placed the sack on the ground, his mother's clothes had made it far heavier than he had expected. 'Aspasia, this is my mother. My Pappa has been killed and her home has been wrecked. Can she stay here? I don't know where else to take her so she'll be safe for a few weeks.'

Maria sank onto the chair that Aspasia indicated. Tassos had insisted they walked as quickly as she was able and the unaccustomed exertion had made her breathless and her heart was pounding uncomfortably.

'I'll make some coffee when I've finished feeding Yiorgo. Tell me what has happened, Tassos.'

'I found my Mamma hiding in the storage space beneath the bed. My Pappa had told her to hide there. He tried to stop the

Germans from ransacking the house and they shot him.'

Aspasia's eyes widened in horror. 'What about the neighbours? Did they shoot them?'

Tassos looked at his mother who shook her head. 'I don't know. I haven't seen any of them. I didn't dare to go out, except to see my husband buried.' Her tears began to fall.

Aspasia shifted Yiorgo to her other breast. 'What do you want me to do?'

'Just let her stay here until it's safe for her to return to Gazi.'

'Pappa won't be very pleased,' she frowned. 'It will be another mouth to feed.'

Tassos removed the pouch from around his neck. 'I can pay you, Aspasia.'

'No, Tassos. That's not necessary.' Maria held up her hand. 'Your Pappa's money box is in the sack. He put it in the storage space with me. If he'd given it to them they wouldn't have shot him,' she added bitterly.

Tassos did not feel as confident as his mother in that assumption. He delved into the sack and felt the metal box beneath his fingers. No wonder the sack had been heavier than he had expected. This was probably what the soldiers had been searching for. Had his father handed it over there was no guarantee his life would have been spared.

'She'll have to share my mattress. It will be a tight squeeze with the children as well.'

For the first time that Tassos could remember Aspasia's grandmother spoke. 'She can share my bed.'

Aspasia shrugged. 'If Grandma is willing then Pappa won't refuse.' She detached Yiorgo from her nipple and closed her blouse. 'Here,' she said, handing the child to Maria. 'Look after him whilst I make the coffee.'

Tassos felt a weight lifting off him as his mother cradled the baby.

'Where's their Pappa?' she asked.

Tassos dropped his eyes. 'They're my children, Mamma.'

'Yours? Is that why you refused to marry Damara? Were you already married?'

Tassos shook his head. 'We're not married. I'm not allowed to get married, remember. If it hadn't been for that stupid doctor when I lost my finger I'd have married Aspasia before Dimitris was born.'

'Why didn't you tell us, Tassos?'

Tassos shrugged. 'Had the villagers found out that they were the children of a leper father Aspasia would have been driven out of the village. Life isn't easy for her as it is. The villagers will have nothing to do with her as she has brought dishonour on her father's house.'

'But you don't have leprosy, Tassos.'

'I know that, but the doctor had me committed. I'll always be a fugitive on the run. I'll leave here before word gets round that Aspasia is entertaining the pedlar.'

'Where will you go?'

'Back on the road, travelling the villages. I'm going up towards Rethymnon. Even if I can't find any goods to sell I can still sharpen blades and mend boots. You don't have to worry about me, Mamma. I'll be back in this area in a few weeks.'

Tassos slipped out of the back door of Aspasia's house and walked down the village street, announcing that he was in town and urging people to bring their knives to be sharpened or their boots to be repaired, but few took him up on his offer. They needed to save their drachmas to purchase basic food requirements that were not only expensive but in short supply.

Tassos took the track across the fields to Tilisos and began to make his way towards Rethymnon. If he was asked to ply his trade he would do so in exchange for a meal, but most days pangs of hunger assailed him, despite foraging from the fields whenever he could. He saw no sign of the Germans who had invaded his country and it was not until he reached Giannoudi that he came across any of the allied troops. Small groups of them were sheltering in the olive groves, looking tired and dispirited. They waved their hands to him and he would wave back, feeling guilty that he had nothing to offer them.

He took the path to Mili and was heartened by meeting a train of donkeys loaded with sacks of flour. He greeted the driver, hoping to be given some news, but the man hurried onwards. He stood to one side to let them pass and was horrified when he saw a German soldier bringing up the rear, his rifle held at readiness.

'Halt,' he was told and obediently Tassos dropped his sack and raised his hands in the air.

'Papers.'

Tassos opened the pouch that hug around his neck and pulled out his identity papers, hoping the soldier would not see the pouch also contained his money.

The German looked at them briefly and Tassos guessed the man could not read Greek. 'Open,' he commanded and pointed to Tassos's sack.

Tassos pulled back the neck and revealed his whetstone and boot repairing kit. The German picked up the knife and indicated with his hands that the sack should be emptied and Tassos hastened to comply. He placed the items on the ground, followed by a roll of leather, his shirt, jacket, cloak and blanket. Still pointing his rifle at Tassos the man unrolled the leather and shook out the cloak and blanket, finding no weapon concealed amongst them.

Tassos pointed to the knife and the roll of leather and held out his hand for its return. Smiling maliciously the German tossed the knife into the bushes that bordered the path and began to hurry after the donkeys.

Cursing him, Tassos replaced his possessions in the sack and began to hunt for his knife. It was well over an hour before he found it and was able to continue on his way. He determined to be alert for any sounds ahead or behind him and if he heard a donkey or footsteps he would hide rather than risk a further encounter.

Costas greeted him with a melancholy expression on his face. 'You're welcome, Tassos. When I heard you approaching I thought I would open the door to a soldier.'

'I met one on the path and he held me at gun point. He took my cobbler's knife and threw it into the bushes.'

'You were lucky he didn't shoot you for carrying a weapon.'

'What are they doing here?'

'Ensuring the supplies of flour get through to the bakers in Rethymnon. They won't go short of food, although the townspeople are queuing for hours to buy some bread.'

Tassos frowned. 'I was hoping I could buy some supplies in Rethymnon. There's nothing to be had in Heraklion.'

'I doubt you'd find anything available there. The town has been bombed and the Germans marched in and took whatever they wanted.'

'But they've not molested you or fired your houses?'

Costas shook his head. 'We're necessary to them. They need the flour. They supervise the mills to make sure we don't hold any back for ourselves and escort us down to Kastellakia. There they load up a lorry and that's the last we see of it.'

'So you're safe here?'

Costas shrugged. 'Who knows? Is anyone safe anywhere these days?'

'I saw some soldiers in the olive groves by Giannoudi. I could go back and ask them to come to help you.'

'What could they do? They're a defeated force on the run. They're wandering all over the place, trying to hide from the Germans and find a road down to the coast. The poor devils are probably walking round in circles getting nowhere.'

'Why doesn't someone take them to the road? It's not that far away.'

'The main road is being strafed from the air. They've been told to avoid it and go by the country routes.' Costas looked at

Tassos. 'You could take them. You know how to get from village to village by using the tracks.'

'Me?'

'Why not? You're not likely to be able to buy any goods to sell so what do you have to lose?'

Tassos shook his head. 'I can't afford to buy food for soldiers even if it's available. I led a group down to Agia Varvara earlier and I ended up well out of pocket.'

'I understand they've been given money to buy provisions. Trouble is, of course, they have no idea what to ask for and no doubt a number are being overcharged due to their ignorance. They need someone to look after them.'

Tassos nodded thoughtfully. He had no desire to join the defeated Greek army or become involved in guerrilla warfare. It was possible that once the allied troops had gathered together on the opposite coast they would be able to launch an offensive and drive the Germans out of Crete. He had nothing to lose by becoming a guide and if they had money for food he would accept a meal as payment for his services.

'I could take them cross country as far as Prasies. I don't know the area any further than that.'

'I'm sure they'd be grateful for your help.'

'I'm not doing it to earn their gratitude. I'm doing it in the hope that they will avenge my father's death.'

Tassos left Mili early the next morning and walked back down the road to Giannoudi where he had seen the military men. As he walked into their midst they eyed him cautiously. He smiled, hoping that would convey he was a friend. He had no idea how he would communicate with them and explain that he could take them from village to village until they were able to continue on their own. He beckoned to them to gather round and half a dozen did so warily, whilst their companions stood with their rifles ready should this be an ambush.

He drew a circle in the air, 'Giannoudi,' he proclaimed and was met by puzzled looks. He pointed to the ground and repeated the name of the village. His fingers made walking motions through the air.

'What's he on about?'

'Maybe he's lost!'

'More like the village simpleton.'

'He doesn't look simple.'

'Where's Brian? He speaks a bit of the lingo. See if he can understand what this chap's on about.'

A tall, thin, man stepped forward. 'Can I help?' he asked in strangely accented Greek.

Tassos frowned. 'I help you. This is Giannoudi. Where are you going?' He repeated the words slowly and the soldier understood the question.

'Preveli,' he answered.

Tassos nodded. He should have guessed their destination. 'Walk with me. Come.' He walked a short distance away from them and beckoned. 'Come. Come with me.'

The man who had communicated with Tassos was addressing the troops and they began to shoulder their rifles and form up silently three abreast whilst Tassos's lips twitched in amusement at their discipline. The thin man took his place at Tassos's side and pointed to his chest.

'Brian,' he announced and Tassos introduced himself in like fashion.

The men conversed in low voices as Tassos led them through the olive trees and on to the dirt track that disappeared into the distance. He wished he had thought to check their water and food supplies. It was going to be a long, hot, walk before they reached Prasies. He allowed them a short respite in the middle of the day when the sun was beating down unmercifully on them. He mimed eating and drinking and turned to Brian for support.

'East, drink, little. Long walk.'

Brian understood and passed the instruction back to the men. Tassos watched in despair as some men drained their water bottles. They were unlikely to find anything more to drink until they reached the village.

As they walked Brian tried to communicate with him and finally Tassos learnt the man had studied ancient Greek. This accounted for the old fashioned and unfamiliar words he used and his stilted accent. In response Tassos spoke slowly, waiting for the man to pick up on a familiar word and understand what he was saying so he could reply. By the time they reached Prasies their comprehension of each other had increased dramatically, but it was a weary group of men, no longer walking three abreast, but struggling to keep up in single file that walked into the village square.

Tassos led them straight to the pump and the men drank gratefully of the cool water, then sank down exhausted at the side of the road. Tassos took Brian to one side.

'Tell the men to stay here. You have drachmas?'

Brian nodded. He wished he could sit down beside the road with the men. Until he had been conscripted into the army he had never indulged in physical exercise of any sort. He had avoided sports whilst at University, preferring to study.

'We buy food,' announced Tassos and led the way over to the small collection of shops. The shopkeepers eyed them warily. They had hardly sufficient to keep the village fed without supplying voracious soldiers. Fruit was plentiful and he bought apples, pears, grapes and figs; there was no bread to be had so he bought the hard rusks that would keep for weeks without mouldering and could be softened in water or milk. Brian carried the food back to the waiting men, who set upon it ravenously, whilst Tassos asked for directions to the next village and how long it would take them to walk there.

'Tell the men we will find somewhere to sleep,' announced Tassos. 'We make an early start. Their water bottles must be full.

It should take us no more than half a day to reach Selli, but it is a very small village. We may not be able to buy any food there so they should save whatever they can for tomorrow.'

'How much further is it to Preveli?' asked Brian and Tassos shrugged.

'I've no idea. I've never been down here before.'

'You mean you don't know your way?'

'I didn't know my way to any of the villages between Rethymnon and Heraklion until I became a pedlar. Once I've followed a track I remember it. Trust me. I've not been lost yet.'

Brian felt his shoulders sag. He had no wish to walk for days under the blistering sun, eking out his water ration and living on fruit and the hard rusks that threatened to break his teeth. He had watched many of his companions killed and others captured; their fate unknown. What he wanted more than anything was to be back in Cambridge with some English rain and able to buy a pack of cigarettes from the corner shop and pint of beer at the local pub.

Tassos led them from village to village, ensuring that each time they entered one the men drank from the water pump and filled their bottles, whilst he went in search of any food that might be available. On reaching Karines, Tassos was advised to take the route that led to Agia Pelagia, which continued on the other side of the main road and would be a more direct to Preveli. Feeling relieved that their final goal was in sight he set off briskly with a trail of miserable soldiers stumbling after him.

They stopped briefly at Frati for Tassos to check his directions and to his surprise the villagers gave freely of whatever provisions they had. They were invited into the taverna and for the first time since disembarking the soldiers were able to enjoy a hot meal that contained both meat and vegetables. The men lingered over the meal and Tassos realised it would be useless to try to make them walk further that day. Not knowing the area, but having been told there was a gorge close by, he did not want to take the wrong road once darkness fell and end up falling into an abyss. The villagers assured him that one more day of walking would see them at Preveli where they would be welcomed.

The news raised Tassos's spirits. If they were going to be welcomed that must mean the troops were gathering to launch a counter offensive against the Germans.

Tassos stood on the hill and scanned the surrounding countryside. He could see no sign of a village and had a sinking feeling that he must have missed the path when skirting the gorge and they were now in the middle of nowhere.

'Where are we?' asked Brian.

'I'm not sure. I'd expected to reach Preveli by now. It must be further than we were led to believe.'

'Why don't we stop here for the night and try to find the village tomorrow?' suggested Brian. 'The men need to rest.'

'I'll walk on a way and see if the village is over the next hill.'

Brian shook his head. 'If you don't come back we're stranded. Wait until tomorrow and we'll walk on together.'

Tassos shook his head. 'I'll leave my sack with you. That way you know I'll be coming back. My tools are in there.' He dumped his sack at the feet of Brian and walked away from the group of disconsolate men.

Tassos rounded the bend in the road and was lost to their sight. Brian sat down, the men looking at him curiously. Why were they stopping here? There was at least another hour of daylight and they were usually expected to take advantage of it before they were allowed to rest.

Nestled down in the hollow of the hills Tassos could see some buildings and his spirits rose. That had to be the village of Preveli. Hurriedly he retraced his steps and shouted to attract Brian's attention. Once the man turned in his direction he began to wave for the men to join him.

'The village is just round the corner in the valley. It's well hidden, but we should be there easily before dark.'

Heartened by the news the men hurried forwards, but as Tassos neared the collection of buildings his heart sank. It was not a village they were approaching, but a monastery. He tried to think positively. The men would be able to have a decent shelter for the night and no doubt the monks would share their food with the travellers. He would be able to find out exactly how much further they could expect to walk the following day.

As they approached the entrance a monk came out to greet them.

'Welcome. There are rooms prepared that you can use. I will alert the kitchen and once you have washed I will escort you to the refectory where there will be food waiting for you.'

Tassos crossed himself and bowed his head to the monk. 'Thank you. We were provided with a good meal at Frati yesterday. The men are in need of rest more than food. Tomorrow we will move on to Preveli.'

The monk raised his eyebrows and looked at Tassos quizzically. 'This is Preveli.'

Tassos looked around him. 'This is a monastery. We are making for the village.'

'There is no village.'

Tassos's shoulders slumped. He must have misunderstood and led the unfortunate men to the wrong location. 'I was told they needed to reach Preveli. Other soldiers had been told to make their way to the village.'

The monk shook his head. 'You obviously misunderstood. They were told to come to Preveli where we will give them sanctuary until a ship arrives in the bay to take them across to Egypt. You have reached your correct destination.'

Tassos felt humbled by his ignorance. 'I was expecting a village on the coast.'

The monk smiled at him sympathetically. 'Follow me. We can talk later about your journey. I am sure the Abbot will wish to know the details. I will ask one of our guests to join you whilst you eat and he can explain our routine to the men.'

As they talked the monk led the way across the courtyard and opened the doors to small cells, furnished simply with two beds and two chairs. 'The men will have to share their accommodation, I'm afraid. We have a number of visitors at the moment.'

Tassos turned to Brian and held up two fingers, pointing to the soldiers and the cells. 'Two men each room,' he said. 'Wash, then we eat.'

Brian nodded. This was not what he had been expecting, but he would be grateful to have a bed and a roof over his head for the night after sleeping on rough ground in the open for so long.

Tassos was invited to enter the Abbot's private room and he stood hesitantly just inside the doorway until he was waved to a seat.

'We are very grateful to you for guiding the men here. We will look after them until such time as they can be taken to a place of safety. Did you encounter any Germans on the road?'

Tassos shook his head. 'I was told they had to travel by country routes as the main road was not safe. I thought the soldiers were mustering here to form an army to attack and dislodge the invaders.'

The Abbot smiled sadly. 'I wish that was the case. No,' he sighed, 'Crete has had to capitulate. We have to bow to our fate and put our faith for our salvation in the hands of the Lord. Provided the Germans do not send their soldiers down here we are relatively safe. I pray that we will have sufficient time for these brave men to be taken off our island. When they have recovered from their ordeal will be the time for them to return and dislodge our enemies.'

'Do you expect the Germans to come down here?'

The Abbot spread his hands. 'I understand they have bombed Chania, Rethymnon and Heraklion and the inhabitants are demoralised and frightened. They are unlikely now to put up any further resistance. Once the Germans feel their hold is secure on those towns they will no doubt wish to extend their influence.'

Tassos thought over the Abbot's words. 'My father had a shop in Heraklion. They burnt it to the ground, ransacked his house and killed him when he tried to stop them. I have taken my mother to a village where I trust she will be safe until I am able to return.'

The Abbot crossed himself. 'I will pray for her, along with everyone else who has been caught up in these horrific events. What are your plans now?'

'I will start my return journey tomorrow. I have been here for two days and I am well fed and rested, thanks to the generosity of your establishment.'

'In return for our generosity would you be willing to do a small errand for me?' The Abbot gazed at Tassos steadily and he felt he could not refuse.

'Of course.'

'I need to pass some information to some,' the Abbot hesitated over the word, 'friends in Gortys. Once there you could join the main road leading back to Heraklion.'

'I don't know my way to Gortys from here,' frowned Tassos.

'It would not be difficult. You would be able to make your way through the villages until you reached Agia Galini and then you would be on the main road to Gortys. Once there you would be able to travel back to Heraklion easily.'

Tassos considered the proposal. There would probably be little difference in the length of time his journey would take, whichever route he used. 'Very well,' he nodded.

July 1941 – May 1945

The Abbot had impressed upon Tassos the importance of delivering the message to the Abbot at Gortys and he had placed the folded piece of paper amongst the bundle of drachmas in his pouch. The message meant nothing to him and he hoped that if he were robbed it would be as meaningless to others. During the two days he had spent at Preveli he had been amazed at the number of soldiers who were sheltering there. He had eaten well, bathed, washed his shirt and patched his worn boots before he bade the men he had led to safety farewell.

Although tempted, he had not dared to delay his journey through the villages by stopping and offering to sharpen blades or repair boots; he hoped the villages he visited after leaving Gortys would require his services and he would have some money to give to Aspasia upon his return to Kavrohori.

The walk to Agia Galini had taken him longer than he had anticipated. On two occasions he had needed to retrace his steps when the track he had been using ended in the middle of a field and he did not feel confident that he would be walking in the right direction if he continued.

Each time he approached a village he looked for any sign of German occupation before he entered a taverna for refreshment and asked for directions to Agia Galini. It was with relief that he finally entered Saktouria and was told Agia Galini was only a day's walk away. Once he had gained the main road to Gortys it should take him no more than three days to cover the distance to the town.

The Abbot in Gortys had greeted him effusively, immediately offering a bed for the night. Tassos handed over the precious scrap of paper and waited whilst the Abbot frowned over the contents.

'I will need to compose a reply to my brother in Preveli and alert others to the current circumstances.'

'I'm not going back that way,' protested Tassos. 'I'm on my way to Heraklion.'

The Abbot smiled benignly. 'I am not asking you to return. I have someone else I can entrust to carry the message. I will only ask you to make a short detour to Protoria. You will be able to travel swiftly using the main road and from there the track up to Heraklion is well used or you can cut across the countryside to rejoin the main road again. It will be no more than two days added to your journey.'

Tassos had agreed, feeling he had no option after the hospitality shown to him and the anger he felt for his father's death at the hands of the Germans.

From Protoria he had followed the tracks back through the villages until he rejoined the main road to Heraklion at Agia Varvara. There he had halted, horrified. German troops were in the town, loading food supplies from the shops on to their lorries, whilst holding the shopkeepers at gunpoint. He had slunk back into the countryside and made a detour. He would have to return to Heraklion by the same route as he had used when he had guided the first group of soldiers down to the town.

Thankful that the way was familiar, he progressed from village to village, stopping briefly to offer his services in exchange for a meal, until he reached Kavrohori and made his way cautiously to Aspasia's house. She and his mother had greeted him joyously.

'We were expecting you back some weeks' ago,' said Maria. 'I was beginning to think the same fate had befallen you as had your father.'

Tassos shook his head and related the reason for his delay. 'I could not refuse to take the messages. In both cases I was asked to do so by the Abbot, and who knows, they could shorten our miserable circumstances.'

Aspasia looked at him tearfully. 'You cannot stay here, Tassos.'

He smiled at her cheerfully. 'I know your father will not have me in his house. I am grateful he has offered shelter to my mother.'

Aspasia shook her head. 'It is not my father. It is the Germans. They visited the village and have a list of all the occupants of Kavrohori. You are not on that list. If they find you here they will take you prisoner or shoot you.'

Tassos looked at his mother. 'Is that true?'

Maria nodded. 'A family up the road gave a meal to a soldier who was passing through. The Germans found him in their outhouse and shot him. Then they shot the family, even the children. You cannot risk staying here if you are not on their list of villagers.'

'I can prove by my papers that I come from Gazi.'

'So why were you not there when they attacked the village? How did you escape when so many were killed? Why were you not here when they came and made a note of all our names?' Aspasia shot the questions at him.

'I was travelling, I'm a pedlar. You know that,' replied Tassos, hurt by her attitude.

Aspasia softened her voice. 'I know; but there is no guarantee they would believe you. If they found out that you had led soldiers to safety and carried messages they would have every reason to shoot you.'

Tassos's face paled. 'I'm putting all of you in danger by being here.' He reached for his sack. 'I'll leave now.'

'Where will you go?' Maria wrung her hands in distress.

Tassos shrugged. 'I don't have an option. I'll make my way back down to Preveli and see if the Abbot needs a messenger boy.'

Tassos became adept at avoiding German patrols as he travelled with messages between one village and another. Sometimes he ended up in an isolated spot and had to wait until a shepherd would approach him and identify himself as the intended recipient of the message. Other times he found himself amongst a group of men who had formed a resistance party in the mountains and they would invite him to join them.

At first he was able to make a meagre living as he passed from village to village and would return to Kavrohori with some drachmas for Aspasia. She assured him they had enough to live on. They had buried his father's metal box containing his savings in the vegetable patch and unless the Germans were going to dig up the whole garden they were unlikely to find it. She showed him where a patch of marjoram was being allowed to spread unchecked.

'It's under there,' she announced. 'We took a little out and have it hidden in the house. It's there for an emergency and if the Germans do come searching they'll be satisfied when they find money in the house and look no further.'

'Do you still have the weapons I made for you?'

Aspasia dropped her eyes. 'I took them apart when the Germans entered the village. Had they found them I would probably have been shot. I still have the blades. If the children are in danger I would use them regardless of the consequences to me.'

'I know you would.' Tassos sighed deeply. 'I wish I could be here with you.'

'I wish you could be, but I'd rather we were apart and I know you're safe than hiding here in the village waiting for the Germans to catch you.'

Tassos did not enlighten her that he had hidden from the Germans on numerous occasions and acting as a messenger between groups of resistance workers was as dangerous as hiding in the village. Caught hiding he would have the chance to talk his way out of the situation or escape. If he fell into German hands with a written message in his possession he would be given no quarter.

Carrying messages had given him the opportunity to become familiar with the central area of Crete and he had never before realised just how large the island was. He now knew where to find streams that contained water all year round, where small caves in the hills would give him shelter and which towns the Germans had commandeered and should be avoided.

Tassos was disconcerted when he was asked to travel from Gortys to Karavados, an area completely unknown to him, and warned he would have to take the village tracks as the main road was being patrolled. He was told to sit by the water pump in Karavados where he would be met by a shepherd. He was to pass the message on to the man who would take it to those hiding out on the Lassithi Plain; then he would be free to return to Gortys and continue up to Heraklion to visit his family if he wished.

After three days on the road Tassos wished he had not accepted the assignment. The countryside was barren and the villages were small and poor. When he finally arrived in Karavados he was hungry and footsore, his boots were badly scratched by the gorse, stones and thorns had worn the soles as thin as paper. He sat beside the water pump, where he had been told he would be met, and cut the leather to begin his repairs. He hoped someone would see him and ask him to effect a repair for them. He no longer carried any goods to sell, and despite offering his services in exchange for a meal, few people accepted his offer. Food was becoming scarce everywhere and he could not blame the villagers for refusing him; their families had to come first.

A man eased himself down on the seat beside him. 'Those boots have seen some wear,' he observed.

'One day I'll have enough money to buy a new pair,' smiled Tassos easily. 'At the moment I'd be happy just to be able to buy some bread.'

'How long did it take you to walk from Gortys?'

Tassos wrinkled his brow. 'About five days. I came over the fields.'

The man nodded. 'Safer that way. When did you last eat?'

'Couple of days ago. Since then I found a couple of windfall apples. The maggots had got to them first, but I was able to slice a bit off.'

'Come with me and I'll make sure you have some food inside you before you start your next journey.'

'Where are taking me? I don't want to walk much further with my boots in this state."

'Not far. The next village, Thomadano. You can patch your boots when we reach there.'

Tassos rolled the leather up and replaced it in his sack. 'I'm willing to sharpen knives or scissors in return for a meal.'

'I'm sure the offer will be appreciated.'

'Is that where you live? Thomadano?'

The man shook his head. 'I come from Magoulas.'

Tassos looked puzzled. 'Where's Magoulas?'

'Lassithi Plain, near enough. Two day's walk. Embaros to Xeniakos then it's almost a straight track to Magoulas. I come down twice a week to see if a messenger has arrived.'

'Any Germans around?'

'You have to keep your eyes open. They tend to arrive unexpectedly. They usually leave me alone.'

Tassos looked at him curiously. 'How's that?'

'I have a flock of sheep with me. I'm just Spiro the shepherd. If they decide they want roast lamb I grumble, but I don't refuse them. It's not my loss.'

'But surely you can't afford to lose your sheep to the Germans just because they want a meal?'

The man shrugged. 'They don't belong to me. I just borrow some whenever it's convenient and drive them in the direction I need to go.'

'Where are they now?'

'Thomadano. I'll take them back with me to Xeniakos.'

Tassos was grateful for the food that he was given, despite it being mostly spinach accompanied by dry rusks. Having cleared his plate he followed Spiro from the taverna and they walked along the road together. Spiro turned into a field where a dozen sheep were gathered in a group. As soon as he released the barrier they walked out onto the road without hesitation.

'They know their way back home,' grinned Spiro. 'We'll part company at the turn to Embaros. You continue on this road and you'll eventually reach Heraklion.'

As Spiro finished the sentence he pushed Tassos to the ground. Bullets spattered the ground near them as a lorry filled with soldiers drove by, taking the opportunity to snipe at the men. Tassos heard Spiro give a grunt and decided the man must have been hit. Once silence reigned Tassos lifted his head. There was no sign of the lorry or any soldiers on foot and the sheep had scattered into the distance.

'They've gone, Spiro. We ought to move. There's no cover here.'

Spiro did not answer and Tassos wriggled out from beneath the man's inert body. There were two bullet holes in his sack, but Spiro had taken a bullet in the head. Tassos crouched beside him. He could see there was no way he could help the man, but what should he do? Should he return to Thomadano and tell the taverna owner of the incident? Would they accuse him of shooting Spiro? He still had the message on him that he had been asked to deliver; no doubt Spiro had been waiting until they parted company to receive it.

Tassos sighed. He had no choice but to find his way to Magoulas, tell the villagers of the man's death and find a way to deliver the message.

Taking a risk, Tassos rose to his feet and ran along the road until he reached a turning that he hoped would lead him to Embaros. From there he could ask directions, although from his conversation with Spiro he remembered the man saying he would walk from there to Xeniakos and then it was a straight track to Magoulas. Constantly looking behind him for any sign of the German army returning Tassos hurried on his way, finally catching up with the small flock of sheep who eyed him warily and moved away from him as he approached.

Tassos covered the ground to Embaros swiftly, following the sheep as they jostled their way through the narrow main street. Spiro had said they knew their way home to Xeniakos. He could follow them and they should lead him on to the next village and there he would ask for directions to Magoulas.

The sheep trotted happily ahead of him, finally jumping a ditch and spreading out over the ground they knew, lowering their heads to search for the few blades of grass that showed through the dry earth. Tassos gave a sigh of relief. At least he could not be accused of sheep stealing.

As he entered the small village he saw groups of women returning from their fields, carrying their implements over their shoulders, but no sign of their men folk. They eyed him warily as he called out a greeting to them, before asking if he was on the right road to Magoulas.

Two women stopped and the others grouped around her. 'Any news?' one asked.

Tassos hesitated. What kind of news were they asking him for? 'Some Germans drove through just before Embonas,' he said.

'That's not news,' she replied scornfully. 'They're up and down the road all the time, in and out of the villages, but it won't do them any good. If you're on your way to the hills take my advice and use the sheep track. It's easier walking and joins the road again just before the fork to the left. Take to the road there and keep going straight ahead and you'll reach Magoulas.'

Tassos thanked her for the directions, pleased that he would be able to walk a sheep trail rather than the road. If the Germans were travelling around the area he would be safer in the countryside than walking openly on a road that they could drive along. He did not want them to shoot at him again; he might not be so fortunate the next time.

By the time darkness fell he decided he was far enough away from the road to rest until it was dawn. He did not want to risk straying from the trail whilst travelling just by the light of the moon. He took a mouthful of water from his bottle, wrapped his blanket around himself and tried to ignore the hunger pangs he was suffering.

Magoulas was large than Tassos had envisaged and he made his way to the taverna, hoping he would be able to buy something to sustain him. To his surprise he was able to purchase some mutton and bean broth accompanied by a small loaf of bread. He enjoyed the unexpected treat and asked the taverna owner if he could have a second bowl of soup.

The taverna owner shook his head. 'Only one bowl available. Others need to be fed, you know.'

'I understand, but I haven't eaten properly in days,' said Tassos miserably.' My last meal was spinach and rusks in Thomadano.'

'What were you doing there? The Germans are on that road.'

'I know. I saw them.' Tassos considered whether he should confide in the taverna owner that Spiro had been shot and he had narrowly missed the same fate. 'I'd gone to meet someone. He said he came from this village.'

The taverna owner raised his eyebrows. 'Would that be Spiro you arranged to meet?'

Tassos nodded.

'I'll have a look in the kitchen and see if there's enough soup to bring you another bowl.'

Tassos waited eagerly for the taverna owner to return, but it was a much younger man who carried the bowl over to him and placed it on the table.

'When you've eaten that we'll go,' he said.

'Go? Go where?'

'I'll take you to the men. You'll not find them without a guide.' Yiorgo sat down opposite Tassos and waited whilst he spooned the broth into his mouth greedily.

Tassos followed Yiorgo along the village street, through a patch of scrub where some thin chickens were pecking at the ground and crawled under a wire fence. They were now in the open countryside and Yiorgo strode unerringly ahead, climbing round boulders that were strewn across the hillside or walking purposefully down into gullies filled with gorse and thistles. Tassos was pleased he had patched his boots whilst in Thomadano, but thought they might well need further attention when they finally reached their destination.

Without warning a man rose up from behind a rock and pointed his rifle at them. Tassos lifted his hands in the air, but Yiorgo seemed unconcerned.

'New recruit,' announced Yiorgo. 'Came from Spiro.'

The man lowered his rifle and nodded towards Tassos. 'Follow me.'

Tassos turned to say farewell to Yiorgo, but the man was already hurrying back down the hillside, leaving Tassos no choice but to follow where the stranger led.

'So tell me where you've come from and how you know Spiro.'

Tassos sat in the entrance to a cave beside a large, bearded man. His shirt and trousers were filthy, but his boots were in good repair. In the waistband of his trousers was an evil looking knife and he toyed with a pistol as he spoke. These must be the mountain men Tassos had heard about. Before the war they had lived by raiding the nearby villages for food and women, their violence terrorising the local community, but now they were united with their fellow Cretans in the common aim of dislodging the Germans from their native land.

Tassos licked his lips. 'I come from a village near Heraklion.'

'You've walked the long way round to join us.'

'I haven't come to join you.'

'You'll be safer with us than wandering around the countryside on your own.'

'I was only asked to take a message to Spiro in Karavados.'

'So where is Spiro?'

'The Germans shot him. We were just walking along the road when some Germans went past and opened fire.'

'Bastards. What's the message?'

Tassos felt in his pocket and pulled out the crumpled piece of paper and handed it to his interrogator who frowned and formed the words with his lips as he read.

'This needs to go to Thranassis. I'll get one of the men to guide you over.'

'Me? If you're going to ask a man to guide me why can't he take it?'

'Do you have a gun? Can you shoot and hit a target?'

Tassos shook his head.

'So you're no use to me. Lakkis can take you over and be back here with us within a few hours. If there's a message to come back to me you can bring it. You'll know your way and we'll be on the lookout for you. Get to know the area around here and you'll not only be safe, but useful.'

Tassos was about to protest further when he saw the man was no longer toying with his pistol, but holding it firmly. Tassos had a nasty suspicion that if he refused the errand he would be shot. He was a virtual prisoner of these wild, lawless men.

Tassos was surprised how quickly he was taken across a stretch of undulating countryside and reached a wooden structure, carefully concealed with turf and leaves. The man guarding the entrance rose at their approach; passed a few quiet words with the man who had led the way and indicated that Tassos should go inside.

With trepidation Tassos walked inside the concealed hut only to find that after a few steps he was in a cave, a flickering pitch torch stuck in the ground to give just enough light for him to see the walls. Walking cautiously, one hand on the wall, Tassos picked his way slowly down the passage until it opened out and he could see groups of men lounging around, some were playing cards or dice, others appeared to be asleep, their hands resting on their rifles.

As he appeared a rifle was pointed at him and he was told to raise his hands and he hastened to obey. A man pushed past him and hurried down the tunnel, returning a few moments later and nodding his head.

'It's safe. Lakkis brought him.'

The rifle that had been pointing at him was lowered, but Tassos still stood with his hands above his head.

'You can put your hands down.' A cultured voice spoke from a dark corner. 'Come and sit here by me and tell me where you've come from.'

Tassos stepped over two sleeping men and made his way to the corner. 'I was asked to take a message to Karavados. I met Spiro there and the Germans shot him. I walked on to Magoulas and then I was brought here.'

'Who sent the message?'

'The Abbot at Gortys.'

Tassos handed the crumpled, dirty piece of paper to the man who picked up a battery torch and let the light fall on the paper. 'How long did it take you to get here?'

Tassos considered his answer. 'Two weeks near enough.'

'Did you walk all the way?' Piercing blue eyes looked at Tassos and he nodded. 'And you stopped to rest?' Again Tassos nodded.

'You did well. You're obviously used to walking.'

'I'm a pedlar. I've walked from village to village for years now.'

'Is that why you became a messenger for the Abbot?'

'Since the fall of Heraklion and Rethymnon I haven't been able to purchase anything to sell.'

'So what are you carrying in your sack?'

'My whetstone and cobbler's tools. I managed to get a bit of work for a while, but no one has any money. I've worked for the price of a meal.'

'So for a meal you agreed to carry a message for the Abbot,' surmised the blue eyed man.

Tassos shook his head. 'I led some soldiers down to Preveli and the Abbot there asked me to take a message for him as I made my return journey. When I arrived back in my village I found a census of the inhabitants had been done and my wife was frightened I would be arrested or shot if the Germans found me there. They'd already shot my father and terrorised my mother. I walked back down to Preveli to offer my services to the Abbot as a messenger.'

'So now you are here are you willing to work as a messenger for me?'

'I don't know this area.'

'But if I gave you a message to take back to Thranassis you would know your way?'

Tassos nodded. 'I could do that, but I wouldn't have found my way here without Lakkis.'

'You're a quick learner. The first few times I send you out I'll give you a guide. You'll soon recognise the landmarks and become familiar with a route. Are you prepared to stay here with us? We won't prevent you from leaving. No one will shoot you in the back as you walk off down the hill. Of course, if a German patrol suddenly gave us a visit we'd know who to blame and come looking for you.' Michael's piercing blue eyes bore into Tassos.

Tassos swallowed a he recognised the threat behind the man's words. 'I'd never tell the Germans where you were.'

'Or the Italians?'

'Italians?'

'They've been left to control this side of the island. The Germans think the villagers over here will cause less trouble than the townsfolk and the Italians will be capable of dealing with any unrest. Quite fortunate for us, really. The Italians are more easily duped and certainly not as vengeful as the Germans.'

'If I agreed to stay here and work for you, would I be able to get up to Heraklion at some time and see my family?'

'You could leave at any time. No one is kept here against their will. If you want to be able to live with your family in a free country again it's your duty to help the resistance in whatever way you can. You don't have to be able to shoot a gun to be useful. For a start you could patch up my men's boots and sharpen our knives. I'm sure the other groups would appreciate a visit from you.'

Tassos nodded. He was quite willing to ply his trade for the benefit of the resistance.

Tassos enjoyed his prolonged stay, hiding in the caves and shelters with the men of the resistance. He quickly remembered the hidden tracks from one hideout to another and began to learn a little English from the men he lived with. Many of the allied troops had reached Preveli too late to be taken aboard a waiting vessel and decided it was preferable to risk their lives with the resistance rather than be taken prisoner. The men he mixed with on a daily basis became his friends, experiencing a camaraderie he had never known before.

He was surprised when resting in a hideout after trekking over the hills towards Flamouriana to suddenly see a face he knew looking down at him.

'I know you. You're To Lose, aren't you?'

'What do you mean? To Lose?'

'It was a catch phrase of yours. One to use and one to lose. You've a finger missing on your left hand.'

Tassos clenched his fist, hiding the gap of his missing finger. He would have to admit his identity to Manolis. The man obviously knew exactly who he was.

'What are you doing here, Manolis? You're a fisherman.'

Manolis squatted down beside him. 'I was until the Germans wrecked my boat. The priest at Aghios Nikolaos asked me to take a message down the coast. I was sent from one village to another until Vasilis finally caught up with me. He persuaded me to sail around to Kato Zakros and one thing led to another. Before I knew it we were going up and down the coast with fugitives or resistance workers and finally ended up at Preveli.'

'I've been there,' Tassos interrupted. 'I became a messenger for the Abbot.'

'He was a good man. He sheltered hundreds of soldiers before the Germans caught up with him. We took him to a village where he would be safe, but he insisted he had to return to Preveli. That was when they smashed my boat. Vasilis said it was too dangerous to stay in the area and he made me walk here. Have you any idea how far it is?'

Tassos nodded. 'I've walked from one side of Crete to the other. I walked here from Gortys. I know just how far it is.'

'Did you work as a pedlar after you escaped?'

Tassos nodded. 'How long was it before my bath tub was discovered and they started searching for me?' he asked.

Manolis grinned. 'They still don't know you're missing. I found a tub floating towards the canal and returned it to the island.'

Tassos gazed at Manolis incredulously. 'They really don't know I've gone?'

Manolis shrugged. 'They might by now, but there was no search in place for you when I was last down there.'

A broad grin spread across Tassos's face. 'Thank you, my friend,'

'Did you make much as a pedlar?'

'Enough to live on,' Tassos replied cautiously.

'Then you owe me a drachma. You sold my aunt six shirt buttons for two drachma. I'd sold you ten for one drachma.'

Tassos shrugged. 'A man has to make a living.'

Manolis held out his hand.

'You can take it off my account. You said you'd left a drachma on there.'

'There's considerably more than that now.'

Tassos frowned. 'How?'

'All the time they don't know you're missing your pension is being credited to your account. You should have a fair amount on there by now.'

Tassos shook his head. 'That's all very well, but how do I get my hands on it?'

'When we've driven the Germans out and life gets back to normal, come and see me in Aghios Nikolaos. I'm sure something can be arranged.' Manolis winked conspiratorially at him.

Tassos took a dice from his pocket. 'Throw of the dice?' he suggested. 'If I throw a six before you the debt is forgotten. I'll go first.'

'Let me see the dice. It probably has six spots on each side and if you throw first you're bound to win.' Manolis looked at the dice, but each side had a different number of spots. He handed it back to Tassos. 'I'd like to look at the drachma. I don't want to find it's some counterfeit money the Germans have been distributing.'

Tassos held the out the drachma for Manolis to inspect and Manolis promptly took it and placed it in his pocket. 'Thanks. '

Tassos looked at him in surprise. 'I thought we were going to throw the dice for it.'

'And no doubt the dice is weighted so you would win.'

Tassos shrugged. 'Oh, well, one to use and one to lose.'

Manolis roared with laughter. 'You're the same old To Lose. Come with me to meet Vasilis. He's an English man. But you'd never know it.'

Tassos followed Manolis round the outcrop of rock to where another hideout had been constructed and over to a man who was deep in conversation with a couple of others. He looked up as Manolis arrived and frowned. The man with Manolis was familiar, but he could not recall seeing him before amongst any of the resistance fighters.

'Am I interrupting anything important?' asked Manolis and Vasilis shook his head.

'Who's your friend?'

'Tassos or To Lose,' grinned Manolis. 'He was a pedlar until he became involved with us.'

Tassos was grateful Manolis had made no mention of his escape from Spinalonga.

Vasilis scrutinized him carefully. 'A pedlar. I met a pedlar once. Handed over a group of lost soldiers to him and asked him to take them to Agia Varvara. Was that you?'

Tassos nodded. 'I left them there to make their way to Gortys and on to Preveli. Did they make it?'

Vasilis shrugged. 'I don't know. I had to get to Aghios Nikolaos and I wasn't at Preveli until later. No doubt Manolis has told you how we ended up here. What's your story?'

Tassos sat with the men, enjoying their comradeship, and grateful for the information Manolis had given him.

Whenever he was asked to take a message in the direction of Heraklion he would extend his journey to incorporate a visit to Kavrohori. He knew that with the number of Germans in the area it was impossible for him to stay there, but it was comforting to know that Aspasia and his mother were safe. It was with a heavy heart that he would walk back to the resistance workers who were living in the area of the Lassithi Plain.

August 1945 – October 1945

Tassos knocked on the door of Aspasia's house, ready to greet her with a broad smile on his face. He had walked from Lagou to the main road that ran along the coast where he had been able to take the bus from Aghios Nikolaos to Heraklion, admitting grudgingly that the Germans had improved the surface of the road. All he had thought about during his journey was their coming reunion.

As she opened the door and he saw her swollen stomach his smile faded and he turned on his heel and began to walk away. He knew she had been the wild girl of the village before the birth of Dimitris but he had believed her when she said she no longer entertained anyone but him.

Aspasia hurried after him as fast as she was able. 'Tassos, wait, Tassos. Please let me explain.'

'What is there to explain? It's obvious.'

Aspasia shook her head, tears filling her eyes. 'I was raped, Tassos. Time and again I was raped, like the other women in the village. This child is nothing to do with me being unfaithful to you. Ask your mother. They raped her as well. She'll confirm I'm telling you the truth.'

'My mother? She was raped?' Tassos looked at Aspasia in horror. 'Where is she? I must go to her.'

'In the house.'

Aspasia watched as he pushed past her and entered the living room. His mother sat on the chair that was once occupied by Aspasia's grandmother,

234

'Mamma.'

Maria looked at her son and crossed herself. 'Thank God you are back with us safe and sound.'

'Aspasia says the Germans raped you. Is that true?'

Maria nodded. 'They raped every woman regardless of her age.'

'Aspasia?'

'Many times. She suffered at their hands and is suffering even now.'

'Why didn't her father stop them? Why didn't she fight them?'

'They shot her father and held the children with rifles pointing at their heads. She had no choice.'

Tassos felt sick. 'I should have been here to help defend you, to look after you.'

Maria shook her head. 'You could have done nothing to stop them. They were animals.' Maria shrugged. 'We were fortunate compared with many. They didn't fire the house. They shot her grandmother. She was screaming uncontrollably.' Maria shuddered, remembering how the old lady's wailing had rung in her ears for days afterwards. 'We could do nothing except wait for them to leave.'

Tassos raised his eyes to Aspasia. 'I'm sorry, Aspasia. I misjudged you. Please forgive me. Say you'll forgive me.'

'You jumped to conclusions and thought the worst of me.' Aspasia's eyes flashed. 'Don't you think it's bad enough for me to be carrying a German's child without you accusing me of being unfaithful? How do you think I feel when I see myself getting larger and larger each day? I prayed for the souls of my Pappa and my grandmother, but hardest of all I prayed that I would not become pregnant. My prayer was not answered,' she finished bitterly.

Tassos swallowed. 'How far are you?'

'Seven months, nine days. Do you want the hours?'

Tassos shook his head. 'I need some time to think. I'd not expected this.'

'And you think I did? I was feeding the children when they burst in. Six of them. They pointed their rifles at the boys' heads and told us to lie on the floor. They pulled Grandma out of her chair and forced her down. Grandma was shrieking. They hurt her. I couldn't go to her and comfort her as I was pinned down with one of them pumping his filthy sperm into me. They shot her to keep her quiet. The boys were crying and I thought they would shoot them. I tried to tell them it was alright, not to be frightened, not to cry. Pappa came in and I thought we would be saved but they held him and made him watch what they were doing. When they were finished they took him outside and shot him too. They were laughing, enjoying our agony and misery.' Aspasia's voice broke and she began to sob uncontrollably.

Tassos took her in his arms and stroked her hair. He had a lump in his throat as he tried to comfort her. 'I love you, Aspasia. No matter what has happened I will always love you. I can't take these awful memories away from you, but I hope you'll trust my love and in time they'll fade. I understand you had no choice. You were thinking of the children.'

Gradually Aspasia quietened and Tassos loosened his arms. He would always love the girl he considered to be his wife, but he needed time to come to terms with the fact that she was carrying another man's child, although unwillingly.

It was only then that Aspasia realised that Tassos had lost a part of his right arm. She looked at him in horror.

'Your arm? You've lost your arm.'

Tassos shrugged. 'Only a part of it. One to use and one to lose. I can manage.' He hoped the loss of his arm would not repulse Aspasia.

'How did it happen? Were you involved in fighting?'

'I was fortunate. It happened just after the Germans capitulated. There were still pockets of them around. They were searching for us and we were searching for them. We had a dozen or more men pinned down and were waiting for them to use up their ammunition before we moved in to capture them. I suppose we'd become over confident and suddenly there was shooting coming from behind us. We were the ones who had been ambushed. Four of our men were killed holding them off whilst those who had been injured made their escape. I'd taken two bullets in my arm and the bone was shattered. At least it wasn't my leg they'd hit so I was able to run.'

'Oh, Tassos.' Aspasia placed her hand gently on the stump of his arm. 'Does it hurt?'

'Not now. It did when they first amputated. The pain was in my arm and hand that was no longer there. The German doctor did a good job, though. I had no infection.'

'A German doctor? I would have expected him to kill you.'

Tassos smiled. 'The doctor was a good man. He insisted he was dedicated to saving lives, not a soldier who thought of nothing but killing and maiming. He had commandeered a house at Kastelli and turned it into a hospital for the German soldiers, but he had never turned away an injured man, whatever his allegiance. I hope when he surrendered he was treated leniently.'

'Can you manage with just one hand?' asked his mother.

Tassos shrugged. 'I can manage most things for myself. I can't sharpen blades or mend boots any more, but I can still carry a sack and sell goods.' Tassos was not prepared to divulge his plans for making his living in the future. He needed to visit the hospital in Heraklion and if the outcome was as he hoped he would travel down to Aghios Nikolaos and have a word with Manolis.

Tassos entered the hospital in Heraklion with trepidation and approached the reception desk.

'I'd like to see a doctor, please.'

'So would everyone else who's waiting. What kind of doctor do you need to speak with?'

Tassos considered. 'A skin doctor, I suppose.'

The receptionist raised her eyebrows and looked pointedly at

Tassos's amputated arm. 'You'd probably do better to see a limb specialist.'

'It has nothing to do with my arm. That is not a problem.'

The receptionist ignored his reply. 'Have you come to be fitted for a prosthesis?'

'No. I'd like to see a skin specialist.'

'Do you already have a prosthesis and are you having an allergic reaction?'

'I've told you, it has nothing to do with my arm.' Tassos was losing patience. 'I need to have tests taken for leprosy.'

The receptionist paled and took a step backwards. 'Go and wait in that cubicle over there. I'll see if there's a doctor free.'

From his seat in the isolation cubicle Tassos could see the receptionist speaking urgently on the telephone and looking in his direction. The other waiting patients were also casting covert glances his way, wondering what horrible disease he was suffering from that necessitated that he was kept away from them.

It was no more than ten minutes when a doctor hurried his way and eyed him up and down suspiciously. 'I understand you wish to have tests for leprosy. Is that correct?'

Tassos nodded.

'What makes you think you may have contracted the disease?'

'I don't think I have leprosy at all, but I would like a certificate from you giving me a clean bill of health.'

The doctor glared at him. 'Are you wasting my time? Why should you wish to have tests for leprosy when you say you don't believe you have the disease? Have any of your family had a confirmatory diagnosis?'

'No, my family are all well. I was diagnosed as a sufferer some years ago and sent to a leprosarium. I have no more signs now than I had then. I am convinced I am not leprous and the diagnosis was incorrect. Please, will you take all the necessary tests?'

'Why was your arm amputated?' asked the doctor suspiciously.

'I was with the resistance during the war. The bones between my elbow and my wrist were shattered. The doctor who performed the operation said I was fit and well in all other respects.'

'If you were in a leprosarium how could you have been fighting with the resistance?' The doctor asked suspiciously.

'I escaped.'

'So you've been living as a fugitive ever since, spreading your disease around.'

Tassos shook his head. 'I'm sure I haven't got leprosy. By now my fingers and toes would be clawed, I would have disfiguring eruptions on my face and body. I have nothing like that. I have a skin condition I have suffered with since I was a child and even that has improved as I've become older. Please, help me.'

Tears were forming in Tassos's eyes. Had he made a terrible mistake in coming to the hospital and asking to be tested?

The doctor shrugged. 'You'd better come with me. If you are confirmed a leprous you'll be sent back to the leprosarium under guard. You'll not have an opportunity to escape again.'

Dutifully Tassos followed the doctor down the corridor and into a small room. 'Undress,' the doctor ordered and began to prepare his instruments on a tray whilst Tassos removed his clothes.

Unprotesting Tassos subjected himself to the intimate examination the doctor gave him. The patches of white skin were examined closely and skin samples taken. A pin was stuck into him whilst his eyes were closed and this time he reacted each time he felt it pierce his skin. Finally a sample of blood was drawn from his left arm and he was told he could get dressed and could return in two weeks for the results.

Thankfully Tassos replaced his clothes and walked out of the hospital. The experience had not been as bad as he had feared. He had been terrified he would be detained in isolation until the results were received or the doctor might have refused his request and transported him straight back to Spinalonga. As he had been allowed to leave it must mean that the doctor was expecting to be able to give him a clean bill of health.

In the two weeks that he had to wait for the results of his tests to come through Tassos took the opportunity to catch the bus from Heraklion to Rethymnon and walked up to Mili to see how Costas was faring now he was no longer under the Germans' control.

'I didn't expect to see you again,' was the greeting he received from Costas. 'You've been away for years. I thought you'd been captured by the Germans or worse.'

'I joined up with the resistance,' explained Tassos. 'I was at the other end of the country.'

'Well, there's work waiting for you.'

Tassos shook his head and held out his arm, his sleeve hanging limply at the end. 'Not any more, I'm afraid.'

Costas frowned. 'How do you plan to make a living? Peddling a few goods won't get you far.'

'I was hoping you might be willing to help me.'

'Me? How can I help? I'm not a pedlar.'

'Do you need someone to lead the donkey trains down to Rethymnon? I've thought about it and that's a job I would be quite capable of doing with only one arm.'

Costas considered. 'Well, I suppose now Zen's gone another leader to take his place wouldn't come amiss. It would free up one of the able bodied youngsters for loading the grain.'

'Where's Zen gone?' asked Tassos.

'Died about a year ago.'

Tassos crossed himself, feeling guilty at the idea that had entered his head. 'What's happened to his house? Have relatives moved in?'

'He hadn't any relatives that I ever heard about. It's standing there empty so you can make use of it for a bed for the night.'

'I'd be grateful.'

Tassos stayed in Mili for three days, confiding in Costas for the first time. He admitted that whilst he had travelled as a pedlar he was a fugitive evading capture and being retuned ignominiously to Spinalonga.

'Do you think I'm leprous?' he asked. 'Do I show any signs?'

Costas shook his head. 'It never crossed my mind.'

'I'm convinced my tests will come back negative. Provided I'm right I'll be back to ask for leading work and if Zen's house is still empty I'd like to live there permanently. If I haven't returned by Easter you'll know I'm back on Spinalonga.'

Nervously Tassos entered the hospital and asked to see the doctor who had taken the tests from him.

The same receptionist was about to ask him questions about his amputation when Tassos cut her short.

'The doctor took skin and blood samples from me. He was sending them to Athens to be tested for leprosy. I've come for the results.'

The receptionist's mouth made a silent "Oh." and she lifted the telephone. 'Please wait in the cubicle over there.'

Tassos's heart sank. If he was being asked to wait in an isolation cubicle it could only mean that his tests were positive. He looked across at the waiting patients, maybe he could slink away without the receptionist noticing and raising the alarm. Before he could put his plan into action the doctor arrived at the cubicle door. He held an envelope that he handed to Tassos who took it with trembling fingers.

'What does it say?'

'It's a certificate giving you a clean bill of health. Your skin condition is caused by eczema.'

'Truly?'

'Open it and see for yourself.'

Tassos allowed himself a weak smile. 'That's something I find very difficult to do with one hand. Could you take it out and show it to me?'

The doctor took the envelope back, removed the sheet of paper and held it up for Tassos to read.

'You know you could have a prosthesis fitted. A hook could help you.'

'I'll think about it,' promised Tassos. 'I have other more important things to deal with at the moment.'

Tassos took a seat nervously at the vacant desk. He was going to have to bluff and lie to obtain an identification card otherwise he would be waiting for months whilst his claim for his disability pension was investigated.

'Name?'

'Tassos'

'Tassos what?'

'Novrakis.'

'Date of birth?'

'I don't remember.'

'What do you mean, you don't remember?'

Tassos shrugged. 'I've had a number of blows to the head and been injured.' He held up the stump of his right arm to prove his claim. 'I don't remember a lot of things.'

The policeman frowned. 'Who would know your date of birth?'

Tassos shrugged. 'I don't know of anyone.'

'What about your parents?'

'I think they were killed during the war. I can't find them.'

'What was your father's occupation?'

'He was a pedlar, like me. I've asked at every village I've been through and no one knows their whereabouts or even remembers seeing them over the past year or so.'

'Where were you born?'

Tassos shook his head. 'On the road. My mother travelled with my father. I could have been born anywhere.'

'Where are you living now?'

Tassos gave a deep sigh. 'I'm a pedlar. I travel around. I don't have a home.'

The policeman looked at the man before him in despair. 'It's against the law now not to have an identity card.'

'I know,' Tassos agreed. 'That's why I've come here. I also need one to draw my disability pension.'

'But you have no documents with you.'

'Because I don't have any to bring,' lied Tassos. If it became necessary to produce his identity papers that were safely in his leather pouch he would return another day and claim to have found them.

'We can't issue you with an identity card if we don't know who you are.'

'So how can I get one?'

The policeman pushed his chair back. 'Wait here.' He went into a back room to consult with a superior officer.

Tassos sat where he was. He knew full well the dilemma he had caused. All the time he claimed to be suffering from amnesia and could not produce any papers proving his identity the onus would be on the police to find out who he was and where he came from. They were hardly likely to investigate him fully, being inundated with requests for identity cards since the legislation came into force.

The policeman returned accompanied by the officer to whom he had explained the situation.

'I understand that we have a problem here.' The officer regarded him gravely.

Tassos nodded. 'It isn't my fault I haven't any papers and can't remember things.'

'Quite. No one is blaming you. Is there anyone you know who could vouch for who you are?'

Tassos shrugged. 'Like who?'

'The priest where you go to church, he would know you.'

Tassos shook his head. 'I know I was a pedlar, like my father. If I went to church it would have been in whatever village I was passing through.'

'What about the doctor who attended to your injury?'

'After my arm was shattered my companions took me to a village where the German doctor cut it off. Once he'd done that I was taken back up into the hills. We had to keep moving.'

'You remember that,' exclaimed the policeman.

'You'd remember it too if you'd had your arm cut off,' remarked Tassos dryly.

'Are any of your former companions in town with you? They would at least be able to confirm that they knew you and had done so for a fair amount of time.'

'They might be, but if so I don't know where to find them.'

The officer sighed. To comply with the law he had no option but to issue a temporary identity card for the man. As a pedlar he could be stopped at any time and asked to prove who he was and without being able to show any identification would end up in jail. It would take a considerable amount of time to check the man out and prove his name was Tassos Novrakis, son of a pedlar. The police had no authority to detain him as to their knowledge he had not committed a crime and come to them voluntarily asking for help. He was certainly not the first man or woman to visit them under similar circumstances.

'We'll give you a temporary card whilst we look into your case. If you remember any details that might help that enquiry you are obliged to tell us. Follow me.'

For the first time Tassos felt alarmed. Was he being arrested?

'We need to measure your height and take a finger print from you. Your religion will be entered as Greek Orthodox unless you have any objection and you will be eligible to vote only in this Municipality.'

Tassos sat and waited whilst a card was written out for him and when it was finally presented he scrutinized it carefully. He had deliberately mispronounced his surname and it was written as Novrakis - the 'o' could easily be changed to 'e'.

Tassos nodded. 'Thank you, sir. Will that enable me to draw my pension?'

'You'll have to go to the ministry and arrange that with them.'

'Can it be paid into a bank account?'

The officer sighed. 'Have you got a bank account?'

Tassos shook his head. 'I can open one.'

'When you've opened the account you'll need to go to the ministry and register for your disability pension. They'll need your bank account details and your signature.'

'I can make my mark. I'm still not adept at using my left hand. Good job I had two. One to use and one to lose.'

Tassos left the police station and made his way to the bank feeling elated. He had done it. He had an official identity card and was able to open a bank account. As he had not produced his original identification papers, had claimed not to know his place or date of birth and had no permanent address it would be difficult for the police to do more than confirm that he had no criminal record. Even if they did investigate him it was unlikely he would be associated with the man who had fled Spinalonga six years earlier as he had accepted the incorrect spelling of his surname.

Carefully he smudged the 'o' in his surname on his identity card, deciding that if he did so no one would be able to accuse him of making an alteration; it had been carelessness by the man who wrote it out.

Opening his bank account was a tedious business and took him over an hour before he finally made a poor attempt at his signature with his left hand. He looked at the small book he had been given showing that he had three drachmas on his account. He placed the book carefully in his pocket although it did not seem like money.

'I'm going to ask for my disability pension to be paid in to this account each week. That's in order, isn't it?' he asked.

The bank clerk nodded. 'You can pay in as much money as you wish to your account. Remember you can never draw out more drachmas than the book shows.'

'I understand that. I'm a pedlar. I travel all over Crete. I'm often away from Heraklion for weeks at a time so am I able to go to the bank in any town and draw money?'

'You'll need to have your identity card with you and you'll be asked to sign you name each time.'

Tassos smiled. 'I can manage that.'

From the bank he made his way to the ministry building that dealt with pension applications and took his place in the queue with the other disabled war veterans. It was no more than a formality to have his weekly pension agreed.

'I'll issue you with a book. Come back next week to collect it. You have to take it to the office where it will be stamped each time you collect you pension.'

Tassos shook his head. 'I was told it could be paid into my bank account. I've opened one and have the details with me.'

'It's not the usual procedure,' frowned the clerk. Very few people actually had a bank account, preferring to have their money in their hand.

'I'm a pedlar,' explained Tassos patiently. 'I travel all over Crete. I might need some money when I'm in Rethymnon or Chania. The bank assured me you could pay it in to my account.'

'You'll have to complete these forms.' The clerk pushed the sheets of paper towards Tassos.

Tassos held up his stump. 'I can't. Can you fill the details in for me, please? I can manage to sign my name.'

The clerk sighed. It was not his job to fill in forms for the applicants.

'Can't you take them away with you and get a relative to help you?'

'I don't have any relatives and I don't know anyone in Heraklion who could help me.' Tassos sighed deeply and looked imploringly at the clerk. 'I'd be very grateful for your help.'

Tassos returned to Kavrohori feeling pleased with himself. He would wait a couple of weeks and then return to Heraklion to make sure his war disability pension had been credited to his bank account as he had requested. Provided that all was in order he would then make the journey down to Aghios Nikolaos and see if he could find Manolis.

Tassos had walked along the waterfront at Aghios Nikolaos looking for any sign of Manolis and finally asked a fisherman where the man usually moored his boat. The area was empty and Tassos sat down a short distance away, prepared to wait until Manolis returned. He had been forced to draw ten drachmas from his bank account to pay his bus fare and enable him to buy a couple of meals, but he could not afford to spend too long in the town. He wanted to return to Kavrohori and ensure all was still well with Aspasia. She was due to give birth in a few more weeks and he hoped Manolis would finally provide the solution to his financial problems and he would be in a position to offer Aspasia a better life.

It was late afternoon when Tassos saw the fishing boat approaching and he could see there was a passenger. He touched the leather pouch he still wore around his neck, containing his original identity papers, his new identity card, bank book and, most importantly, the papers from the Heraklion hospital confirming he was not suffering from leprosy.

He waited patiently whilst Manolis moored and handed the doctor ashore before walking towards them.

'Good afternoon, Doctor, Manolis.'

Doctor Stavros showed no sign of recognition, but Manolis grinned at him. 'Hello, To Lose. Hoping to sell some more buttons to my aunt?'

Tassos shook his head and held out his amputated arm. 'I haven't brought my sack with me. I was hoping you'd be able to join me for a drink and give me some advice. When we met up in the mountains you suggested I visited you after the war.'

Doctor Stavros cleared his throat. 'I'll be off home and leave you old friends together. Next week at the usual time, Manolis.'

'If you could wait just a moment, Doctor. I have something I would like to show you.'

Doctor Stavros sighed. It had been a long and tiring day examining the men and women on Spinalonga who had survived the war years. All of them were suffering from malnutrition and many were taking longer to recover than others. Father Minos had given him a list with the names and dates of death of those who had succumbed during the years when the doctor had been forbidden to visit and he was gradually updating the medical records he held. His current patients were few, compared with those he had tended in the past. Now he was being delayed from his meal and glass of raki by a man who presumably wanted to show him his amputation.

From the pouch around his neck Tassos removed his clean bill of health and held it out for the doctor to read. Doctor Stavros placed his glasses on his nose and looked at the paper. He read the document; then looked at Tassos.

'Why should I be interested in this?'

Tassos smiled thinly. 'You don't remember me, do you? Week after week I came to you and asked you to take leprosy tests, but you always had some excuse. I'd been sent to Spinalonga and in your eyes that confirmed I was a leper. I knew I didn't have leprosy, but you wouldn't listen to me.'

Doctor Stavros took of his glasses and rubbed his hand over his head. His familiar headache was starting. 'I didn't have the facilities for taking tests. I still don't.'

'So if I hadn't escaped I would still be over there, condemned to spend the remainder of my life as an outcast when there was nothing wrong with me at all.'

'It was not my fault. I did not make the original diagnosis.'

'Nor were you prepared to challenge it. I am planning to sue you and the medical authorities for misdiagnosis and wrongful imprisonment. You ruined my life and now I'm going to make sure you pay for it.'

Doctor Stavros picked up his medical bag from the quay where Manolis had deposited it. His head was really throbbing now. 'This is not the kind of conversation that should take place on the waterfront,' he managed to say with dignity. 'Come and see me tomorrow at my surgery and we can discuss the matter.'

He strode away, leaving Tassos to replace his papers safely into his pouch.

'Do you mean that?' asked Manolis. 'Are you really planning to sue?'

'That depends upon you, my friend. If we can go somewhere quiet for a drink I'll explain my requirements.'

'So you want me to transfer the balance on your account to your bank account?' Manolis pursed his lips. 'I'm not sure if I have the authority to do that.'

'I'd be happy to accept it in cash. I'm sure the doctor would agree that it was preferable for me to have my money than for me to sue him and the government for double or triple the amount. What happens to the balance held by you when someone dies? It goes back to the government. Well they're not getting their hands on my money.'

Manolis frowned. Each week the doctor had handed him a list of names that should be deleted from the ledgers he kept and a letter to take to the bank to enable the government to reclaim the sizeable balances held in the name of a deceased patient.

'I'll see what I can do. I'll have a look at the ledger tonight and see how much you're owed. I could go to the doctor with you tomorrow.'

'According to me I'm owed one thousand eight hundred and forty one drachmas. I'd like every drachma.'

Manolis nodded. The amount Tassos was planning to claim was very little. He had been sending much more than that back to the government each week.

After leaving Tassos in the taverna Manolis had decided to make a call on the doctor. He had the ledger page showing Tassos's account before him and he pointed to the sum accumulated to the doctor.

'He's not asking for more than he's entitled to. Had he been on the island he could have spent it. If he goes ahead with his threat to sue the government he could ask for additional compensation and they could decide to award him a good deal more. All I need from you is a letter authorising the transfer to his bank account.'

Grudgingly Doctor Stavros agreed. He had no wish to be taken to court and accused of medical negligence. He could also be asked how he had been ignorant of a patient's escape from the island for so long. He drew a red line across the page that held Tassos's medical notes. It was not his money.

Tassos returned to Heraklion, still not convinced that the figures written in his bank book were actual drachmas and he would be able to hold the notes in his hand. He took up a stance before the young counter clerk.

'I'd like to withdraw some money,' he told the cashier and was handed a form to complete.

Tassos shook his head. 'I'm sorry.' He held up his amputated arm. 'I'm not able to write properly with my left hand. Would you be good enough to fill in the details for me?'

The cashier looked at the bank book and filled in Tassos's name and account number. 'How much?' he asked.

Tassos licked his lips. 'One thousand eight hundred and fifty drachmas.'

'How much?'

Tassos repeated the amount and the cashier frowned. 'It isn't usual for a customer to withdraw such a large amount at one time.'

'I have a purchase to make and the vendor is insisting on cash. I understand I can draw out as much as I like provided the money is available on my account.'

'I'll have to speak to my superior for permission.'

'I'm happy to wait whilst you check with him.' Sweat was beginning to form on Tassos's brow. What would he do if they refused him?

An older man accompanied the clerk back to the desk and smiled at Tassos. 'If you would come with me for a moment, sir.'

'Is there a problem?' asked Tassos anxiously.

The man led the way into a small side room and waved Tassos to a seat. 'I understand you wish to withdraw a sizeable sum from your bank account.' Tassos nodded. 'I will need to see your identity card before I can authorise the release of the money.'

Tassos passed the card to the manager and waited whilst he scrutinized it carefully before handing it back. 'Are you able to sign your name on the withdrawal form? If not I can act as a witness to your mark.'

'I can manage a signature of sorts.'

Tassos scrawled his name and the manager compared it with the one in the bank book. There was no valid reason to refuse to give the man the amount of money he had requested.

'I will ask the cashier to bring the money in to you.' He sighed and hoped no one else would come in that day and ask for a large withdrawal. It would be embarrassing to have to admit that the bank did not have sufficient money on the premises.

The baby let out a thin wail and Tassos rose from the chair in the yard. What were they going to do with this child? They could not drown it as you would an unwanted kitten or puppy, but it was a German child. He did not know if he would have the courage to place his hand over the child's face and smother it. He felt such a surge of anger against the unknown father that he had to close his eyes and hold on to the chair to keep his balance. Regardless of the consequences if he ever found the man responsible he would kill him.

He waited until his mother called him from the door to say he could go in and reluctantly he entered the living room. His eyes were drawn to Aspasia who had placed the child to her breast and was looking down with an expression of love and joy on her face that surprised Tassos.

'It's a little girl,' she said, wearily. 'She's beautiful.'

Tassos looked down at the small form, expecting to feel his hatred surging through him. Instead he felt nothing but affection and tenderness. She was so tiny and helpless. He stroked Aspasia's damp hair and smiled at her.

'A little sister for the boys.'

Aspasia looked at him, her eyes widening in surprise.

'They don't need to know I'm not her father and nor does she.'

'You mean, you'll bring her up as if she were your own?' Aspasia asked incredulously.

Tassos nodded. 'It's not her fault. She's innocent. She didn't ask to be brought into the world in this way.'

'The villagers will delight in telling her.'

Tassos shook his head. 'We're getting married if you'll accept a cripple for a husband. I have the papers from the hospital to confirm that I am not a leper. I'm a free man; no longer a fugitive. As soon as you've regained your strength we're leaving Kavrohori. I'll not have anyone look askance at my wife again or tell this little girl that she's a German bastard. Our boys will take my name and no longer be considered as by blows of a casual liaison.'

Tears slid quietly down Aspasia's cheeks and Tassos wiped them away with his finger. 'May I hold her for a moment? I never had a chance to hold the boys when they were tiny.'

Aspasia cried quietly as she placed the baby in the crook of Tassos's arm. She had never expected him to accept the child as his own. After her initial outburst to him they had never discussed the child again, and he had not treated her as his wife and shared her mattress. When he had disappeared for weeks at a time she thought he had taken up with a woman in another village. How she had misjudged him.

8th – 11th April 2010

'My biggest concern is how to keep Grandma in the dark. I don't think she suspects anything at the moment. I want to make sure that my grandmother and Uncle Andreas are a complete surprise for her,' said Marianne with a worried frown. 'I'm not sure how we are going to organise that.'

'Easy,' said John. 'We insist Grandma stays in her room whilst you and Bryony are finishing off the food and things. Once everyone is here I'll bring Grandma through to the lounge.'

'You don't think it will be too much for her? I wouldn't want her to have a heart attack from over excitement.'

'Mum, wouldn't you rather that happened than she died without ever seeing her children again?'

Marianne looked at her son. 'John, you are so callous on occasions.'

'No, I'm thinking practically. She has to go one day and I'd like to think she was happy to the very last minute of her life. Don't worry. I'm sure everything will go according to plan and be perfect.'

'I certainly hope so. Two parties in two days! That's more than enough for anyone, let alone someone her age.'

'She doesn't know that. She thinks it's our party that day. Just make sure she stays resting during the morning. If she's too tired to come to the girls' party we'll all understand. Hers is more important. She'll never be a hundred again.'

Marianne shrugged resignedly. 'I suppose you're right.'

'Of course I am.' John gave his mother a quick hug. 'The girls aren't likely to remember if their great great grandmother was there for their first birthday party.'

Mark breathed a deep sigh of relief. So far their journey, although tedious, had gone according to plan. Paul and Teri were no more than half an hour late flying into Kennedy airport and the flight to Heathrow had left on time. He had managed a couple of hours sleep and then sat fretting about their luggage having been transferred safely whilst the others slept soundly oblivious to his concerns.

Whilst Mark had tried to obtain confirmation that their luggage had been loaded onto the flight to Heraklion Paul went in search of the latest novel by his favourite author and the two girls browsed the boutiques and Duty Free shop. They had met up for a late breakfast, but he had found it difficult to do justice to the English breakfast they all ordered, watching the flight announcement screen continually. There were a number of flights departing for Heraklion and Mark watched their flight number moving steadily up the screen until finally a gate number was shown.

He had hurried them along the maze of passage ways and into the departure lounge, only to find they were waiting in there for over half an hour and his haste to get them there was unnecessary. Now they had finally reached Heraklion he felt he could relax. It was just a question of collecting the hire car and driving down to Elounda.

'I don't remember it being as busy as this when we came with Mum and Dad,' said Paul. 'How did they cope with us amongst all these crowds of people?'

Mark shrugged. 'I doubt if it was as busy then. Wait here with the luggage whilst I find out where we collect the car.' He extracted the hire contract papers from a folder and looked around for the Hertz sign. 'I'm going over there,' he announced. 'Looks like there's a queue, of course, so I don't know how long this will take. Don't move from here.'

'Shall I get a trolley?' asked Ronnie. 'We don't know how far we're going to have to drag these cases.'

'Let's wait until Mark comes back. The cars can't be very far away.'

'I'm getting one anyway,' Ronnie announced. 'We can always abandon it if we don't need it.'

She walked over to the line of parked trolleys and wheeled it over to them. 'Load up,' she ordered Paul. 'We ought to show Mark that we can think and organise ourselves. Just because he took charge of booking the tickets he seems to think we've never arrived at an airport before. It's a wonder he hasn't tied us together.'

'He's just concerned that he won't be able to find us again. You'd feel pretty foolish having explained to a Greek official that you'd lost three adults only to find they'd gone off to the loo.'

'Actually that could be a good idea. We don't know how long this drive will take us and if there's anywhere convenient to stop on the way. Come on, Ronnie. We'll leave Paul here and he can look after the luggage until we get back, then we'll take over.'

'Don't get lost,' called Paul and Teri waved a hand at him.

Mark waited impatiently in the queue, but when a man tried to force himself in front of him he stretched out his arm. 'I'm sorry, sir. I was here before you.' He handed his papers to the assistant, ignoring the muttering that was taking place behind him in Greek.

A form was presented to him along with a set of car keys.

'Please sign. This gives you details of the car you are hiring. In the unlikely event that the car should develop a fault the number to telephone is here.' He pointed to a series of numbers. 'Keep this with you at all times. It is a legal document and if you are stopped by the police you will need to produce it along with your passport and driving licence. Follow the signs that say 'Car Hire – Parking' and you will find your car waiting for you. It has a full tank of petrol. At the end of your hire period you should return it to the same area with a full tank and deposit the keys back with us. Drive carefully, sir, and enjoy your stay in Crete.'

Before Mark could ask for any further information the man had held out his hand for the papers being offered by the impatient Greek behind him.

Mark walked back to where Paul and the girls were waiting for him. 'We follow the signs to the parking area,' he announced. 'Everyone ready?'

They nodded and Paul proceeded to push the trolley and the small procession forced their way between the coaches who were loading up people and luggage and the taxis that seemed to appear from nowhere.

'Good idea of yours to get a trolley,' said Teri. 'It's bad enough getting through these crowds without having to manoeuvre a case.'

Once they had moved a short distance away from the terminal building the people thinned and they were able to move more easily. Mark strode ahead, consulting the paper he had been given and looking at the number plates on the cars, finally stopping and checking he was correct.

'I hope we'll fit in,' he said. 'It isn't very big.'

'We'll manage,' Paul assured him. 'Marianne said it was only about an hour's drive. It doesn't matter if we're a bit cramped.'

'Should you 'phone them to say that we're here?' asked Teri.

Paul shook his head. 'If we hit a traffic jam we could be delayed and then they'd be worried something had happened to us. Better to just turn up.'

Annita sat in her room, Elias's photograph in her hands. 'Well, Elias, it's going to be a busy day tomorrow. John and Nicola have organised a big party for the girls. Nicola promised her mother they would have one as she didn't have a big white wedding. I'm not sure who will be there. Giovanni told me his brother and Francesca are coming from Italy and Marisa is so excited at the thought of seeing him. She doesn't like Francesca, never has. Says she tries to organise her and tell her what to do.

'I don't know Nicola's grandparents at all, but I'm sure they'll be nice people. Marianne said Mrs Duggan was such a help to her when she travelled over to Athens to be with Elizabeth after the shooting. I'm sure Mrs Duggan was only too pleased Marianne agreed to go with her. Such a good thing that she did.' Annita chuckled to herself. 'Her mother wasn't very happy when she said she was staying out in Greece and marrying Giovanni.' Annita sighed heavily. 'We just have to accept that our children go off to different parts of the world and sometimes we never see them again.

'Marianne says her sister and husband are coming. I'm surprised Helena agreed to make the journey. Despite being twins those two girls drifted apart once Helena married. Only natural, I suppose. It will be quite a gathering, Vasilis and Cathy are coming down from Heraklion, and of course Marjorie has come over from England. That has made Saffie happy. Provided the little girls don't decide to be shy and cry whenever anyone speaks to them it should all go very well. I'm quite looking forward to it. I just wish you could be here to enjoy the day with me, Elias, and I don't get too tired.'

Mark drew up outside the self catering apartments. They looked deserted. 'I presume we're in the right place. It looks closed.'

'Maybe we passed it,' suggested Paul.

Mark shook his head. 'According to the directions I was sent the apartments are at the far end of Plaka just behind the shops. The sign said Plaka and these are the only shops I saw.'

'Why don't you 'phone them? They might be waiting for us to call and say we're here before they unlock.'

Mark pulled out his mobile and consulted the list of telephone numbers he had been sent. 'Which one?'

'Giovanni or Marianne, I would think. If you can't get either of them try the one for John.'

Mark nodded and proceeded to press in the numbers, hoping Giovanni was there to take the call.

'Hi, is that Giovanni? It's Mark here. We followed your directions and we're sitting outside some self catering apartments in Plaka but there's no one around.'

'You are earlier than we expected. I will be with you in five minutes.' Giovanni closed his mobile. He had hoped Marianne would have been able to go up to meet her nephews and their partners, but she and Bryony were working together in the kitchen preparing some of the food for the following day. Now he had the onerous task of making them welcome and he did not approve of their chosen relationships.

'Well, I guess we're in the right place,' said Mark. 'Giovanni said he would be with us in a matter of minutes so we may as well get the luggage out.'

'It looks quite nice,' said Teri. 'It's a shame there's no swimming pool.'

'The sea is just over there so why do they need a pool? Besides, it would probably be freezing at this time of year.'

'Some of the hotels we passed had pools although they were near the sea.'

'Yes, and did you see anyone in them? I didn't, but I saw one or two people in the sea.'

'I think the view is beautiful,' said Ronnie. 'I'll let you all go off walking and I'll stay here and paint.'

'You won't want to paint every day any more than we will want to walk every day,' replied Mark.

'You don't know what I will want to do.'

Mark shrugged and turned away. He was not quite sure of his relationship with Veronica. She could often be argumentative and confrontational when he made a casual passing remark. After each one of their blazing rows he vowed to finish the relationship, but if he was totally honest with himself he was frightened of being without a companion.

Giovanni drew up with a squeal of brakes. He pulled the keys to the apartments from the glove compartment and took in the young people who were standing waiting for him. There were two young men and two girls. He let out a sigh of relief; he had been expecting four men. The situation was not going to be embarrassing for him as he had feared.

The two boys greeted their great grandmother, both surprised that she should remember which of them was Paul and which was Mark. They introduced Teri and Ronnie to her and the four were taken over to meet Bryony and Marcus before duly admiring the twin girls presented by Nicola and John. Uncle Yannis greeted them shyly in his halting English and Ourania bobbed her head in acknowledgement before drawing Marisa forward.

'Giovanni. Mamma,' she said and Marisa shook their hands before commenting quietly in Greek to Ourania who smiled.

'Giovanni,' called Ourania, 'Come and explain; we were expecting four young men. Why do the ladies have names that belong to boys?'

'They are in disguise,' said John in Greek and Giovanni was forced suppress a smile at the expressions on Ourania and Marisa's faces.

'Behave yourself, John,' said Giovanni sternly. 'Of course they are not in disguise. The ladies' names are Teresa and Veronica. They have been shortened to Teri and Ronnie, in the same way that John has shortened Nicola to Nick.'

The girls heard their names and turned to look at Giovanni. 'Dad's just explaining that your names have been shortened. Grandmother Marisa was expecting you to be boys.'

'Well, I hope we haven't disappointed her. I'm never going to remember everyone's name and who speaks English,' said Teri.

'Don't worry about it. When everyone else arrives they'll all speak English, except Dimitris and Antonia from the village. You won't be stuck in a corner trying to make conversation in a language you don't understand. Mum's arranged for you to go to a taverna for a meal tonight. She and Dad and Bryony and Marcus will be with you so you'll have no problem ordering or making conversation.'

'What about the rest of you?'

'You don't have to worry about us. Aunt Ourania will see to Grandma and Nick and I will be here just in case there are any problems. We're happy to leave the girls with Mum or Bryony, but they'd be a bit much for the older generation.'

'I think twins would be a bit much for me at any time,' commented Ronnie. 'I'm not used to small children.'

'Nor was I until these two arrived. Do you want to hold Jo? She's becoming a real heavyweight.'

Ronnie looked at John doubtfully. 'I don't want to drop her.'

'You won't drop her. If she wriggles too much just sit her down on the floor. She'll try to climb up your leg. They're both just finding their feet. Another week or two and they'll be running around.'

'So how do you plan to spend your time after the parties?' asked Marianne. She was pleased she had decided on a taverna meal rather than catering at home. It gave her the opportunity to sit and talk without having to keep rushing out to the kitchen to replenish plates.

Mark sat back in his chair. 'We're rather hoping you will be able to help us. We've looked on the internet, of course, and I've bought a map, but I thought you'd probably know the best places for sightseeing and walking.'

Marianne looked at Giovanni. 'I think we're probably the very last people to ask. We can tell you where the tourists go, but we haven't been sightseeing ourselves for years. There is Spinalonga, of course, that's easy. John can take you over there, but further afield, well, there's Knossos, obviously and the other sites that will be marked on the map or mentioned in a guide book.'

'Saffie would be the person to ask,' Bryony leaned forward eagerly. 'She's done so much exploring in her car.'

'I don't think she's done much walking, though.'

'What about Samaria?' asked Paul. 'That sounded really interesting.'

Giovanni shook his head. 'It's a bit early in the year yet. There's still a danger of flash floods and I don't know when the boats start operating. You wouldn't want to walk to the coast and have to turn around and walk back.'

'There's the little gorge outside Heraklion,' suggested Marianne and laughed. 'Giovanni slipped down the side and then accused me of pushing him.'

Giovanni took his wife's hand. 'Did I ever take my revenge? I remember I ruined my suit.'

'Many times! You can talk to Saffron tomorrow at the party. She'll be able to give you directions to the scenic parts and the most attractive villages in the area. As you have a car you can just drive and stop wherever takes you fancy.'

'Wait until Mum arrives and hears we're going to be driving around. She'll have a fit.'

Marianne looked at her nephew in surprise. 'Why shouldn't you drive over here? Most of the tourists hire a car.'

'She forgets we're no longer little boys. We'll have to spend some time with Mum and Dad, but I'm pleased they'll only be here for the one week. She'll nag us the whole time to mind the roads and be careful who we talk to.' Paul pulled a face.

'We'll be firm with her. We have Grandma's party tomorrow, then the one for the girls the following day. Why don't we spend the Monday with Mum and Dad?' suggested Mark. 'It will give us a chance to see our grandmother and the girls can have the car to run around in once they've dropped us. We could go to Knossos on the Tuesday. If John was free to take us to Spinalonga on the Wednesday that would be great. Thursday we could meet up with the parents in the afternoon and go for a meal in the evening and then they'll be going back to Heraklion on Friday ready for their flight home. Once they've left we're free to do as we please and Mum won't be able to say that we neglected her.'

'Whatever you arrange to do is fine with us. I shall just be relieved when these parties are over.'

'Can we help at all?' asked Teri.

Marianne shook her head. 'We are organised. Bryony and I have been cooking like maniacs for a week and placing food in the freezer. There are only fresh salads to be made tomorrow morning. Everything else just has to be heated up. It won't be a sit down meal, just finger buffet.'

Annita sat in her wheelchair waiting impatiently for Marianne or Bryony to come and collect her. After helping her to dress Marianne had assured her one of them would be back for her as soon as everything was in readiness. The time was passing and she was sure she had heard cars drawing up outside. If neither of them had come within the next ten minutes she would disregard their request and make her own way to the lounge. She tapped her fingers impatiently on the arm of the chair, checked she had changed her slippers for a pair of shoes, looked in the mirror to make sure her hair was tidy and looked back at the door again. She could hear voices and laughter from people she did not recognise. They had obviously forgotten her. Setting her lips in a determined line Annita propelled herself to the doorway and pressed the automatic switch to open the door. As it swung back she saw John was there, the twins in his arms.

'I was just coming to get you, Grandma. Mum and Bryony are busy laying out the food so I've been given the job. Can I put these two onto your lap? I can't push you and hold them.'

'I can manage to wheel myself.'

'I know you can, but it will be quicker if I do it and the first car is just arriving.' John placed the girls on his great grandmother's lap. 'It will only be for a few minutes, just hang on to them.'

Swiftly he walked with Annita from her room into the lounge. The chairs and tables had been pushed back towards the walls, one table near the door was loaded with glasses and bottles and Marcus stood there, always willing to act as bar tender despite being teetotal.

'Hold on to the girls a few minutes longer whilst I get you a drink.' John stepped back, but instead of going towards the table of drinks he picked up his camera and took a series of photographs, hoping that in one of them he would have both the girls looking in his direction.

Annita looked around as Nicola relieved her of the twins. There were so many people. That looked like her daughter Elena standing there, and was that Andreas? Marianne was ushering them both towards her and it *was* Elena and Andreas. Annita felt the tears coming into her eyes and stretched out her arms. Fancy them bothering to come all this way to attend a party for the twins.

Giovanni banged on the table with a spoon and the general conversation gradually stopped and the guests looked in his direction.

'I would like to welcome everyone and thank you for coming,' he said, beaming. 'Today the party is for Grandma. As you all know she is a hundred this month and we could not let that milestone go unmarked. Please, raise your glasses to Annita.'

Bryony pressed a glass of champagne into her grandmother's hand. 'Everyone wants to spend time with you, but they will all be here for a few days so there's no need to overtire yourself.'

'I thought it was for the girls you were throwing a party,' Annita said, bemused.

'That's tomorrow. Today is your day. Enjoy it, Grandma.'

Once Annita had greeted all the members of her family who had arrived from America John insisted there had to be a family photograph. He fussed around, ensuring that Annita was flanked by Elena and Andreas. There were too many ladies wearing shades of pink or red for his liking and he finally solved the problem by placing a man between each one, finally putting the twin girls back in Annita's arms and allowing Vasi to take the photograph so he could be included.

Throughout the afternoon he took photographs of family members chatting, drinking, laughing and generally enjoying themselves, mostly with his great grandmother as the central figure. Finally Annita called Marianne over to her.

'I'm exhausted. Can you ask Giovanni to call for silence? I just want to thank everyone, then I'm going for a rest.'

Annita waited until she had the attention of her guests. 'Excuse me not standing but I think at my age I'm allowed to stay in my chair. I want to thank all of you, particularly the American contingent, for coming to Crete to make this such a special occasion for me. I also have to thank Marianne for the organisation and everyone else who contributed to the arrangements. I have to go for a rest now, but I'd like you all to continue to enjoy yourselves and I'll be with you again in a couple of hours.'

Before Annita retired to her room John called for one last photograph and insisted that everyone, a relative or just a friend should be included.

'Can't it wait?' murmured Marianne. 'Grandma is so tired.'

'If I don't take it now some people may have left when she comes back to join us. I promise I'll be quick.'

Marianne finally kicked off her shoes and flopped down in an armchair. 'Thank goodness they've all gone at last. I'm exhausted, and we've got to do it all again tomorrow.'

'That will be easier,' Giovanni assured her. 'We won't be trying to keep a big secret from Grandma. Do you think she enjoyed herself?'

Marianne nodded. 'She was terribly tired when she eventually agreed to go to bed, but she kept saying how wonderful it was that Elena and Andreas had bothered to come over. What did you think about Andrew turning up out of the blue?'

'I'm pleased Vasilis had enough rooms set aside. He could have made his presence known a little earlier.'

'He said he didn't know until the last minute that he would be able to come,' Marianne defended her brother.

'I'll have to add the cost of his room to the hotel bill when I pay Vasilis,' muttered Giovanni gloomily.

'At least he's staying in the self catering,' Marianne reminded him and yawned hugely. 'I'm off to bed. Teri and Ronnie were very good and loaded the dishwasher for me whilst Saffie washed the glasses so there's nothing more for me to do tonight.'

'Well, girls, what do you want to do today?' asked Mark.

'Sleep,' groaned Teri. 'I think the travelling is catching up with me.'

'You can sleep tomorrow whilst Paul and I are with Mum and Dad. I thought we could go down into Elounda and have a look at the town.'

'Will there be anything open? It's Sunday, remember. People in Greece go to church on a Sunday.'

Mark shrugged. 'Won't hurt to drive down and get our bearings. We can always drive around a bit and see something of the countryside. We have to be back just after lunch anyway for the twins' party. It must be quite awful to have two babies around all the time. I hope they won't spend the afternoon yelling their heads off.'

'They were very good yesterday,' Ronnie reminded him. 'I'm sure Nicola will take them away if they do start to be a nuisance. I know it's a party for them, but they're hardly going to know that.'

'I hope there won't be other children there rushing around. You know what children's parties are like – mayhem.' Mark looked at his watch. 'Well, if we are going down to the town we'd best get a move on. Half an hour enough for everyone to be ready?'

Mark drove down to the car park in the square at Elounda. 'Anyone got any change? There's a sign saying we have to pay.'

'You may not need change. It says tickets that way and on top of that little building there's another notice that says tickets.'

'Suppose it's closed?' asked Mark.

'Then you put a note on the windscreen.'

'They'll probably not understand and give us a fine anyway,' replied Mark gloomily.

'I'll go,' said Ronnie and set off towards the kiosk.

The man inside smiled at her. 'Yes?' he said in English.

'Parking ticket?' said Ronnie hopefully.

'Put inside on windscreen. Stay all day.'

Ronnie handed him a note and checked the change she was given. 'Thank you very much.'

'You are welcome. Have a good day.'

Waving the ticket she returned to the car. 'No problem,' she announced. 'We put it inside on the windscreen and we can stay here all day if we want.'

Mark raised his eyebrows. 'Are you sure about that?'

'Go and ask if you don't believe me. Now, where shall we go, into the town or over to the sea?'

'Let's see what the town has to offer.'

They walked down to the church, passed a bar and a collection of small shops and after that the road began to climb up the hill and it appeared to be residential. They waited for a gap in the traffic and crossed to the other side of the square where there were a variety of shops, mostly selling souvenirs or beach goods, with a couple advertising themselves as supermarkets. There were open fronted bars, the chairs and tables spilling outwards, and nearly all of them occupied.

'So much for my assumption that everything would be closed because it's Sunday,' observed Teri.

'Couldn't we go back over to the square and walk along by the sea? It looks far less crowded over there,' asked Ronnie as she stepped off the pavement to avoid a woman with a buggy. 'Maybe it's so busy here at the moment because everyone has just come from church. It could quieten down in an hour or so.'

They followed her back across the road to the waterfront. It was still busy, but not as congested as the other side of the road.

'We've got a couple of hours, why don't we see how far round the bay we can walk?' suggested Paul. 'There may be nothing to see, but I certainly can't face pushing my way through all those people. That sidewalk is so narrow you have to keep going into the road. Sooner or later one of us will be hit by a car.'

They followed him along to the end of the square where there were some tavernas, the owners insisting they had the best and freshest food to try to entice them inside. Paul hesitated.

'It looks as if we walk on through there. I just hope they won't think we're going to stop for a meal.'

'If it isn't a thoroughfare I'm sure we won't be the first to have made a mistake. Lead on and let's see what happens.'

'There might be somewhere decent to stop for lunch,' said Mark hopefully.

'You can't be hungry yet,' exclaimed Ronnie.

'I'm not, but it could be as well to have somewhere in mind.'

People were using the forecourts of the tavernas as a walkway to avoid the climb up the hill and down again. The group wandered through trying to look at the dishes advertised without the owners noticing.

'They all seem to have much the same on offer,' remarked Teri. 'I suppose we could go back to that one where Marianne took us. I enjoyed my meal there.'

'It may only be open in the evenings. We don't want to walk back there and find it's closed.'

'We should have checked as we drove past.'

'There are plenty to choose from. As you say, they all seem to be offering the same dishes.'

'There are a couple of interesting looking restaurants along there. What do you think about eating out on the water?'

Teri looked doubtful. 'Will we feel them moving? I don't want to end up feeling sea sick.'

'They'll only move if there's an earthquake,' Ronnie pointed to the rocks that were built out supporting the walkways. 'They're not floating restaurants.'

'Mark. Paul.'

The men stopped in their tracks. 'It's Mum,' said Paul glumly. 'We'll have to go over. We can't pretend not to have seen her.'

Mark went forward and planted a kiss on his mother's cheek. 'Hi, Dad.'

'Pull up a chair,' Helena ordered, 'and you can join us for a pre lunch drink.' She completely ignored the two girls.

'Actually we were going for a walk,' protested Paul.

'You can do that any time, not that there's anything to see around here. I can't think how Marianne can bear to be buried away here. At least if she was in Athens there would be some shops to look at. The ones they have here are useless.'

'If you were in Athens you wouldn't have this wonderful view of the bay,' remarked Paul.

Helena shrugged. 'They've quite a decent menu here.' She raised her hand to the bar tender. 'What do you want to drink, boys?'

'Where's Grandma and Uncle Andreas?'

'They said they would stay in the lounge at our hotel. It's just a bit further along. I think they found yesterday rather too much for them and they want to rest before we have to go through it all again today.'

'Great Grandma seemed to cope. I think it was a great idea to have a party each day.'

Helena sniffed. 'Lot of fuss about nothing. Grandma probably won't remember after a couple of days and those girls certainly won't. We only came because mother insisted she had to come and we felt she should be looked after. Now, have you boys made up your mind what you'd like to drink?'

'I'll have a coke,' said Mark.

'Me too. What about you two girls? What would you like?'

Teri and Ronnie exchanged glances. They had been totally excluded by their partners' mother.

'Actually,' said Teri, 'I'd just as soon continue walking for a while. You stay here with your parents and have lunch. We'll meet you back here in a couple of hours or so. Come on, Ronnie.'

The girls walked away, leaving Helena with a satisfied smile on her face and the boys feeling totally discomfited.

Once a short distance away from the hotel Ronnie let out a breath. 'I do not understand why Mark allows his mother to dictate to him. He's not a little boy. All he had to say was no thanks, we're going for a walk.'

'Paul did try.'

'Not hard enough. I tell you, if Mark and I stay together I will never have that woman in my house. She could at least have had the manners to say hello to us.'

'Do you think you and Mark will stay together?'

Ronnie shrugged. 'Who knows? Look there's the old uncle and their grandmother. Should we go over and say hello or just wave?'

'Wave,' decided Teri. 'They probably won't remember who we are. If they're still there when we come back we can always say a quick hello and tell them we're off for lunch. How far do you want to walk?'

'There are some old mills over there. Why don't we walk that far and if there's nothing of interest turn back? We need to look out for a taverna where we can have a meal. I absolutely refuse to sit and eat with Mark's mother and I don't want to be forced to make difficult conversation with his grandmother.'

Together the girls walked to where a stone bridge spanned a shallow canal. Ronnie looked around. 'I guess the locals cut a way through years ago so they didn't have to sail out and around the peninsula.'

Teri peered into the water. 'It isn't very deep.'

'It's probably silted up now, but then their fishing boats weren't that big years ago. More like rowing boats with a sail. I doubt if it's used at all now.'

'Is that a taverna I see over there?' Teri pointed to where tables and chairs were placed inside a wooden shelter close to the canal. 'Shall we see what they're offering?'

'Why not? Even if it's horrible we'll tell the boys it was marvellous and insist it was better than the meal they had,' Ronnie grinned.

'It can't be that bad. There are a number of people sitting there.'

'They could just be drinking. Come on, let's take a chance.'

A man came forward as the girls took a seat at a table. 'What would you like, ladies?'

Teri looked at him in surprise. 'You speak English?'

He shrugged. 'I have a number of different languages. It is necessary when you have visitors from all over the world. You are American – yes?'

'How did you know?'

He smiled. 'You get to know by the way the tourists dress which country they come from. Now would you like a special fish? Or lobster, freshly caught.' He pointed to the net at the side of the canal bank where a number of lobsters were contained.

Teri shook her head. 'We don't want anything too much to eat. We've a party to go to this afternoon. There's bound to be loads of food. There was yesterday.'

'Ah, Mr Giovanni's big party. You are relations?'

'No, just friends.'

'The old lady? She enjoyed the party?'

'She certainly seemed to. You know her?'

'Everyone knows her. She is the oldest lady in Elounda. Now, if you do not want a big meal I suggest you have a salad and my special chips. To accompany you can have cheese balls, meat balls, souvlaki, calamari, omelette.' He shrugged. 'The choice is yours.'

'Maybe just omelette and chips,' said Teri.

Ronnie nodded. 'Could we have a salad between us?'

'Of course. And something to drink? A small beer would be good.'

Ronnie shook her head. 'Fresh orange juice for me, please. We'll be drinking wine this afternoon.'

Teri looked at her watch. 'We ought to get back to the boys. I want to have a shower and wash my hair. If they're not ready to leave we can have a taxi.'

'Why don't we take the car? Let them have a taxi. I'll pay and tell the man how much we enjoyed those scrumptious chips.'

'We could bring the boys here. Tell them we're taking them for fish and chips.' Teri grinned mischievously.

Ronnie nodded. 'One day next week after their mother's gone home. If Mark and Paul are planning to spend some time with their relatives tomorrow, what are we going to do?'

'They said we could drop them and go off in the car.'

'We can have a look at the map. I don't fancy driving too far afield. Maybe there's a bit more to Elounda than we saw this morning. We could drive in to the next town, what's it called, Aghios something, it looked to be a fair size.'

'I'm easy. Provided we see Knossos and go out to that island at some point I really don't mind where we go tomorrow.'

'Girls, I'm relying on you to be as good today as you were yesterday. This is your party.'

'Yes,' joined in John. 'Bad behaviour and we'll never give you another.' He smiled at Elisabetta as she tried to avoid having her socks put on. 'You've got to start off being properly dressed. I know you'll have them off as soon as possible.'

'Pap, pap, pap,' she said back to him.

'It's time you learnt to say Pappa,' he admonished her. He picked her sock up from the floor and began to put it on a second time. 'No, this is not a game. This is getting dressed ready for your party.'

271

'I think they had enough of being dressed up yesterday,' observed Nicola. 'Once they've made their entrance I think I'll bring them back and put their jeans on. They can crawl around in those. If they try whilst they're wearing dresses their knees get all caught up. Here, you hold Jo and I'll finish Lisa. I should have thought and bought something new to wear today. I wore this dress yesterday.'

'No one will notice. They'll be too busy admiring these two.'

'Have I got time to change?'

'By the time you've changed these two will need to be changed again.'

'I wish I could lose a bit more weight. All my clothes feel tight.'

'They don't look too tight. Actually, you are looking particularly radiant and beautiful.' John leaned across and kissed Nicola on the nape of her neck. 'I'm so glad it's this year and not last. I was so miserable. I was sure I was going to lose my sight.'

'We owe Doctor Gharcia a big thank you.'

'And Saff,' added John. 'Thank goodness she insisted I went to England.'

'Do you think her shop will be a success?'

'I hope so. She'll certainly be selling a few different items from the other souvenir shops. I just hope I she'll be happy with the photo of Spinalonga. It's small enough now to fit a box lid and still looks decent.'

'Suppose the other gift shops copy her idea?'

'She's taken out copyright. If they start to appear in the other shops she can claim infringement and compensation. Is Lisa ready? Jo's trying to kick her shoes off again. I'm sure a number of guests are already here and once they've been admired and photographed they can have their ordinary clothes put back on. I wish I could put on my jeans and a T-shirt. I'm not used to being all formal in a suit.'

Nicola giggled. 'We should have put in the invitation that it was casual wear only.'

'I'm not sure how well that would have gone down with the older generation. What do you think of Mark and Paul?'

'I've hardly had a chance to speak to them, but they seem to be nice enough. I'm not sure about your Uncle Andrew.'

'I'm going to try to get an opportunity to talk to him today. I'd like to know what he does that made it so difficult for him to know if he would be able to come over.'

'Probably wondered if it was worth making the effort. After all, he doesn't know us. Come on; let's make a grand entrance with these two. I'm really looking forward to tomorrow when everything will be back to normal.'

Mark finally saw Saffron alone out on the patio and took the opportunity to gain her attention.

'You're Saffie, aren't you? I know I've been introduced to everyone, but I'm hopeless at remembering names.'

Saffron smiled at him sympathetically. 'I'm having the same trouble. I don't know Nicola's family at all and I hardly remember my American relatives.'

'Marianne said you would know the best places to visit whilst we're here.'

'Me?' Saffron looked at Mark in surprise.

'She said you've driven around the area so would be able to tell us which walking trails were the best. Giovanni said the Samaria could be risky to attempt at this time of year.'

Saffron nodded. 'So I've heard. I can tell you about the villages, but I've only been a little way along the walking trails. I've usually parked the car, gone a short distance and turned back. I didn't feel it was safe to go far on my own.'

'Why?'

'Suppose you twisted your ankle? You could lay there for hours before another walker came by.'

'You could use your mobile.'

'If you're in a gorge you can't always get a signal. You can't

273

always get one anyway if you're out in a deserted part of the country.'

'Driving down nowhere looked deserted.'

'That's because you were on the main road. Once you turn off for the villages there are often some very lonely parts and you can't rely on the signs giving you accurate information. I was used to driving in England before I came here. If you over-shot your turn you could always find another that you would take you back. It's not the same over here. In the very rural areas a road will take you to a village and then you have to return to the main road to travel on to the next one. The locals tend to walk from one village to the next across the fields provided it isn't too far away.'

'So which villages do you recommend we visit?'

'Why don't you visit us at our house first? Drive into Elounda and park there; then walk up the hill so you can visit Kato Elounda and Pano Elounda. We're just a short distance further up. You could come for lunch and walk back to Elounda through Pines and down to Mavrikiano.'

Mark frowned. 'We planned to spend some of the time tomorrow with Mum and Dad and had planned Knossos and Spinalonga for Tuesday and Wednesday, then another visit to the parents on Thursday before they leave.'

'There's no pressure,' smiled Saffron. 'I understand you're going to be here for another two weeks. I'll be along at Plaka sorting out the shop. I want to be ready to open in another week when the season gets underway properly. I'll give you my mobile number and if you call me we can arrange a date. If it doesn't fit in with everyone else's plans then just say so. I won't be offended.'

Mark calculated rapidly. 'Suppose we made that a definite date for Friday? If I brought the map with me you could point out the prettiest villages or those that have something interesting that we ought to see. I'm sure Mum will try to insist that we drive up to the airport to see them off and I really see no point in doing that. It's a total waste of a day. If I tell her we're booked to have lunch with you she won't be able to argue.'

'I'll look forward to it.'

'Oh, will we need our walking gear?' asked Mark as an afterthought.

'Not for the walk to and from me. I suggest you wear long trousers and sturdy shoes if you walk through any of the gorges. Summer visitors seem to think beach wear is appropriate and come back stung or bitten by insects and their feet cut by stones.'

'I don't think it's warm enough for shorts and T's yet. We were hoping to be able to swim whilst we were here.'

'It could be in a couple of weeks. You can always ask John if you could borrow some wet suits.'

Mark nodded. 'I'll tell them we're visiting you on Friday.'

12th April 2010

'Well, I'm certainly glad the parties are over. Now maybe we can get back to our normal lives,' said Giovanni as he pulled his T-shirt over his head.

Marianne smiled. 'You have to admit you enjoyed playing the part of the proud grandfather.'

'I was not play acting,' answered Giovanni indignantly. 'I am proud to be the grandfather to two such lovely little girls.'

'It's good to see John and Nicola so happy after last year. John is going to have the girls this morning so Nicola can go and spend some time with her family at the hotel.'

'Why don't they come here?' asked Giovanni.

Marianne shook her head. 'The girls will be perfectly happy if she isn't around, but if they see her they will want her attention. She deserves a complete break, even if it is only for a few hours. Elizabeth and Nicolas are coming here on Tuesday, so you two will have plenty of time to talk together. I expect Eleanor will be with them and I find her difficult. She's nothing like Nicola.'

'You're nothing like Helena so that shouldn't be a surprise to you.'

'That girl with Mark didn't seem too happy yesterday. She said she and Teri had gone along to the canal and had lunch there whilst the boys had lunch with their parents.'

Giovanni raised his eyebrows. 'I thought they said they had arranged to spend today with Helena and Greg.'

'Apparently they walked down towards the causeway and

Helena and Greg were there. Helena insisted the boys stayed and had lunch with them.'

'Why did they not all have lunch together?'

'From the way Ronnie spoke I don't think the girls were invited. At least they're off to Knossos tomorrow and going to Spinalonga with John on Wednesday so that should give them a bit of breathing space. I was going to ask Helena and Greg to come for lunch on Thursday, but Mark said they would be leaving during the morning for Vasi to drive them all back to Heraklion. I'll see if they'd like to come on Wednesday instead and bring Andrew.'

'Why don't you ask them for Tuesday evening?'

'Uncle Andreas and my grandmother are coming that afternoon. They want to see Grandma, of course, and catch up properly with her but I thought she ought to have a rest today. They can stay as late as they like and I'm happy to include them in a meal, but I thought it would be easier with the generations split up.'

'What about Angelo and Francesca?'

'They're coming tonight. I haven't forgotten, them Giovanni. I've just tried to arrange things so that everyone has some quality time with the people most important to them.'

Giovanni smiled in admiration at his wife's organisational skills.

'No, Mark, I am not going with you to visit your parents today and nor is Teri. Your mother was really quite rude to both of us on Sunday. She didn't even bother to say hello.'

'I'm sure it was unintentional.'

'Are you? I'm not. I know she doesn't have to like me, but she can at least be polite. You said we could have the car and Teri and I are planning to do a bit of exploring on our own. You have our mobile numbers so you can call us when you plan to return to the apartments. You can have a taxi back and we'll meet you here.'

'It would obviously be more convenient for you and Teri if

we had a taxi down to them,' Mark said sulkily.

'I'm quite happy to drive you down to their hotel in Elounda. I'll wave to them from the car and if your mother should ask you can tell her we thought she would appreciate some quality time on her own with her two little boys. I'm ready to leave whenever you are. I told Teri we'd be off between ten thirty and eleven.' Ronnie picked up her purse and the keys to the hire car. 'I'll see you down by the car.'

Paul put his arm around Teri's shoulders. 'I'm sorry we were caught by my mother yesterday.'

'You could have been firmer and insisted you accompanied us on our walk.'

Paul shrugged. 'I know, but it's difficult to refuse her and Mark always gives in to her. I didn't want to upset him so that there was an atmosphere between us.'

'You didn't mind about upsetting me, though?'

'I didn't think you would mind as you were with Ronnie. I wouldn't have left you on your own.'

'Well that's something to be thankful for, I suppose.'

'What are you two planning to do today whilst we visit?' Paul wanted to change the subject.

'We're taking the car and exploring.'

Paul frowned. 'Will you be safe, going off on your own?'

'That didn't seem to worry you yesterday,' replied Teri acidly.

'That was different. You were just walking locally. You could end up anywhere in the car, run out of petrol, have a puncture, get lost.'

'Well, if any of that happens to us we have our mobile 'phones. I'm sure we'd be able to contact someone and get some help.' Teri shrugged off his concerns. 'Just remember we're going to Knossos on Tuesday and over to Spinalonga with John on Wednesday, so make sure you don't arrange to meet your mother on either of those days. I know Mark's arranged something with Saffron for

Friday. I do wish he'd consult us first. We may have been planning to do something different.'

'Such as?'

'I don't know, but this is supposed to be a joint holiday where we decide together what we want to do each day,' complained Teri.

'It will be,' promised Paul. 'It's just this week that everything is a bit up in the air, with the parties and everything. Once Mum and Dad have gone back we'll sit down and plan properly.'

'So now we've dumped those two safely into their mother's arms, where shall we go?' asked Ronnie.

'Let's go back to the square and park up. We can have a wander around, then drive in to Aghios Nikolaos. When we've had enough we can drive back to the apartments and have a walk around Plaka. We've hardly looked at the area since we arrived.'

Ronnie nodded. 'Fine. We can always have lunch here if we see anywhere that takes our fancy.'

'You know what would be really sensible? If we found a taverna where they spoke English and we could ask where we should go. We could drive around and miss something interesting if we just take off.'

'Good idea. Let's walk along by the harbour for a start. It seems terribly busy down there and I'd like to know why. Maybe a fisherman has just brought his catch in.' Ronnie stood still and admired the expanse of the bay. 'I'll have to spend some time painting whilst I'm here. The colours are wonderful.'

'Won't Mark mind if you're not out with us?'

'Too bad. Did he ask if we minded him spending time with his family? He's like his mother in many ways. Expects everyone to do what he wants when he wants.'

Teri nodded. 'I know. I had words with Paul this morning about visiting Saffron on Friday. Apparently she's suggested a walk through a couple of villages, have lunch with her and to walk back a different way. Actually I'd quite like to see Saffron's house, but Mark didn't ask us if we wanted to do that, he just informed us that was the plan.'

'I agree. We both object to Mark making arrangements on everyone else's behalf, so in future whatever we do has to be a majority decision. Look, there are boat trips. Shall we go on one?'

Teri shook her head. 'Not much point. They all say they're going to Spinalonga and we're going there with John on Wednesday.'

'Over to the town, then. Do you think the church will be open? I'd like to have a quick look inside.'

The girls looked inside the church and admired the ornate decoration before crossing over the road and looking in a shop that was advertising natural sponges and olive oil soap along with other chemist's sundries. Teri was tempted immediately, but Ronnie pulled her away.

'You don't need to buy the first ones you see. There are bound to be other shops selling local produce. I can see one with sponges hanging outside over there.'

They crossed the road again to the parade of shops, interspersed with tavernas, that was opposite the car park. They investigated the small shops that called themselves supermarkets and came out giggling.

'They have a fantastic variety of goods in there, but not very much of anything. I'm used to seeing a whole aisle devoted to cereals or different kinds of bread.'

'They probably know what the locals like and if you're a tourist you just buy whatever is available and make do. We ought to think about stocking up at the apartment. I gave Mark the last of the bacon for breakfast this morning.'

'Shouldn't we buy it from the general store by the apartments?'

'We don't know what time it's open. We can buy a few bits and pieces here today and then ask John when we see him on Wednesday.'

'We don't want to get anything yet.' Teri grabbed Ronnie's

arm as she was about to re-enter the supermarket. 'We don't want to leave it in the trunk of the car all day. They won't close before five and we're bound to be back here by then.'

They walked to the bottom of the hill, looking up the side roads, and then back over to the square. On the corner was a jeweller and they ogled the ostentatious jewellery that was on display, before deciding it would be far too expensive.

Teri shrugged. 'Well, I guess that's Elounda. Shall we go along to that bar we passed and have a look at their menu? They were speaking English so we could ask them about Aghios Nikolaos.'

The two girls followed the signs indicating a car park in a side street half way up the hill in Aghios Nikolaos, paid the charge and walked up to the square.

'Well, there's certainly more here than in Elounda,' observed Teri.

'Yeah, more, but more of the same. All the shops seem to be selling exactly the same souvenirs and beach goods as those in Elounda.'

'I think we give this town up. I hope some of the others are more exciting.'

'We have only seen this bit. Let's walk down the hill and have a look at that pool we passed in the car, then we could continue round to the waterfront and see if anything is happening there. We really shouldn't judge the place until we've seen a bit more.' Ronnie led the way past a war memorial and into the small public garden.

'Why don't we sit down for a minute and have a look at the map?' suggested Teri. 'We don't want to walk down the hill and find there's no way to get round to where we parked the car and have to walk back up again.'

'There has to be a way round.' Ronnie joined her on the seat and they looked at the map together. Ronnie traced a line with her finger. 'Down to that pool or lake and then if we go around there we should be down by the sea. There has to be a turning off which will lead us back to the car park.'

Teri folded up the map. 'I'll believe you. Why do you think that old lady is crossing herself in front of that tree stump?' she asked in an undertone.

Ronnie shrugged. 'I don't know. Maybe it has some significance to her. It looks as if some of the trees have been cut down. What a shame. I hope they plant some more to take their place. Come on, let's move.'

The shops flanking the road leading down to the pool were no more interesting to the girls than the ones they had seen earlier, but once they reached the pedestrianised area Ronnie sucked in her breath.

'Now this is pretty.' Small boats floated on the lake and a steep hill rose up at the end of the pool. 'I wonder if we can walk all the way round and come out the other side of the bridge?'

'There's only one way to find out. Goodness, everywhere down here appears to be an eating place.'

'There is a leather shop over there.' Ronnie pointed to where a vast collection of leather bags and sandals were hung outside a narrow entrance. 'Shall we have a look?'

Teri shook her head. 'You can, if you want. I find the smell of leather shops overpowering. I'll wait outside.'

'I'll only be a minute.' Ronnie negotiated the steep steps that led down from the opening into a large room, crammed with leather goods of every description. A number of assistants were in evidence, serving customers or replacing items that had been rejected on the shelves. The smell of leather pervaded the atmosphere and Ronnie felt her head begin to throb. She turned and forced her way back up the steps against the prospective customers who were coming down and rejoined Teri in the fresh air.

'You were wise to stay outside,' she admitted. 'I'd love to have poked around down there, but the smell made me feel quite ill. Fancy having to work somewhere like that all day.'

'I doubt if they notice it. A bit like working in a fish shop. After a while you don't notice the smell of fish.'

'That's what it reminded me of,' remarked Ronnie. 'An overpowering smell of fish. Come on, let's move further away. Maybe there's a perfume shop around here somewhere and I could squirt myself with a sample.'

Despite walking to the end of the paved way there did not appear to be anything more interesting than shops selling souvenirs or leather goods unless they wanted to stop for an ice cream or a meal.

'I feel quite cheated,' remarked Teri. 'I don't know quite what I was expecting, but something more than there is here. Now we have to walk the same way back. Why hasn't someone built a bridge across?'

'Probably so you have to pass all those tavernas again and second time around you will succumb and go in for a meal.'

'Actually I wouldn't mind having a drink. It's considerably warmer down here. It must be because of the cliff.'

'How about the Cave Bar? It's the nearest and I'm sure they're all much the same.'

Teri nodded and followed Ronnie into the dark interior.

'Wow! It really is a cave.'

'It is the Cave Bar,' a pained voice from the darkness informed them.

'Yes, I know it said that outside, but I was expecting a conventional bar inside.' As Teri's eyes became accustomed to the dim light she could see it was the bar tender who had spoken.

'Why spoil something that is natural?' the bar tender asked. 'What would you like to drink, ladies?'

'Small beer for me,' replied Ronnie.

'And the same for me,' added Teri.

'Have a seat.' He waved his hand towards the wall where small tables, each with a nightlight burning in the centre, were surrounded by seats.

Within minutes the bar tender came bustling over, placed a bowl of nuts and another of olives on the table and proceeded to uncap the beer bottles.

'You are staying in Aghios Nikolaos?' he asked.

'No,' Teri shook her head. 'We're just visiting for the afternoon. We're actually staying in Elounda.'

'Elounda, very pretty.'

Ronnie nodded. 'It's beautiful.'

'Where do you come from?'

'The States. What about you?'

'Aghios Nikolaos.'

'You speak excellent English.'

The bar tender shrugged. 'We learn at school and from the tourists we learn the other languages. It is necessary to understand the drink they ask for.'

'So you can tell us where we should visit whilst we're here.'

'You are by the pool; up the hill leads to the square. There is the war memorial and gardens.' He waved his hand to the right. 'The other side of the pool there is the museum and here is the cave.'

'We've been up to the memorial and the gardens.' Ronnie hesitated. 'Whilst we were there we saw a lady crossing herself before a tree stump. Why would she do that?'

The bar tender's face took on an expression of sadness. 'Her husband, her son, maybe her brother or her father would have been hung from the tree or tied there and shot.'

'What?'

'It was during the war. Many men were massacred there, women also when they pleaded for the lives of their loved ones.'

'That's awful.'

The bar tender shrugged. 'That is war.'

'Why have they cut down the trees?' asked Teri. 'Do they think people will forget if they are no longer there to remind them?'

'No, the people will not forget. The generation will pass on, but their children will remember and their children's children. Some trees had to go; they had become sick and dangerous; ready to fall, but the stumps have been left to mark their places.'

'So the memorial is to those people who died up there?'

'To them and to others also. Everywhere people died. Every village has a memorial. Whole families perished. You would like to see something?'

Ronnie and Teri exchanged glances. Was he going to show them photographs of dead people or even a preserved body?

'What is it?' asked Ronnie.

'You follow me.' The bar tender picked up a torch from behind the bar and beckoned to them. 'You are in the cave. This is not just a crack in the hillside that has been made into a bar. This is the cave where the resistance hid to escape reprisals.' He switched on the torch and shone it onto the wall. 'You see,' his finger pointed out the lettering. 'The names of the brave men and women who fought against our brutal invaders.'

Teri and Ronnie looked at the Greek lettering, unable to translate the names, but able to recognise that many were the same.

'Whole families,' murmured Ronnie and the bar tender nodded.

'My grandfather.' He pointed to a name. 'My grandfather's brother and his son.' He switched off the torch. 'You have seen enough?'

Teri nodded. 'Yes, thank you.'

The girls returned to their seat, both in a sombre mood. 'I think this is somewhere we should bring Mark and Paul,' said Ronnie. 'We'll walk round the pool and come in here for a drink.'

Teri drained her glass. 'Shall we walk back to the bridge and see what the other side of the pool has to offer? The bar tender said the museum was over that side.'

'May as well.'

The other side of the pool was almost a mirror image, everywhere seemed to be a bar or taverna interspersed with small gift shops or offering scooters for hire. They followed the signs for the museum, paid their entrance fee and entered the rooms where the artefacts were displayed. Most of them had been found in the bay and claimed to be from the sunken city of Olous. Particularly fine artefacts that had been found locally were shown only in photographs, the originals being in the museum in Heraklion. The photograph of an early Christian mosaic decorated one wall and Ronnie looked at it curiously.

'I'd like to see that. I wonder if you have to dive down.'

Teri looked at her sceptically. 'You would hardly be able to make it out if it was underwater. Look the notice says it can be reached by crossing the canal and walking behind the taverna. Do you think that was where we had lunch yesterday? I didn't see any signs.'

'We could drive back that way and ask. The man there spoke decent English.'

Teri nodded. 'We'll finish looking around in here and then collect the car, drive back to Elounda and out to that restaurant. If we're able to see the mosaic and this sunken city it won't be a completely wasted day.'

'It wasn't wasted,' argued Ronnie. 'We've seen the town, walked around the pool and been into that cave bar. It was definitely better than having to try to make polite conversation to the boys' parents.'

Ronnie drove back along the road towards Elounda, stopping to take a photograph of the bay. 'You really appreciate just how beautiful this area is when you're up here. I was so busy looking at the map to make sure we were on the right road that I didn't really take much notice when we arrived.'

'We could drive up the road on the other side of Plaka and see what the view is like from there. It could be better.'

Ronnie shook her head. 'It may be as good, but certainly not better. If the boys haven't phoned we could do that when we've found the mosaic.'

They continued down into the small town and ended up in the square. 'How do we get down onto that road that leads to the canal?' asked Ronnie. 'When we walked we went through over there where the tavernas are, but you can't drive through there.'

'There must be a turning further up and we missed it.'

Ronnie drove around the square and slowly back up the hill.

'There,' said Teri. 'Down that steep hill.'

'What!' Ronnie exclaimed in annoyance. 'I'm on the wrong side of the road and can't see if anything is coming round the bend. I'll have to find a place to turn and come back down.'

They had to drive a considerable distance back up the hill until Ronnie decided she had sufficient vision of the on-coming traffic to make a turn.

'I'll go slowly. Keep an eye open for the turning.'

'You could start indicating now. It can't be much further. Yes, down there.'

Ronnie manoeuvred the car around the corner and down the short steep hill and they were down on the sea road where they had walked the previous day.

'Drive as fast as you can past the hotels,' said Teri. 'We don't want them to spot us if they're sitting outside.'

'Don't even look that way. If they ask us later we can say you were looking at the map and I was concentrating on driving.'

Teri giggled. 'I hope they haven't decided to walk over to this taverna.'

'One thing is for sure, they won't have walked. If they decided to come over here Helena would have insisted they had a taxi.'

'Maybe this wasn't such a good idea.'

'Before we park we'll look around. If there's any sign of them we'll drive away immediately.'

'Why do I feel like a naughty school girl playing hooky?' asked Teri.

'Did you skip lessons?'

'Once or twice, then Mum found out and I was grounded for two weeks and given extra school work. I decided it wasn't worth it.'

'Why did you do it? Didn't you like school?'

Teri shrugged. 'Friends were doing it and getting away with it. I went along with them so I didn't lose face. It wasn't really much fun. We had to keep a look out the whole time for neighbours who knew us.'

'Well, we seem to be safe enough. There's only a few people here and no sign of anyone we know.' Ronnie parked the car a short distance from the taverna and the girls walked over and took a seat.

The owner appeared and greeted them as old friends. 'You have come to see me again, that is good. What can I get for you today? You would like some more chips?'

Teri shook her heads. 'We've just stopped for a drink and to ask you where the mosaic and underwater city are.'

He waved his hand to a path beside the taverna. 'The mosaic is there. Olous is under the sea. I do not think you will be able to see that today. It needs to be very calm and the water clear. You had a good party yesterday and today you would like a small beer, yes?'

'Why not?' said Ronnie. 'We're only driving back to Plaka and I'm sure a small beer won't make me intoxicated.'

'You are staying with Mr Giovanni?'

'We're in the self catering apartments.'

'They are good?'

'Very good. We have no complaints.'

'Mr Giovanni has made many improvements since the big fire. I will bring you the beer.'

'Did you know about a fire at the apartments?' asked Ronnie and Teri shook her head.

'When was the fire?' she asked as two beers were placed on the table along with a bowl of olives and another of nuts.

The owner shrugged. 'Two seasons ago. Everything had to go and he had to build again. Now it will not burn.' With a smile the owner moved on to serve some customers who had taken a seat further down and they heard him speaking in French to them.

'I can't drink all this in one go,' protested Teri as she took a handful of nuts. 'Why don't we go up and look at the mosaic? We haven't paid him yet, so if we tell him we'll be back I'm sure our drinks will still be here.'

Teri waved to the man and pointed to their drinks and the path leading to the mosaic. He nodded, obviously used to his customers wandering off and returning a short while later.

The girls peered over the wire fence at the mosaic; it was damaged and not as complete as the photograph in the museum had indicated.

'It should have a roof to protect it,' frowned Ronnie. 'If they leave it open like that all year round they'll eventually have nothing left for people to look at.'

Teri looked around. 'I wonder where it was in relation to the city that sank? It must have been inside a building originally, but there are no signs of any walls.'

Ronnie shrugged. 'Maybe Giovanni will know. We can ask him the next time we see him. Have you seen enough? If we want to drive up the hill from Plaka we ought to make a move.'

Teri nodded. 'We still have our beer to finish and I'd like some more of those nuts.'

'Yes, we don't want the boys 'phoning to say they're back at the apartments until we've been up there and had a walk around Plaka.'

The view from the hill above Plaka was no less magnificent than it had been from the other side of Elounda. Spinalonga showed up more clearly, and people could be seen walking around on the island.

'I'm longing to go over there,' sighed Teri. 'I've read the guide book, but I understand that John has much more information. They had a relative over there, I believe.'

'Really? Mark's never mentioned it to me.'

'His mother has probably forbidden him.'

'Why should she do that?'

'Well, you realise he would have had leprosy? She's probably terribly ashamed to admit that they had a leper in the family.'

'Would she have known him?'

Teri shrugged. 'I've no idea, but I think it doubtful. I'm sure John will tell us all about him or her. Down to Plaka now and then home?'

Teri nodded. 'Yes, I feel as if I've had enough for today. I'm not sure if it's the beer or the parties that are catching up with me.'

'Probably both. I doubt we'll be very long looking around Plaka, so you might be able to get in a late siesta.'

'At the moment that is a very appealing idea.'

They parked the car back at the apartments and Teri groaned. 'We forgot to buy any food.'

'Don't worry. We're off to Knossos tomorrow. We'll make do with coffee and stop somewhere on the way for a breakfast unless the store is open.' Ronnie tried the door, finding it firmly closed. 'Just coffee it is, then.'

They walked past the small row of shops, only two of them displaying goods in their windows. 'It's not warm enough yet to get enthusiastic about beach wear,' said Teri as she moved to the shop two doors along. 'I do like that.' She pointed to a cream dress with brown saddle stitching around the hem and neckline. 'Can you see how much the price tag says?'

'The shop's closed so however much it is you'll have to look another time. That seems to be about it for shops. If we go down there we can walk back by way of the sea.'

'That island looks so close from here. I'm surprised the lepers didn't swim over to the mainland.'

'Probably not fit enough. If you had limbs that had become useless you'd probably not risk swimming. This would be a lovely place to sit and eat and there are a number of tavernas. I expect they all serve locally caught fish.'

'I wonder if their chips are as good as those we had yesterday.'

'That seems to be it. End of Plaka. That road should take us back up to the apartments. We might as well head back; then you can have your siesta.'

'There are some shops up here. Oh, look, Ronnie. I'd love to have that enormous vase.'

'I'd like to see you trying to get it into the luggage rack on the 'plane. Where would you put it?'

'I've no idea,' smiled Teri, 'but I'd still like to have it. Actually there are some other beautiful vases in there. I'd like to come back when they're open and have a proper look.'

'I'm not sure if I'd dare go in. Suppose I broke something?'

'I expect they're insured.'

They crossed to the other side of the road and looked in the window of the gift shop there. A woman could be seen unpacking items and she looked up as their shadows fell across the window. She waved and came across to unlock the door.

'We're caught now,' murmured Ronnie. 'We'll have to go in. We'll say we haven't any money with us if she starts the hard sell.'

'There might be something worth having.'

'If so we can always come back another time. Oh, it's Saffron, isn't it?'

'That's right,' smiled Saffron, 'and although I know you are Teri and Ronnie you'll have to remind me which one of you is which. There were rather a lot of people at the parties that I'd never met before. You met Marjorie, didn't you? She's helping me to get sorted out. Come in and have a look around. I'd planned on opening this week but some of the stock hadn't arrived. Everything is a bit upside down. Would you like a coffee or a cold drink?'

Teri and Ronnie followed her dutifully into the shop.

'We had a beer a short while ago, thanks.'

'Where are Mark and Paul? Not interested in looking around shops?

'They've spent today with their parents. What are you selling here?'

'Souvenirs, jewellery, books. Have a look over there whilst we do some more unpacking and try to decide the best places to put them. Tell me what you think of the items. Would you buy any of them to take back home? I'm not trying to sell to you, I just want your opinion.'

'I want that enormous vase in the shop across the road,' smiled Teri.

'I'm sure Uncle Yannis would be only too pleased to sell it to you.'

'Uncle Yannis? The man we met at the party?'

Saffron nodded. 'It's his wife's shop really. They had one for years in Aghios Nikolaos and decided to move down here when Giovanni rebuilt.'

'And you've opened up in competition with him?'

Saffron shook her head. 'He certainly wouldn't allow me to do that. I had to show him everything I proposed to stock. If he said no, that was it, and I had to think of something else.'

'Bit unfair, wasn't it?'

'Not really. He has a reputation for selling high quality glass and ceramics, along with decent leather and silk goods. It wouldn't be right if I had cheap imitations that I was selling for less. I could ruin his business. What have you two been doing all day on your own?'

Ronnie proceeded to relay the details of their day to Saffron and Marjorie whilst Teri browsed amongst the books. 'Can I buy this one?' she asked, holding up a volume. 'I've nearly finished the book I brought with me.'

'Of course you may have it. No charge.'

Teri shook her head. 'I insist on paying for it. If we were strangers you would not give your goods away.' She grinned at Ronnie. 'Do you think if I went to Uncle Yannis's shop and asked if I could buy that vase he would be prepared to give it to me?'

'You would have no chance there,' Saffron warned her. 'He would reduce the price for you, but he would still make sure he was making a sizeable profit. He is an excellent businessman.'

Teri placed the Euros for the book on the counter and Saffron handed her one Euro back. 'Cost price to you.'

Ronnie suppressed a smile. After Saffron's remark about her uncle she was probably still making a profit on the sale of the book.

'Mark said you've invited us for lunch on Friday,' said Ronnie. 'I thought you had visitors staying with you. We don't want to intrude or put you out.'

'Vasilis and Cathy returned to Heraklion today. Vasi will be down at the hotel ensuring that all is in order, so there will only be Marjorie with me.'

'What time should we arrive?' asked Teri.

'As it suits you. Mark was asking me about walking trails. I suggested you visited the local villages on foot and had lunch with me. I had to admit I had never walked any of the trails properly, but he's going to bring the map and I can give you a rough idea of how long it takes to drive to places from here.'

'That will be really helpful. We don't want to find we've spent so long driving that there's no time to walk.'

Saffron's mobile rang and she looked at the number displayed. 'Excuse me. I must answer. Hello, Vasi. Is there a problem?'

'I just wished to know where you and Marjorie wished to eat tonight.'

'You decide. We'll be home in another half an hour.' Saffron closed her mobile. 'I'm sorry about that. Had I not answered Vasi would have thought there was something wrong and come rushing over.'

'We mustn't delay you. We ought to get back and have a shower so we leave the bathroom free for the boys when they arrive. We'll see you on Friday, and thanks for the book.'

Paul emerged from the bathroom, a towel wrapped around his waist. 'Well, Mum can't complain. We've certainly done our duty and spent all day with them.'

'I'm surprised she didn't expect you to spend Tuesday and Wednesday with them as well.'

'She tried, but I told her we're going to Knossos tomorrow. She suggested she and Dad came with us, but I told her there was no room in the car. I thought for a moment that Mark was going to suggest that we hired a second one so we could take them.'

Teri shook her head. 'I don't think Ronnie would have been very happy about that. I'm sure she would have insisted that she and I drove up together and you two spent the time with your parents. You know that as soon as you arrived your mother would need a cold drink and would manage to sit there for ages, then say it was time for lunch. You'd be lucky to get into the site before it closed.'

'Well they're not coming. They'll have to amuse themselves tomorrow. Marianne has invited them for lunch on Wednesday and I'm sure Mum wouldn't want to come to Spinalonga with us. She can spend some time with her grandmother. Uncle Andreas and Grandma are going for lunch tomorrow. We'll give Mum and Dad another quick visit on Thursday morning before they go up to Heraklion and after we've seen Saffron on Friday we can make some proper plans for our walking trips.'

Andreas had spent the afternoon talking to Annita, whilst his sister sat and listened to them. Having enquired about her mother's health and described how she usually spent her days Elena could not think of any other conversation. She could not boast about her grandsons as they appeared to have mixed in well with their relatives, describing their occupations and ambitions.

Andreas was delighted to find his mother was still so mentally alert.

'It's just walking around that's such a problem; so frustrating having to use a wheelchair most of the time. If people are standing near you talking the words go over your head and you can't hear them properly. Then they think you're deaf and start shouting.

I'm very fortunate to be here. Had I still been in that care home in New Orleans I probably wouldn't have anyone to hold a sensible conversation with!'

Andreas nodded sympathetically. He knew what it was like to care for someone who had no real comprehension. Laurie's Alzheimer's had progressed until he became no more than an inanimate body sitting in a wheelchair saying senseless words in response to anything Andreas said to him. When Andreas could no longer cope with nursing him he had reluctantly had him admitted to a care home, but had spent many hours sitting beside his long time companion just holding his hand. He had dreaded finding his mother in a similar mental state, despite Marianne's assurances that she was only a little forgetful on occasions.

'So what have you been doing with yourself recently?' asked Annita.

Andreas shrugged. 'I can't seem to settle and concentrate on writing. The ideas are not coming as they used to. Getting old, I suppose. I'm treating these few days over here as a holiday. Giovanni told me there's a television series being made about Spinalonga and they're using one of the villages for some of the scenes. It's only up the hill so I wandered up and had a look. Then I thought I'd like to go over and have a look at the island. They run trips out from Elounda.'

'Why don't you ask John to take you? He's going over on Wednesday with Helena's boys and their partners. They seem like two nice girls.'

'Do you think they'd mind if I tagged along?'

'I'm sure they wouldn't and John is a mine of information about the island. He's spent most of the winter trying to trace a man who lived over there before the war. According to Yannis's notebooks he escaped and then disappeared. John's met a dead end. Apparently the man surfaced after the war and claimed all his back pension, but he can't find out anything more about him.'

'Really?' Andreas sat thoughtfully. 'Would John talk to me

about him?'

'I'm sure he would. What are you thinking?'

'Well,' Andreas leaned back and closed his eyes. 'It has given me the germ of an idea. It might be too ambitious.'

'Tell me,' commanded Annita.

'I'm thinking a play could open with the man on the island planning to leave. I don't know how he would do so yet.'

'In his bath tub,' interrupted Annita. 'That's how they used to come over to the mainland.'

Andreas nodded. 'Then I'd have to think how he managed to make a living and avoided being found and sent back. The stage could be in two parts; one side is his life and the other is John trying to find him. I could write it as a monologue for each actor until the final scene where the stage becomes one and they meet. No, a monologue won't be right. There will have to be some other characters that make an appearance to help the plot along.'

Annita smiled at her son. She could tell by the look of intense concentration on his face that he was already envisaging the final production.

14th - 16th April 2010

'Did you enjoy your visit to Knossos yesterday?' asked John as his American cousins climbed out of their car.

'It was superb,' said Paul. 'I think we went round the site twice. We'd just think we'd seen everything when one of us would say 'did you see' and we went back to have another look. We should have had a meal before we went in as we didn't leave until they closed. We were all starving by then so went to one of the tavernas opposite and regretted it.'

'Not good?' John raised his eyebrows.

'Nothing actually *wrong* with it, but I got the impression that it had all been cooked a good deal earlier and we had the reheated remains.'

'They probably cater mainly for a lunch time trade. Anyone still at the site when it closed would probably be staying in Heraklion and in a hurry to return to their hotel.' John looked at his watch. 'I asked Uncle Andreas to be here at ten. It's five past now. I hope he won't be much later.'

'Uncle Andreas? He's coming with us?' Paul frowned. This could be like being at Knossos with his mother, moving at a snail's pace and seeing next to nothing.

'The only chance he has is today as they are leaving tomorrow. According to Grandma he's desperate to go over and see the island. He walked up into the village where they've created a pretty good replica of the main street and should start filming any time now. Oh, here he is.'

A taxi drew in and Uncle Andreas climbed out, pushed a note into the driver's hand and spoke to him in Greek. The driver glowered at him and reversed out of the drive way with a squeal of tyres.

'I'm so sorry if I kept you waiting,' apologised Andreas. 'The taxi arrived late; then he tried to overcharge me and expected a tip. I told him he had asked the wrong man.'

'All ready?' asked John. 'You've all got a pullover with you? It can be pretty chilly out on the sea.' He helped his uncle into the waiting boat and checked that the others were seated.

Andreas looked at Spinalonga. 'Is this where the island is closest to the shore?' he asked.

'Plaka is actually the nearest place. It's only a thirty minute trip from here. You'll be fine even if you're not a good sailor.'

Andreas shook his head. 'So if you escaped from Spinalonga where would you expect to land?'

John looked at his uncle curiously. 'That would depend upon the currents, but somewhere along this stretch of coast. When we're on the island you'll see just how close we are to Plaka.'

'So once you'd landed where would you go then?'

John shrugged. 'Probably up into the hills to hide.'

'My mother said they used their bath tubs. Is that so?'

'They were pretty resourceful. The trouble was that once a bath tub was spotted a search was carried out and they were brought back. Their freedom was short lived.'

'Except for one, I understand.' Andreas looked at John. 'My mother said you'd spent the winter trying to find out what happened to a man who left and was never found.'

'How does Grandma always know everything?' John shook his head. 'I asked her a few questions, but she really couldn't help me. I expect she asked Nick what I was up to.'

'Was your grandmother the relative who lived over here?' asked Ronnie curiously as they drew closer to the island with the Venetian walls towering above them.

John laughed. 'Grandma has always refused to set foot on the island. Nick and I were planning to get married over there and I think she was terribly relieved when the weather was too bad for us to make the trip across. No, it was her cousin who had leprosy. I'll tell you all about him when we've moored and are in the square. He was a great character. I'm tremendously proud to claim him as an ancestor.'

'Mother's never mentioned him. He can't be related to us,' stated Mark.

'He's a distant blood relative to you; he would be your great uncle once removed as he was Grandma's cousin. I'll show you a copy of the family tree later and you can see where you connect up,' announced John smugly.

Mark rolled his eyes and shook his head. 'At least he isn't a direct antecedent, thank goodness.'

'What difference would it make if he was?' asked Ronnie.

'Well,' Mark shifted somewhat uncomfortably on the wooden seat. 'You don't really want people like that in the family.'

'Like what? The man was ill. It's not like being a criminal. I'd be more proud of him than I am of one of my ancestors.'

John raised his eyebrows. 'Do tell, Ronnie.'

'He was a forger. He forged people's signatures so he could get hold of their money.'

'What happened to him?'

'He's serving time. He won't be out for another five years.'

Mark looked at her in horror. 'You've never told me you had a criminal in the family.'

'You've never told me you had a leper,' she replied tartly.

'Yes, but.....'

'But nothing. He decided it was easier to forge a signature than paint a picture. I'm grateful for the talent he passed down to me, but I'm certainly not proud of him.'

Mark swallowed hard. 'Who was - is he, Ronnie?'

'My father.'

'Your *father*! I thought you said your mother was a widow.'

'She is. When my father was convicted she divorced him. My stepfather died in a climbing accident.'

John was trying hard to curb his amusement. Despite the situation being tragic for Ronnie, Mark's reaction was comical. He wondered what Mark would say if he knew one of his aunts had worked as a prostitute and the other was a murderess. To have a father convicted of forgery and serving a jail sentence for his crime was almost insignificant.

John moored the boat securely and helped his passengers ashore. 'Follow me. We go through the tunnel and then we'll be in the main square of the village. I'll tell you about old Uncle Yannis's life over here, how they all suffered during the war and how Grandma played such an important role in their lives later on. You can go in and out of their houses and feel their presence.' He saw Uncle Andreas cross himself. 'We'll visit the church and light a candle to their memory, the memory of courageous men and women who fought not only their disease, but the conditions they found over here when they first arrived.'

Once through the tunnel and into the square John climbed up on a block of stone. 'I like to stand here when I talk to people,' he explained. 'Old Uncle Yannis used to stand on a block of stone in the square to talk to the villagers. I like to think I'm standing in his footsteps.'

Teri caught her breath and blinked back a tear. There was something very poignant about the way John spoke and she longed to know more. This was living, recent history, not like Knossos, where so much was based on speculation and assumption.

They followed John as he led the way around the island, showing them the old quay where the food supplies and water barrels were off loaded and the room where everything that left the island had to be disinfected. He pointed across the water.

'There's Plaka, Uncle Andreas. When Old Uncle Yannis lived

over here the family farm was where the self catering apartments are now. Aunt Anna used to come down every day and wave to him. She used to bring Uncle Yannis and my Grandmother Marisa down with her. They visited him regularly. My grandmother was married over here and according to my parents I was conceived over here. Maybe that is why I love this island. It is a part of me.' John grinned at the evident disapproval on Mark's face.

'I'm going in to light a candle,' announced John as they reached the church. 'You're all welcome to do the same, but under no obligation.'

Uncle Andreas followed his nephew inside immediately. Mark and Paul looked at each other, shrugged and followed them, whilst Teri and Ronnie appeared uncertain.

'We're not of the Greek Orthodox faith,' said Teri. 'Is it all right for us to light a candle?'

'Certainly,' nodded John. 'If you're lighting it in the memory of a loved one you can follow any faith or none at all.' He lit a candle and held it for the others to light theirs and they placed them firmly in the tray of sand.

Uncle Andreas still had his candle in his hand. He had walked down to the altar and was now on his knees. John touched Paul on his shoulder and nodded towards the doorway. Understanding they trooped back outside into the sunshine.

'I'm sure he won't be long,' John assured them. 'Look. Over there are the washing troughs. The doctor had those built so they could wash their clothes and those curved tunnels are the old Venetian water conduits.'

'Did a priest come over from the mainland to hold the services?' asked Ronnie curiously.

John shook his head. 'A remarkable priest, Father Minos, devoted his life to the people of this island. He was healthy, but he came over here and lived as one of them, not only tending to their spiritual needs, but helping with the rebuilding. He no longer received a stipend from the church, only the same amount of pension as the lepers were given. What did he do with his? He saved up and bought a bell for the church.' John pointed to where a large bell was mounted.

'Does it still ring?' asked Ronnie.

'I'm sure it does.'

Mark stretched out his hand.

'No,' said John sharply and Mark looked at him in surprise. 'I'm superstitious. Father Minos used to ring it to call a meeting or for a service. He also rang it to announce a death in the community. I don't want to go home and tell Grandma that Uncle Andreas is not coming back.'

'Thank you for your concern for me.' Andreas stood smiling behind them. 'Actually I would have no objection to ending my days here.'

'I would object very strongly if you decided to do that today.' John spoke sternly, but inwardly he was shaking. Did his uncle have some sort of premonition? 'Shall we continue? We'll climb up to the hospital and you'll be able to look down on the buildings, then come down and walk to the end of the inhabited village.'

Both Ronnie and Teri shuddered at the inside of the hospital.

'Fancy having to spend your days in here! It's so dank and cheerless.'

'It was better than having to spend the time in your house relying on a neighbour to help you. Spiro organised a nursing rota and the people were as well cared for as possible.'

'Can we move on?' asked Teri. 'I really feel uncomfortable and depressed in here.'

John led them back down to the main path and along to where the apartment buildings were falling into disrepair. 'These were built after the war by the government. On the ground floor there was a kitchen and communal dining room and the bedrooms upstairs. Any newcomers were allocated rooms here. The older inhabitants refused to move from their houses.'

They continued to the end of the path that finally rounded

the island and led back down towards the tunnel where they had entered. The path narrowed, steep rocks reached up above them and sea stretched away into the distance.

'All right, Uncle? Do you want to continue or would you rather go back and wait for us?'

Andreas looked at his young nephew scornfully. 'It can't be any further to walk on than to walk back. Of course I'm coming with you.'

John nodded approvingly. 'I'll start to tell you about Tassos, the man who managed to get away. There's not a lot to say about this side of the island, except that it's beautiful. The sea is such a brilliant blue during the summer that it hurts your eyes to look at it. In the winter or during a storm the water is grey and the foam churns against the rocks, the wind blowing strongly enough to carry you down into it. It's somewhat unlikely that you'd be able to clamber out.'

As they followed the path down to the graveyard John told Andreas how he had read Old Uncle Yannis's notebooks and the escape of Tassos had intrigued him.

'I couldn't imagine that he had been found and returned to the island and Old Uncle Yannis wouldn't mention it. I finally managed to find out that after the war he had withdrawn all his pension arrears that had accrued and then he disappeared again. I don't know where to start looking for him now and it's doubtful if he's still alive.'

'When we get back to the house would you mind if I made some notes?'

John shrugged. 'Not at all. You can always e-mail me if you have any questions. If you suddenly come up with a brilliant idea for me to find him please let me know.'

Andreas smiled. 'I doubt very much that I'll do that, but I do think this story has all the makings of a very fine play. I wish my father was still alive. He'd be able to tell me all the medical terms so I could baffle my audience and then disclose the common name for a complaint.'

John smiled, remembering how Saffron had interpreted the abbreviated notes that he had copied from the medical records.

John pointed out the old Turkish graveyard as they passed and then led them to the small cemetery that had been used by the lepers. 'We're not allowed access now. The authorities say it's dangerous. I don't actually believe them. At one time all the graves were open. The bones had been removed,' John hastened to assure them. 'They've filled them in so no one could fall into them now.'

'How deep were they?' asked Paul.

'A couple of feet, no more. There's very little depth of soil over here and even the effort of digging a shallow grave would have been too much for many of them.'

'What did they do with the bones they removed?' asked Teri.

'They placed them in the tower along with the others. Old Uncle Yannis is in there, along with his first wife and adopted daughter.'

'So everyone who went back to Athens has been returned here for burial?' remarked Paul.

John shook his head. 'By coincidence Old Uncle Yannis was visiting the island with Nicolas and Elena. That's Nick's father and aunt, not your grandmother. Old Uncle sat down to wait whilst they climbed to the top of the hill and when they returned he had died. Earlier Nicolas had rung the church bell.' He gave Mark a stern glance.

Teri shivered, despite the day being warm. 'So that is why you wouldn't let Mark ring it.'

John smiled sheepishly. 'I told you, I'm superstitious. Anyway,' he continued, 'Aunt Anna insisted her brother was brought back to the island.'

'Was that allowed?' frowned Mark.

'As far as I know no one asked permission. There was a private service over here for him and then they held one in the church at Plaka and placed a coffin in the grave.'

'So he isn't actually over here. They just had a service here.'

John shook his head. 'His body was placed in the tower and the empty coffin in the grave.'

'Suppose the authorities found out?' asked Ronnie, wide eyed at the thought of the subterfuge.

'Well, if they'd found out at the time they would probably have insisted that his body was recovered and placed in the graveyard at the church. If they found out now they wouldn't have a hope of knowing which bones were his.'

'Surely they would be the ones at the top.'

'Don't forget they cleared these graves and put the bones in the tower. They would have been the ones on the top. Even if they had known Old Uncle was there they wouldn't have been able to be certain which skull was his. It could have rolled away as the body disintegrated.'

Teri shuddered. 'Do we need to have this conversation? You're making me feel quite squeamish.'

John smiled at her. 'Sorry. You did ask what happened to the bones.'

Teri smiled guiltily. 'You just didn't give me the answer I was expecting.'

'Why did Nicolas and Elena want to climb up the hill?'

John waved his arm. 'There's a path that takes you up to the remains of the Venetian fortress and you have a spectacular view. I don't mind waiting if you want to climb up there.'

Andreas nodded. 'You young ones go if you want. I'll be quite happy to sit here and talk to John.'

'Might as well,' said Paul. 'We may never get another opportunity.'

'I wish I was younger so I could join them,' sighed Andreas as he sat down on the grass beside John. 'Now tell me more about this man Tassos.'

When they finally left the island John sailed round the side that was open to the ravages of the sea.

'This gives you an idea how clever the Venetians were. They used the cliffs and natural rock formations as part of their defence systems. It would have been virtually impossible for an attacker to gain entry to the fortress from the seaward side and once they tried to sail into the bay they would have been blown out of the water. Wherever you see crenulations is where they had a cannon placed. It took the Turks twenty six years to finally capture Spinalonga,' ended John with a touch of pride in his voice.

'We'll sail over to Plaka and have a late lunch. I know a couple of them are open this week and they serve good, fresh fish. After lunch we'll walk up to the shops. I'm hoping Saff will be there. I've something to show her.'

Teri winked at Ronnie. They had not mentioned to their respective partners that they had already visited the area briefly.

'So what do you think, Saff? Is that box good enough?'

Saffron picked up the small wooden box and carefully examined the photograph of Spinalonga that John had glued to the lid and then secured with a silver trim.

'It's beautiful, John. It's even better than I had hoped.'

'What about these?'

John produced three more boxes, each with a different photograph on the lid. They were the same as the larger photographs Saffron had displayed.

Saffron shook her head. 'They don't appeal to me at all, but I'm sure some of the tourists will think them wonderful. Why would you want a photograph of a donkey when you can have one of Spinalonga?'

'Many people are animal lovers.'

'Yes, fine, so buy a photograph, but not in preference to Spinalonga.'

'You're biased,' John grinned. 'Do you want me to make some more like this or only with the island?'

Saffron considered. 'How about twenty of the donkey, twenty

of the church and forty of Spinalonga? That uses up all the blank boxes. I'll order some more and when I know which designs are the most popular I'll ask you to make up another batch. That man in England who paints the enamels sent me a quote. I can't possibly afford to buy them, although I'm sure he's offering them to me at a good price. I'm going to ask Giovanni to offer them to Uncle Yannis. If he wants them he might be willing for me to have the hand painted miniature pots.'

John smiled at Saffron's naivety. There was no way his uncle would give up an article he would expect to sell in his shop at a profit.

'So,' said John as he steered the boat away from the jetty at Plaka. 'You've been to Knossos and Spinalonga. What are you planning next?'

'A quick visit to Mum and Dad to say goodbye to them tomorrow, then just a general exploration of the area. The girls say they have something to show us.'

John raised his eyebrows and looked at them. Teri shook her head.

'We'll tell you when the boys are not around. We want it to be a complete surprise.'

'Saffron has invited us up for lunch on Friday. We're going to leave the car in Elounda and she says we just walk up the hill. There are two more villages called Elounda. One of them is where they're making the film.'

'Well worth a visit,' interrupted Andreas. 'I was interested in the filming, of course, but those two little villages appear almost unspoilt. They don't look as if they've changed for a hundred years.'

'Or the inhabitants,' chuckled John. 'It's mostly the elderly villagers who live up there. Many of them were born in the house they live in. They refuse to leave their homes and come down to live with their children in the town.'

'I can't say I blame them,' said Ronnie. 'They have deep roots.'

John nodded. 'That's true, but when they can no longer look after themselves they expect their children to move back up there with them. It can cause a good deal of friction in the family.'

Ronnie nodded. She knew how she would feel if she was ever expected to move in to look after Mark's mother.

As they drew in to the private landing stage at Uncle Yannis's they could see Helena and Greg sitting on the patio with Marianne and Giovanni.

'I'm surprised to see your parents still here.' John looked at his watch. 'Well, I suppose it isn't that late. They're probably thinking they can share your taxi back to Elounda. I was planning to drive you home, Uncle, so they'll just have to squeeze in with us if they want a ride.'

'That's very good of you, John, but I'd be quite happy to have a taxi.'

'I won't hear of it. I'll drive you home. I go down each evening to collect my dog and take him for a run.'

'What kind of dog do you have?' asked Ronnie.

John grinned. 'The ugliest mongrel you've ever set eyes on. He's gorgeous and so intelligent. I'd have him up at the house but Aunt Ourania's frightened of dogs and he'd probably chase her precious cat.'

As they stepped from the boat onto the jetty Helena came hurrying towards them.

'Thank goodness you're back. Have you heard?'

'Heard what?' asked Mark. 'What's happened?'

John looked over anxiously towards the patio. His parents seemed relaxed and not unduly concerned.

'The volcano.'

'Where?'

'Iceland I believe.'

'Oh,' Mark smiled, 'I thought you meant here.'

'No, but it might as well be. All the flights to London have been cancelled.'

'Cancelled. Why?' Mark looked towards his father for enlightenment.

'Ash in the air they said.'

'It means we're going to be stuck over here. What are we going to do?' Helena wrung her hands.

'There's nothing you can do except wait for the airports to re-open,' replied Paul.

'No, I mean what are we going to do with ourselves stuck down here? There's nothing at all to do.'

'What would you be doing in New Orleans next week?' asked Greg patiently.

'I've an appointment at the beauticians, lunch with Noreen and we're out to dinner the following Saturday with the Lange-Ellisons. I need to have time to decide whether I have something suitable to wear or if I need to go shopping.'

John had a problem controlling his laughter and looked at his mother who was trying not to smile.

'We're waiting for Vasilis to 'phone. He said he would check the situation out with the airlines. Everything could be back to normal by tomorrow. We can't make any decisions until we've heard from him,' said Marianne.

'Well, better to know about it now than when you get to the airport. You could be sitting there for days waiting.' John shook his head at his aunt. 'There's absolutely *nothing* to do at the airport.' He picked up an empty bottle from the table. 'Fancy a drink anyone?'

'I'd love a beer,' said Teri and Ronnie nodded in agreement.

Helena looked at them scathingly. 'Whoever's driving must only have a soft drink.'

Paul shrugged. 'Well, I'm having a beer whether I'm driving or not. I'm sure one won't put me over the limit, besides, we're only going a short distance up the road.'

Mark hesitated; then nodded. 'Yes, I'll have one too.' They neither of them admitted they had enjoyed a glass of beer with

309

their late lunch.

Helena glared at John. The boy was a bad influence.

It was an hour before Vasilis telephoned to say that all flights that would need to pass through the volcanic ash cloud had been cancelled. If the ash entered the aeroplane engines they could fail and cause a catastrophic disaster.

'I'm afraid that means you could be stuck on Crete for a while.' Giovanni smiled at his sister-in-law. 'Vasilis has promised to keep us informed of any developments and we'll check the internet continually for updates.'

Marianne frowned. 'What about our bookings for next week? Have they been cancelled?'

'Bound to be. If flights are not leaving, others can't arrive.' John rose from the table. 'I'd better check if Nick has finished giving the girls' their tea and see if I'm on bath duty.'

Andrew arrived carrying his holdall as John was about to leave the patio. He walked over to Giovanni, looking concerned.

'Would you be able to call a taxi for me, please? I couldn't find any local numbers and I need to get to the airport as soon as possible.'

Giovanni frowned. 'The flights are grounded temporarily.'

Andrew nodded. 'I know. I need to get to Spain. Other arrangements have been made for me to travel on from there.'

Helena looked at her brother in delight. 'We could all come with you.'

Andrew shook his head. 'That's not possible.' He turned back to Giovanni. 'I'm sorry to be leaving you so abruptly. I enjoyed my visit and I'd like to return one day. Marianne, it's been a pleasure to be here with the family. Is it possible to say goodbye to Grandma before I leave?'

'Of course. She'd never forgive you if you left without seeing her. Giovanni will call you when the taxi arrives. Leave your bag there.'

John looked at his father and raised his eyebrows. What was so special about Andrew that arrangements could be made for him to return to America?

'I don't see why we couldn't leave with Andrew,' said Helena petulantly. 'Obviously there's no problem with flights from Spain. It's only over here, of course, that there's a panic.'

'Do Nick's parents know?' asked John. 'I doubt that a delay will make any difference to her grandparents, but I expect her father is due back at school on Monday.'

'Greg's also due back in the office on Monday,' Helena reminded her nephew. 'Special arrangements should be made for people who need to get back.'

John shook his head. 'Well, I'll leave you to sort out those special arrangements whilst I have a word with Nick.'

As John crossed the lounge to the rooms he and Nicola occupied Andrew was just emerging from his grandmother's room. John held out his hand.

'Sorry you're having to rush off. I haven't really had time to get to know you. Tell me, what work you do that enables you to get preferential treatment?'

'I work in the White House.'

'Really? Doing what?'

Andrew shook his head. 'I'm just a clerk who deals with mundane paperwork each day.'

'Yeah,' said John sceptically, 'and I'm the Greek Prime Minister.'

'Rather you than me,' smiled Andrew. 'That sounds like my taxi. Say goodbye to your wife and children for me.' Andrew hurried back to the patio to collect his bag.

'I'm sure Mum and Dad don't know or they would have called me,' frowned Nicola. 'They were planning to take my grandparents up to Kritsa today to show them the village and drive back across country to take in some of the other villages before arriving here to say goodbye. They shouldn't be much longer as they know the girls will have to go to bed.'

'Am I on bath duty?' asked John.

'Yes, but we'll wait until they've left. No doubt they'll want to hold them for a few minutes.'

'If the girls allow them to. All they want to do now is haul themselves around the furniture. Cuddling days are gone and I missed most of them,' reflected John sadly as Elisabetta attempted to climb up his leg.

'How has Aunt Helena taken the news?'

'It's a disaster as far as she's concerned, but I tell you what is interesting, Andrew has managed to get a flight to Spain and 'arrangements' have been made for him to get back to Washington. Did you know he worked at the White House?'

Nicola shook her head. 'What does he do?'

'He claimed he was just a clerk.'

'He probably is.'

'So why is he being given priority arrangements? I would have thought a clerk getting back to work on time was less important than your father being in school.'

Nicola shrugged. 'Carry Lisa out to the patio for me. It's so difficult carrying both of them at once now they're so big.'

'You'll have to have a yoke with a carrying bag on each side.'

Nicola looked at John with mock sternness. 'I spent months looking like an elephant and now you want me to look like a donkey! It will be easier once they can both walk a short distance. I thought it was difficult managing whilst they were babies, but at least I could put them down and they'd be where I'd left them. Now if I turn my back they're gone.'

John placed Elisabetta on his mother's lap and she immediately wriggled to get down on the ground.

'Let her go, Marianne. We'll watch what she gets up to.'

'So, what's the plan now?' John looked at his assembled relations.

'We've looked on the internet and it appears that Italy, Spain and Greece are not affected at the moment, but the ash cloud is travelling over France and Germany. It could easily come down here. Angelo and Francesca shouldn't have a problem.'

'Maybe we could go to Italy,' suggested Helena.

Greg shook his head. 'There's no point in doing that. We still wouldn't be able to get a flight to Heathrow.'

Helena pouted and turned her back on her husband. 'At least you boys are all right. You're on holiday over here.'

'That's a point.' Marianne turned to Giovanni and spoke in Greek. 'We ought to check with Vasi and see if it's possible for everyone to stay on at his hotel. If he has other guests arriving he may need their rooms.'

'In that case your sister could be camping on the beach! I'll 'phone him now, but if they can't fly out other visitors can't fly in.'

'That depends where they're coming from. We should have room at the self catering if he can't keep them.'

'That would certainly make one person very happy!'

'My grandparents wouldn't mind,' said Nicola who had been following the conversation.

'It would not be a problem for me either,' Andreas added. 'In fact if this ash cloud means I have to stay in this delightful area for another week I shall be only too pleased. I have no reason to rush back to New York. May I suggest, provided your friend has rooms at his hotel, that my sister, niece and her husband go to Heraklion? I feel they would pass their time more happily in the city.'

John wagged his finger at his uncle. 'I have a suspicion that you would prefer some distance between you. I didn't realise you spoke Greek so fluently. Good job we didn't say anything detrimental about you.'

'It would not be the first time I had been insulted,' smiled Andreas easily. 'I will be quite happy to move into a self catering unit. My needs are simple. I have a coffee and croissant for breakfast and can take a taxi into Elounda for my meals.'

'I wouldn't hear of it,' Marianne replied immediately. 'You'll be welcome to come down and have your meals with us.'

'What are you saying about me?' asked Helena and Marianne looked at her sister in surprise.

'Nothing. Uncle Andreas suggested you might prefer to stay in Heraklion.'

'That would be far better. We could all stay up in Heraklion at that nice hotel where we spent our first night. I was looking forward to going back there. It was so comfortable. You boys would like it there. They have a gymnasium on the premises.'

Ronnie fixed Mark with a steely glare and was relieved when he answered his mother.

'No, Mum, we've arranged to stay down here and have a walking holiday.'

'You have the car. You could always drive out from Heraklion each day.'

Paul shook his head. 'We made our plans some time ago. If we'd wanted to spend the time sitting in a hotel with you and Dad we wouldn't have asked the girls to come with us and we would only have stayed the week.'

Teri smiled at him gratefully. Having visited Knossos, the only attraction Heraklion held for her now was a visit to the museum.

'I'm sure my parents won't want to go to Heraklion,' said Nicola firmly. 'Uncle Andreas wants to stay here and there's no reason why Aunt Elena can't get a flight home to Athens as she planned. Uncle Angelo and Francesca don't appear to have a problem returning to Italy so that would just be two rooms you had to ask Vasilis to reserve.'

Elena spoke up timidly. 'I'd like to stay here. I'd wanted to come for two weeks, but Helena said it wasn't a good idea. I'll be able to spend some more time with my mother and I don't mind staying in the self catering units.'

'Don't be silly, mother,' said Helena immediately. 'You'll

come to Heraklion with us.'

Elena looked between her two daughters. 'No, I'll stay here if Marianne doesn't mind.'

Marianne reached out and squeezed her mother's hand. 'I'd be only too delighted for you to stay longer. I'm sure Grandma will be thrilled.'

Giovanni ran a hand over his thinning hair. 'I'll phone Vasilis and make a provisional booking for longer than the one night for Helena and Greg. We'll see what the situation is tomorrow before we make any firm arrangements. Ouch!' Giovanni lifted Joanna's hand from his leg. 'I don't mind you using me as a climbing frame, but you are *not* to pinch.'

Joanna smiled angelically up at her grandfather and he lifted her up onto his lap where she made a grab for the empty glasses.

Mark drove back to the self catering apartments. 'What happens if this ash cloud gets worse?' he asked dolefully.

Paul shrugged. 'Well, there's nothing we can do about it.'

'I know,' frowned Mark. 'I'm just concerned about Mum and Dad. Do you think we should go up and stay with them in Heraklion until the flights are back to normal?'

'Mark,' Ronnie's voice was icy. 'You are not attached to your mother by your umbilical cord. If you go up to Heraklion to be with your parents I will be taking the first available flight from here to the States and you can expect to find your belongings on the step when you get home. They're adults. They have each other and their relatives speak Greek.'

'Ronnie's right,' insisted Teri. 'This was arranged as a holiday for the four of us. Your parents were not included and they don't need you to look after them.'

'It's just the way Mum is.' Paul tried to smooth over the awkward situation that was developing.

'Yes, and I'm the way I am,' replied Ronnie. 'If you're planning to spend *our* holiday dancing attendance on your mother you're on your own. Teri and I will find somewhere else to stay and hire a car. You can do as you please.'

'This ash problem is getting worse.' Giovanni pointed to the diagram on the computer screen. 'I'm getting mails continually from the travel agents asking us to accommodate guests until the travel restrictions are lifted. That's all very well, but what happens if tourists from Italy and Spain arrive and their rooms are occupied by other Europeans?'

Marianne peered over his shoulder. 'Hopefully that won't happen. I'll look at our booking lists. Even having moved the relatives into the self catering we should have a few spare units and it has freed up rooms for Vasi.'

Giovanni shook his head. 'If we have to start turning new bookings away we'll be losing money. I told John we could give everyone a free stay for a week. I can't start charging them for extra days when it's no fault of theirs that they're stuck over here indefinitely.'

'Look on the positive side, they'll need food. They'll be buying supplies from the taverna or going there for a quick meal. John went up early and he 'phoned a while ago to say he'd been busy and needed some more bread. Marcus has driven in to Elounda and will take it up to him.'

'This situation could go on for months.'

'If it does I'm sure the travel agents will arrange ships to transport their customers. After all, they'll be losing money also,' Marianne tried to console her husband.

'Even when the crisis is over people could decide not to come here in case it happens again.'

'And a number of people who wanted to come and were unable to get a booking will be only too pleased to take their place. There really is no point in you worrying over it. Personally I'm delighted that Elizabeth and Nicolas are staying longer. We'll have a proper chance to catch up.'

Giovanni smiled at his wife. 'That is a bonus. I find Eleanor a bit of a trial. She doesn't seem to be interested in anything.'

'She's the wrong age group. She could do with a companion of her own age.'

'Thank goodness Helena decided she wanted to go to Heraklion. I don't know how Greg puts up with her. Nothing is ever right for her.'

'I think Greg's used to it and doesn't take a lot of notice. I wonder what she will find to complain about at the Central? I'll warn Vasilis or he'll be terribly hurt and think he's letting his customers down.'

'We should have sent her to one of the hotels that caters for the lorry drivers,' grinned Giovanni. 'Then she may have had cause for complaint.'

Mark took Paul to one side. 'I 'phoned Mum this morning and she said she had slept a little better, despite the fact that the hotel is right in the centre of the town and she is so worried about getting home.'

'I honestly don't know what her panic is. You heard what her plans were for next week. They can all be put off until a later date except the dinner with the Lange-Ellisons. They'll just have to send their apologies and explain they were unable to return. Just don't talk about them in front of the girls. It will only end up with you and Ronnie having a row. She is right, you know, Mum doesn't need you to look after her, she has Dad with her.'

'I thought if they were stuck there for any length of time we could go up to Heraklion. I know the girls would like to go to the museum.'

'So would I,' replied Paul, 'But I think we should plan that for after Mum and Dad have gone home. You'll go off to see Mum and I'll be obliged to go with you. We'll never get to the museum and the girls will give us hell. I really enjoyed yesterday when we went over to the Causeway. The girls were so proud of themselves for finding that taverna and the mosaic.'

'Today could be boring. How long do you think we'll have to stay at Saffron's?'

'She's giving us lunch and we're going to look at the map and decide where we want to go. We'll have to stay a couple of hours at least.'

Mark shrugged. 'Let's hope these Elounda villages she's recommended are worth seeing.'

'Uncle Andreas said the one they're using for that film set was interesting. It really is like Spinalonga.'

'I hope she'll be able to recommend some decent places to walk.'

'What about visiting some of the other sites?' suggested Paul. 'She should be able to tell us if they are worth the drive. Knossos isn't the only one on the map.'

'I'll go along with whatever you and the girls want.'

'With a good grace, I hope, or everyone will be miserable.'

Saffron opened the gates as her visitors arrived and walked down the drive to greet them.

'Wow!' said Ronnie. 'This is some house.'

'Vasi's father built it for Cathy after they were married.'

'So why aren't they living here now?' asked Teri.

'The stairs became too much for Cathy. She had a couple of falls and they thought it more practical to buy Vasi's flat from him. It also meant that Vasilis was closer to the hotel in Heraklion. Anyway, come in and tell me what you thought of Kato and Pano Elounda.'

'I loved them,' announced Ronnie. 'I could spend all day every day there painting and sketching.'

'That's about all there is to do in them,' said Mark gloomily. 'How on earth do people pass their time?'

Saffron smiled. 'It's mostly the old folk who live there now. They walk down to Elounda for their shopping, then they have the house to clean and washing to be done along with preparing a meal. They most of them have a little garden where they grow vegetables and herbs, some of them still go to their fields so they find plenty to occupy themselves.'

'That's all very well now they're old, but what did they do when they were young?' asked Mark.

Saffron's lips twitched in amusement. 'Much the same. You have to remember these are country people. Even now many of them will never have visited Heraklion. A bus journey to Aghios Nikolaos is a big event for them and they'll talk about it before they go and for some time after they return. Now, come round to the patio. I've left Marjorie supervising the lunch.'

'Have some of them truly not been to Heraklion?' asked Teri in surprise.

Saffron shook her head. 'They see no reason to go up there. Very few of them would see the attraction of Knossos or visiting the museum and why would they go up there to shop when they can buy everything they need locally? Have a seat. It's a shame it isn't warm enough yet to swim or we could sit down by the pool.'

Paul looked down the expanse of garden to where a swimming pool glinted invitingly. 'I'd have brought my trunks if I'd known you had a pool,' he said longingly.

Saffron laughed at him. 'It would be freezing. Lambros has only just filled it and it will probably be June before we use it. Sometimes it can be warm enough for a quick swim in May, but I wouldn't recommend it. Now, what would you like to drink? I've fruit juice or beer and we'll open a bottle of wine to have with our lunch.'

'I'll have a small beer,' decided Paul. 'If you are going to tell us about some good walks I'll need to keep a clear head or I'll not remember where you told us to go.' He spread the map out on the table. 'We don't want to spend too much time driving so we're really only looking at the area around here at the moment. We plan to drive up to Rethymnon next week and stay there for a couple of days so we can see something of the area around there.'

'Well,' Saffron considered. 'You have to remember that I have no experience of the walking, but I can recommend some interesting villages and there is Kritsa Gorge. Most of the dedicated walkers take to a goat path or donkey trail and go into the hills or just stop by a dried up river bed and walk along that.'

'I'm not sure we're that dedicated,' Teri shook her head. 'I enjoy walking provided there is something to see along the way or a beautiful view at the end. I don't want to walk from one hill to the next just for the sake of it.'

Saffron nodded. 'I suggest you drive to some of the villages along the coast or a short distance into the hills. I would recommend that you go to Gournia to see the ancient settlement there. You could walk up a trail to Vasiliki and have lunch in the old town, then take the path to Faneromenis Monastery and back to Gournia. That's virtually a round trip. Another day you could go to Kritsa, that's a beautiful old town, and walk the gorge there or go to the site of Lato. I wouldn't suggest you try to do both in one day. If you went to Lato you could walk to Hamilo for a meal or start from Hamilo and walk to Lato and back. Remember I'm only giving you ideas. You don't have to go by the routes I propose.'

Paul wrote down the names of the villages and the routes Saffron had suggested. 'It makes sense to take your advice. We'll need somewhere to stop off for a meal and walking should be enjoyable. We don't want to end up in the middle of nowhere, but nor do we want to be walking along a road.'

'You'll see dirt roads and tracks going off just about everywhere. Many of them just lead into the fields. It's a better idea to make for a village rather than just turn off and hope you'll arrive somewhere. You ought to think about driving up to the Lassithi Plateau. The villages up there are interesting and some of the views are spectacular. Again, if you drive up towards Heraklion there are a number of caves that can be visited.'

Teri shook her head. 'I'm definitely not a cave person. I don't like to think of all the weight above me. I know it's irrational and you others can go if you want and I'll wait for you.'

'We'll put caves at the bottom of our list for when we've run out of other things to do,' Paul smiled.

'I don't think you'll run out of places to go. When you're up at Rethymnon you ought to visit the gorge at Mili. It is different from the others and quite beautiful. The river still runs through and everywhere is lush and green.'

'Have you been there?' asked Mark.

Saffron shook her head. 'Not to walk the trail. I went to have a look at the church and walked down to the river.'

Ronnie nodded enthusiastically. 'I'm taking photographs the whole time. I just wish I could stay here for longer and spend the time painting. It's an artist's paradise.'

'Marjorie suggested turning the house into a centre for walkers and artists.'

'What's stopping you?'

'It would need a considerable amount of work to make it suitable. There are only three large bedrooms at present. They could be divided to make six, but then we would need someone to run it.'

'Well if you decide to go ahead with the idea just let me know.'

'You'd come all the way back and stay here so you could paint?'

Ronnie shook her head. 'No, I'd be willing to live here and run it for you.'

'Really?' Saffron smiled. 'What about your work in the States?'

'I'm only a customer advisor in real estate. I spend most of my time at the computer typing up contracts or answering the 'phone.'

Mark scowled. 'You'd very soon be bored out of your mind living here.'

Ronnie shook her head. 'I'd be living in a beautiful place, a bit of cleaning and cooking and then the rest of the day is mine to spend painting. My idea of heaven.'

'If you did use the house for holiday makers where would you and Vasi live?' asked Teri.

'A little house down in the town would suit me. I don't need anything grand. Provided there was a room where Marjorie could come and stay I'd be happy.'

'So, shall we add Mili to our list?' asked Mark, trying to divert the conversation away from Vasi's house.

'Sounds like a good idea. Anywhere else you can think of Saffron?'

19th - 28th April 2010

Giovanni drew up outside the self catering apartments. He had been relieved when he had heard on the news that the ash cloud from the Icelandic volcano was dispersing and flights should be able to resume within the next couple of days.

He knocked on the door of the apartment occupied by Paul and Teri, hoping they had not already left to drive to Rethymnon. Teri answered, a towel wrapped around herself, her hair hanging limp and damp.

'I'm sorry,' Giovanni apologised. 'I have disturbed you.'

'Not at all. I've just finished in the shower and Paul is having his. If you can give me a moment I'll give him a shout and put some clothes on.'

Giovanni smiled. It would have been more sensible to have telephoned as Marianne had suggested, but he had needed to come up to the apartments to replace a faulty catch on a window.

'There's no need for me to come in. I just wanted to let you know the latest news about the ash. It appears to be clearing and they think flights will be able to start again in the next few days.'

'Oh, that is good news. I'm sure Mark will be most relieved to know his mother will be able to return home soon.'

'Along with everyone else who has been stranded, no doubt. That was all I came to tell you. Enjoy your time in Rethymnon.' Giovanni walked back to his car to collect his tools and the new window catch.

Teri relayed Giovanni's news to Paul when he came out from the shower.

'I'm not going to tell Mark yet. He'll only 'phone Mum and she'll keep him talking for hours. We don't want to be hanging around here for too long. We said we'd be ready at ten and it's nearly that now.'

Teri hesitated, knowing she could well regret her decision. 'Why don't we call in on them briefly on our way? I do mean *briefly*, Paul. An hour at the most.'

Paul smiled at her. 'I'm sure Mum would appreciate it.' He squeezed Teri's shoulders. 'Are you prepared to pacify Ronnie?'

Terri nodded. 'I suggest you two spend some time with your parents and Ronnie and I will go and have a look at the Venetian fortress. We really can't spend too long in Heraklion today if we want to reach Rethymnon this afternoon.'

'The fort may not be open, it's Monday, remember.'

'Oh, well,' Teri shrugged. 'I'm sure we'll find something to occupy us.'

'Do you think Giovanni minded that we had changed our weeks around? I know we said originally that we would spend this week down here, but it really makes more sense to go further afield whilst we're still fresh. If we don't want to go anywhere next week we can sit here in the gardens. If we're in a hotel in the town we'll be obliged to go out somewhere.'

'I don't think it mattered to Giovanni one bit. He allocated two apartments to us for the three weeks and we have to pay him for two weeks whether we're here or not. Are you ready?'

Paul patted his pockets. 'Car keys, apartment keys, wallet, mobile. Yes, I've got everything. The map is in the car.'

Ronnie could hardly disguise her delight. Mark had entered the Central Hotel in Heraklion only to be told by Vasilis that his parents were out. Helena had decided she had to go shopping as it was likely they would be leaving the following day.

'As if she hasn't had plenty of time to shop,' grumbled Mark. 'We should have called to say we were coming.'

'Why don't we have a coffee at the hotel? You could call them from here and say we'll wait at the hotel until,' Paul looked at his watch, 'twelve thirty. We really should leave then if we want to find somewhere to eat and reach Rethymnon at a reasonable time.'

Vasilis joined them and asked their plans for the day. Paul explained they were headed for Rethymnon and had only called in to say goodbye to their parents. Vasilis had smiled to himself. It would be a relief when the lady left. She had been such a nuisance to the reception staff, asking them continually to contact the airlines to see if there were any flights available.

'And what are your plans whilst you are in Rethymnon?' asked Vasilis.

'We thought we ought to go to Chania and see Souda Bay and the cemeteries. It depends upon time, really. We only plan to spend a day there. From Rethymnon we want to drive down to Spili; there's a walking trail there and there are a couple of other walks we want to do whilst we are that end of the country.'

Vasilis nodded. Walking held no attraction for him. 'Could I ask a favour of you when you leave Chania?'

'Of course.' Paul's heart sank. Were they going to be asked to go miles out of their way to call on some old Greek lady and have to spend hours trying to talk to her?

'Just before you reach Chania there is a country road. A short distance down that road is a large memorial. I would be very grateful if you would place some flowers there. My wife's father had it erected in memory of his first wife and his son. I will be able to give you exact directions.'

Paul nodded. It would be churlish of him to refuse the simple request.

'I still can't get hold of Mum,' complained Mark. 'It says her 'phone is switched off.'

'Try Dad,' said Paul laconically.

'I have, and I've left a message on his voice mail.'

Paul looked at his watch. 'They have ten more minutes to

put in an appearance and then we are leaving. They could have decided to go out somewhere for the whole day.'

Ronnie and Teri kept glancing surreptitiously at their watches and rose immediately the allotted time was up.

'Come on,' said Ronnie. 'I'm hungry and I don't want to eat in Heraklion. I want to stop in one of the villages.'

'Good idea,' Teri followed her lead. 'Let's get back to the car and see where we should make for.'

Smiling to himself Paul followed them, whilst Mark tried to contact his mother again.

Whilst they were eating lunch in Paleokastro Mark's 'phone rang.

'Where are you? What's wrong? Has something happened?' They could all hear his mother's anguished voice.

'There's nothing wrong, Mum. We were passing through Heraklion and just thought we'd call in to say goodbye as you should be leaving tomorrow.'

'Where are you now?'

'I'm not sure, Paleo something.'

'Well come back,' Helena commanded.

Paul and the girls shook their heads vehemently.

'That's not possible, Mum. We're on our way to Rethymnon. We waited for you and tried to 'phone you and Dad.'

'I was having a fish pedicure. My feet feel wonderful now. I wanted your father to have one as well, but he refused. Silly man. Then I had my hair washed and dried. I'm not terribly pleased with the result; the girl took no notice when I told her what to do.'

'I left a message on Dad's voice mail.'

'He forgot to bring his 'phone out with him and mine was switched off. If you come back to Heraklion we can have dinner this evening. I'll book a table with Vasilis.'

'No, Mum. We will be in Rethymnon. We can't have dinner with you.'

Ronnie rolled her eyes. Mark's mother was unbelievable. She

was sure Marianne did not try to rule John's life.

'I'll get the bill,' she announced in a loud voice. 'We really do have to leave *now*.'

Mark was still explaining to his mother that they were unable to return to Heraklion when they climbed back into the car. Paul revved the engine and the girls opened the windows to allow the noise of the traffic to come in.

Mark frowned. 'I can't hear you, Mum. There's too much noise and my battery is getting low. I'll have to phone you back when I've recharged it.'

Ronnie smiled to herself; if the battery to Mark's 'phone really was low she would make quite sure he could not find his charger.

'Plan of campaign, then.' Paul spread the map out on the table. They had walked from their hotel down to the picturesque waterfront at Rethymnon and finally, after much deliberation and looking at the fish on display had finally settled for a meal at the Seven Brothers.

'Do you really think they are brothers?' asked Teri. 'I keep looking to see if I can spot any resemblance between them.'

'Provided we have a good meal I don't mind whether they're brothers or not. Now, where do you want to go tomorrow? Walking or Chania?'

'Chania,' said Ronnie immediately. 'I feel that is almost a duty visit. I'm not sure if I will enjoy looking around cemeteries and realising just how many young men lost their lives.'

Paul nodded. 'We can see if we can find the memorial Vasilis asked me to place flowers on as we drive back. The fresher they are the longer they'll last. He's given me exact directions, so it should be easy enough to find and is hardly out of our way.'

'I'll take a photo,' promised Ronnie. 'That way he'll know we really did bother to go there.'

'Suppose we can't find it?' queried Teri.

'Then I don't take a photo. Simple. What shall we do the next days?'

'How about walking Agiou Andoniou Gorge and then Prasiano Gorge the following day? It looks as if the two meet up, but it could be too ambitious to try to walk the whole length and walk back in one day. Then we could drive down to Spili and there's a walk shown there. We don't have to do it, of course. See how we feel. Then we go to Mili Gorge on our final full day. How does that sound? Everyone in agreement?'

'That was a good idea of yours, Paul, to drive back to Heraklion on the old road. I really enjoyed stopping at all those villages.'

'Blame Ronnie for all our stops,' grinned Paul. 'She was the one who insisted that she had to have a photograph of every war memorial.'

'I also photographed the houses and some of the spring flowers,' replied Ronnie. 'I find everywhere so interesting and so very different from back home. I can understand why Marianne decided to stay and live out here.'

'You don't think Giovanni had anything to do with her decision?' asked Teri.

'I'm sure he did,' smiled Ronnie. 'Actually I'm looking forward to being back in Elounda at the apartments. I feel quite at home there, more so than when I was in Rethymnon. Do you think we should call in and say that we're back?'

Mark shook his head. 'If we stop they could think we were after a meal. Why don't we freshen up and then go down to the waterfront and eat where we had lunch with Mum and Dad? We can call in on the way back. We ought to offer to take them out for a meal before we leave and we could arrange a date.'

Ronnie sighed heavily. 'Only one more week. I'm not looking forward to being back in the States and having to go to work each day.'

'We'll make the most of our last few days. How about if we walk Kritsa Gorge tomorrow?' suggested Paul. 'The temperature has certainly risen since we arrived and we don't want it too hot for walking. With a bit of luck we might be able to get in a swim before we leave.'

'Well, I'm ready. I've filled our water bottles and made a couple of ham rolls for each of us.'

'Sun screen? Insect repellent?' asked Paul.

Teri nodded. 'They're in the bag, along with my sun hat.'

Paul skimmed his own hat across the room to her. 'Pop mine in as well. I doubt if I'll need it but I don't want to come back with sunstroke.'

Mark led the way along Kritsa gorge and looked at the massive boulders that now barred their way.

'Are you sure we're in the right place?' he asked.

Teri nodded. 'The sign said Kritsa Gorge.'

'Do you really want to climb up there? If it's like that all the way it will be tough going.'

'Tapes is about ten miles away. Do you want to drive up and meet us there?' asked Ronnie mischievously. 'We won't tell on you.'

'Of course not,' replied Mark, disgruntled. 'I was thinking of you two girls.'

'Well, if we find the going to hard you and Paul will have to give us a piggy back.' Ronnie winked at Teri. 'Come on, let's show these wimps how it's done.'

Ronnie placed her back against a large rock and proceeded to place her feet on the one opposite, pushing herself upwards until she was able to find a handhold on the top of the rock and scramble up the last two feet.

'Wait there,' called Paul. 'Let me come up next then I can give Teri a hand.'

Ronnie moved over cautiously on the boulder. If it was going to be climbing like this all the way she was not sure if they should continue. She peered over the edge of the rock and could see others lower down that she should be able to climb down to unassisted. When she jumped off the lowest one the dried river bed lay before her, littered with large stones and small rocks, tufts of grass growing out between the crevices, but certainly negotiable.

'Come on,' she called. 'It's only that first bit that's difficult.' She stood and waited until they climbed down to join her.

'That was extremely reckless of you,' Mark reprimanded her. 'Suppose you had fallen or trapped your foot between the rocks and we hadn't been able to reach you.'

'You forget I used to go rock climbing with my stepfather,' replied Ronnie.

'Yes, and he was killed on a mountain.'

Ronnie glared at him. 'That was totally uncalled for, Mark. My stepfather died due to an avalanche. Only one of the climbers survived.'

Mark had the grace to look embarrassed and Teri pushed her way to Ronnie's side. 'Come on, Ronnie. We'll show them the way. We girls will stick together. The last one to the end of the gorge has to buy dinner tonight.'

The walking was arduous, underfoot the stones would move unexpectedly, throwing them off balance, some boulders blocked the path completely and they had to inch their way around them or scramble along the bank, clinging to tufts of grass. At times the walls of the gorge overhung, giving a tunnel effect.

'Do you think it's like this all the way?' asked Teri and Ronnie shook her head.

'I have no idea, but I think it could be sensible to find an alternative route back.'

The path became easier for a while, then more large boulders blocked the way. Ronnie sized them up and decided they could be climbed.

'I'll go first,' she glared at Mark, daring him to argue with her. She stood at the top and directed Paul where the best places were to put his feet and find a handhold until he stood beside her.

'It looks pretty easy again now,' she said. 'I'll climb down whilst you help the others up. Get Teri to pass her bag up to you.'

The river bed widened out and climbed upwards, their pace slowing as they became hot and tired.

'We *must* be nearly there,' groaned Teri. 'We've been walking for hours. I don't think this village of Tapes exists.'

Ronnie pointed to a metal sign. 'According to that it does. Another one and a half hours. We must have already walked for three hours. A doddle.'

'Except that a metal fence is barring our way.' Mark stopped and mopped his brow. 'Can we climb over?'

'Could be easier to walk round.' Ronnie pointed to where a path took off diagonally and a line of stones formed an arrow. 'Maybe it isn't safe to walk any further and that's why they've put the fence there.'

'Provided this path leads *somewhere*.'

'Preferably to Tapes,' muttered Mark.

Ronnie strode on ahead, refusing to admit that she was as hot and weary as her companions. She was relieved when a small taverna came into sight and she quickened her pace. They ordered beer to drink and Teri asked if they were able to refill their water bottles.

The owner shook his head. 'I have bottles.' He pointed to the large, well stocked fridge.

'We obviously have no choice. I wonder if he can tell us an easier route for going back.'

Teri collected four bottles of water and asked for directions. The taverna owner pointed out the way to the donkey path that would lead them back down to Kritsa. Thanking him, Teri pulled some Euros from her pocket and was then horrified when she saw the cost of the beer and water was double the amount she had expected to pay.

'Let's go,' she said. 'We can't afford to eat here. However hot those ham rolls may have become we'll have to make do or wait until we get back to Kritsa and go to a taverna there.'

The donkey path was certainly easier to negotiate than the gorge had been. It wound gradually down the hillside to a valley where olive trees were growing, long stretches of it being cobbled and in other places they were walking on grass.

'We should have come up this way,' commented Paul. 'It would have been easier than climbing over those rocks.'

'Then we wouldn't have walked the gorge,' pointed out Ronnie.

'That was more like mountaineering than walking,' commented Teri.

'You don't mind if I sit out on your patio and paint?' asked Ronnie. 'The others have decided they want a lazy day after our exertions at Kritsa.'

'Not a bit,' smiled Marianne. 'We'll make sure the girls leave you alone. The only talent they have at the moment is to make a mess everywhere. I dread to think what would happen if they were let loose with paints. Come in and help yourself to a drink whenever you fancy. I'll give you a shout when the lunch is ready.'

'I don't expect you to feed me,' protested Ronnie.

'I have to make lunch for everyone else. It's only a snack and one more mouth won't make any difference.'

Ronnie smiled gratefully. It was a relief to be away from her friends for a few hours and be able to indulge herself in her love of art. She had brought a box of watercolour paints and some coloured pencils that could be dipped in water to simulate paint with her to Crete and she hoped she would be able to achieve the desired effect with them. She adjusted the umbrella behind her, opened her pad to the first blank page and looked across the bay. She would sketch in the outline of the arm of land opposite, then colour it in dark blue with some black lines to indicate where the hollows occurred. The sky, with the sun rising, would be the brilliant red that she had witnessed early one morning. She would have liked to wake Mark to show him the beauty she was experiencing, but knew he would not appreciate being disturbed.

If she was successful in that attempt she would then do another similar with the sun golden this time and shining on the water. Maybe she would add a small boat, the owner going off to fish and she would show the causeway with the windmills standing out starkly in the early morning light. Totally engrossed, she worked swiftly, and did not notice John walk up behind her.

He waited until she lifted her hand from the paper to look into the distance. 'Mum said to bring you out a drink. She's sure you haven't been in for one.'

Ronnie started guiltily. The drink Marianne had given her earlier stood untouched at her side. 'Thanks. I was concentrating so hard I hadn't even realised I was thirsty.'

'Have you done all those this morning?' John looked at the paintings Ronnie had completed. 'May I have a look?'

Ronnie waved her hand towards them. 'Feel free. They're pretty basic.'

John studied each one closely. 'These are fabulous,' he said finally. 'You could easily make your living as an artist.'

'Flattery will get you everywhere,' smiled Ronnie.

'No, I really mean it. If Saff had some of these for sale in her shop the tourists would be falling over themselves to buy them. Actually, would you mind if I 'phoned her? If she's at the shop it will only take her a minute or two to get here. I'd like her to see these.'

Ronnie shrugged. 'By all means.' She picked up her brush again and drew a line denoting the edge of a building.

'I wish I could paint,' sighed John. 'Dad lets me loose on the walls of the apartments, but that's about it.' John selected Saffron's number and waited until she answered. 'Saff, can you come to the house for five minutes? I'd like you to see something.'

John stood and watched Ronnie covering the sheet of paper with swift, accomplished brush strokes until Saffron drew up in her car. He hurried over to her.

'Did you realise how well Ronnie could paint? She's done some beautiful pictures of the hills with the sun coming up and her painting of Spinalonga is a marvel. Come and see.'

John led Saffron over to the table where Ronnie still sat painting and picked up the collection of views she had completed earlier.

'I knew she was an artist, but I'd not seen any of her work.' Saffron scrutinized them carefully. 'Is she willing to sell these? They're just the kind of thing I'm looking for as an addition to the shop.'

'You'd have to ask her, but this is what I really want you to see. I think she's just about finished.'

Ronnie looked up and smiled at Saffron. 'I'm having a wonderful day. The light here is so good; it shows the detail so well.'

Saffron drew in her breath. 'That is amazing.' She looked at the small picture of Spinalonga. 'How long did it take you to paint that?'

'About an hour.'

'An hour! Is that all? What about the others?'

'Half an hour after I'd done the first one. It was just a question of copying the outline and using different colours to denote the time of day.'

'So how many could you paint in a day?' asked Saffron thoughtfully.

'I've no idea. If I just copied the same one over and over I could probably complete about thirty, but why would I want that many?'

'Would you be willing to sell them?'

'Take whichever ones you want.'

Saffron shook her head. 'I'd want to sell them on in the shop. I do wish you were staying out here. You could sit outside the shop and paint and I just know that tourists would stop to look and there could be a notice to say your paintings were available to buy in my shop.'

'Look, Saff, you haven't looked at this one yet.' John pointed to the painting Ronnie had just completed of Spinalonga. 'Could you paint that on the lid of a wooden box?' asked John.

'I'd have to use a different medium, but there's no reason why not.'

'There's your answer, Saff. Ronnie could paint boxes and they'd fetch twice as much as the ones with a photograph.'

'I doubt it; they'd be more likely to buy your photographs.'

John shook his head. 'My photographs are all the same, just reproduced time and again. Each one of your paintings is individual and slightly different. There would never be two identical.'

Ronnie laughed. 'Almost identical. If I was painting the same scene over and over again they would all probably look identical, but there would be subtle differences. I wouldn't always have the same amount of paint on the brush.'

Saffron replaced the paintings on the table. 'I'm serious, Ronnie. If you wanted to spend a season over here I'd certainly buy your paintings.'

'Truly?'

Saffron nodded. 'I'm sure I'd be able to sell them for at least ten, if not twelve Euros each. How much would you charge me? Remember you'd have to take into account your materials and have enough to live on.'

Ronnie laughed and shook her head. 'Thanks for the offer, but I'm flying home on Saturday. I'm hardly going to be able to complete enough by then to stock your shop for the season.'

'May I buy the ones you have done? If you'll sign them I can advertise them as limited editions.'

'People will think I'm a famous artist.'

'Ronnie, with the quality of your work you *should* be a famous artist. Work out how much you want me to pay you for these and I can bring the money up tomorrow. If you're not around I can always leave it with John or Marianne to pass on to you.'

'Are you serious?'

'Perfectly. There are ten paintings of the peninsula and one of Spinalonga. Would a hundred Euros be enough or would you expect more?'

Ronnie frowned. 'I honestly wouldn't know what to charge. I've never sold a painting before,' she admitted. 'A hundred sounds more than fair to me.'

'I'll pay you the same for any others you are able to complete before you leave,' promised Saffron. 'I want to get back and show these to Marjorie, so I'll see you tomorrow.'

Ronnie looked at John. 'Do you really think my little paintings will sell?'

John nodded. 'I'm sure they will. People buy my photos, but I'm sure they'd rather have an individually signed painting.'

'But you take incredibly good photos. I've felt quite embarrassed showing you our poor attempts whilst we've been over here.'

'They're a good record of your visit. That's the main thing. I have the time to wait for the light to be just right or try again another day if I want something to be perfect.'

'Do you want to see the ones we took when we went to Rethymnon?' asked Ronnie. 'I have the disc with me.'

'Love to. Can I put them up on my computer?'

'Of course. If there's anything there that could be of use to you feel free to take a copy.'

'I'd ask you first.' John took the disc that Ronnie held out to him.

'No need. Just help yourself.'

Ronnie picked up her brush. She now wished John would go away and leave her alone. No doubt Marianne would soon be calling her for lunch and she would have to be polite and sit at the table until the meal was ended. It would be a waste of the clear afternoon light and she wanted to capture Spinalonga as the sun moved round in the sky, casting shadows in different places.

When the sun began to go down she would return her attention to the hills opposite and try to reproduce the way they became pink, then purple and finally dark blue before disappearing into the darkness of the night.

John began to look through the photographs Ronnie had taken. There were the conventional views of the gorge on the main road to Heraklion, the village of Paleokastro where they had stopped for lunch and then Rethymnon itself with the waterfront and fish restaurants. Giovanni had told them where they would find the lyra workshop and there were numerous photographs of the instruments and Giorgos Papalexakis working on them.

The following day they had driven to Chania, visiting the cemeteries at Maleme and absorbing the history of the war that had raged in Crete. On their return to Rethymnon they had stopped, at Vasilis's request, and laid some flowers at the foot of the memorial to Basil Hurst's first wife and child, both of whom had been so brutally killed. There were some other flowers in evidence and John made a mental note to ask Vasi if he or his father had visited recently.

Many of the photos showed one or more of their group at the taverna where they had stopped for a meal, village houses and war memorials and John skipped past them rapidly. They held no interest at all for him. They had spent a day walking along the Agiou Andoniou Gorge and the following day had started their walk in Prasiano Gorge, hoping they would eventually reach the place where they had turned back the previous day. A day of comparative rest had followed where they had driven down to Spili in the morning and only walked a short distance that afternoon.

On their last day in the area they had driven to Kastellakia and on to the new village of Mili. From there they had taken a path through lush greenery, unlike the other boulder strewn dry river beds they had visited. Ronnie had taken photographs of old mills, the river rushing around their disused wheels and deserted buildings, the sunlight coming through the leaves to shine on their neglected walls.

To John's surprise they had entered a modern taverna and Ronnie had taken photographs from the veranda of the river below, and the stark rock walls rising on the other side. Through a clearing in the trees a tiny church could be seen built into the rock face. She had taken a photograph of an old man, sitting with a rug across his knees, smiling benignly at her, a woman standing protectively a short distance away.

John smiled. It must be pleasant to spend ones days sitting in a taverna in such idyllic surroundings. He moved on to the next photograph, then frowned and returned to the one of the old man and zoomed in for a closer look. He was sure, unless it was a trick of the light; that the man had no index finger on his left hand. Desperately trying to focus more clearly and enlarge the photograph to see the man's hand, John finally had to give up. He was making something out of nothing. There were probably hundreds of old men who had a finger missing. He would ask Ronnie if she had noticed the defect.

Leaving the disc in the computer and the photograph on the screen John went back to the patio where Ronnie was engrossed. Without looking up she spoke to John.

'I can feel you standing there, John. What did you think of the photos?'

'When you can conveniently stop for a moment I'd like to ask you about one of them.'

Ronnie nodded and continued to shade the walls of the fortress on Spinalonga, finally placing her brush to one side. 'I've told you, if you want one just take a copy. You don't have to ask my permission.' She stretched her hands above her head. 'Actually I ought to walk around for a bit. I tend to forget how the time goes. I've probably not moved for a couple of hours or more.'

'Come and have a look at this photo. It says "Mili Gorge" and you seem to be at a taverna.'

'It was beautiful there.'

'It looks it,' John answered impatiently. 'Who was the old man sitting there?'

Ronnie shrugged. 'I've no idea.'

John almost pushed her down into the seat in front of the computer. 'Look, is his finger missing?'

'I didn't really notice. It gave me a bit of a turn when he waved goodbye and he had a hook instead of a hand.'

'Ronnie,' John spoke in an awed voice. 'I think you've found Tassos.'

'Nick, Nick, I've found Tassos.' John rushed into their room and Nicola frowned at him in annoyance and put her finger to her lips.

'Quiet. I've just got the girls to sleep and Lisa's been so fretful all morning. I think she's cutting another tooth.'

'I'm sorry,' said John contritely. 'I didn't think. I was so excited. I'm sure Ronnie has found Tassos.'

'Where?'

'At Mili. They went to a taverna there. The old man waved goodbye and he had a hook instead of a hand.'

'John, any number of men who have lost a hand could have a hook.'

'*And* have a finger missing on their left hand? I'm sure it's him. I'm going to ask Dad if I can have the day off to go up to Rethymnon tomorrow. You don't mind, do you, Nick?'

'If I said I did mind and asked you not to go you'd be unbearable to live with. If it is Tassos then you've finally found him. If it isn't him you'll just have to stop searching and accept that he disappeared without a trace.'

'I'm going to ask Ronnie the easiest way to get there. I don't want to spend hours negotiating a woodland trail if there's a quicker route.'

'Why don't you ask Saffie? She'll probably know better than they do.'

'You're brilliant, Nick.' With a broad smile on his face, John returned to where Ronnie was still painting.

29th April 2010

'Saff, I'm at Kastellakia. There's a hand written sign that says Mili is up a cart track. Is that where I need to go?'

'Positive. I took a side road that had a sign for Mili. I hadn't gone very far when I saw there were houses down in the valley and a tiny church. I thought that was Mili and walked down to have a look. The place appeared deserted except for a couple of houses and a taverna. I walked around for a bit and then returned to the car and drove on. Apparently that's the old village of Mili. The new one is some kilometres up the road.'

John took the turning onto the unmade road where the sign indicated the way to the village of Mili. Almost immediately he could look down into a lush valley. A wire fence ran along the side of the narrow road and John could see a small church perched precariously below him. He continued until there was a convenient lay by for him to draw into and park.

He crossed the road and looked down, a path wound its way down the hillside, passing the church and disappearing amongst the trees. John walked carefully down the worn track, catching elusive glimpses of houses and accompanied continually by the sound of running water. He peered through the undergrowth, finally locating a small waterfall, no higher than eight inches; the water ran into a pool and trickled away in a slow stream. He parted the branches of a low tree and stood beside it.

A strange feeling of peace came over him. It was almost like being in a different world, so quiet, not even the buzz of insects or bird song to break the silence. He relaxed against a tree; the whole area had a mystic quality and he wondered if Cathy's father had ever visited and if this pool had inspired him to write the fairy stories that had enthralled children.

He was not sure how long he remained standing there, drinking in the beauty and serenity, before he returned to the path. He passed some derelict houses, looking dark and depressing, and walked on down the narrow track until it suddenly widened out and he saw the taverna. There was no sign of anyone patronising the establishment and he looked at his watch. It was nearly eleven. If it catered for those visitors who walked the trail it would surely be opening very soon.

Steps led up to a wide veranda with wooden tables and chairs. Here the sunlight penetrated through the trees and John walked forwards to take advantage of the warmth. He had not realised how chilled he had become whilst standing by the pool. As he did so he saw the old man sitting at a table at the far end and his heart skipped a beat. Had he actually found Tassos?

'Are you Tassos Nevrakis?'

Tassos held up his hand and his stump. 'I can't deny it. Who wants to know?'

John sat down opposite the man and held out his hand. 'You don't know how pleased I am to finally find you.'

Tassos raised his eyebrows. 'Why have you been looking for me? Are you from the government?'

'No, I'm Yannis Christoforakis's great nephew. I know you were on Spinalonga with him and you managed to escape. I just want to know how you managed to evade the authorities so successfully.'

Tassos chuckled. 'You should ask Manolis.'

'Manolis died a few years ago.'

Tassos crossed himself. 'Shame. He was a good man.'

John did not think Tassos would want to know that Manolis

had committed suicide after the death of his wife.

Tassos smiled. 'It's a long story. Stassa,' he called, 'a drink for our guest.'

An elderly woman leaned out from a doorway and nodded.

'What do you want to know?' asked Tassos.

'Everything. Tell me exactly what happened to you. Right from when you first left the island.'

'Are you planning to write a book?' Tassos regarded John suspiciously.

John shook his head. 'Goodness, no. I'm only interested in photography, mostly wildlife. I'd hoped to work for National Geographic magazine, but I had an accident that affected my sight. I thought it was out of the question; then Nick had the girls so I can't go running off all over the world to take photos of exotic butterflies or caterpillars, besides, I enjoy being at home with them.'

'Nick?' queried Tassos.

'My wife,' John announced proudly. 'We have twin girls just over a year old.'

Tassos nodded and sighed. 'This could take a while. Tell Stassa you'll be here for lunch.'

John sat back and listened, enthralled as Tassos related the story of his wandering life and his experiences with the resistance.

'It was bad luck that I should lose half my arm just as the Germans were about to surrender.' He shrugged. 'One to use and one to lose. Could have been worse. It could have been both of them.'

'Was that when you decided to go to the hospital and ask for tests?' asked John.

Tassos shook his head. 'I made that decision after I had returned to Kavrohori. The only way I could give Aspasia a decent life was to marry her, and to do that I had to be cleared of infection. I got to thinking, even if I could marry her, the villagers would say I'd done it so I had someone to look after me. We needed to leave Kavrohori and start again where no one knew us.'

'So you became a donkey driver.'

'What else can a man with one arm do? I could have walked the streets selling lottery tickets, I suppose. I remembered Manolis saying I had plenty of money on my account as a leprosy patient. It was my money, so I decided I would claim it. I opened a bank account in Heraklion ostensibly for my war pension to be paid into.' Tassos winked. 'I claimed I was still working as a pedlar so might need to draw money from different towns. I took the bus down to Aghios Nikolaos and saw Manolis and Doctor Stavros and said I wanted my pension arrears paid in to my bank account.'

Tassos leaned back in his chair. 'You should have seen the look on the doctor's face when he realised who I was. He didn't like it when I showed him my papers proving I was negative. He tried to make excuses for not taking samples and having them properly tested. I told him if my pension wasn't paid I planned to sue the medical authorities. I'm sure that's why he agreed to authorise the payment. He was frightened that if I complained to the government he would lose his job.'

'And as soon as it was paid in to the bank you drew it out. Why didn't you leave it in there to gain interest?'

'I didn't trust them. I wanted that cash in my hand. I knew they wouldn't be able to find me easily as I hadn't given them any address, but if the money was sitting in the bank they might be able to take it from my account.'

'But you still had your war disability pension paid in to the bank?'

'Until the end of the year. Then I withdrew that amount and closed the account. I opened a new one at a different bank in Rethymnon. I felt safe enough to tell them my address. I was living here then with my wife and family, working as a donkey driver.'

'And you've lived here ever since?'

Tassos nodded. 'When I first discovered the village of Mili I thought it was paradise, so green, so lush, vegetables and fruits growing like weeds. Nothing like the area around Heraklion where I'd lived as a boy and I'd never seen anywhere else like it during all my travels. We moved into Zen's cottage. It was cramped, with my mother and the three children, but we managed.'

'Surely with all that money you could have bought one of the larger houses down here?'

Tassos shook his head. 'At that time they were all occupied. They belonged to the millers and the donkey drivers. Most of them still do.'

'So why does no one live here?'

'We live here,' stated Tassos proudly. 'We refused to be frightened and move away.'

'Why were the others frightened?'

'It was during the winters. For a few years in succession we had a lot of rain. It fed the streams and springs that flow into this river. The river was so high we could not cross from one side of the gorge to the other. The mills on the opposite side from us began to take their sacks up to the road and an open lorry would collect them. It was much quicker than walking the trail with a loaded donkey.

'Each year as the water receded we could see where the sides of the gorge had been eroded. Rocks began to fall. Each year the erosion became worse and word went round that the whole gorge would collapse into the river and drown us all. At first the women and children were sent away for safety, then the men began to join them, coming each day to work and returning to a neighbouring village at the end of the day.

'Finally they decided they would build a new village. One by one the families left their houses down here and moved away. I refused to leave paradise. My boys moved on. Dimitris lives in Rethymnon, he has a shoe shop there, and Yiorgo is a taxi driver in Chania. Aspasia and Anastasia stayed here with me. This was where we belonged. There were no donkeys now for me to lead and I had only my war pension to live on.'

'How did you manage?'

'Living here you need very little. All your vegetables and fruit are outside your door. We had lived on my wages as a donkey driver and before we left Kavrohori Aspasia had dug up my father's box from under the marjoram so there was money available for an emergency.'

'What about your pension money that you had drawn in cash?'

'I had that untouched. I wanted to make sure that when I died Aspasia would have enough money to live on. Sadly she went before me. Anastasia promised her mother that she would never leave me to fend for myself. When Babbis asked her to marry him she said he had to live here so she could continue to care for me. He was a bus driver. He would leave his scooter the other side of the valley and ride in to Rethymnon to go to work each day. Then he had the idea to open up the old taverna and I gave him my pension money to do repairs, buy modern kitchen equipment, tables and chairs, glasses, cups, plates.' Tassos spread his hands. 'Everything. He hoped that when the original villagers came down to check on their houses or collect produce they would call in and spend a few drachmas. Until the taverna began to bring in a living he continued to drive his bus. Now the walkers patronise us and we are open in the evenings. The villagers come down and also many visitors who are staying in Rethymnon come for a meal.'

'So the taverna is a success?'

Tassos nodded. 'Babbis has built on an extension to cope with the increasing trade. Times have been hard, but I know my daughter won't go hungry when I'm gone.'

'Ronnie, Ronnie.' John rushed over as he saw her come out of the apartments. He flung his arms around her and kissed her soundly. 'Ronnie, you're a marvel. You had found Tassos.'

'Really?' Ronnie looked at him in delight. 'That old man was actually him?'

John nodded, still holding her hand. ''He told me his life story. It's fascinating. Come and sit over here with me and I'll tell you.'

Mark watched John lead Ronnie to a seat on the patio outside the general store and taverna from their apartment window. She had said she was only going out to the car to collect her bag to place her artist's materials safely inside. He stood and watched as Ronnie listened intently to all John said. She showed no sign of returning and he finally gave up watching them, checked his mobile to see if he had missed any calls, decided it was too early in the day to call his mother and returned to the window.

They had risen from the seats and Ronnie's face was aglow with pleasure. John kissed her on both cheeks and she walked over to the car, collected her bag and waved her hand in farewell.

Mark opened the door as she arrived back in their apartment. 'That took you a long time to collect a bag,' he remarked.

'I was talking to John.'

'I saw exactly what you were up to with John. I think it's disgusting. He's a married man with tiny children and there are you two having an affair. You should know better how to behave even if he doesn't.'

Ronnie looked at Mark in amazement. 'We're not having an affair. Don't be stupid.'

'I saw you. You were all over each other.'

'Mark, *if* John and I were having an affair we'd hardly conduct a liaison outside the apartment windows in full view of everyone. John was telling me that he had met that old man at Mili Gorge and he was the one he'd been searching for.'

'He could have told you that without slobbering all over you. I never liked him when we were boys together. My mother was right when she said he was unruly and disobedient. You could tell even then how he was going to turn out.'

'Your mother is not the oracle. There's nothing wrong with John. He's a decent, hard working young man who takes his responsibilities seriously.'

'Meaning that I'm not?'

Ronnie sighed. 'If you think I'm the kind of girl to go on holiday with her partner and then cheats on him with his married cousin you just don't know me very well. There's no future for us together without trust and you obviously don't trust me.'

Mark tried to put his arms around her. 'There's no need to be like that, Ron. My mother always says ....'

'I've had enough of you *and* your mother. When we return to the States you have two days to clear your belongings from my apartment and find somewhere else to live. We're finished, Mark.'

Ronnie picked up her bag and walked out of the apartment whilst Mark looked after her in consternation. Where was he going to find somewhere else to live at such short notice?

Ronnie walked over to the taverna and general store where John had just started preparing a breakfast for a family.

'May I help myself to a coffee?' asked Ronnie.

'Take a seat. I'll bring it in a minute.'

Ronnie shook her head. 'I'll need to get to know my way around. I could be asked to lend a hand occasionally.'

John gave her a puzzled look as she helped herself and sat at a table in the corner.

'What's up, Ron?' asked John as he walked past.

'I'll talk to you later when you've finished serving,'

Ronnie nursed her cup in her hands. Leaving Mark eventually had been inevitable, but to give up her apartment and regular job to take a chance on making her living as an artist in Crete was bordering on the insane.

3rd May 2010

Annita sat in her room. She had told Marianne that she was feeling tired and would get dressed later. Bryony had brought her breakfast in, but she had little appetite that morning. She reached out and took Elias's photograph from beside her bed.

'Oh, Elias, what it is to be old and tired. My family gave me the most wonderful party and it was such a surprise, but it really seems to have completely worn me out. I truly thought it was going to be a party just for the little girls. They are beautiful, a credit to John and Nicola. It's sad that I won't be around to see them grow up, but I have so much to be thankful for.

'I do hope it will be a good season for Giovanni and Marianne this year. They've certainly had some problems, what with the fire and then John having to go to England for his medical treatment. A good job Marianne thought about suing that awful boy's father. They would never have managed all the rebuilding otherwise.

'I'd like Saffron's shop to be a success. I'd also like to know that she and Vasi were going to be married. Maybe Bryony could have a word with her. She thinks a lot of Bryony, always has done.

'I must remind John to write to Andreas and tell him he has found this man Tassos. It would be good for Andreas to write another successful play. He needs something to occupy him now he no longer has Laurie.

'He and Elena seemed to be good company for each other when Helena and Greg had gone to Heraklion. Elena really should not let her daughter dictate to her. She's quite capable of thinking for herself and making her own decisions.

'I'll have just a little longer in bed, then ring my bell and tell Marianne I'm ready to get up.'

Elias's photograph had slipped from Annita's fingers and her head dropped forward.

Giovanni sat in the office with Marianne whilst she checked their computer bookings for the following weeks.

'Considering the ash problem that affected Europe we've only had three cancellations. It could have been far worse, particularly if it had lasted longer.'

'I just wish we had some more bookings. We're well down on this time last year. At this rate we'll be lucky if we manage to cover our overheads,' remarked Giovanni gloomily.

'Now our families have finally gone home, I'll contact the travel companies and see if I can drum up some more business. It could be worth our while to offer seven nights for the price of six until the end of June. If that is successful we can increase the prices a little in July for new bookings to cover the loss. What do you think, Giovanni?'

'I leave you in charge of bookings. You do whatever you think is best.'

'I don't know what happened between Mark and Ronnie, but they must have had a terrible row. I don't think they were speaking to each other.'

'Apparently Ronnie is planning to come back over here. She's going to work as an artist on commission for Saffron. She's asked me if I'll give her a special rate at one of the apartments for the season.'

'And will you?'

Giovanni shrugged. 'She'll pay the same rate as everyone else, but I'll tell her it includes her water and electricity. That way she'll think she's getting a good deal and it means a guaranteed booking until the end of October.'

'What will she do then? Go back to the States?'

'I don't know her long term plans. They probably depend upon the success of Saffron's shop.'

'With the number of visitors who are coming to this area whilst that film is being made Saffron should be successful.'

'I hope so. I just wish they'd stay down here and not just visit for the day.'

Giovanni began to open his post. He read the letter through a second time and threw it to one side in disgust.

'The bank says they're increasing the interest charged on loans by twenty per cent with immediate effect and they've already increased the business tax. The cost of electricity and oil has already doubled this season. We might as well close down now.'

Marianne patted her husband's shoulder. 'Don't worry so much, Giovanni. We've always managed to come through somehow. I'll see if Grandma is ready to get up, then I'll make some coffee and get on to the travel firms.'

Marianne entered her grandmother's room and stopped in horror. It was obvious that her grandmother was no longer with them.

'Giovanni, Giovanni, come quick. 'Phone the doctor. Grandma ....' Marianne's voice broke and Giovanni placed his arms around his wife and held her tightly.

If you have enjoyed reading Tassos, you will be pleased to know that the next book – Ronnie – is planned for publication in June 2014.

Read on for a 'taster' of what is to come.

RONNIE

May 2010

Ronnie opened the door of her apartment and moved to one side to allow Mark to take their cases in. They had hardly spoken since Mark had accused her of having an affair with John. During their flight she had feigned sleep or sat and talked quietly to Teri about her decision.

'I'll put the kettle on,' she announced, 'unless you'd like something stronger? Then we need to sit and talk.'

'That will make a change after hardly speaking to me for the last few days.'

Ronnie ignored the jibe. She was not prepared to start a row. She knew the acrimonious accusations would start as soon as she told Mark she was returning to Crete.

She returned from the kitchen carrying two glasses and a bottle of wine. 'I forgot we wouldn't have any fresh milk. We'll have to make do with this or water.'

Mark poured a glass for each of them. 'I've had enough water recently.'

Ronnie sat across the room from him and took a mouthful from her glass. 'I've changed my mind, Mark.'

Mark smirked. 'I thought you would see sense.'

Ronnie looked at him levelly. 'You don't have to pack your belongings. I will be packing mine. You can stay here and take over the agreement for the apartment if you want. I will tell the agency tomorrow that I'm cancelling.'

'You can't do that!'

Ronnie shrugged. 'I can. I have to give them a month's notice of cancellation so I won't be staying here after the end of the month. I'll leave it up to you if you want to go to the agency. If you decide to move on you will have to be out by the end of May, the same as me.'

'I can't afford this apartment on my own,' protested Mark.

'That is your problem. I've subsidised you long enough. I've been paying three quarters of the rent, remember, and most of the utility bills. You'll either have to find someone to share it with you or ask your parents for a loan. You could always go back home to live for your final year at Uni. The choice is yours.'

'Where are you going?'

'I've decided I'll take Saffron up on her offer. I'm going back to Crete to work as an artist.'

'You're going back to be with John, aren't you? I was right,' declared Mark triumphantly, 'you are having an affair with him.'

'I have no plans at all with John. I've always wanted to be an artist and this is my opportunity.'

'I won't let you.'

'You won't let me?' Ronnie raised her eyebrows. 'You are not my keeper. I will do as I please.'

'You'll never make enough as an artist to live on. Then what will you do when you're destitute?'

'If it doesn't work out I can always come back to the States. At least I will have taken the opportunity rather than spend the rest of my life working in a mundane job and regretting I didn't have enough courage to take a chance.'

'You're talking a load of rubbish. Do you really think tourists are going to buy your daubing of sunsets?'

'Saffron seems to think they will. I won't know until I've tried.' Ronnie finished the last of her wine. 'I'm going to start packing up. I'll pass you out a blanket and pillow and you can bed down on the sofa.'

'Ronnie, I can't sleep here. I'm too tall to sleep on the sofa.'

'Then you'll just have to bend your knees.'

Giovanni sat in the office with Marianne whilst she checked their computer bookings for the following weeks.

'Considering the ash problem that affected Europe we've only had three cancellations. It could have been far worse, particularly if it had lasted longer.'

'I just wish we had some more bookings. We're well down on this time last year. At this rate we'll be lucky if we manage to cover our overheads,' remarked Giovanni gloomily.

'Now our families have finally gone home, I'll contact the travel companies and see if I can drum up some more business. It could be worth our while to offer seven nights for the price of six until the end of June. If that is successful we can increase the prices a little in July for new bookings to cover the loss. What do you think, Giovanni?'

'I leave you in charge of bookings. You do whatever you think is best.'

'I don't know what happened between Mark and Ronnie, but they must have had a terrible row. I don't think they were speaking to each other.'

'Apparently Ronnie is planning to come back over here. She's going to work as an artist on commission for Saffron. She's asked me if I'll give her a special rate at one of the apartments for the season.'

'And will you?'

Giovanni shrugged. 'She'll pay the same rate as everyone else, but I'll tell her it includes her water and electricity. That way she'll think she's getting a good deal and it means a guaranteed booking until the end of October.'

'What will she do then? Go back to the States?'

'I don't know her long term plans. They probably depend upon the success of Saffron's shop.'

'With the number of visitors who are coming to this area whilst that film is being made Saffron should be successful.'

'I hope so. I just wish they'd stay down here and not just visit for the day.'

Giovanni began to open his post. He read the letter through a second time and threw it to one side in disgust.

'The bank says they're increasing the interest charged on loans by twenty per cent with immediate effect and they've already increased the business tax. The cost of electricity and oil has already doubled this season. We might as well close down now.'

Marianne patted her husband's shoulder. 'Don't worry so much, Giovanni. We've always managed to come through somehow. I'll see if Grandma is ready to get up, then I'll make some coffee and get on to the travel firms.'

Marianne entered her grandmother's room and stopped in horror. It was obvious that her grandmother was no longer with them.

'Giovanni, Giovanni, come quick. 'Phone the doctor. Grandma ....' Marianne's voice broke and Giovanni placed his arms around his wife and held her tightly.

'You can't possibly expect us to drop everything and come rushing back to Crete whenever you call. We haven't got that kind of money, you know.'

Marianne did not remind her sister that they only needed their air fare and they would be accommodated free in the self catering apartments.

'We could get stuck over there again with another ash cloud or something. That was terribly inconvenient, and after John's disgusting behaviour I'm sure the boys won't want to come.'

'What do you mean? What did John do?'

Helena snorted. 'Don't tell me you don't know. He and Ronnie are having an affair. Mark saw them together. He's thrown her out, of course.'

'Oh, no, now wait a moment, Helena. John is certainly not having an affair with anyone. Saffron offered Ronnie a job as an artist, painting pictures of the area for her to sell in her shop.

Ronnie has taken her up on her offer and before she left she arranged with Giovanni to rent a self catering apartment for the rest of the season.'

'Very convenient for them, I'm sure,' scoffed Helena. 'If you hadn't decided to give grandmother that party and get her over excited and over tired she'd probably still be alive now.'

Marianne felt the tears coming into her eyes. Surely no one could blame Annita's death on a party that had been held three weeks earlier.

'And don't expect mother to come over,' continued Helena, 'and I'm sure Uncle Andreas won't come either. I suggest you just go ahead with whatever arrangements you need to make and get grandmother's funeral over and done with.'

Marianne took a deep breath. 'Mother has already arranged to meet Uncle Andreas in New York and fly out with him.'

'What! How dare you speak to her before talking to me?'

'I don't have to ask your permission to speak to our mother. She had every right to know before you. I called her and Uncle Andreas before anyone else and it was her decision. I tried to 'phone you yesterday but you were out and I left a message asking you to call me back.'

'I was busy yesterday. I'm having to spend some time with Mark. He needs my support. I'll speak to mother and tell her it's out of the question for her to come over. She's too old to be gallivanting around like that.'

'Helena, she's only seventy. Grandma was her mother and if she wants to come over to be at her funeral she has every right. Uncle Andreas will look after her.'

'I'll hold you directly responsible if anything happens to her,' threatened Helena.

'There's no reason why anything untoward should happen to her. What's wrong with you? You never used to be like this.'

'There's nothing wrong with me. If you hadn't gone off to Crete, got yourself pregnant and then married that Giovanni man, you'd be over here helping me to look after mother. You've managed to evade your responsibilities very nicely.'

Marianne took a deep breath. 'I think we ought to end this conversation right now, before either of us says anything more hurtful to each other. Goodbye.'

Marianne dropped her head into her hands. Had she evaded her responsibilities? She didn't think so. She had taken care of Giovanni's Aunt Anna and Uncle Yiorgo, then her grandmother. She now had Giovanni's mother living there with Uncle Yannis and Aunt Ourania and she knew that eventually she would be responsible for caring for them as they became older and incapable of looking after themselves. Helena did not look after their mother; Elena was quite capable of living alone and looking after herself.

Despite being convinced that John was not having an affair she would have to drive up to the taverna and ask him for clarification of Helena's accusation. Surely she had not invented the story from spite?

'John, I have to ask you this for my own peace of mind. Are you having an affair with Ronnie?'

John looked at his mother in amazement. 'Whatever gave you that daft idea?'

'Your Aunt Helena said Ronnie and Mark have parted and it was due to you. Ronnie told me she was coming back here to work as an artist on commission from Saffron. Is that an excuse to be here near you?'

'If it is, it's news to me. I am definitely not having an affair with Ronnie or anyone else. Why would I even consider such foolishness when I have Nick and the girls?'

'Helena said Mark saw you and Ronnie together. He wouldn't have made that up surely.'

'Mark's an idiot. When I came back from speaking to Tassos I threw my arms around Ronnie and kissed her. Had Mark found Tassos I would probably have kissed him!' John squeezed his mother's shoulders. 'I'll be interested to hear Ronnie's version of events when she does come. I bet it doesn't tally with Aunt Helena's and I'm sure Aunt Helena is only too pleased they're no longer together. I heard that she was really rude to both the girls. I think Teri is a little more acceptable to her as she's with Paul, but no girl will be good enough for her precious little Mark.'

To be continued .....

For up-to-date information about the titles in this continuing saga of a Cretan family, see the website:

www. beryldarbybooks. com

For up-to-date information about the titles in this continuing saga of a Cretan family, see the website:

www. beryldarbybooks. com

MANOLIS

A supplementary title to the saga of a Cretan family

CATHY

The sequel to *Manolis*

For up-to-date information about the titles in this continuing saga of a Cretan family, see the website:

www.
beryldarbybooks.
com

VASI

The tenth book in a continuing saga of a Cretan family

ALECOS

The sequel to *Vasi*

Beryl Darby

JOHN

The eighth book in a continuing saga of a Cretan family

For up-to-date information
about the titles in this
continuing saga of a Cretan
family, see the website:

www.
beryldarbybooks.
com

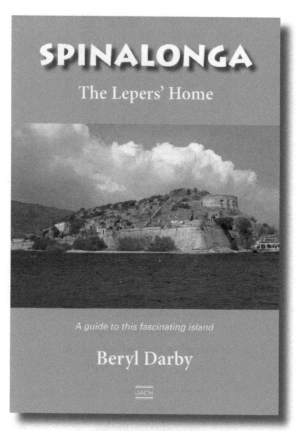

SPINALONGA

The Lepers' Home

A guide to this fascinating island

Beryl Darby

JACH

**Beryl Darby's guide to this
fascinating island**

www.beryldarbybooks.com